# THE
# SECRET BOOK
# OF
# FLORA LEA

## ALSO BY PATTI CALLAHAN HENRY

# THE
# SECRET
# BOOK
## OF
# FLORA LEA

*A Novel*

# PATTI CALLAHAN
# HENRY

**ATRIA** BOOKS

NEW YORK   LONDON   TORONTO   SYDNEY   NEW DELHI

An Imprint of Simon & Schuster, Inc.
1230 Avenue of the Americas
New York, NY 10020

First Atria Books hardcover edition May 2023

**ATRIA** B O O K S and colophon are trademarks of Simon & Schuster, Inc.

For information about special discounts for bulk purchases, please contact Simon & Schuster Special Sales at 1-866-506-1949 or business@simonandschuster.com.

The Simon & Schuster Speakers Bureau can bring authors to your live event. For more information or to book an event, contact the Simon & Schuster Speakers Bureau at 1-866-248-3049 or visit our website at www.simonspeakers.com.

*Interior design by Kyoko Watanabe*

Endpaper illustrations by The Devonshire Collections, Chatsworth. Reproduced by permission of Chatsworth Settlement Trustees/Bridgeman Images, San Diego Museum of Art, USA© San Diego Museum of Art/Gift of Robert A. and Karen Hoehn/Bridgeman Images, Natural History Museum, London, UK© Natural History Museum, London/Bridgeman Images, Los Angeles County of Art, CA, USA/ Bridgeman Images and © William Salt Library/Bridgeman Images

Manufactured in the United States of America

5  7  9  10  8  6  4

Library of Congress Cataloging-in-Publication Data
Names: Henry, Patti Callahan author.
Title: The secret book of Flora Lea : a novel / Patti Callahan Henry.
Description: First Atria Books hardcover edition. | New York : Atria Books, 2023.
Identifiers: LCCN 2022052496 (print) | LCCN 2022052497 (ebook) | ISBN 9781668011836 (hardcover) | ISBN 9781668011850 (ebook)
Subjects: LCGFT: Novels.
Classification: LCC PS3608.E578 S43 2023 (print) | LCC PS3608.E578 (ebook) | DDC 813/.6–dc23/eng/20221116
LC record available at https://lccn.loc.gov/2022052496
LC ebook record available at https://lccn.loc.gov/2022052497

ISBN 978-1-6680-1183-6
ISBN 978-1-6680-1185-0 (ebook)

*To the fierce and wise women of* Friends and Fiction,
*Mary Kay Andrews, Kristin Harmel,*
*Kristy Woodson Harvey, and Meg Walker*

Said the river: imagine everything you can imagine,
then keep on going . . .

MARY OLIVER

# CHAPTER 1

*Not very long ago and not very far away, there once was and still is an invisible place right here with us. And if you are born knowing, you will find your way through the woodlands to the shimmering doors that lead to the land made just and exactly for you.*

HAZEL MERSEY LINDEN, 1939

## October 1940
## Binsey, Oxfordshire

On a red blanket by the river, six-year-old Flora Lea Linden awakens alone, a dome of blue sky above her and birdsong wild about her. *Someone called my name?* She glances around the green expanse, at the churning water of the River Thames furrowed with winks and puckers as it nearly overflows its banks, taking to the sea anything or anyone who dares to enter its rush.

The river surges toward Oxford where students hurry to and from tutors under pinnacled towers standing guard over cobblestone streets. Then the waters bend and curve, gathering force, bouncing against the stone walls and locks of England until they reach London, where bombs are plummeting to city streets, delivering ruination, where smoldering cathedrals and crushed homes litter the river with their ember and ash.

*Did someone call my name?* Flora sits and rubs her eyes. She's not exactly alone. She has Berry, her stuffed teddy. And she isn't frightened. Why should she be? Her older sister, Hazel, told her many times that these woodlands belong to them, that the shadowed glade and the sacred sunlit puddles where the canopy of trees opens wide is a safe place meant for the two sisters, created just for them.

She stands and carefully steps closer to the river. Hazel refuses to go with Flora to Whisperwood anymore, so what's she to do but go alone? It's hers!—not to be abandoned: the glowing castle and the grove of alder, the chattering squirrels and animated trees.

Hazel had told Flora that the glinting lights on the river were stars and galaxies, rushing to meet the sea. Hazel had ordered her not to ever *become* the river, as they became other woodland creatures, nor should Flora ever drink from the river. If she did, she was told, she would never find her way back to Mum or Bridie or their warm cottage in the heather-strewn fields.

This enchanting river was—like the apple in the Bible—forbidden.

But Flora doesn't believe this beautiful, starry river can be dangerous. She clings to Berry by his worn, furry paw and ventures nearer to the water's rush, thrilled at her boldness. No one knows what might happen to her on this adventure or who she might become.

She hears a voice nearby in the woods, familiar, but Flora ignores it.

The way here was through a shimmering door, and Hazel was too busy to see it. The river is Flora's companion, her friend, and this intimacy has her creeping ever closer to its edge.

Hazel never wants them to pretend to be bunnies, so that's what she's decided today. Flora will be a bunny.

She stares down at the river's churned-up waters, looking for stars but seeing only mud and silt, humps of river-smoothed rocks underwater. She skids down on a soggy, earthy incline, her wellies slipping where the browned grasses of October change to mud. Falling on her bum, Flora laughs.

*What an adventure!*

Berry slips from her hand as her palms and fingers dig into the wet earth to keep herself from tumbling into the frigid waters. She scoots closer, wanting to grab Berry. He's too close to the river.

"It's okay," she says as she reaches for his paw, repeating her sister's words: "It's our land. We're always safe in Whisperwood."

# CHAPTER 2

## March 1960

Until Hazel Linden untied the frayed red velvet ribbon on the parchment-bound portfolio, her last day at Hogan's Rare Book Shoppe in Blooms-bury was as ordinary as any workday spent organizing, sorting, and protecting the store's remarkable inventory—that's of course if you called working among the most rare and collectible books and literary memorabilia in England ordinary.

Hazel noticed every detail of her final workday at the shop with a bit of melancholy, and a note of the dramatic. This would be the last time she'd shelve *The Hobbit* with its snow-capped mountain cover.

The last time she'd enjoy watching a crisp March day punctuated by bursts of quick bright rain from inside the warm, dim-lit shop with its display of leather-bound volumes behind tall, wavy windows that over-looked Charing Cross Road.

The store glistened with dark green walls that could almost appear black and brass sconces with their arms bent over the shelves. Photos of famous authors in black lacquer frames hung on the wall behind the register. A mother and daughter, Jane-ites Hazel called them, both in bright red rain slickers, were currently swooning over an edition of *Pride and Prejudice* they could never afford. The aroma of pulp and dust and history mixed with the sweet scent of the lilacs, ones she'd clipped from her backyard hedgerow and arranged in a vase on the checkout counter.

She took it all in from behind the ancient cash register wearing a new Mary Quant knockoff she'd bought at the street fair in Notting Hill, her shoulder-brushing tawny hair now with newly fringed bangs not quite looking like the photo she'd taken to the salon. A slight drummy feeling pounded behind her eyes. She shouldn't have had the final whiskey last night. (It was always that final whiskey that did her in.) But it was worth the morning's dull fuzziness for the fun she'd had at the pub with fellow booksellers Tim and Poppy. They'd morbidly called it Hazel's "going-away wake."

"To us, you're dead," Poppy declared with laughter. This was followed by cheers and lifted pints for her employment at Sotheby's. Her new job on the international team of specialists in rare books and manuscripts in English literature was a job they all had wanted but it was Hazel who had been offered it. Her colleagues were awfully good to her about it when she well knew that in their place, she'd be green with envy.

Tim chimed in. "But you must work with that insufferable Lord Arthur Dickson. I have to say a well-placed surname, to be accurate." He faux-shuddered.

Hazel shook her head and lightly hit Tim's shoulder. "A small price to pay to see private collections and be part of the London auctions."

"Seriously, it's not the same as the shop. It's much stuffier and quite snobby," Tim told her. "With us, the glory of the trade is that no two days are the same. I can tell you won't have nearly the jolly fun you have with us."

"I'm sure I won't. But I will come see you all the time. I promise. I'm not moving or leaving the city."

Poppy twirled her pint glass between her palms. "I'd rather be assigned the atlas and maps specialty."

"Don't give up," Hazel said. "Maybe one day you will be."

Poppy shrugged and took a long sip of her pint. "Girls like me don't end up at Sotheby's, even though I knew from the first moment I walked into Hogan's what I'd been designed for."

"That's not true," Hazel said, but what was true was that she had mixed feelings leaving Hogan's for Sotheby's. Taking the dreamed-of job in rare literary collections meant she was forsaking the safety and coziness of the shop. When she'd started there, she'd thought it a quick stop, an after-university job to keep her afloat until . . . until what? She hadn't known. After the war, no one in England had known what might be next.

Now, on her last day she would leave behind the shop and her wonderful colleagues there: the elderly owner, Edwin Hogan, and his sixty-year-old son, Tim, who'd been waiting to take over the store for far too long. There was also Poppy, the youngest of them at twenty-five, who'd been working there since she was eighteen years old. As a teen, Poppy had wandered into the store so often, leafing through old copies of *Alice's Adventures in Wonderland* for hours, that Edwin had finally told her she needed to start working there or get out. It wasn't until later that Hazel discovered Poppy had not been loitering; she'd nowhere else to go. She'd been a war orphan who'd aged out of the London Orphan School near Hampshire, sleeping in parks or on the couches of old pals who might let her stay for a while. She'd been looking for a job, but no one was willing to give her a chance.

Edwin gave her a new life. He taught her what he'd taught all of them: Cultivate a love of fine and rare books in a customer and you didn't just have a sale that day but also a devoted customer for decades. Poppy took it to heart and she now lived in a two-bedroom flat with four other women and dreamed of a future.

Hazel promised all three of them that she'd stop by often. They were, after all, as close as family.

"Hazel!"

Hazel looked up. Edwin, ninety-two years old and somehow looking even older, hobbled from the back room, silver cane clicking his familiar walking rhythm on the parquet floor. "There are a few new arrivals in the back. Please process them and place them in the safe."

No squishy sentimentality for Edwin, not even on her final day. But she knew that beneath that gruff white beard and narrowed pale watery-blue eyes beat a heart soft as a down pillow. She'd seen it in the gentle words he spoke to a patron who needed to sell his prized first edition of Wilde's *The Importance of Being Earnest,* in the manner in which he'd saved Poppy from the streets, in the flash of tears when his great-grandchildren burst into the store, even as he sternly told them, "Do not touch a bloody thing with your sticky fingers."

"I'll get right to it, sir."

This was her favorite part of the job, unwrapping and cataloging what had arrived through the back door. She would check each volume against the Book Auction Reference catalog bound in red cloth, and then with each pull of a string or tearing of the packing tape she'd reveal a new treasure. And although this would be the last shipment she would handle here, the last time she'd hope to dig through boxes donated by an old professor to find something worthy, there might be rarer, fancier ones to come at Sotheby's. She smiled, felt the thrill of her new employment: the largest auction house in the world.

Loss and gain. As nearly every myth told: birth, death, rebirth. One thing dying, another born. An old job. A new one.

*You're so dramatic.* She could hear the words of her love, Barnaby, cloaked in admiration.

She pushed open the swinging green-painted door with her palm pressed to the same spot as always. After fifteen years, there might be a permanent but unseen handprint.

Four packages in brown paper and twine crowded a pine table at the center of the dusty room. For Hazel, this part of the job was like Christmas. Edwin had a wonderful knack for locating interesting volumes before anyone else even knew they were available. "To be a proper bookseller you need a researcher's brain, knowing which questions to ask and where to find the answers."

A thick black leather logbook sat open at the left side of the packages. Edwin's tight script filled thin lines of the grid. It had taken Hazel almost a year to decipher his handwriting, like learning hieroglyphics. How long would it take the next employee to understand Edwin as she did?

To the right of each entry in the tattered logbook ran two columns for Hazel's own neat entries: quality and ID number. She cataloged the condition of everything that came through the back door, assigned it an inventory number, then stashed the item in the safe until Edwin decided where and how it would be displayed.

She read the list.

1. First edition Dickens *A Christmas Carol*
2. Handwritten letter from Hemingway to Fitzgerald, 1932
3. A signed (but not first) edition of Tolkien's *The Hobbit*
4. A first edition of Bertrand Russell's *History of Western Philosophy* with the dust jacket made of a WWII map
5. A signed first edition fairy tale by American author Peggy Andrews with original hand-painted illustrations by Pauline Baynes

Edwin adored nabbing the original illustrations for books, for they only grew in value with time. The more popular the book, the more the original drawings became a coveted item for collectors. But it wasn't always about a first edition; to Tim especially it was about the journey of the actual book. Tim valued each one not for its number in the printing order but for the narrative of who had held, loved, and even handed down the book itself. This package with Baynes's paintings sounded intriguing, so Hazel saved it for last.

She slipped on a pair of white gloves, and thirty minutes passed as she cataloged each of the items. Dickens's *A Christmas Carol*'s canvas cover was slightly ripped at the bottom right and had a bit of discoloration on its front left corner. But other than those small defects, it was a glorious edition that would be displayed in the locked glass case of the main showroom. Hazel jotted down the facts in the ledger and set the book aside. She opened the Hemingway letter, checked it for stains or rips, compared the signatures to originals in the files. *The Hobbit*: in perfect condition and obviously kept as a treasure, not as a book to be read and loved. Then the Russell book with a prime example of how, during the paper shortage after WWII, old maps were used as dust jackets. This one was of Stettin, with routes and roads clearly mapped, and a warning: "For the War and Navy Departments only."

Her mind wandered. Tonight she and Barnaby had a dinner planned with her mum, stepdad, and half brother. How could she get out of it? She couldn't, Barnaby would remind her, then kiss her to let her know he was on her side.

And after that: freedom! She had three glorious weeks of holiday before starting the new job.

She planned to luxuriate in the empty days ahead of her. She might board a train to Scotland or a ferry to Ireland. She might escape to Brighton Beach and sit on a patio with a book and nothing else to do but read. And yet she hadn't made any plans but for one: to take a weeklong trip with Barnaby to Paris. Hotel reserved. Ferry tickets purchased. She'd drink fancy cocktails at bars, not pubs. She'd ascend the Eiffel Tower, amble through the Louvre, hopefully make mad love in their hotel room overlooking the Tuileries. She'd saved her pence and pounds for two new dresses now hanging in her closet, awaiting this trip.

Spring in Paris.

"Hazel?" Tim's voice snapped her out of her dream, the last package still taped tight.

"Someone's out here looking for you," he called.

She made her way down the dark back hallway to the main room to find waiting for her a tall man with a black felt hat and an overcoat dripping with rain. Next to him, a woman with raven hair was dressed nearly all in red from her coat to her hat.

"May I help you?" Hazel asked.

"My colleague at Foyles sent me here and said to ask for you," said the man. "You might know about an edition of the 1928 privately printed Auden poems? I hope you do."

"Ah, Tim always says that optimism is an essential quality in a book collector," Hazel said with a confident smile. She motioned for him to follow her to the showroom's back corner, where the red pamphlet was locked tight.

The woman stayed put and Hazel barely noticed her again, even after the man had purchased the pamphlet. She slipped it into a waxed envelope.

"A collector?" she asked, curious.

"No." He shook his head. "My love." He motioned out the front window where Hazel saw the woman who had been with him, her face now raised to the sun. "She's enamored of Auden, and it's for our wedding day."

"Time will say nothing but I told you so." Hazel quoted Auden with a smile.

"That's one of my favorites," he said. "And yet her favorite is 'Let the more loving one be me.' "

"Ah, that's so lovely," Hazel said. "Many happy returns."

By the time she'd finished with the besotted groom, Edwin was off to run an errand and Tim was crouched down, reorganizing a shelf of children's books that had been scattered on the floor by an unattended toddler.

Before she could head to the back room, the door's bell rang its tinny song, and Hazel turned to find her dearest friend, Kelty, and her daughter, Midge, an eight-year-old sprite.

She smiled at Midge, her legs long and the rest of her body trying to catch up in bits and spurts, her auburn hair springing free from two braids just as Kelty's had done all those years ago when Hazel met her during the evacuation.

Images often came back to Hazel that way—quick as hummingbirds— memories of that September day, cold and clear, the day they filed out of Bloomsbury to board trains.

"Auntie Hazel!" Midge threw her arms around Hazel's waist. "Mum said I could get two books today at Foyles. Two!"

"Well, that's jolly," Hazel said, leaning in as Kelty greeted her with a peck on the cheek.

"Just on our way back from school and thought we'd stop by." Kelty wore an emerald dress with a cinched waist and patent leather shoes, looking more like a student than a mum. Her auburn hair was pulled back in a high ponytail with a wide green headband. Every single man looked at her twice—some, a third time.

Midge bounced on her toes. "I'm going in the back to stare at Swallows and Amazons since you won't let me touch it," she said.

"Not now, love," Kelty said. "We're meeting your father." Then to Hazel, "You know her book love is your fault."

"I gladly take full credit." Hazel took a fake bow with a wide sweep of her hand toward Midge, who giggled.

"Come with us?" Kelty asked with hope.

Hazel nodded toward the back room. "I still have work to do."

"I thought so. Well, we just wanted to stop in and see you on your last day at Hogan's. Can't let it go by without some kind of recognition, can we?"

Hazel kissed her godchild on the cheek and gently pulled her pigtails. "See you both tomorrow? I have dinner with Mum and Alastair tonight."

"Good luck there," Kelty said with a hug.

Hazel watched them leave, Kelty holding Midge's hand as she skipped out the door. A surge of love and regret washed over her. How she loved them, but also how she'd resisted having a child of her own, a family of her own. But now a new life was unfurling. She and Barnaby were finally talking of marriage.

There was so much good ahead. After so much loss.

With Tim in the main room, Hazel returned to the packages in the back. She rested her hand on the rectangular bulk of the last one. *The last one*, she noted to herself, then laughed at her dramatic rendering of a simple job.

The carton had arrived from America with bright red airmail stamps. Hazel zipped off the tape to find a parchment-bound portfolio wrapped in red velvet ribbon. She could always tell when a book had been saved for money or for love, and this was love.

She pulled at the end of the ribbon and it gently fell away.

White gloves on, she opened the portfolio to find a stack of hand-colored drawings on thick cotton paper, each one separated by tissue paper.

The illustration on top was an enchanting rendering of two girls holding hands and running through thick emerald woodlands, their pigtails flying behind them, their dresses covered in yellow roses. On the right side was a river. In the background, a glistening white castle where red and green pennants flew from the tops of towers.

Hazel's breath puddled in her chest. She suddenly felt dizzy, untethered. Goose bumps prickled the back of her neck. Her world narrowed to the pile of illustrations on the pine table.

She bent closer. What was it? What was it about this drawing that made it feel as if one might fall into the scene, into the obviously magical land? Small woodland creatures—chipmunks, birds, squirrels, butterfly, beaver—hid among mint green leaves and gnarled branches. An owl, large and looming on a branch above, watched over the girls.

Hazel shivered.

The river, on closer inspection, was glittered with what looked like stars.

Stars.

A river of stars.

Hazel set her white gloved hands on the table and steadied herself. It wasn't possible. Of course it wasn't. She was being fanciful. Too theatrical. There could be other imagined lands with starry rivers. Of course there could be.

She carefully lifted the pile of thick papers and peeked at the book beneath. The title: *Whisperwood and the River of Stars. By Peggy Andrews.* The green-and-blue cover featured the illustration of the girls.

"It can't be," Hazel said quietly. "No."

*Whisperwood* belonged to her and her lost sister, Flora. It was a private realm that had sprung to life between them, a make-believe world to endure through the worst of the war, a place to find comfort where little existed.

And it had disappeared with Flora into the river.

For the first time in twenty years, in pure astonishment, Hazel said the name out loud. "Whisperwood."

# CHAPTER 3

## September 1939

Hazel and Flora sat in the soft grass in their back garden in Bloomsbury, England. The flat had been too quiet, too grim by far. The wireless turned off in case of bad news Mum didn't want the girls to hear and Mum with the telltale tear-swollen eyes she tried to hide from her daughters. They heard her through the thick plaster walls, crying herself to sleep, or maybe never sleeping at all.

But that afternoon in the back garden a brilliant day shone around them, allowing a moment of reprieve. The gold, cracked-brown, and crimson leaves carpeted the grass, which was surrounded by brick walls taller than their papa had been. The enclosed space was no bigger than Hazel's classroom at Bloomsbury School. The girls were waiting for their mum to come home from her shift at the Royal Voluntary Service. Mum absolutely would not, she'd told her daughters, allow herself to be useless when Britain needed her.

Bombs could fall from the sky any day now. At school, Hazel watched scratchy films on the roll-up screen, black-and-white footage of airplanes in the sky, their bellies opening to release cylinders that plummeted to the ground and exploded in fiery destruction. Hazel imagined bombs landing on her, her sister, her house, her mum—on all of her beloved Bloomsbury.

Every morning Hazel awoke safe and sound, yet she wondered, would this be the day? Would this be the day they prepared for at school, the day that posters on London lampposts warned about, the day when they sent the children away to safety, far from their mums and their flats and everything they knew and loved?

It was called Operation Pied Piper, a nursery rhyme name for a horror of an idea.

Hazel heard that some families had sent their children to relatives in America, but the Lindens didn't have any far-off aunts or grands in safe places. She wanted to be brave, but the thought of leaving Bloomsbury and Mecklenburgh Square and their two-bedroom flat in the mansion on the oval park with the lamplit paths kept her jittery and sleepless. If bombs eventually fell from the sky, she didn't understand why going somewhere else would matter so much. The sky domed over everything. There was nowhere to hide.

While Flora dozed in her lap, the memory of the day Papa left intruded like an unwelcome visitor, which it often did when she was quiet.

"You ask too many questions and think too many things," Papa had said with a laugh. He'd stood in front of Hazel and Flora in his drab-olive military jacket. "Don't be bothering your mum with all your questions. Save them for school. She has enough to worry about without trying to dash about finding answers to obscure inquiries." He'd leaned down and kissed Hazel's forehead, a sweet sad smile for just her.

Hazel had nodded through her tears, but she'd wanted to scream, "Don't leave! If you leave, everything will come undone!" She'd known it to be true.

But she hadn't been able to stop anything that was coming their way because outside a honk blared, and through the floor-to-ceiling windows, they could see the long black car at the curb outside their London flat waiting for Papa. Cold rain spit down, tinkling against the windowpanes.

Hazel had grabbed the edges of Papa's stiff uniform's sleeve, and four-year-old Flora had clung to his left leg, so that if he walked he'd drag them out the front door and they'd bounce down the marble steps to the rain-slick pavement facing the garden square. Mum stood behind the sisters, not even trying to hide her weeping. "Girls, your papa *must* leave now."

"No," Flora had said with simplicity and assuredness.

Papa had crouched down and lifted Flora, the only way she'd release his leg, and she'd nuzzled his neck. His thick black hair, a blessing of the Irish he'd told them, hidden beneath his olive-and-brown cap. Hazel had been envious of her little sister, but Hazel was too old by far to be held that way by her father. Instead of weeping like her mum, Hazel had frozen her words stuck below a scrim of ice as cold and silver as the edges of Kensington Gardens' Round Pond in dead winter.

Papa had pried Flora's arms from his neck and kissed her cheeks before handing her to Mum. "I promise to return to my girls." He'd looked to Mum with a gaze so fiercely desperate that Hazel couldn't help but hope that someday a man would look at her the same.

"I love you all so much. Now be good. Help your mum, do what she says, and I will see you soon. Watch out for each other." His face had quivered as if a little earthquake were happening beneath the skin, and this, more than his leaving, made Hazel feel light-headed, terrified.

Kisses all around and then he was gone. He'd walked out the door with every promise to return, but that was the last time they'd seen him. During RAF training one fiery faulty engine took his life.

That was a year ago. Hazel, Mum, and Flora stood, arms around each other, for some time after Papa threw his brown duffel bag over his shoulder and closed the door behind him. Finally Mum exhaled, wiped her face of the tears with the back of her palm. "Well, girls, it's time to set the table. Dinner is almost ready."

So, Hazel thought, *that's how we do this. We pretend. We pretend all is well and we go about our dinners and days until he returns.* But the telegram of his death arrived only a week later, and since then the house and the world had grown dimmer and quieter. War inched toward them and now they could smell its breath in the air.

Now Papa was gone for good and their knapsacks were packed and waiting, gas masks hanging from the straps like snout-nose monsters. They'd been fitted at school—Hazel's dark black and Flora with the preschool version, which was a red-and-blue Mickey Mouse mask designed to keep young children from being frightened of them, but it didn't work. They were scary.

Now, in the back garden with Flora, Hazel didn't want to think about having to leave, but of course she thought of little else.

"Tell me a story," her sister said, waking and stretching, snuggling closer to Hazel, tucking her ragged stuffed teddy under her arm. Flora was so sweet with her wild blond curls, large brown eyes, and those lush eyelashes that almost touched her eyebrows. A sprinkle of freckles spread across her nose and cheeks. And the distinctive birthmark on the inside of her arm, two inches from the inside of her wrist. Hazel said the brown marks looked like rabbit ears; Mum said butterfly wings and Papa said angel wings. Mum once told Hazel that her grandmother had the same mark, and that it was an ancestral gift, not a mistake. That night alone in the washroom, Hazel had scanned her body, or as much of it as she could see, looking for her own ancestral mark. There was none to be found.

Every afternoon now, Hazel was left with her sister, and that was fine by her, that was the easy part. Thinking up *new* stories was the hard part.

The back garden's flowers clung to late summer colors. The cornflowers and Queen Anne's lace bowed close to the ground while the lettuces in Mum's garden withered brown around the edges. Rose bushes spilled pink and red blossoms at the base of the brick wall they shared with neighbors on three sides. Hazel inhaled, feeling words growing and rising from within.

"Not so long ago and not so far away, there was once, and still is, an invisible place that is right here beside us."

Flora laughed in delight. Stories seemed to be Flora's pacifier, the way that Hazel could get her little sister to sit still, to stop thrumming with the live-wire energy that kept her restless. This was the answer to Flora's distress and sleepless nights, her startling at every noise and siren—stories. *This* was how to get through the fear.

Flora, with her five-year-old lisp, asked, "Ith invisible *and* here?"

"Yes! Right here and—incredibly enough—at the same time in another place." Hazel saw it now: No one would decide for them where they'd stay until the war was over. She herself would decide where they stayed. She didn't know much about this new place, not yet. The discovery would come in the telling.

"How can a place be two places?" Flora asked.

"Magic," Hazel answered matter-of-factly. "In this land, anything can happen, we can be anything we desire"—she clapped her hands—"a river full of stars runs right through it."

"I want to go." Flora sat straight and set Berry the teddy on the ground in a slump. "How do we get there?"

"Keep an eye out for the secret doorways. They're hidden everywhere, and only visible to those who are worthy." Hazel paused. "Fortunately, we are worthy."

Flora smiled, sat straighter. "Can we go there?"

"Yes!"

"Where is it?"

Hazel stared to the cloudless sky to find the answer, hoping her imagination might provide it. She thought of Neverland, Wonderland, the Hundred Acre Wood. You had to fly or fall into those secret places.

"Under the rocks?" Flora bent forward, placing her hands on the patchy lawn. "Or is it up high, even higher than the airplanes?"

"No," Hazel said without a doubt, though she couldn't say how she knew. Then she saw an iridescent glow at the edge of the hanging white sheets. "It's always here," she said, "but we can't see it until we walk through the door. Look!" Hazel pointed at the chestnut tree with its brown conkers covered in spiky, green shells hanging from the branches. "The entry shimmers because light sneaks out around the doorway. The air quivers."

"I'm scared," said Flora.

"Don't be. Sure, some woodlands are frightening. Ours is not. It's magic and belongs to us. This land is on our side. It is . . . safe."

Flora wrinkled her nose, popping the paw of her stuffed and ragged Berry between her thumb and forefinger, rubbing it.

"What's the place called?" whispered Flora, her eyes appearing even bigger than usual.

Hazel imagined a woodland, a river, a castle far off. In this place, there were no wars or heartbreak. You could do as you please, become whatever you like.

Flora yanked the ends of Hazel's curls.

"Hazel, what's it called?"

Naming was not to be taken lightly. Flora and Hazel and their mum, Camellia—they'd all been named after plants. Lea and Mersey, their middle names, born of their parents' childhood rivers. "Don't forget," Papa had told his daughters, "you are of earth and water. Both of you. Also of love. Our love." And then he'd pulled Mum to him so tightly that she'd blushed and swatted him away.

The name of their new land came to Hazel right as prayer, a name that already existed, that had waited for them, a name of secrets, of the earth and its rivers, just like the two sisters.

"It's called Whisperwood and the River of Stars."

Hazel took her sister's hand and they stood, walked to the chestnut tree in the corner, and set their hands on its interlacing furrows of bark, rough beneath their palms.

"Close your eyes," Hazel said, and the sisters sat on the grass again, Flora curled against Hazel like a puppy. "This kingdom is made of flowers and rivers and trees—like us."

"Let's go now!" Flora said.

"Once through the door, we can be whatever we choose. We'll have an adventure, but we must return here unless—"

"Unless what?" Flora whispered. "What if we get lost?"

"No one gets lost in Whisperwood."

"Can we stay?" She lifted her face to Hazel, sunlight falling through the leaves, leaving a lace pattern on Flora's cheeks.

Hazel considered it. "Not at first . . . maybe one day, when we choose what we were meant to be. But only then." She scooted closer to the tree, wishing for a hidey-hole, something to enter to take them away. Above them a blackbird, alone and plaintive with its slash of orange beak in the emerald leaves, sang out its distinctive chirpy song.

Flora looked up. "What will we be? Will we be birds?"

"We'll know when the time comes. We just keep trying until we find what's meant for us."

"Will both of us be the same thing?" Flora nestled closer, as if this would guarantee they'd become the same. "I might be a bird and you might be a skunk."

Hazel burst into laughter. "A skunk? Why me?"

Flora nuzzled closer. "Becuth you smell."

Hazel bounced her sister off her lap. "Stop!"

"You don't really," Flora said, and moved closer. "Now what's next?"

Sometimes when Hazel made stories for Flora, what happened next in the plot came flying at her like a secret only she could hear. Other times the story hid in shadows, not ready to reveal itself.

Hazel told her sister the truth. "I don't know. Maybe we are meant to be the same thing, maybe not. But I can tell you that there is always an owl watching over us."

"How do we get in?"

A low cloud tucked itself around the sun like a sheet of linen, so they both shivered before Hazel said, "We enter by whispering its name three times. *Whisperwood. Whisperwood. Whisperwood.*" She paused to create suspense.

"We are here at last," said Hazel. "Isn't it beautiful, Flora? The woodlands are so green, and the river sparkles with stars, and oh, oh! Ahead is the castle!"

"What are we what are we what are we?" Flora trilled impatiently.

"We're . . . bluebirds!"

Opening one eye to look at her sister, a warm feeling spread across Hazel's chest, under her ribs. Flora lay back upon the grass and smiled, her eyes shut so tight her tiny face wrinkled. She raised her arms and flapped them. Yes, this was the way out of worry and fear.

Hazel's voice guided them through forests with branches so immense and sturdy they looked as if they could pick up the sisters and hold them. At the riverbank, they watched dazzling, floating constellations and shooting comets beneath fast-flowing crystalline water.

"Today we'll meet the chipmunk in the red jacket," Hazel explained. "Oh, look, Flora, we are flying over the forest, higher than all the trees. There's where the Thames meets the sea. We can see everything."

They lay quietly together, becoming birds, experiencing their own world in their own minds. As she lifted wings over a vibrant land of her own making, Hazel realized that she'd found a never-ending tale that could be told again and again.

So far gone in their imaginary land, the sisters were startled by their mum's call.

Hazel and Flora opened their eyes to see Mum standing above them, the sunlight behind her creating a nimbus. She wore a pink-and-yellow flowered dress and her long amber curls tumbled down her back, alive in the wind.

Was there another mum in all the world more beautiful than theirs? Hazel doubted it very much.

And yet something was amiss. With her lipstick a slash of red in alabaster, Mum's mouth was a crooked line, quivering and struggling to become straight. Her eyes were alert and her black eyeliner was smudged.

In her hand was a square of cream-colored paper, flapping in the breeze.

# CHAPTER 4

## March 1960

Hazel lifted the book called *Whisperwood* with great care, as if it might disintegrate in her hands. The cover illustration was appealing and whimsical, yet hinted of danger. The river sparkled as any river made of stars must.

Flora.

Was her Flora alive? Was her sister somewhere, telling this story to the world?

Woozy, Hazel flipped over the book and read the copy.

*Whenever they spot a shimmering door seen by no one else, twin orphans Audrey and Janey Burton escape the cruelty of the orphanage where they live. Walking through this entrance, the sisters find themselves in the Kingdom of Whisperwood, where they can become anyone or anything they desire. But after every adventure Audrey and Janey must return to the gloomy rooms of the Shire Orphanage—that is, until they discover who they are meant to be in Whisperwood.*

"Shire." She and Flora lived in Oxfordshire during the evacuation.

She opened the first page.

*Dedication: To Linda Andrews, my mother, who is the beginning of all good stories.*

Who the bloody hell was Linda Andrews? She could not have known this story. No one knew anything about this tale. Yes, her six-year-old sister's disappearance had been covered in the newspapers when it happened in 1940: how she had been lost during the Blitz when they had been sent to the countryside to live without their parents, like so many other children from London.

No one had dared imagine Flora would disappear into thin air—or into the River Thames, if the police were to be believed. At the time the terror of war was the imminent threat, not a little girl's disappearance.

On that autumn morning of 1940, as Hazel and Flora had meandered from the Aberdeens' stone cottage, winding along the woodland path through the damp heather to sit on the wide green meadow beside the River Thames, Hazel had not been paying attention to nature's silent and secret messages as Bridie Aberdeen had taught them.

If she had, she might have noticed the river was moving unusually swift and sure following the previous night's storm, rushing madly past the sisters, carrying away far too quickly the bent twigs they threw into it.

It's possible that the beady-eyed crow who looked down at them, cawing in a chatter near human, was a messenger of doom. Or the owl who, for the past days, had been hooting during daytime hours meant to remind her to pay attention.

The night before, sleep had come so reluctantly that Hazel had wanted to kick her sister from the bed so she could have it to herself. Was it possible that *this* was the reason it had happened—because Hazel had wished her sister gone, if only for a wink, before she'd fallen to sleep?

But for all the details that appeared in retrospect, in the twenty years Hazel had been picking them out of her memory like pills off a sweater, she still believed she'd missed a hint, a clue, a footprint, a note— something that would one day surface and solve the mystery of Flora's disappearance.

Now, in the back room of the small Rare Book Shoppe, the past overcame her. She'd been searching for her sister for twenty years, ever since she'd disappeared when she was six years old from the hamlet of Binsey, and now Hazel had a clue, something to grasp on to, and she was not letting go.

She shoved the other parcels into the safe, engaged the bolt, and twirled the combination. She had only one thought: *This book will lead me to Flora.*

Hazel refolded the *Whisperwood* portfolio up tight, tied the velvet ribbon, and slipped the entire parcel into her leather satchel. Heart pounding, she walked out the back door of Hogan's Rare Book Shoppe, letting the heavy metal door slam and lock behind her.

The loamy spring afternoon was filled with mist, like a veil between the present and the past. She rushed out of the cobblestone alleyway to the front of the bookshop. A group of eight tourists in thick walking shoes and yellow rain slickers followed a stout woman tour guide into the store. Through the wavy glass of the window, Hazel spied Tim inside at the front desk, his head bent over a ledger. He lifted his head as the crowd entered.

He couldn't see Hazel and she ran down the sidewalk. She rushed past the bicycles in blue, green, and red that stood side by side or lazily leaned against each other at the rental stand. Londoners strolled past her as if she didn't even exist.

Possible explanations for the parcel in her satchel rushed at her too quickly, a rainstorm she was trying to catch in a thimble. Was Peggy really Flora? Had Flora told someone? Had Flora truly lived as Hazel and her mum had always barely, but daringly, hoped?

She turned onto Charing Cross, running on the pavement toward the British Museum, and then toward her Bloomsbury home at Mecklenburgh Square. She dashed past the pharmacy with the deep red awning and the café with the scrolled iron tables where couples noodled together over frothy pints. She passed through leafy-green Mecklenburgh Square to the Georgian mansions snuggled next to the edge of its manicured grass, the leaves unfolding, yawning with new spring life.

Hazel arrived at her flat, her childhood home. The building had been built for grandeur in the 1800s, then turned to flats when Londoners chose more posh neighborhoods. In the late 1930s Papa had nabbed the best flat for his family. Through bombings and wars, it still stood, though now it was pockmarked and worse for wear, still showing the scars of a traumatic time for all Londoners—the Second World War.

Hazel always noticed the scars when she walked to the luminescent building, its slightly stained stones and ornate columns on the second level rising to the third, the paint-chipped iron railings and gates protecting its glistening, black-painted doorways and tall windows, one of which was still cracked from a long-ago bombing. She would never look away. To look away was to deny those days, even deny the loss of Flora.

She dug her keys from her satchel, unlocked the door, and hurried inside.

Hazel's flat was ground level, and better for it, Papa had always said. Ornate plaster trim skimmed the edges of tall ceilings, windows yawning open to a back garden and a living room big enough for built-in pine bookshelves to cover every wall and either side of the working stone fireplace, which was stained with decades of soot.

Hazel shed her green mackintosh, hung it on the peg by the front door. The flat's furniture was either bought at a secondhand store or handed down from her mum, comfortable, plush, and almost all of it covered in flowered fabric, as if Hazel's mum meant to bring the garden inside. Books were everywhere, on sagging shelves, side tables, piled against the wall.

Mail was scattered on the floor where it had been dropped through a slot in the door. Magazines. Bills. Advertisements for a new jazz club in Soho. Hazel lifted the lot of it and dropped the pile on the coffee table. The glossy cover of *Vanity Fair* with a photo of a woman in a yellow suit and a yellow hat holding daffodils. Then the magazine's tagline: "For the Younger, Smarter Woman."

Hazel laughed. Younger. Smarter. Sure thing.

Her mum had subscribed to the magazine for Hazel every Christmas with hope Hazel would read the articles on fashion, weddings, and womanhood. She never did. And in this edition: "16 Pages of Going Away Clothes for the Bride!" And for God's sake, another installment of the *Lost Children of Pied Piper* by Dorothy Bellamy, who focused each month on one child who'd been lost during the evacuation of London's children. The insistent journalist had been hounding Hazel to talk to her about Flora for a year now.

Hazel dropped the magazine into the trash bin on her way to the kitchen. She would never, not ever, answer questions about that day and night to anyone but her family and the chief inspector who'd been there the day Flora disappeared, the man she still kept in touch with, Aiden Davies.

She rushed across wide pine floors to the bright yellow kitchen, dropping her satchel on the oak breakfast table before flipping on the overhead light. Above the kitchen sink, a window looked onto a back alley where a stone wall separated her house from the neighbors'. Ivy grew along the crumbling wall and two trash cans leaned heavily against it like drunken bums who'd found themselves halfway home, then collapsed. She set a blue porcelain kettle on the two-burner stove and lit the gas. She waited for the kettle's steamy song.

She needed to calm down or she'd find herself breathing into a paper bag. She turned on the wireless, finding a station playing baroque music. The kettle sang and she poured the boiling water over the Darjeeling tea bag in her favorite porcelain cup with the tiny pink flowers around the edge. She dropped in two sugars, recalling when rationing left them without such luxury.

She slipped the package from her bag and set it on the tabletop, which was scarred with years of knife marks, ink stains, and a dent or two where a pot had been dropped.

She opened the package, untied the ribbon, and set the pile of illustrations to the side. She picked up the book. The spine read: Henry-Todd Publishing, New York, New York. She glanced at the flap—there was no smiling picture of the author as there usually was. Hazel wanted to search her face and features for any sign of Flora. There was no biography but this: *Peggy Andrews lives in Massachusetts. This is her debut novel.*

It was as if they wanted to keep her a secret; it was as if . . . was it possible . . . that they were hiding her true identity? They could bloody well try, but this Peggy woman was telling Hazel's story, and Hazel was going to find her.

If she were honest, there were a few people who might have heard her and Flora tell of their secret land of Whisperwood. But only a very few. And they would *not* have run off to America to write this story.

Would they?

There was nothing to do now but read.

There must be a rational explanation.

*"If you were born worthy, and we all are and don't always know it, you will find your way through the forest glade to the doors that await you. When entering, you will find a land made for you,"* Audrey said to her sister, Janey.

The beginning wasn't exactly right—the wording had shifted a bit from the opening Hazel always used like an incantation when she was telling the story to Flora. She kept reading.

*The sisters sat in a sunny garden on a bright red blanket, a brief respite from the Shire Orphanage where Madame Bullynose was waiting to collect the blackberries they had been ordered to gather.*

Hazel laughed. Madame Bullynose! That was cheeky—definitely not part of Hazel's original story. So there were embellishments. But the garden and the red blanket—that was Flora's and hers.

*"Everyone is born with this knowing," said Audrey. "But the adults, with their wounds and their lists and the trivial things that seem to matter to them but really do not matter at all, forget about this knowing. They let pain and loss and heartache block the doorways."*

*Janey whispered, "But the children remember."*

With the wireless music rising and falling, with the sweet chirping of birds outside and her tea growing cold at her side, Hazel read of two girls named Audrey and Janey who lived on a spit of land on a bayside in Cape Cod, Massachusetts.

The girls searched cranberry bogs and bays to find shimmering doors leading to another world. It wasn't England, but there was a starry river and wild hills of heather, cliffs, boulders, and rocks. And there were also sand dunes that spilled onto wide beaches and ponds of snapping turtles and giant fish, lakes with endless bottoms.

The illustrations on every few pages enhanced the story with clarity and whimsy.

As the story continued, the girls met characters from fairy tales. They met Hansel and Gretel and warned them not to enter the woods, explaining that they would be locked up and fed sweets by an old woman who wanted to eat them. Pages later, the two sisters met Snow White and told her not to eat any apples.

By changing the middle of these stories, the sisters made better endings. Endings they liked. The three little pigs might roast the wolf for dinner or Goldilocks might adopt the three bears. Peggy Andrews's orphans weren't just wandering through Whisperwood taking in the sights, they were changing centuries-old stories to suit their fancies.

Two hours later, Hazel sat back in her chair. This American author knew their secret story; was it possible Flora had told it, was even the author? Sure, the author had changed some parts, but then again, how much could a six-year-old remember?

She closed the cover. "How do you exist?"

Through the years, with Flora's absence a soft wound in the center of her body, the low buzz of loss and mystery inside of her, Hazel had often wondered if Whisperwood had gone on without her and Flora, if the land they'd made together had its own adventures while she lived her real life. Whisperwood was fantasy, no different than any of the books Hazel had loved, *Alice's Adventures in Wonderland*, *Peter Pan*, *The Hobbit*, or The Chronicles of Narnia . . . but Whisperwood was long gone, faded to gossamer.

Hazel had thought about writing the tale in one of her many notebooks, but she'd tossed her childhood writings into the river after Flora disappeared. She'd considered peeking back through the shimmering door to see if their land had lived on. But each time she thought about it, a great fear stayed her.

Why would she visit the land that made Flora disappear? Or the woods that put her in danger, the river that possibly drowned her sister?

Yet somehow their river of dreams and stories had flowed to America.

What the bloody hell was Hazel supposed to do now?

She could have ignored the book. She could put the novel and illustrations in Edwin's safe, shaking her head at the odd synchronicity of the fairy tale, attributing its existence to the universal unconscious that Jung espoused, the mystery of imagination.

But she couldn't turn away from her own tingle of knowing.

This was indisputably her Whisperwood.

How would she find the author? There weren't many options: She could call the publishing house or fly across the ocean and comb the entire state of Massachusetts. She could hardly call an operator in America and ask, "Do you know a Peggy Andrews in Massachusetts?" Was there a phone book of Massachusetts residents in the British Library? If there was, how many Andrews would she find?

Hazel spread the original drawings in a fan across the table. They were beautiful originals; collector's items; one of a kind. And with that, the truth hammered into her chest: She had walked out of her place of employment without a word, stealing valuable signed illustrations by the prominent Pauline Baynes of Narnia fame along with a signed first edition fairy tale. She had just committed a crime.

Edwin could have phoned Scotland Yard for less than what she'd just done.

A thief, and yet . . .

This was *her* fairy tale.

It belonged to her.

And to Flora.

Taking the book and picture collection was thoughtless at best, a crime at worst. But Flora was the reason Hazel still listened to every whisper and goose-flesh moment, to the trill of something amiss or a magpie's call, the way a friend stirred their tea clockwise or anticlockwise. Within her an unrelenting alertness kept her noticing the books that happened to fall into her hands or song lyrics that struck her just so, to the hoot of an owl during daylight that might mean something rare. Her heart always scanning, even when she was consciously unaware, for something that might point the way to Flora.

# CHAPTER 5

## March 1960

There was a jangling noise, loud and insistent. After two more rings, Hazel realized the noise came from the telephone on the kitchen wall.

She lifted the green plastic receiver from its cradle with a "Hallo."

"Hazel, are you quite all right?"

Tim. He sounded worried.

"I am. Yes."

A hot blush of fear rose on her neck. He already knew.

"You left without saying goodbye." Silence, a beat she couldn't read. "But I understand, my friend. I am terrible at goodbyes myself. And it's not as if you're *really* leaving. You're still here in London. Just not here in the store." He laughed, but it was an uncomfortable sound as if he'd never done it before.

"I'm sorry," she said. "I'm terrible at farewells, you're right. And a bit hungover from last night. The pub was the better goodbye, as it is."

"Agreed," he said. "The store was rushed with a tour group, and I didn't even realize you'd left. We will miss you so very much. I know you have holiday but promise to tell us all about your first day at Sotheby's, will you?"

"I promise. And Tim, I am so sorry." She hesitated. This was her chance to confess what she'd done, to tell him that she'd carried the parcel through the back door, that she'd taken the portfolio by accident. Anyway, she'd return it tomorrow.

But she didn't say a word.

"No need for apology. Be well, Hazel. London is changing so quickly, and I guess things are expected to change here, too."

She hung up with a trembling hand. Yes, it was a new decade.

London was shifting beneath their feet, changing in ways she saw in quick flashes: music with a new beat, transistor radios, the crowds in Soho, the hemlines rising and the hair falling, the aristocrats mixing with the commoners on the street and in the pubs. Whispers of a drug blotted on tissue paper that could take anyone to a new world.

Londoners had finally come to believe there would be no more war. The brief respite between the first and second wars had trained them to wait for the next, but now, fifteen years later, they were relaxing, the divots and hollows of war being filled in with concrete and hope.

And Hazel, too, was moving on.

Until this.

All these years of keeping in touch with Chief Inspector Aiden Davies to make sure he didn't forget Flora, the annual dig through the trunk in the hall closet to reread newspaper articles and relive the day to find a hint or clue she'd missed, and now this. She decided to write down every possible way this book might have been written by an American author, then found its way to Hogan's Rare Book Shoppe.

She opened the pine hutch on the far wall of the kitchen and from the bottom shelf grabbed a robin's-egg-colored notebook. It was one of the myriad notebooks that found their way into her home from almost every stationery shop and bookstore in London: blue and red, paisley and cream, palm-sized and large. They filled her cabinets, drawers, and countertops.

What she was meant to write in the notebooks she was never entirely sure, but there they were, blank and waiting for her when she was ready to use them. Her desire to write stories had been extinguished the day Flora disappeared, but that didn't stop Hazel from buying these lovely notebooks. And that didn't keep her from regularly heading straight from work along Charing Cross Road to Gerrard Street and into the Legrain coffee shop, where serious, studious writers gathered.

She wanted to be one of them, be one of the patrons who called themselves writers or authors. She wanted to be one of the women who wrote books that found their way to the shelves of libraries and bookshops. She wanted to be . . . an author. But it was a ridiculous dream, especially since she couldn't even begin a story since the day Flora disappeared. The empty notebooks piled around her flat, the lists she made of ideas and to-do lists were the only remnants of her urge to put words to paper.

From the bottom shelf she picked up her green clay inkpot and her prized silver engraved nib pen. Then she carefully placed the illustrations in a pile at the far edge of the table. The top drawing, matching the cover of the book, glimmered under a vellum cover sheet.

She opened to the first unlined blank page, her pen lingering as an ink-tear dropped to the blank paper.

*People who might know of Whisperwood:*

1. *Harry Aberdeen*
2. *Bridie Aberdeen*
3. *Mum*
4.

Hazel closed her eyes and tried to remember who'd been near when she and Flora had whispered the story to each other. They had never told the story in a public place, so it couldn't be kind Father Fenelly with his black shirts and white collar, or the pinched-faced teacher named Miss Slife, or the four wide-eyed nurses or the gentle pub master, Mr. Nolan, neither the teasing twins nor the awful frizzy-haired hag nor—

A knock on her flat door, and Hazel dropped the pen. She stood and walked into the living room.

Thank goodness it was Barnaby, with his wind-whipped black hair under his green felt cap, his kind blue-gray eyes, his cheery voice and sharp cheekbones, and the silver scar that ran along his left cheek that told a story of a bomb on his childhood street in Hampstead Heath. *His* parents had refused to send him away, taking their chances.

"Hello, love," he said, hugging her close, nuzzling her neck with his stubbly dark beard. The man could grow a beard between breakfast and lunch.

"A nice surprise," she said, kissing him.

She was a bit disoriented.

"Surprise? We are meant for dinner with your mum and stepdad in half an hour."

"Oh no . . ."

"You forgot?" He tapped her nose.

"I did. Can we cancel? I'm not up for Mum and blowhard Alastair right now."

He grinned. "I have no problem canceling." Already he was unbuttoning his gray wool coat, hanging it on the peg by the door, plopping his cap on the bench to settle in.

"Make a drink," she said. "And I'll make the call. I have something to tell you."

He raised his eyebrows. "That sounds mysterious."

"A story," she said.

"My favorite." He moved to the silver bar cart with the bottles of Macallan's and Jameson, the Relsky and the Gordon's glittering like jewels among the Waterford highball glasses.

Hazel went back into the kitchen and picked up the phone to call her mum, who would be unhappy at the change in plans.

———

## London, 1957

Hazel arrived early at the white stone building on Bond Street: Sotheby's Auction House. Just entering the famed establishment gave her a thrill. Inside she found the cavernous auction room with its open beamed ceilings of gleaming dark wood, a burlwood podium squatted at the front. Voices overlapped in the din.

A black canvas sign hung crooked on the wood-paneled wall to the left, declaring the auction for the day: RARE BOOKS, MANUSCRIPTS, AND AUTHOR MEMORABILIA.

Hazel registered at a long linen-covered table and took her paddle: Number 42.

"Excuse me, excuse me," she mumbled as she sidled past others to an empty seat.

She wouldn't buy anything. She never did. She didn't have the money. But she did have enough love for books and manuscripts to want to see it all in person, to scope out anything Edwin might have missed.

Today there would be letters from Charles Dickens to Elizabeth Gaskill, a few original manuscript pages of *The Hobbit*, and—the most interesting—a silver engraved fountain pen from Virginia Woolf's estate. It couldn't be said what she wrote with it, but Hazel imagined the essay "A Room of One's Own."

The gavel banged on the pedestal and the room fell to silence. A tall man with a bald head, shiny under the overhead lights, called out, "Come to order. We'll begin with item zero-six-zero on page two. A first edition of *Alice's Adventures in Wonderland*."

The pages of auction brochures rustled, and the frenzy was on: paddles raised, voices calling out, bids placed while the room grew louder. A man arriving late sidled in on the left side of Hazel. He fumbled with his satchel, dropped it as papers fell out and scattered on the floor.

"Fuck," he said. He cringed and bowed his head. "Sorry." He shoved his papers back into his satchel and shook his head. "Bloody rotten train," he said, then was fully focused on the brochure for a moment before turning his attention to the man at the podium.

Hazel stared at the silver scar running along his left cheek, wondering about its story. The man's curly hair was brushed back with pomade, comb marks evident. She guessed early thirties, same as her, but she'd been wrong before. He wore a focused expression and had a chiseled chin. When he slanted his eyes in her direction, she looked away. She'd been caught staring.

She absolutely would not swoon over another man who would become shut up in another room down a long hallway of doors she always ended up closing—sometimes slamming. Another man whom she'd need to tell, "I'm just not ready for this." Another man who'd want her to move in with him and take her away from Mecklenburgh Square.

He raised his paddle for a few items but never won.

"Do I know you?" she quietly asked him between artifacts.

"I don't think so," he said with a smile that radiated kindness. "I'm Barnaby Yardley."

"I'm Hazel," she said, and feeling like she had to explain why she was there, she added, "Hogan's Rare Book Shoppe."

"Ah, my father's favorite."

Then there it was: Virginia's pen held high in the air by the man in the black gown. The author had lived on the same Bloomsbury square where Hazel lived now, yet Virginia Woolf's apartment had been bombed and destroyed. Hazel thought of Virginia despondent and hopeless. In spite of the beautiful words she wrote she still filled her pockets with rocks and took herself to the River Ouse to drown.

Hazel's paddle was in the air. She realized it only after she'd done it.

Then the man called Barnaby raised his as well.

On the next round of bids, she again raised her paddle.

So did he.

Hazel twisted in her seat and faced him. The only way she'd be able to purchase that pen was if her mum gave her more money. And she was determined that would never happen again. Even for Virginia Woolf's pen.

Barnaby Yardley won the bid and Hazel stood, feeling deflated.

Once outside, a humid summer day pressed down on her shoulders and Hazel walked home with her hands in fists, her leather satchel bouncing against her hip. Who was that guy who'd purchased the pen she coveted? He was an ass. A prig. A man most likely with family money who'd no idea what it was like to scrape pounds together for the gas bill in winter.

Two days later, he arrived at Hogan's Rare Book Shoppe. She was unlocking the cabinet to bring out a first edition of Orwell's *Nineteen Eighty-Four* for an order in America.

"Well, hallo there," he said with a grin.

It took a moment for her to place him as he wore a gray felt hat pulled low on his forehead. A University of London crest was sewn on his jacket pocket.

A professor, she guessed.

She nodded at him but didn't answer. She had books to shelve, messages to answer, an angry customer who'd bought a book with missing pages.

"I'm sorry," he said.

"Excuse me?" She held the Orwell novel and backed away a few inches.

"Sorry for outbidding you."

Ah, she realized, it was the dreamy dope from the auction. She waved the book, yet didn't move.

He smiled. "It's fascinating seeing the remnants of our literary heroes, isn't it?"

"It is," she said. "Like digging up fossils to see how things developed."

"Exactly!" he said, and smiled so kindly that she felt warm.

An odd pause, then he asked, "Was there a particular reason you wanted that pen?"

Hazel tilted her head and really looked at the man. He seemed sincere. "I wanted it for loads of reasons, none of which are logical or intellectual. And it's most likely best that I didn't win it."

"Tell me one reason you wanted it," he said.

"Adeline Virginia Woolf once lived in the building next to me during the war, yet her building was destroyed and mine wasn't. She once sat in that flat and wrote books. She tried to save her own life with words and she never was quite able to do so, eventually walking into a river and . . ."

Did he have a quick flash of tears? She wasn't sure. He nodded. "That's so sad, yet the world still has her work now."

"That's so true." Hazel nodded, warming to him now, but hesitant. "What would it be like if we didn't have *To the Lighthouse*."

"Or *Mrs. Dalloway*," he said.

From a room over, someone called Hazel's name and she glanced backward and then looked to Barnaby. "I need to get back to work." She couldn't resist a parting shot. "Enjoy your pen."

"Hazel, would you like to have dinner with me tonight?"

Turned out he wasn't an ass. Or a prig. He was a professor of British medieval literature. He was also from an aristocratic family who spent holidays in a run-down stone castle in Scotland where they hunted stag and grouse. In Hampstead Heath, the Yardleys owned a mid-eighteenth-century brown brick house with a rooftop overlooking London and a library where Barnaby's father's literary collection had grown to be one of the most famous in England. He'd bought quite a few books from Hogan's.

It didn't matter that she had every intention of resisting his charms. After a dessert of crème brûlée, he'd presented her with the pen in a blue velvet box. "I thought I was buying this for my father's collection, but instead I was buying it for you."

———

Barnaby stood at the brass bar cart in her living room, twirling a Waterford highball between his palms, lamplight catching the cut glass and amber whiskey. He smiled at her when she entered the room and handed the glass to her. "I have a feeling this story you're set to tell me might need this."

"It might," she said.

They sat facing each other on the saggy flowered couch. Hazel leaned on the armrest and cradled her drink without taking a sip. "It's about my sister," she said.

His thick dark eyebrows rose, making furrows on his forehead, and he leaned forward. "Your lost sister. Is there news?"

"Of a sort." Hazel shifted on the couch and set her whiskey on a dainty side table.

"Today I found a book. One that's been released in America. A fairy tale."

He nodded for her to go on. He knew about Flora, of course. Everyone did. There had been newspaper articles—the lost girl of Pied Piper who was never found, no matter how many search parties went out, no matter how many times they dredged the river. The tale of Flora had become a ghost story, an Oxford, Binsey, and Bloomsbury legend.

But Hazel had never told Barnaby the full truth. She'd never told *anyone* the full truth. Not even Kelty. She closed her eyes, pressed her fingertips to her temples. Opening her eyes, she looked at the man she loved so very much and started again.

"When Flora and I were children," she said, "fourteen and five years old in 1939, England had just declared war on Germany. London was on edge. Papa had already been . . . was already gone . . . you know, the training accident." She cringed. "And then Flora and I were sent to the countryside to live with strangers."

"Yes, darling, I know." Barnaby took her hand.

"Well, I'd tell Flora stories to keep her happy, to distract her."

"Fairy stories? Like of the wee folk?"

"Not exactly. It was more, like, an endless story, an imaginary land for the two of us. Whisperwood and the River of Stars was only ours."

"Whisperwood?"

She cringed at the dip in the tone of his voice. Barnaby was hurt that she'd never told him about any of this. Hazel was well attuned to disappointment in others. She picked up on any and all ways she didn't please someone.

"Yes, and, Barnaby, Whisperwood is also the name of this new book written by an American author named Peggy Andrews. It's not just the title that's similar, so is the actual land and parts of the story."

"Oh, Hazel, honey, you think this author might be your sister?"

She stared at him and saw it, as evident as a lighthouse in fog: pity. Pulling away her hand, she sat straighter. "I don't know what to think. But I want to know how our story made its way to America. I'm confused . . . no one knows this tale. What if—?"

"What if she's alive," he finished for her.

Hazel nodded but barely, reluctant to let in too much—or any— hope. Still, while Barnaby stared at her, her wish seemed to grow, the thrill of the idea that Flora might be alive, an incredible ending to a long saga.

"This is stunning," he said, "but can you be sure no one else knew the story? Not the woman you lived with or the boy or—"

"Bridie and Harry," she interrupted. "No. They never knew about Whisperwood."

"You're sure?" He scooted across the couch to take her hands once more. He ran his thumb across the top of her hand.

"I am mostly sure."

"I'm trying to see where you are going with this. Do you think that if you track down this author you'll find Flora or perhaps learn what happened to her?"

"It occurred to me. Yes."

"Maybe you should finally call that woman who writes the lost children articles. Maybe she can help."

"Dorothy Bellamy? Are you serious? She romanticizes these lost children. She writes fluff pieces for the younger, professional woman." Hazel mocked the tagline and rolled her eyes. "How in the hell would it help to tell her this?"

"I don't know. She's a reporter, right? Did you ever talk to her?"

"No, and I won't. She can write me ten thousand more letters or call Aiden Davies a million more times." Hazel shook her head. "For God's sake, Barnaby, she calls Flora 'The River Child.' I don't want Flora to be some doomed legend, some Juliet or Isolde. I want her to be *alive*." Hazel paused because she knew what Barnaby was thinking. "She is not the child they found in the river near Wallingford in 1956. That was not her. I don't care what they say—they never positively identified that body as her. All they know is that it was a skeleton of a five- to six-year-old female. There was no way to look for distinguishing marks."

"Like bunny ears," he said with compassion.

"Yes."

Logic might insist it could be Flora's remains, that she'd floated undetected in marsh and tides to settle there, but Hazel refused to believe it.

"I want anything you want, I do," said Barnaby, "but I bet a great many people knew this story of yours. The adults around you? The teachers? Your mum? I don't want you to get your hopes up too much. The survival of a story is not the same as the survival of your sister."

"Thank you, professor," Hazel said, a bite of anger in her voice.

"*Whoa*, there. Don't take this out on me. It's only a book, a fairy tale."

"Which one is a fairy tale, Barnaby? The one about finding Flora, or the book by Peggy Andrews? Because either way, it is never, ever *only* a fairy tale." She hadn't meant to sound so harsh. She lowered her voice. "You think it's a coincidence, don't you? What you'd call synchronicity. The universal unconscious, I know. All of that is well and good in theory but I am currently faced with this one thing, Barnaby: This story *could* be mine. It could be Flora's. Surely that must *mean* something."

"Oh, Hazel." He held her close and she smelled the woody aroma of cigarettes that infused all his clothes. He pulled back and kissed her softly. "They bloody well called the scheme Operation Pied Piper. Not very well thought out when you consider what happened to the children in the Grimm's fairy tale." He stood and walked to the bar, poured himself another finger of whiskey.

"I know." She took a swallow of her own whiskey, the warmth flowing down. How could she explain to Barnaby how it had all felt; how it felt even now to know she'd lost her sister. The dread. The panic. The jealousy of other people having small children at their side. How she'd awaken with a pounding heart knowing she lost something but for a sacred few moments not remembering what it was. The despair eased through the years, but not much. As she grew older, nothing quelled the memories: not liquor, not men, not stories or books or the distractions of friends and parties.

At twenty-five years old, she'd realized that all she could do with the ache and the shame was to live with it, allow it to walk next to her like a shadow, a ghost, a living memory. Some days, she'd turn to that loss and acknowledge it, and sometimes, for blessed hours, she would forget, but then the shadow would fall long and fast onto her soul and she'd remember this: She lost her sister. "Watch out for each other" would echo down the long halls of her heart and she'd shudder as she did now.

"Do you have the new book here?" asked Barnaby.

"I do." She stood and took his hand, leading him down the narrow dark blue hallway to the sunny room in back, which smelled of tea, rosemary, and a tinge of lavender from the potted plants on her windowsill, a scent memory of Binsey.

# CHAPTER 6

## September 1939

Hazel had known the minute she saw the note in Mum's hand flapping in the breeze that something terrible had happened—the evacuation notice had come through. Tears ran down Mum's cheek and she didn't bother to wipe them away.

"It's an order from the government," Mum had explained. "Germany invaded Poland and now . . . this."

OPERATION Pied Piper: EVACUATION OF ALL CHILDREN FROM LONDON IMMEDIATELY.

While Mum and Flora slept, Hazel awoke to the gentle pattering of rain on the window. Slipping out of bed, her bare feet sank into the sheepskin rug and her new plaid flannel nightgown, which was a bit too long, dragged along the floor.

In the dark of night, Hazel tiptoed into the living room, quieter than a feather falling. Light from the lamppost outside filled the room with a hazy glow, just enough to help her locate what she needed: *Grimm's Fairy Tales*.

She remembered a snowy afternoon long ago, before Flora was born. Hazel had sat on her papa's lap as he read the story of Cinderella from his family's pale blue Brothers Grimm book. Mum had been cooking in the kitchen and the world was right and true—even as the birds pecked out the eyeballs of the evil stepsisters.

"Theo!" Mum had appeared suddenly at their side, grabbing the colorful book from Hazel's father's hands. "Don't scare her. She's too young for such grisly tales."

Papa had pulled Hazel close and kissed the top of her head. "Hazel knows that fairy tales aren't real."

Mum had dragged a wooden chair from the corner with a high screeching sound, stood on its seat in her stocking feet, and slipped the book onto the top shelf where Hazel couldn't reach it.

Now, Hazel looked up and there it was, exactly where Mum had put it all those years ago on the top bookshelf to the right of the hearth. Inside those blue covers, she knew, was the story of the Pied Piper.

She brought the same wooden chair to the bookshelves, stood on it, and grabbed the book from its spot. She carried the book to a cozy corner chair covered in chintz, curled her legs beneath her, and read by the outdoor lamppost light.

Hazel soon found the story she was looking for. A piper who arrived in a German city named Hamelin was given the job of luring the town's hated rats to a river to be drowned. By doing this, the Pied Piper saved the town.

That was good, wasn't it? The Pied Piper saved the town!

She read on.

Then the mayor of Hamelin refused to pay the colorfully attired piper. In return, the man donned a bright red cap, played his seductive flute tune, and led the town's children into the hills and valleys and rivers beyond, never to be seen again.

Only two children—blind and lame, who could not follow the piper—were spared. The rest of the town's children disappeared forever.

Hazel let out a cry of despair, then quickly covered her mouth. If she was looking for comfort in this story, it was not to be found. No Pied Piper would take them away forever. She would protect Flora until their return to Bloomsbury.

She would have to make up her own stories.

Hazel awoke the next morning, scared and not wanting to show it. Flora was curled next to her; she'd wiggled free of her own tangled sheets in the middle of the night and climbed into Hazel's bed.

The sounds of Mum cooking breakfast seeped under the bedroom door: the clang of pans, her singing, the whistle of the kettle. Flora still slept as she rounded into Hazel, back-to-back. Hazel rolled over and put her arms around her little sister, causing her to stir. Flora twisted around to face her.

"No!" she said firmly.

"I know," Hazel replied in a whisper, knowing exactly what Flora's declaration meant. Do not get up. Do not take me from this place. Do not let this be the morning we must leave.

"Not yet?" she asked.

"No, sleep a little longer," said Hazel.

A sword of sunlight sliced through the thin slat of open curtain and landed between Flora and Hazel. Hazel reached over and rested her hand on the sunlight to cover it, ensuring nothing came between them.

After breakfast, Mum snapped a photo of the two sisters on the front stoop. Then they walked to the Argyle School where Hazel and Flora joined the children marching to the train station. The air was wet and cold, the kind of weather that moves to the bones. Mums, fathers, and children were crowded together as they followed the teachers through thin alleyways and up ascending streets. Gas masks swung from knapsacks like huge insect heads, terrifying Hazel each time she accidently glanced at one. Girls with bows in their hair wore swing coats and scarves pulled tight around necks. A growing crowd behind them propelled them forward.

They passed women and men who stopped what they were doing to sadly observe the desultory line of children marching past, as if they were harbingers of doom. Shopkeepers watched the procession while others leaned against iron lampposts, some of them waving at the children even as they taped huge X-patterns across their windows so they would not shatter when the bombs dropped. Bloomsbury Park—with the sitting statue of Charles James Fox that the girls had climbed around and hidden behind—was empty. Hazel imagined the brightly dressed Pied Piper leading them away from family and home.

Her knapsack seemed to grow heavier by the minute. Weeks ago, she'd packed it with Mum and Flora, only half expecting to ever actually carry it to the train station. They'd ticked through the printed list from the government.

Gas mask.

Plimsolls.

Identity card and ration book.

Toothbrush.

Comb.

Spare socks.

Mackintosh.

Hazel hoisted her bag higher as lines of children from other schools and other areas converged on the train station's platform.

Mum held on to the sisters' hands; Flora on one side, with her teddy bear dangling from her tight grip, its ragged paw dragging on the ground, and Hazel on the other. Their teacher, Miss Plink, hurried ahead of them, and they hustled to keep up. Miss Plink held a sign for Hazel's class, and then they were on the edge of the platform, as people pushed and shoved and cried out for friends or parents. Flora was allowed to go with Miss Plink's class and stay with Hazel.

Mum, Flora, and Hazel stood silently clinging to each other.

From her jersey pocket Mum produced two tags fastened with strings. She slipped them around her daughters' necks as if the girls were luggage.

Hazel lifted hers from her chest and turned it round to read:

**Name:** Hazel Mersey Linden

**Address:** Bloomsbury, London

**Date of Birth:** June 2, 1925

**School Attended:** Argyle School

Then on the back of it.

**DESTINATION:**

And here there were three lines, one for County, one for Parish, and one for Burgh. They were blank because no one knew where they would end up.

From behind came a great surge of people. Hazel felt herself falling forward toward the tracks. She grabbed Mum's coat, and Mum clutched Hazel's arm. Hazel stared at the weeds growing between the shiny gray metal rails and then just like that, the train arrived with a noisy clamor, screeching, bearing down, smoking like it was on fire and emitting great puffs of white clouds.

Mum let out a cry, then placed her hand over her mouth.

"All aboard!" shouted a man's gravelly voice.

This was it. This was the leaving. "Where is this train going?" Hazel asked.

"I don't know," Mum said, her voice choked, "but, Hazel, send me your postcard the minute you arrive. You must let me know you are safe."

Miss Plink's voice hollered, "Climb aboard! Children, get on!"

One by one, members of Hazel's class along with their younger siblings climbed the stairs from the platform onto the railcar. Mum hugged her daughters and did not even attempt to hide the tears pouring down her face. "I will not rest until I hear from you."

"I love you so much," Hazel said, thinking that it could be the last thing she ever said to her mum.

Mum hugged her girls while others behind them were pushing.

"Where are we going?" Hazel asked again.

Miss Plink stood above Hazel at the top of the stairs and held out her hand to pull Hazel up. "We won't know until we get there," Miss Plink told her. "They keep the destination secret so there aren't any records; it is to keep you safe. You can send a postcard as soon as you arrive."

The train lurched forward, its whistle screamed. Another was due to arrive just after. Hazel thought about chance and luck, and how other children would get on the next train to take them somewhere different. Was her best luck on this train or the next? How could she ever know?

Hazel and Flora stumbled down the aisle and found two empty seats as the train picked up speed. Flora's hair had come loose from the sweet pink ribbon Mum had put in and Hazel took the bow from Flora's hair and tucked it into her jersey pocket.

The train was stuffy. Too many people filled it with their fearful breathing. Hazel squeezed Flora's hand. Her eyes were so wide, taking in the other frightened children, the battered suitcases and ragged knapsacks, the pillowcases stuffed with clothes.

"Hazel, will there be a river of stars?" her sister asked.

"Absolutely," Hazel stated, attempting the authority of a grown-up telling lies.

Flora fell asleep in Hazel's lap while Hazel stared out the window. Train stations flew by without names on them—identifying signs had been removed to confound the enemy seeking to find their way. They switched tracks, and Hazel grew confused about what direction they were headed. She finally closed her eyes but never really slept. At last, she felt the train grind to a stop.

The Linden sisters climbed off the train onto a wooden platform, holding their knapsacks while Flora also clung to Berry. The afternoon sun was high and bright. Hazel couldn't say how long they'd been traveling. It had been an hour . . . or five? It might have been the next day.

They stood with their classmates, close together, arm to arm, sacks bumping and jostling, but no one said a word. In the eerie quiet, they followed Miss Plink inside the station.

A black sign with white enamel letters hung on the wall—OXFORD.

Oxford, England, was a place Hazel had heard quite a bit about. Papa attended university here at Christ Church and Mum had visited him from London during his schooldays. This was a setting as legendary as Whisperwood and had always seemed just as imaginary. Until now, Bloomsbury was the only *real* place.

In Oxford, Mum and Papa had fallen in love.

But the scene Hazel now beheld was nothing like she'd imagined Oxford. Children were crowded and crunched together. Flora was quietly crying, Hazel held her hand. She needed to be brave. There was no one else to look to for help.

This may have been the loneliest Hazel had ever been. It was a hollowed-out feeling. If getting through this wartime was up to her, they were doomed.

"Are we staying here?" Flora asked.

Hazel answered honestly. "I don't know." She attempted a smile. "Let's eat the snacks Mum made us."

Flora nodded and wiped tears from her face with the back of her hand. Hazel kissed Flora's cheek and tasted the salty fear. Next to them, a young boy wept, the groin and inside of his pants stained where he'd wet himself. Hazel reached over and patted his shoulder, yet he paid her no mind, insulated in his misery.

Across the station, Miss Plink spoke to a man in a blue stiff uniform. Hazel kept Miss Plink in her sights as she guided Flora a few steps away to a wooden crate to sit upon. They undid the parcel Mum had prepared: two boiled eggs, a square of cheese, two pieces of bread. A note was bent three times into a rectangle.

Flora looked up to Hazel. "Read it."

"Let's save it for later, when we find out where we'll be."

Flora picked up the note and stuffed it into the pocket of her mackintosh.

"Don't lose it!" Hazel said in a voice too stern. Flora's lip trembled.

"I won't," she said.

In silence, they ate their cheese, their bread, their eggs, and—finally, slowly—two tiny squares of chocolate.

"Miss Plink's class, follow me!" called out an echoing male voice with a thick Cockney accent.

Another classmate, a tall boy named Padraig Logan, raised his hand just as if they were in a classroom and Miss Plink had asked them to solve the math problem on the board.

"Yes, Padraig?" Miss Plink asked.

"Where are we going?" His voice shook, and this scared Hazel as much as anything had, for Padraig was the class clown. With his wild dark hair and blue eyes that looked like tiny globes, he was the jokester who always made them laugh.

"We'll be heading first to the town hall at city center. Once we get there, a lovely family will choose you and take you home. All will be well."

Hazel did not quite believe Miss Plink, and she stared at the white enamel sign, emblazoned with black letters: OXFORD.

# CHAPTER 7

## March 1960

Barnaby put his drink down, then placed his palms on either side of the book, leaning over to stare at its cover. Standing next to him, Hazel needed to look away, at something other than his reaction. Behind him on the yellow linoleum kitchen counter sat her eggcup from this morning, crusted yellow at its edge. An upside-down spoon was at its side. The saltshaker was shaped like a lamb. Her simple world before she'd found the book.

"What a gorgeous cover," he said.

"Isn't it?" She took a swig of the whiskey.

"Those?" Barnaby pointed to the pile of drawings.

A drop of her stomach: She should have tucked them away. He would know what they were worth.

"These are the original illustrations," she said. "I took them from the shop."

"You took them? As in, Edwin and Tim don't know you have them?" She cringed. "It was a mistake."

His eyebrows drew down and in. "I'd say it's a mistake. Let's take them back right now."

"We should. Yes, we should," she said. "I haven't even looked at all of them yet. Maybe we can do it in the morning?"

"Hazel, you aren't thinking straight."

"Agreed." She didn't need him telling her this. Here stood the man who *never* became frayed at the edges or angry or desolate. Barnaby was steady and true. But bloody equanimity was not what she needed at the moment.

"Are you all right?" he asked. "You're worrying me." He touched her forehead with the back of his hand.

His tenderness calmed the core of her panic. She reached for his hand. "I'm okay. I just . . . this is all so baffling. I very much need to figure out what's happening."

"You need to take these originals back or you won't be able to figure out anything but how to get your next meal in Holloway."

His mention of the women's prison was meant to be funny. She sat on the metal kitchen chair with the bright lemon vinyl, a new addition from the consignment shop. "I need to think this through."

Barnaby swept his hand across the illustrations. He leaned closer. "My God. Are they Pauline Baynes's art?"

"Yes."

"Originals?"

"Yes."

"Take them back now, Hazel."

"Can we just stop talking about the illustrations for one minute? Talk about the story. About the book. About how and why it exists? About Peggy Andrews?"

Barnaby reached into his pocket and yanked out a red crumpled packet of cigarettes. He placed a cigarette between his lips; it took three matches before he lit it, exhaled two plumes through his nose. "Okay, let's talk about the story."

Hazel nodded and picked up the book, handed it to him. "Look at it. Read the back. Whatever you are reading is what I made up, what I told Flora."

He read silently, his cigarette ash falling onto the table. Hazel grabbed the green glass ashtray from the hutch and slipped it under his hand, these small rituals ingrained after three years together. It was a long time to date when nearly all of her friends were married and having their second and third babies. But they'd agreed they weren't ready. Not yet. Soon, though.

Keeping Barnaby from a more formal union with Hazel was a

disastrous heartbreak after his first marriage had dissolved. Their child had died at birth, and his wife, Maggie, had come undone, as might be expected. She'd fled Barnaby and returned to her family in Ireland, refusing to speak with him, then waiting nearly three years before signing the divorce papers. Hazel thought she wanted everything that marriage and family meant, but she also hesitated at the idea of giving up her flat and her freedom.

Hazel rarely if ever visited Barnaby's flat, a cramped one bedroom near London University. It was beautiful to be sure, a sixteenth-century building divided into flats with high ceilings and wide planked oak floors, and yet it was also crowded with his ex-wife's boxes and belongings that she still refused to retrieve.

But Hazel hoped for what awaited when she and Barnaby went to Paris: a sapphire-and-diamond ring that had once belonged to his grandmother who had died after Maggie left Barnaby. Grandmother's ring sat in the vault in his parents' stately Hampstead Heath home and was promised to him if he ever married again.

Barnaby looked up. "Hazel, this is exactly the story you just told me."

"Yes."

He pressed his lips together. "Someone must have heard you tell it."

"No."

He set his elbows on the table, took in another inhalation of his cigarette, and reached for his highball. His eyes were on her, not his drink. His hand reached for the glass and caught the crystal's rim, just enough movement to knock it over.

The whiskey transformed into an amber river flowing across the scarred table. Hazel watched in horror from the kitchen sink, then lunged toward the table, grabbing the pile of illustrations.

But not in time.

"Fuck!" Barnaby jumped to stand, snatched a tea towel with its cross-stitched map of London, a Christmas present from her mum.

They collided in their frantic movements, pages flying across the floor, white wings of fallen birds, and Hazel crying out, "No!"

Barnaby wiped the liquid off the table and looked down at Hazel, crawling on the floor, gathering the pages. "Are they okay?" he asked.

"I think so." Hazel crouched, picking them up one by one, examining each of the twenty drawings, piling them on the pine sideboard. Two girls opening the gates of a castle. Two rabbits with girls' faces. A tree arching its branched arms to pick the girls up. A fox hidden in the emerald grass. An owl flying behind the sisters to watch over them. Each illustration both enchanting and whimsical.

Then a stone cottage so like the home in Binsey that Hazel fell to her bottom, staring at the drawing, feeling Barnaby's keen gaze fixed upon her. In the picture, smoke curled from the chimney, and window boxes overflowed with blooms of nearly every color. The door was bright blue, the flagstone pathway crooked, the white fence with climbing roses weaving in and out of the slats. And in the corner, the bottom left corner, was an amber-colored splotch of earth.

Not earth. Whiskey.

She lifted it, and he took it from her. "Fuck," he repeated, the only language he had left.

"It's just one," she said.

"No." He pointed to the corner of the kitchen near the icebox. He walked toward it, picked up the drawing of a tree with a riven opening at its bottom, two girls' faces peeking out from their hiding place in its hollow. A dark splotch on the top left corner, a stain over the sun.

They stood in silence, guiltily holding the two damaged illustrations.

A knock came hard and fast at the front door. Barnaby set the drawing on the kitchen counter and peeked out the side window with a view to the front door.

"A bobby," he said.

Heat rushed through Hazel, adrenaline fiery and quick. "Answer it," she said. "Now. I'll hide them."

"That makes it worse, Hazel."

"What am I to do? Tell them? Are you kidding me? Ruin everything? Sotheby's? Hogan's? You might have been joking about prison, but it's real."

"Edwin loves you. He wouldn't do that." Barnaby shut the lace curtain over the window. "He'll understand."

"Edwin is the most principled man I've ever met. He also loves his artifacts and rare book collection more than he loves me. More than he loves anyone. Trust me." Hazel exhaled through pursed lips. "Give me time. I've got to find out why this all exists."

Barnaby walked toward the living room.

Hazel gathered the papers and the book, shoved them back into their parcel, then paused stock-still to ponder her predicament.

Here was her choice: to walk out and offer the parcel to the police and say, "I am so sorry. It was a mistake." Or she could stash the package in the back of the hutch where a secret door hid important family papers. That meant hoping she'd find answers before answers found her.

# CHAPTER 8

March 1960

"Hazel!" Barnaby called from the living room. She closed her eyes and steadied herself. Had he already told the police? Had her calm, principled boyfriend told the truth?

She walked into the living room to see Barnaby smiling and laughing with a bobby in his dark blue uniform and hat in his hand. Hazel stood quietly, nodding at the bobby.

"Detective Martin has a complaint from your neighbor above about a barking dog."

Hazel laughed, a jittery sound. "Well, since I don't have a dog . . ." She smiled but felt it shake.

"Sorry to bother you, ma'am." The bobby rolled his eyes. "As if we don't have more important things to worry about than a dog keeping a young child from going to bed. Seems the child believes some yappy dog is a werewolf, and the mum can't get her to settle."

"At least the kid has a good imagination." Barnaby clapped the bobby's shoulder before walking him out and shutting the door, locking it with the top bolt.

Hazel dropped to the couch and buried her face in her hands. The rush of fear and tears rose in one hiccup of a sob.

"It's all right," he said. "He's gone."

Hazel looked up. "No, it's not. Not one bit all right."

"Oh, Hazel." Barnaby stood over her and held out his hand. She took it, rising to face him. He drew her closer, running his hand up the back of her neck and grasping her hair. Desire rose hot and nimble. "I can make it all right for you," he said, flicking his tongue against her earlobe. Before she could make sure his cigarette had burned out in the ashtray, they were in bed.

The thrill of protecting her seemed to energize him. Their lovemaking was as urgent as in those early days. Momentarily, the troublesome world faded away for Hazel. Fear translated to desire, lies to truth. As he came inside her, her legs spread and her hips arched to meet him, she melted into him.

This was love.

The past was an anchor; she needed to cut the line.

The past. Harry.

God, no. Not here, not now. She would not think of Harry as Barnaby rolled over and pulled her closer, spooning his body around hers. "God, I love you," he said.

"I love you madly," she said seconds later, but he'd already fallen fast into sleep.

She was wide awake, as if she'd drunk too many cups of tea. Whisperwood had pried open a closed and decaying memory box filled with thoughts of Flora, Oxford, the woman who took them in, and Harry—the boy she lived with during the evacuation; the boy who'd been with her when she lost Flora, the boy who'd become her best friend, and the one she'd never forgotten but also desperately tried to forget.

She slipped from bed, jittery and jangled.

She walked into the blue bathroom with the tall silver mirror and stared at her face. Hazel never thought of herself as beautiful, although others had said so. But sometimes, when the light was just right and she caught a glimpse of her unguarded self in the mirror, she believed she *could* be beautiful. Or at least maybe in some other era, she might have been, when the style would suit her brown eyes and wavy tawny hair, wild about her freckled face.

She turned on the shower and stepped into scalding water. She soaped up, washed her hair until she felt the cigarette smoke was gone, the lather slinking down the drain in thin spidery lines as moonlight sifted through the bathroom window. She climbed out, wiggled her toes in the bathroom rug, and lifted her pink bathrobe from the hook behind the door. She was quiet even though she knew it would take a good hard shake to wake Barnaby. He slept like the dead, especially after whiskey and lovemaking. She belted her robe and tiptoed into the living room.

Now that she was calmer and the world dark and quiet, she realized what was at stake: not only being arrested but losing the Sotheby's job. All of it had been jeopardized with an impulsive decision and a knock of whiskey.

She searched for solutions. Only two of the twenty illustrations were damaged. She might return them as if they'd never been gone. If Edwin ever noticed two were missing, he'd blame the sender.

But Hazel could not lie to him or to Tim. She couldn't sneak it all back in the dark iron safe like nothing had happened. She would have to face Edwin and the truth.

Just not yet.

She thought of those who believed Flora's story was over: Aiden Davies had been the one to ring her and Mum in 1956. It had been sixteen years since Flora disappeared and Aiden Davies was the one to call and say, "We believe we've found her."

They'd found the skeletal remains of a young girl, looking to be the same age as Flora. Hazel had rushed to Oxford with Mum, listened to Aiden's regretful explanations of facts and figures: 213 miles of River Thames, and every week someone was found dead in it. As he'd promised after Flora disappeared, Aiden had walked the shoreline from Binsey to Wallingford hundreds of times, searching the steely waters for a hint or clue to Flora's whereabouts, asking local townspeople, leaving photos. But on the sixth of December, 1956, a group of teens had snuck out under the full moon with a bottle of Jameson and came across what remained of a body at the marshy edge of the river.

In the stuffy office at the Thames Valley Police Station in Oxford, Mum and Hazel sat in metal chairs, rusting at their edges, and faced Aiden across his cluttered desk. "You can't prove it's her," Mum had said clearly, clinging to her black patent leather purse on her lap.

Neither of them had looked at the body, or what remained, for who could do such a thing? There was nothing to identify so why gaze on a small decomposed body? No rabbit-eared birthmark or curly blond hair.

"She's about the right age and—" said Aiden.

"How can you know that?" Hazel had sprung up. "You say you searched miles and miles of river, you would have seen Flora years before now."

Aiden's voice was patient and tinged with his own sorrow. He didn't want this to be the end of their story any more than they did. "The width of the river, the strength of the current—that river does not surrender its secrets easily. I am so sorry."

Hazel and Mum had left Aiden Davies, both of them stoic in their belief that this body did not solve the mystery of Flora. They had no proof but their own feelings, and for Aiden that wasn't enough.

And maybe Aiden Davies was right; that child's skeleton and remains found on the riverbank could have told the truth: Flora might have perished. But deep down Hazel didn't believe it. True, she could damn well be fooling herself to avoid the despair of acknowledging Flora's death. But until there was proof, she was going to continue to live with the hope that Flora had survived.

Hazel shivered. The oak grandfather clock in the hallway ticked its metronome: eleven o'clock.

Hazel calculated the time in New York City—six p.m. She entered the kitchen, picked the phone from its cradle, turned the dial, and was transferred through a few switchboards. Then came the swishing noise of the sea, really just the static reception, and at long last a man answered a phone at what was likely a tall building in Manhattan. She wasn't sure why she'd expected a woman.

Hazel calculated that each minute of this conversation was costing more than she could afford, but then again, she'd stolen a first edition book and original artwork. What was an international phone call in the scheme of things? "My name is Hazel Linden." She cleared her throat as she slipped into a stronger British accent she hoped would impress this American. "I am a bookseller at Hogan's Rare Book Shoppe in London."

"And?" His tone was brusque.

"Well, today, I unpacked the extraordinary book by your author Peggy Andrews. I am hoping you might put me in touch with her."

"I can get you whatever materials you might need. *Why* do you need to be in touch?"

For this, Hazel was unprepared, so she blurted out, "I need to talk to her about her book."

"Is this for an interview?"

"Yes." Hazel fell into the excuse with relief. "We publish a bookshop newsletter."

"Ms. Andrews is extremely private. I am not permitted to give out her information in any way. But you can write her, care of us at Henry-Todd Publishing."

"Would you mind so very much just asking her to return my call?"

"She doesn't have a phone, or if she does, she hasn't given me the number."

"Oh."

"Listen," the man said, sympathetically noting her disappointment. "Write her at our address, and your letter will be forwarded." He rattled off the address of some skyscraper in New York City, along with the name of a publicist.

"Thank you," Hazel said. "In the meantime, I have a few questions I'm hoping you can answer," she pressed, even as she heard other phones ringing and the shuffling of paper.

"Maybe, if you can make it quick."

"Of course. Can you tell me how old Ms. Andrews is?"

"It says here that she'll be twenty-five in April."

Flora's birthday was in July. Peggy Andrews was at least a year younger than Flora would have been.

"And what does she look like?" Hazel asked.

Now he was thinking Hazel was creepy; she felt the shift in his silence. "Can you mail me a photo? Please."

"If you want to contact the author, mail a letter here to the publishing house." He hung up. Just like she imagined a busy New Yorker might do.

She slammed down her own phone.

Maybe she'd just jump on an airplane and fly to America, or book passage on a ship and find this woman who lived somewhere in Massachusetts. More information—that's what she needed.

She clicked on the small lamp at the edge of the hutch, retrieved a sheet of her best fine linen stationery and her nib pen. Find the author and she would find Flora. Or at least find out *about* Flora.

What was she to say in a letter? How much of the truth to tell? *Whisperwood is my story. It is my sister's story. It is not yours and how did you come by it?*

No. Hazel could not be aggressive, or Peggy Andrews might become even more elusive. Hazel had to be kind and inquisitive.

Curious.

She set her pen to the paper. *When I was a child, I made up this very story with this very same name: Whisperwood and The River of Stars. I am curious how . . .*

When finished, she sat back and read it twice, satisfied that it hit the right notes. Respectful so that maybe she'd receive a response and then . . . maybe . . . Peggy Andrews would tell her more.

# CHAPTER 9

September 1939

Outside the Oxford train station, the cadre of exiled children walked in yet another line, this time past taxis and flashing red lights, over zebra crosswalks, and down a very long street. Along the way, the city's grand steeples came into view. Its buildings were made of bulky stone, the fences of wrought iron. Streets curved around the high wooden gates of Oxford's many colleges. The river of children flowed past cafés humming with business while students in black robes rushed past them before pausing with pity to stare.

The beauty of the city rose tall and mighty with pinnacles and towers, with arched and vectored windows carved into stone. A hopeful lightness grew in Hazel's chest. They weren't headed to the terrible part of a fairy tale with hags, witches, and dragons. She might, after all, have climbed onto the right train, the one with the good fortune. The townspeople crowding these sidewalks waved flags, cheering the children, as if they'd done something special, as if they were the ones to finally win the war.

"Welcome to Oxford!" a boy called out. Hazel stopped to look at him. He was possibly her age, taller, though, with a mop of curls that looked as if they could never be brushed out. He wore a faded gray wool jacket and a flat cap of black. He waved wildly at all the passing children.

Hazel hiked her knapsack higher on her shoulders and *snap*—the strap broke and her bag tumbled to the cobblestone street. Other children coming fast behind her stepped on her bag as her belongings scattered: her black sneakers and white cotton underthings, her yellow flowered dress and wood toothbrush. Feet trampled over all of it as she cried out, scrambling to recover her meager belongings among squashed cigarette cases, wrinkled toffee papers, and greasy newspapers once holding chips.

Sweeping it all into her hands, she attempted to shove the pile into her canvas bag. Then hands were there, everywhere, and all around her. She cried out and shoved someone away—no one would take the few things that belonged to her! Rough and soft hands grasped her knapsack. Flora gripped Hazel's dress hem so as not to get caught in the tidal rush.

Hazel pushed hard at a body leaning over her, his hand picking up her hairbrush. She looked up to see the boy who'd hollered welcome. Hazel's shove sent him to his bum. But he laughed, a full sound.

"I'm just trying to help. Here!" He gave her the brush, then a white shirt with a Peter Pan collar—her favorite, muddied by footprints.

With the crowd moving around them, Hazel jammed her things into the knapsack. It had been so neatly packed and was now a mess. Deep sobs she'd managed to suppress all day threatened. The boy stood and held out the knapsack to Hazel.

She got to her feet and took it from him. "Thank you."

"You're very welcome."

Flora pulled at Hazel's hand, pointing to their class moving away.

Hazel cast a last glance at the boy and ran toward the back of their group, pushing and shoving until they reached Miss Plink. Within minutes, they arrived at the town hall where families would choose which children they wanted to take home, like puppies for the kids or cows for their farm.

———

"He'll do," said a man's deep voice.

Hazel held to Flora as tightly as her strength allowed while she watched the man in mud-flecked pants point at an older boy who wore overalls and a defiant grimace. Hazel undid her coat and wrapped one side around Flora so everyone would know they were one unit. Indivisible.

A woman, her gray hair wild and wiry, her clothes hanging about her like a potato sack with faded flowers, came to stand in front of Hazel and Flora. She stared at Flora with an intensity that made Hazel pull her coat closer around her sister. "What a lovely child!" Her voice was syrupy and slurred, a sickening sound.

"They are sisters," said the man with the notebook and the uniform. "They go together."

The woman looked down at Hazel, her eyes beady and dark like one of the crows perched on their backyard wall at home that dove for shiny things. Hazel wasn't shiny, she knew that. But Flora was as glittery as a six-pence, as a diamond—a treasure. Her blond hair and button nose and wide eyes drew in everyone. Hazel didn't measure up.

The hag—the word that bubbled into Hazel's mind—turned away and hobbled down the row until she reached a girl with auburn hair so bright it looked on fire, falling over her shoulders in braids. Her face down, her dress crumpled in her little fists.

"You!" squawked the woman.

The girl's tear-streaked face looked up.

"What's your name, child?"

"Kelty Monroe."

"I choose you."

"No!" the girl cried out as the hag raised her hand for an officer.

"I'll take this one," the woman told the officer, wagging her finger Kelty's way.

Hazel looked away, a bird of fear swooping and diving in her chest.

The room was full of children, some from her class and school, and just as many who Hazel didn't recognize. They sat on benches crowded into the room while locals strolled through and selected children to billet at their home. A table ran across the far wall, with covered dishes of food for those not chosen by dinnertime. Some farmers first picked out the boys in their gray serge shorts or tweed pants. Childless families wanted cute girls in frilly lace dresses who looked like Shirley Temple or who were young enough to treat like dollies.

But who wanted a fourteen-year-old girl and her sister?

Hazel couldn't tell if her stomach pangs were hunger or fear. What if no one chose them and she and Flora were left sitting on these hard benches while all the others went home with kind families to sit down at warm meals?

On the wall hung a poster, its top left corner undone and flapping. It featured a picture of a woman walking through rubble in a bombed-out city, smoke pouring from damaged buildings' windows, a horrible scene. The bedraggled woman carried a baby while two dirt-smudged children clung to her coat as she trudged through this wasteland. On a beautiful blue background dissonant to the photo were the words THIS COULD BE YOU! CARING FOR EVACUEES IS A NATIONAL SERVICE. And just below, it read in smaller letters ISSUED BY THE MINISTRY OF HEALTH.

So, she and Flora had an official name: They were evacuees.

A woman in a blue dirndl skirt flaring out, smiling stiff and awkward like it was hard work, handed an enamel cup of milk to both girls and one chocolate biscuit each. They drank and ate eagerly. All the windows in this stuffy room with its low-slung beams were closed. Fresh autumn air was locked outside by thick doors that kept opening and shutting as adults arrived and left with children.

The smell of sweat and damp wool filled the air, and Flora said, "Take me to our land."

"Not now," Hazel whispered.

"Then tell another story, one where Mum takes us home."

"She's at home," Hazel said, unable to make the leap into frivolous fantasy when reality loomed too ominously before them. Adults passed them in a line, sizing them up like tomatoes in the market.

"Make Mum be here," Flora said. "Bring her here to get us."

But Hazel couldn't find the beginning of such a story. Her shoulders slumped as a pretty woman in a bright blue dress walked toward them in the line. Chestnut hair fell to her shoulders past her lace collar, and she wore a jaunty red hat cocked to one side. Her green eyes scrutinized the benches as if she were looking for her own child.

"Choose us," Hazel whispered.

Flora looked up from Hazel's shoulder and sat straight, Hazel's coat dropping open. The woman smiled at them as she moved past. Then, next to the woman, Hazel spotted the boy who'd helped her in the street.

He was with the beautiful woman. When he looked at Hazel, his face broke into a smile.

"You!" he said.

"Yes, me," Hazel said in return.

"I'm Harry." He stopped in front of Hazel and—even though there was no wind, not even the slightest breeze in that staid room—his hair seemed to move. "What's your name?"

His mum, or whom Hazel assumed was his mum in the blue dress, had moved down the benches, smiling and nodding to hopeful children who either clung to each other or their dolls, blankets, and teddy bears.

Hazel lifted her chin, not wanting to show her fear. "I am Hazel Mersey Linden."

"Mum!" Harry called, all the while his gaze remaining on Hazel.

"Yes, darling?" She turned, now about six children down the bench.

"Come here, please?" he asked.

She was quickly at his side, her red lipstick so bright that Hazel could have read her words as easily as hearing them.

"What is it?" she asked.

"I want you to meet Hazel."

The lady with the lipstick and the red hat and the flowery dress glanced at Hazel, then at Flora. She smiled so kindly that Hazel's hopes rose. She looked like the sort of lady who would be friends with their mum, the sort who laughed and made things in the stove that smelled like home, the kind of person who might read them books and draw pictures on blank sheets of paper with colored pencils.

"Hello, Hazel." She looked back to Harry. "We need to choose a boy, son. Someone to help us. We can't take home two girls." Her voice was not cruel when she said it, not like the mean-faced hag with the wiry hair. She was kind even in her denial of his request.

Hazel's heart fell. She squeezed Flora so tightly that her sister yelped.

"Mum," Harry said in a playful voice as if they were outside in a game, "we don't need more boys. We have me."

She laughed and it sounded just as Hazel would have imagined: spritely and full of fun. The woman paused a few heartbeats, but that time felt as long and winding as the train ride here—the place Hazel's parents had fallen in love, the place where Hazel and Flora were to live until Britain stopped the cruel man named Hitler and they could safely go home.

"Girls," she said with a smile and a tilt of the head. "Where are you from?"

Flora answered before Hazel could open her mouth. "London, ma'am, Bloomsbury."

"Well, I certainly do love Bloomsbury." She turned to the boy. "Harry, that's where Virginia Woolf was part of the Bloomsbury Group."

Harry looked at Hazel. "Mum's quite enamored of the Bloomsbury Group. Mum's very Bohemian, secretly wishes she had been part of them—instead, she's stuck being my mum."

"Oh stop, you!" She gently kissed his cheek, and he didn't pull away. This amazed Hazel: a boy who did not pull away from his mum's affections in public, a boy who used words like *enamored* and *Bohemian*.

"And your parents?" the woman asked.

"Mum is working for the British Service, and Papa is already..." Hazel still couldn't say a word that held such finality: *dead.*

"I'm so sorry," the woman said, reading between the trembling lines in Hazel's voice. "As for the billet, I only have one extra bed," she said. "I'm sorry."

Flora popped off the bench, clinging to her bear with all her might, her fists tight around its hind legs. "We can share," she said, voice trembling.

Hazel nodded. "It would be no trouble at all."

The woman crouched down to look Flora in the eye. "Well, if it suits you, then of course you shall come home with us."

Hazel felt her mouth drop open with surprise and relief.

Flora looked at Harry's mum. "And Hazel can tell you stories. She tells the best stories!"

"That sounds wonderful," said the lady. "My name is Bridgette Aberdeen."

"I'm Hazel Mersey Linden."

"I'm Flora Lea Linden."

Their introductions overlapped.

"Lovely to meet you both."

Hazel saw Flora through Mrs. Aberdeen's eyes: an adorable child with an air of naivete and kindness. Flora was the best of them, not just of the Linden family but of all the children who'd arrived by train that day.

Bridgette Aberdeen stood and adjusted her hat. She raised her hand to the officer at the end of the bench. "These two children will be coming home with us."

# CHAPTER 10

## March 1960

Morning entered Hazel's Bloomsbury bedroom with flashes of light seeping through the tea-colored lace curtains. Far off, in the land of the awake, a phone endlessly jangled. She slipped her right leg across the sheets, seeking Barnaby. She slid her leg farther, then her hand reached for his comfort but found the space empty. She turned over and stared at a dented down pillow where he'd been.

The previous day rushed at her with a stomach-drop of dread.

She'd eventually climbed into bed at one a.m. Barnaby had been asleep.

That annoying noise. She stumbled in her half sleep to answer the phone endlessly ringing in the kitchen. "Hallo."

"Good morning, Hazel."

Edwin Hogan.

"Good morning," she said, attempting levity in her voice. "Am I late for work?" she asked, hoping for a jolly joke, but knowing immediately why he'd called.

"We have a problem."

"Oh?" She placed her hand over her heart, felt its power against her chest.

"Someone found their way into the back room and stole a package yesterday. It was chaos, Tim told me. A tour group. A young couple

buying an Auden. A mother and daughter. I am calling to ask if you noticed anything out of place or happened to hear their names?"

Her mind scrambled and she set her heart to tell the truth when he
spoke again. "I have called Scotland Yard." A pause. "Did you lock the
parcel in the safe with the others?"

"No," she said. "I left one out for Tim." The lie came so easily that
bile rose in her throat. She bent over and cradled the receiver between
her ear and shoulder, placed her hands on her knees. Who was this
woman lying and stealing, all for a fairy tale and in futile hopes of a living sister? Where was Barnaby? They had to return these illustrations,
somehow sneak them into the bookshop's back room.

"Hazel, you know better than to leave a package out . . . unattended."

"What was stolen?" she asked with a glimmer of false hope it might
be something else.

"There is a new fairy tale taking America by storm. I secured the
original illustrations. Baynes's illustrations. Once Britain discovers the
book, they will be worth a pretty pence. But now they're gone. Did you
see them?"

As if there were a small box to hold lies and she was filling it up too
fast, she told a partial truth. "I did see it. But I didn't look all the way
through them at the time . . . I left."

"Just left?"

"Yes."

"Why, Hazel?"

"I was upset, Edwin. I thought, well, I don't know exactly what I
thought. I was emotional. Forgive me."

"If you remember anything at all, will you please let me know? If you
can recall anyone who found their way into the back room?"

"I will certainly think about it."

"Do you know where Poppy was?" he asked. "I can't find her this
morning."

"No, but Edwin, there is no way she'd do such a thing. Not after all
these years, not after what you did for her."

"I have to go now, Hazel. The chief detective has arrived. Please call
us if you think of anything."

He hung up without a goodbye, and Hazel ran for the bathroom, dry heaved over the toilet, and then sank to the gray tile floor. The winding roses wallpaper, red and yellow and green, blurred in her vision and she rested her forehead on her bent knees. Would they blame Poppy or the in-love man who bought the Auden book for his fiancée, or Tim?

It was too late to return the parcel. It was too late to tell the truth. But she could not let them blame beautiful and innocent Poppy.

Thirty minutes later, in tweed trousers and a pale blue sweater, with the letter to Peggy Andrews in her pocket, Hazel grabbed her red felt coat from the peg by the front door where she found a note taped to the wood panel. "Sorry I had to run out. An early tutoring session and I did not want to wake you. Meet you at 10:30 at Legrain. Mad love, B."

Hazel dropped the note on the entryway bench and walked outside.

The March day was rising warm and crisp. Hazel stopped for a moment before hustling down the sidewalk. One block later she reached the red postbox on the corner of Doughty and slipped in the letter.

It brought her back to the day she'd written the postcard to Mum from Binsey. *We are safe and warm with a lovely family. You do not need to worry . . .*

The first part was right and true, the second an unintentional lie.

When she and Flora had arrived in Binsey, she'd anticipated one kind of story, but it became another. Now Hazel knew what she had to do, knew what was required of her. If any good was to come of this Whisperwood discovery, it could not be borne of a lie.

# CHAPTER 11

## September 1939

Hazel and Flora rode in the backseat of Mrs. Aberdeen's blue Flying Nine. Outside, the sky was low and dove gray, spitting bursts of rain. Wipers flapped noisily across the windshield. Hedges brushed against the car, explaining all its scratches. Hat in her lap, Mrs. Aberdeen drove with both hands on the wheel, singing with complete abandon a song on the radio about being too marvelous for words.

In the front passenger seat, Harry twice turned around and smiled at the sisters, rolling his eyes as if to say he knew his mum was nutty, but what could you do? Flora and Hazel scooted as close to each other as possible, holding hands; Berry was squashed between them, his furry face aimed toward the front windshield as if watching where they were going, how many turns down this curvy road it took to get to the Aberdeen house.

Hazel stared at Mrs. Aberdeen, evaluating how to tell her mum about the lady who took them. She had creamy white skin as if she'd never been in the sun. Her mouth had a little bow in it like Harry's, and when she sang in her lilting voice, the corners of her mouth rose in a smile. Her hair tumbled over her shoulders and danced with the terrible bouncing of this car that felt as if it might fall to bits over every bump.

Flora and Hazel had never been to the Oxfordshire countryside, and Flora stared out the windows without a word. The landscape in twilight had Hazel almost believing that Whisperwood was possible, that there were shimmering doors scattered here and there. Her feet itched to get out of the car, to run through these heather fields and rolling hills, bounding over lichen-covered rocks. She imagined the growing shadows on the grassy fields as silver pools of water. *You only had to look for such things.* She hugged Flora. "We're going to be all right," Hazel said.

Flora yanked Berry from his stuck place and tucked him into her lap. "I know."

Soon, they bumped along a long gravel drive with so many ruts and dips the car felt like it might collapse into a heap. When they came to a quick stop, Mrs. Aberdeen trilled, as if this were the last line to the song she'd been singing all along, "Welcome to the Aberdeen cottage."

The sisters climbed out of the car onto the gravel and stared at the quaint stone cottage. The house was aglow. The sunset behind it turned its stones near silver. An inside light left on filled the windows with lemony hues. The front door was painted a bright blue. Under windows on either side of the door, window boxes were wild with green leafy plants and red and yellow flowers that rambunctiously overflowed their edges.

This cottage appeared to have sprouted from the earth. Ivy ran along the side of the house and crept toward the left window. The roof was tiled in dark slate and its copper chimney pot looked set aflame by the setting sun, tossing bright arrows across the roofline. Around the cottage, the landscape poured over mounds and hills in green and brown waves. There was not another house in sight.

"Hurry now. It's getting dark, and I want to get you settled," Mrs. Aberdeen said. "We'll have a look about tomorrow. Come, come."

The sisters followed, with Harry behind, who was carrying their packs into the house.

Moss held together an entryway path of flagstones that wound around two alder trees whose yellow leaves fell to the ground while others clung tenaciously to the branches. Hedges at the front of the house sprouted every which way.

A great wind came from behind them, sending the sisters through the front door along with a swirl of leaves, small sticks, and moss. Mrs.

Aberdeen let out a tinkling sort of laugh. "Well, the land must be welcoming you home."

Hazel took in the view of the cozy home with a riverstone fireplace big enough to walk into, ample firewood stacked next to it. The mantel itself was fashioned of a log cut in half. Above were open beams and bumpy plaster walls glistening white. And everywhere there were books: on wooden side tables and shelves, on the floor and stacked in corners. The cozy living room also held a large, overstuffed couch and two plump chairs with a floral pattern of red and blue flowers. Instead of a proper coffee table there was a trunk and upon it, more books. The rug was a crisscross of ivy on an arbor. The riotousness of it should have felt chaotic but didn't. The cottage whispered comfort.

"You can't say home," Flora said, resolute while her lips trembled. "It's not our home."

Mrs. Aberdeen dropped her big tapestry purse on an entryway bench and leaned down, set her hands on her knees to face Flora. "Oh, dear, you are so very right. It is not your home. But I hope you find you love it anyway. I should have been more careful with my words. Let me try again." Mrs. Aberdeen stood and cleared her throat. "Welcome to the Aberdeen cottage, home of Bridgette and Harry Aberdeen." She curtsied and grinned.

Flora laughed.

"We must send Mum a postcard right away," Hazel said. "We have to let her know we are safe. It's . . ." She tried to remember the word. "Imperative."

Mrs. Aberdeen looked at Hazel and ruffled her hair as if she'd known her all Hazel's life, not less than an hour. "We shall do that first thing in the morning. For now, let's get you something warm to eat and settled in your room. What a day you must have had today!"

Harry picked up the packs he'd dropped in the entryway and tossed them over his shoulder. "It's back here." He nodded toward the hallway.

The sisters followed him across dark wood floors gleaming under lamplight. Framed photos of Harry at all ages covered the hallway walls. Hazel didn't have time to stop and stare at them but knew that she would. They took a right and found themselves in a kitchen, a square and solid room with windows at its far end looking out to a garden in dusk. Hazel saw arbors and pathways and a red barn, a vegetable garden with willow cages.

A brick hearth fireplace with charred logs was along the right wall and Hazel believed she'd never seen anything so glorious: a small hearth in the kitchen. *The kitchen!* On another wall was a door to a tiny bathroom, then one going outside, and a closed door with a bright egg-shaped brass knob.

The kitchen was soaked in green: its counters, the AGA stove putting off heat, the curtains over the sink made of pale checkered emerald and the countertops of mint. The wooden cupboard's open shelves sagged, overcrowded with plates and mugs and glasses and linens. A round and dark wood table and centered upon it was a flowered teapot and a vase of purple thistles.

Harry opened the closed door, nudging it with a shove of his hip. Hazel followed him as Flora lingered in the kitchen, walking to the table and touching the edge of the prickly thorns. Hazel entered the room behind Harry.

Harry dropped their knapsacks on the bed covered in quilts of mismatched patterns that dominated the rectangular room. "This is yours."

A wardrobe of dark wood and a dresser draped with frilly lace laid across were against the left wall. Two windows offered a view of the back fields.

"It's beautiful," Hazel said, and she wasn't just trying to be nice. She was too tired for nice.

Hazel sat on the bed as Flora walked in. "Oh!" Her exclamation at the sight of their room was of delight, and she ran to Hazel and climbed into her lap.

Relief rolled over Hazel: safe in a house such as this with a bed such as this while the war raged. But could she be so happy while Mum was most likely sitting at the kitchen table with tears flowing down her face, wondering where her daughters were and if they were safe?

Harry smiled at them, that same grin she'd seen when she'd dropped her knapsack in the street and hands were grabbing at her things and then suddenly there he was. "Mum says dinner is in twenty minutes, so if you want to wash up, the bathroom's right outside your door." He made a funny face. "We'll be sharing. We only have one."

Hazel drew Flora close, and she set Berry on the pillow. "I'll unpack, and we'll come out for dinner."

Harry lingered at the door until Hazel asked, "Do you need something else?"

"No, I'm just glad you're here," he said, and the door clicked shut. He was gone.

Flora let go of Hazel and plopped onto the bed they'd be sharing, lying back. "It's so soft!"

Hazel pressed her hand onto the mattress and smiled. "It is lovely, even if it feels a million miles away. It seems farther away than just a train ride from London."

"Tell me a story," Flora said. "Please."

"Dinner's coming up," Hazel told her. "I'll tell you one before we go to sleep tonight."

"Okay." Flora popped up, her dress swinging as she twirled in the middle of the room. "Our room!"

From outside came the sounds of Mrs. Aberdeen in the kitchen, banging pots and pans, the duller thump of pottery and the soft sound of the wireless playing music instead of the bleak voice of Prime Minister Chamberlain. Scents of rosemary and lavender sifted into the room. At the window, Hazel looked at the shapes of the land, lumps and spikes in the descending night. A river was out there, its soft hush rushing past.

The music on the radio was turned up as Guy Lombardo sang about September in the rain, and Harry's laughter interrupted the notes.

"She plays a lot of music," Hazel said.

Flora walked to the door and placed her hand on it as if it were the magic door of Whisperwood. She wasn't quite ready to push it open and enter, not yet. "I like it," she said.

"Me too," said Hazel. "I like it a lot."

"Can we read Mum's note now?" Flora twisted her dress hem in her hands, anxious.

"Yes, let's." Hazel fished the note out of Flora's mackintosh that hung on the wooden peg by the door and unfolded it. She read it out loud. "I love you both so much. Be brave and watch out for each other. I will visit you as soon as I can. All my love forever, Mum."

"Watch out for each other," Flora said out loud, and then turned her face up to Hazel. "I will watch out for you."

Hazel almost laughed but she could see the sincerity and knew it would hurt her sister. She kissed her nose. "Time to unpack."

She tossed their knapsacks onto the end of the bed and pulled out their scant belongings: their white underthings and folded socks and pressed shirts. Her white shirt and a flowered dress were streaked with mud from the fall in the street. She set them on the dresser and folded them neatly; she would clean them. She was in charge now. She neatly placed the rest in an empty drawer of the pine dresser. Hazel put their jackets and two matching blue dresses, which Mum had made on the black Singer sewing machine, in the wardrobe to join other raincoats and wool sweaters.

Even at home they'd never had much, just a few dresses and all the sweaters and coats they needed to stay warm, but here they had even less, and Hazel wanted it to be neat—as if Mum had put things away in their proper place. She would need to be Mum for Flora, and sister and storyteller.

*Watch out for each other.*

The words echoed in Hazel's mind and she drew Flora close, hugged her tightly, and kissed the top of her head.

"Let go!" Flora said, yet she clung so tightly that Hazel couldn't have let go if she wanted to.

# CHAPTER 12

**March 1960**

Hogan's Rare Book Shoppe's bell tinkled as Hazel walked into the store. At the counter, Poppy stood at the register in a bright red dress, her dark hair in a tight and low ponytail, her brow furrowed in concern as she talked to two men standing side by side at the checkout counter, both in blue, both police inspectors with notebooks and stern looks.

Hazel clutched her satchel tighter and, with confidence she didn't have, she waved hello to Poppy and headed straight to the back hallway. She pressed her hand on the green swinging door and pushed it open.

Tim stood and Edwin sat on a chair, but both were bent over a ledger at the long oak table, their heads close to each other, nearly touching. Edwin's bald head had the white stubble of age while Tim's thick black hair shone under the hanging brass light. They wore nearly matching tweed jackets; only if she looked closely would she see how the patterns were slightly different. They lifted their gazes in unison to see her.

"Hazel!" Tim's voice filled with happiness. "Did you change your mind? See the error of your ways, and you're returning to us instead of working at the monster of Sotheby's?"

She tried to smile but nothing happened. "I've made an error . . . a bad one. I'm sorry." She dropped her satchel on the table and unlatched the brass locks. She slipped out the parcel and put it in front of them both. "I took it," she said.

That's how easy it was to confess. You just say it. You just drop it onto the table and tell the truth and what comes, comes, she thought.

Edwin's face moved in waves, confusion to anger. Tim rubbed his hand up and down his left cheek. Hazel stood perfectly still. She would take what came to her. "You can go tell the bobbies out there. I'm so sorry. I didn't mean to. I was . . . I think I can explain."

She'd seen the look with Edwin before; he had a decision to make. He was determining whether he would turn soft or hard. And no one ever knew which way it would go. "You can explain?"

"It's difficult, but I can try."

"Why don't I go get Chief Inspector Norman out there to come talk to us? Maybe you can explain it to him?" Edwin's face turned red, his bulbous nose aflame, his eyes rheumy with anger.

"Father," Tim said softly, placing his hand on his father's freckled arm where his shirtsleeve had been rolled up. "This is Hazel. There has to be a good explanation."

Edwin stared at her as if doubting the woman standing in front of him was the same person who had worked for him for fifteen years, who'd spent holidays with him, his wife, and their extended family. And Hazel actually felt like a different woman, like someone else altogether.

"It was impulsive and wrong," she said.

She then told them the truth, slowly and methodically. She told them of Whisperwood, of Flora, of the world turning upside down when she found the book yesterday.

When she finished, only the wheeze of the radiator filled the room. She tried to read their expressions. Edwin looked up first and, yes, those were tears in his eyes. "My dear God, Hazel, what you have been through."

"I'm not alone, Edwin. What all of us endured in those days was a horror. You lost two sons. You lost half of your store to a bomb and rebuilt it. I'm no different, and I have no excuse for what I've done, but I want you to please understand."

"What am I to do now?" Edwin looked to his son. "Those inspectors out there are questioning Poppy, calling customers from that day."

"Go tell them I stole the parcel." Hazel bowed her head. "I did."

Edwin grabbed his silver cane that had been leaning against the oak table. He walked out, the click-click-tack rhythm of his walk. Tears gathered in her chest, a ballooning feeling that meant she would not be able to stop from crying if she started.

Tim's voice. "It's going to be okay. Father would never have you arrested."

Hazel wiped her face and looked at Tim. "Do you really believe that?"

Tim didn't answer but came to her side and together they stared down at the drawings.

"I haven't even told you the worst part," she said.

"There's more?"

"I ruined two of them." She would not betray Barnaby.

Before she could say more Edwin entered the back room with the tallest of the two bobbies. A man with earth-brown skin, warm eyes, and his blue police hat low on his broad forehead. He held a notebook and she saw the names and notes scribbled on the pages: Poppy among them.

"This is Hazel Linden," said Edwin. "Our most valuable employee, until she left us for a new job at Sotheby's. She is here to confess that she took the parcel."

The bobby cleared his throat. "Is that true?" he asked.

"Yes." She pointed at the table, her voice shaking. "I've returned it."

"Did you steal it to take to Sotheby's?" he asked. "Earn yourself a bit of money on the side at your ex-employer's expense? Just one last stick-it to the boss?"

"No!"

"No!"

Tim and Hazel answered in unison.

"Nothing like that," she said. "It was an accident. A . . . an emotional accident."

"First time I've heard that one," he said. "An emotional accident."

Edwin leaned on his cane. "Of course I don't want to press charges."

The bobby set his gaze on Hazel. "Didn't Tim call you and ask about the illustrations? Ask if you knew anything about them? Edwin also?"

Hazel swallowed. "Yes, and I lied. I panicked. But I'm here now." She looked to Tim and he bit his bottom lip, shook his head no. He knew she was about to confess what she'd done to the two ruined illustrations.

"Inspector," Tim said. "It's all been one long hellish night and day. It's cleared up now and we can dismiss it. We'll deal with it from here."

"It doesn't work exactly that way," the inspector said. "She might have confessed but she stole valuable merchandise."

"And brought it back," Tim said. "Can we just move on?"

The inspector shoved his hat on his head, put his notebook back in his pocket, and walked out without another word.

Hazel exhaled as the swinging door closed. "Edwin, I am so sorry. So, so sorry. But there's more I need to tell you."

"Father," Tim dove in. "Two have been damaged. Accidentally damaged."

Edwin closed his eyes for a moment, steadied himself with his left hand on the oak table. Then opened his eyes. "Hazel, this parcel and its contents now belong to you. But you must pay for them."

"You know I don't have that kind of money."

"You'll find it," he said. "I know you will. Barnaby or your mother. But there are . . ."

"I know," she said. "There are consequences. There always are. I will find a way to pay for them, Edwin. I promise. But it won't be from Barnaby or Mother."

Tim coughed a laugh. "Maybe with your big new fancy job."

She heard the hurt in his laugh. "Tim . . ."

"Listen to me," Edwin said, his voice and face softening. "Stories and books tend to find their rightful owners. I've always said so. And this time isn't any different. Now go find out why this woman has your story. Find out if your sister survived." He lifted his cane and walked to the dark gray metal filing cabinet, opened a drawer with a high screech of its ancient rust, and lifted out a file. He returned and set it on the table, opened it. Inside was a handwritten receipt from Henry-Todd Publishing in New York.

Hazel glanced at it and turned away. It would take her years to repay the cost of these illustrations and a signed first edition of a limited production. Years.

Edwin lifted the yellow receipt and handed it to Hazel. "This is now yours."

She nodded and attempted to stay the tears.

"If you look closely, there is something there you might need."

Her gaze scanned the receipt. And there it was as if under a spotlight, a phone number and address in Cape Cod, Massachusetts, with one name: Linda Andrews.

———

It was 11 a.m. in London, 6 a.m. in America. Hazel would need to bide her time before she called.

Hazel calculated the times as she headed home, carrying the parcel safe in her satchel. If she hadn't confessed she wouldn't have this phone number. The exorbitant price of the package was worth the priceless digits of a phone somewhere in Massachusetts where a woman named Peggy Andrews wrote about Whisperwood.

Rain fell in soft sheets but Hazel didn't bother to lift her umbrella. Who cared how wet she became? She had a number, a way to find the American author.

Midway home she remembered she was meant to meet Barnaby for coffee at Legrain, where authors and screenwriters scribbled in notebooks and sipped cappuccinos as the brass fixtures steamed and hissed. Men with smoldering cigarettes and women in cardigans and red lipstick, rock-large earrings under jaunty hats, excitedly discussed Kingsley Amis and Graham Greene, Willa Cather and John Steinbeck.

Hazel loved the Soho coffee shops, listening in on conversations while sipping coffee, a notebook open containing nothing but lists and to-dos and scraps of overheard dialogue and things she'd noticed: the slip of a girl's eye toward a sexy man with another woman, the rip of paper when a just-written paragraph went astray, the astrologer with the hoop earrings and red scarf in the corner, giving readings to those willing to shell over a few pence.

But Hazel had better things to rush toward at the moment: her own story. Barnaby would be teaching by now, and there was nothing to do but keep going. She'd explain later.

She opened the front door, dripping rain on the pine floors, setting her satchel on the front bench, and digging out the yellow Henry-Todd Publishing receipt. Rushing, she slipped on the envelopes that had been dropped through the front door slot. Her legs flying east and west, she landed hard on the wooden floors, her left wrist taking the brunt of the fall. "Bloody hell!"

She straightened herself and stood, picking up the mail, sifting through it before she dumped it on the pine sideboard in the lamplit hallway on the way to the kitchen. *Dorothy Bellamy*, one of the return addresses declared. My God, would the journalist never give up? Could she possibly have anything new to ask? This was the fourth letter. Hazel ripped open the envelope.

*Dear Ms. Linden,*

*Please hear me out about the River Child. I am unsure if you've read my other stories, but I make a solemn promise to honor your sister in this story, as I have all the other children. But I can't do that unless you or your mother speak to me. Each essay and story in the series is a recounting of one lost child's life in . . .*

Hazel didn't read another word, ripped the letter in half, and tossed it in the trash can at the edge of the table. "Nope, not hearing you out."

Shaking out her left wrist, she began to pick up around the flat. She had at least three hours until she could call the number in America, where it would be 9 a.m. She sorted mail, folded clothes, made the bed, swept, and emptied out the trash. These were menial tasks to keep her mind from flying in a thousand directions.

Finally, Hazel lifted the phone's green receiver. She turned the plastic dial with her right finger until the operator's voice came on, clicking through numerous switchboards. The female-robotic voice twice told

Hazel to try again later and Hazel refused. Finally, "Andrews residence," the soft female voice said.

"May I please speak with Peggy?" Hazel asked, pacing the kitchen as the curly cord stretched across and back like an accordion.

"This is Peggy speaking, but I am having trouble hearing you."

"My name is Hazel Linden. I'm calling from London; I am sorry you can't hear well."

"London." The woman's voice stated the city as if she'd never heard of it.

"I am a bookseller at a rare book shop here in Bloomsbury. And your Whisperwood novel, along with the original illustrations, have found their way to our shop."

"Is that so? Originals?"

"Yes."

"Oh, I had no idea," she said. "How curious."

Hazel needed to hurry, to ask quickly for not only was the price of every minute long distance exorbitant, but she could also not risk losing this woman who might hang up on her, walk away from the conversation. This was her first lead in twenty years; how could she find her way into it to get an answer? "I need to ask you how you know of this story, of Whisperwood."

"How I know of it? I wrote it." The woman's voice with her clipped American accent grew instantly cold.

"And it's absolutely wonderful," Hazel soothed her.

"Did you say you have the original illustrations?"

"Yes."

"I see."

"Ms. Andrews, I need to know how you first heard of Whisper-wood."

"And why is that?"

"Because, you see . . . because it was once *my* story. It was a story I made up to keep my five-year-old sister calm when we were evacuees, and now it's found its way to you, but my sister is gone. She was lost during the war. I have never told anyone of Whisperwood. I am trying to understand how this story made its way to you."

There was nothing but the staticky sound of miles between them.

"I am sorry about your sister," the woman stated, "but this story is *not* yours."

A rustling, a movement on the other end, and then the muffled sound of the woman calling out, "No one, Mother. A wrong number."

"Peggy?" Hazel called her name, suddenly frantic. Maybe she shouldn't have just dumped the information, but what else was she to do? "Can you please tell me where you first heard this story? It could mean life or death for a girl long ago . . ."

No response.

"Please take my number and if you think of anything." Hazel rattled off her phone number. "My name is Hazel Linden." She once more stated her number.

A woman's voice in the background called out, "Peggy?"

"Sorry, I believe you have the wrong number. Do not call again."

A click of disconnection, and Hazel dropped the phone. It dangled on the kitchen wall, swinging back and forth.

# CHAPTER 13

## March 1960
## Cape Cod, Massachusetts

Peggy Andrews set the drab-gray telephone receiver into the cradle that hung on the wall. She stood, stunned, in the kitchen of the ramshackle cottage of worn cedar shakes on the shoreline of Cape Cod, Massachusetts. Mother called her name from the other room.

"Wrong number," Peggy called out, scribbling down the telephone number the woman named Hazel had given her.

She took the phone off the hook and set the receiver on the counter, its black cord stretched from the wall. Who calls someone at nine in the morning? What was wrong with this lady?

*I need to ask you how you know of this story.*

*I have never told anyone of Whisperwood.*

*Life or death for a girl.*

*My sister.*

Peggy stared out the window. The wind was thrashing the sand along the shoreline in gold dervishes of the sunshine. No one had informed the weather that it was springtime, that the world had tilted toward longer and sunnier days in the northeast. The gray-blue whip of wave washed up and retreated from the beach. With the wind, the tall sea oat grasses waved on the dunes. The tide was coming in.

She glanced at the phone, a *buzz-buzz-buzz* coming from its headset.

A woman in London had read Whisperwood and claimed to be the one who'd created the land and river.

How disturbing and utterly frightening.

What could this woman possibly want? There were so many wackos in the world. Mother had warned her all her life about such people, and she was right. That's why they lived in near seclusion on this small spit of land.

She shuddered at the thought of this woman stalking her.

So unsettling.

She thought of the Lindbergh baby taken from its crib. Peggy's mom had told her the story countless times—until Peggy turned ten years old and begged her to stop. "Enough! I know what happened." She never had to hear that story again. But like all stories, it stuck in Peggy's imagination.

A slip of anxiety rose in her throat and Peggy swallowed it. She would not allow this silly British bookseller to ruin a beautiful morning just as she was set to sit and write. She picked up the scrap of paper with the phone number, crumpled it into a ball, and tossed it into the trash beneath the sink.

Peggy and Mother had negotiated owning the original illustrations with their advance, so who had sold them to someone in England? Peggy thought Mother had them in the safety deposit box at the bank in town. But she would not ask because to ask would mean telling Mother about the phone call. And Peggy wasn't ready to upset her mother when all was going so very well.

It had taken a long while for Mother to grieve both the husband she lost in Pearl Harbor and her sister, Maria, to an early death three years after they'd moved to her house on Cape Cod to be with her. Mother told Peggy many times that they were lucky to have Maria's house, but she'd give it all away to have Maria alive and well. And now, the success of Whisperwood had seemed to awaken her mother, Linda, bring her back to Peggy in full color, and she didn't want to risk changing that.

Peggy sat, pulled out her lined notebook, and began to write, to fall into the world of Whisperwood, a land that belonged to her and to her mother. This is where she belonged and she would not allow some bizarre phone call to set her off this task.

Later that day, as early evening arrived, Peggy stood in the kitchen and listened to the *click-clack slap* of the Olympia that came from the sunroom where Mother was typing today's pages. Peggy heard her laugh; she'd obviously just reached the part where the sisters turned into skunks.

Peggy went in search of her tennis shoes for a walk on the beach, something she did every day after reaching her page quota. No matter the weather, Peggy walked.

Whisperwood was to be a series. The first book had already sold so well that the publishing house was going back for a fourth printing. They'd called, begging Peggy to write faster, write more. Bonuses were offered, and Peggy was producing as quickly as possible. First editions were already going for large sums. These stories, they were her life's work. How could this strange bookseller claim otherwise?

Her blue tennis shoes on, and her dark hair, long enough to catch in her waistband if she wasn't careful, pulled back in a ponytail, Peggy slipped on a red wool cap and was out the kitchen door. On the screened porch, she grabbed her slicker from the hook and wound her soft-worn gray scarf around her neck.

The screen door slapped shut with a *swish-slap*. She began listing all that she should think about on this walk: what to cook for dinner, the next plot point in the story—then the phone call from Hazel Linden that morning.

No. Peggy would not think about that.

Peggy walked along the shoreline. As the tide rose, she dodged incoming white-edged waves, skirted clear tidal pools dimpled with the breathing bubbles of hidden sea creatures, and thought about the next chapter. After being skunks, what would the sisters turn into next?

Since she was a child, she'd been told she had trouble separating what's real from what's imaginary. Maybe so, but it had led to a career that most young women her age—twenty-four years old—couldn't dream of. But yes, her story world often seemed more vital than the world she objectively knew was real.

More than once it had occurred to Peggy that if she thought about her own life as much as she pondered the fates of the two orphaned sisters, she wouldn't still be living with her mother. Maybe instead, as the new decade emerged, Peggy would be out having the time of her life with the rest of her peers in New York or Boston. Maybe she'd be the one in London.

She laughed at the absurdity. She'd barely left the state of Massachusetts much less the country but for that one high school field trip to Niagara Falls on the Canadian side of the border.

A conch shell, pink on the inside and barnacle-crusted on the outside, revealed itself with a receding wave. Peggy picked it up. One more to add to the collection that ran along the screen porch's wooden edge. She closed her hand around it and bent her head down, the wind gaining speed, lifting her hair and the edges of her jacket. Maybe a storm was coming?

At the horizon nothing but blue sky rested easy on the water. She was working herself up, thinking storms were coming and some kook from Britain would fly to America and snatch away her writing career. The thought was ridiculous. Still, she would remind herself to call the publishing house and tell them to never, ever, give out her personal information.

"Pegs!"

She spun around, the wind now at her back, her ponytail flapping. Only one person called her Pegs: Wren Parker, literally the boy next door. They'd grown up in houses twenty yards apart. There wasn't much they hadn't seen of each other's lives. They'd gone to different colleges— she'd stayed close by and taken classes at Quincy College right in Cape Cod, and he'd left for Harvard.

"Wren," she said, "what are you doing home?"

"Job hunting," he said, jogging to catch up with her. "I saw you through the window and thought I'd come out and say hey!"

"Well, hey," she said with a smile. How many times through the years this same refrain—*I saw you through the window and thought I'd come out and say hey.*

"How's your book doin'?" he asked.

"Really great." She cringed. "Did that sound braggy? I didn't mean it that way. But it's selling so much better than I ever thought it would. I mean, Wren, I really believed that only two people would read it: my mom and maybe you."

"I read it, for sure."

He took a couple jogging steps and stood in front of her, stopping so she'd have to walk around him if she didn't want to face him. She still thought of Wren Parker as a boy, an annoying one at that, the kid who slipped sand into her potato chip bag, who jumped from behind sand dunes and the sides of houses to make her scream.

But there he stood, a foot taller than her five feet. His hair was cut in that silly floppy way that everyone was wearing, an imitation of James Dean. His dark brown eyes had a hazel ring around them—that much hadn't changed.

He wore a thick fishermen's sweater, a style that had been worn by generations of his Massachusetts oyster-farming family. His grin was teasing. He dared her to walk around him. She stopped and stood firm. "Well," she said. "What did you think of it?"

"I loved every page. And you know I don't read stories like that. I'd rather read about Robinson Crusoe or a story where the Jolly Roger flag rises in rebellion." He lifted his arm as if holding a sword. "But, damn, Pegs, it was so good."

"Thanks. That means a lot to me."

He turned on his heels and started walking again in silence for a minute, the sea breathing next to them.

Their hands brushed, and she wondered for a second if he would take hers in his. But that would never happen. Wren Parker was the guy who dated the homecoming queen. He was the shortstop of the Cape Cod Baseball League team and the guy who could steer a sailboat through a fierce storm and return unscathed. He was *not* the guy who would take Peggy Andrews's hand. Instead, he treated her like the sister he didn't have.

When she'd been excluded at school, he'd drawn her in by asking her to sit at the lunch table with her soggy bologna sandwich. When she hadn't been invited to the prom, he assumed she'd be sad and asked her. Of course she'd refused; the idea of dressing up and making nice for hours and hours on end was too much to bear. When a storm hit and they all lost electricity, he brought over candles and matches.

Once Peggy had dreamed that Wren Parker told her he loved her— not those town girls with dewy skin and glossed lips. But that was long ago. Far as Peggy knew, he was still dating the blue-eyed girl from

Hyannis Port he'd met during a baseball tournament. Even now he could be hunting for a diamond ring so he could get down on one knee.

"How's the job hunt?" she asked.

"It's good. I have to decide whether I will take a job with OSHA here in Cape Cod or spread my wings." He jumped ahead of her, walking backward while talking. He was so full of energy Peggy wondered that he didn't self-combust.

"Where would those wings take you?"

"I'm pretending I can change into something—you know, like your book."

"Oh, oh, I get it." Peggy spread her palms and pushed gently at his chest, and he kept his backward stride.

He turned to walk next to her again. "I have a job offer in California. I got a month to decide."

"Why a month?"

"Because I have one more paper to finish before I'll have my degree." He nudged her with his shoulder. "Maybe you could ghostwrite it for me?"

"No time," she said with a laugh. "The editor wants my next book two months early. I get a huge bonus if I finish it, so I'm working really hard."

"I was kidding, Pegs."

"I know. I know."

"Someday, I just know it, I am going to get you to lighten up."

"I'm lightened," she said defensively. "Look, I'm out walking the beach, I'm light as a feather."

He laughed loudly and she loved when his booming laughter hit the sky. He looked her in the eyes. "You seem sad. Is everything okay?"

"I got a weird call today, and I'm trying to shake it off. Walk it off."

"And I interrupted."

"That's okay," she said, and she meant it. Anyone else interrupting her long evening walk would have annoyed her, but not Wren.

"Who called?"

"It was this woman from London . . ." Peggy trailed off, not for suspense but to find a way to explain it to Wren. The waves massaged the sand, rising higher now, the wind behind them. "Anyway, she said that the story of Whisperwood was hers. That it was her childhood land."

"Could that possibly be true?"

"There's no way. Mother and I made it up. It's been ours for all my life. That's why I keep her so involved. She told me the first story way back when I was a kid, to keep me calm after Dad died, to give me something of my own."

"Oh..."

"Sometimes I'd add to the story and get to see my dad in Whisperwood, but eventually I turned it into a land for the adventures of the orphaned sisters."

"It's all quite amazing. To think that you can just make all of that out of air, out of nothing. Did you tell your mother about the call?"

His tone of voice over the word *mother* was the tone he'd always used—it carried disdain. Although Peggy knew why, she still hated it. Mother had never been kind to Wren. She didn't tell Peggy when Wren called. She didn't let him in the house if Peggy was working. For one full year after he'd been with a group of town kids who'd jumped off the pier and one of the boys drowned, Mother forbade Peggy to see him.

She didn't like Wren, and she knew Peggy did.

"No, I haven't told her. You can imagine how she'd react. I'm sure it's nothing, anyway."

They walked a bit in silence. She knew what was coming. Wren was busy. He had to go. He always did. He moved at a hundred miles an hour while she was at walking pace.

But that wasn't what happened.

"So, Pegs, are you dating anyone these days?"

She came to a halt. "These days? As if I've ever dated anyone?"

"Come on, you must be seeing someone. You're practically a celebrity, and there's so much going on in Provincetown. The music scene is off the chain and you're—"

"I'm what?" She started walking again.

"So cute."

She didn't laugh. "Puppies are cute, and you're nuts."

"It's possible," he said, eyes twinkling.

"Are you dating anyone, Mr. Parker?"

His stride slowed, an easier pace, and for that Peggy was grateful.

"Sort of. I think she thinks we're dating, but I just thought we went out to dance a few times."

"I bet she wears dresses with daisies on them, and her hair is blond and swings in a perfect ponytail."

He laughed so hard that he had to stop and bend over, his hands on his knees. "Oh my God, you called that right."

"Of course I did. And she has a cute nickname like Doll or Babykins."

He didn't laugh this time. A sheer gust came from behind, almost blowing them forward, and they halted, braced against it. A briny aroma washed over them. "I'm sorry I interrupted your quiet time," he said.

"It's okay," she said. "I thought I'd brainstorm the next scene with the orphans, but I just kept thinking about that weird phone call. So thanks for putting an end to that."

"Why would a woman in England call you about your fairy tale if there wasn't at least—in some way—a kernel of truth? Don't ignore it. Find out what she wants."

"It's too weird."

"What are you scared of?"

"Nothing. What do you mean by that?"

"Is there a reason you don't want to understand what she wants, that you might possibly be frightened of where it leads?" He shrugged. "Hey, what do I know? I'm just a guy who wants to dive beneath the waves and find out what is going on under there."

He'd meant no harm. "You are *not* just a guy," she said, the words out of her mouth and into the world before she could take them back.

"Well, well," he said with a grin. "You finally recognize such a thing?"

She lightly punched him in the arm. "Stop. You know what I meant."

"I'm hoping I do."

# CHAPTER 14

## March 1960

Hazel paced the kitchen, the disconnected phone still dangling. Peggy Andrews had hung up on her. Now what?

She presently owned a parcel of damaged original illustrations she couldn't afford and she'd missed coffee with Barnaby, who'd worry. Her thoughts were spinning at a dizzying speed, and she had no idea what to do next.

She found herself at the end of the hallway, where she opened the linen closet door and pulled out a wooden trunk with tarnished brass latches. She tossed aside the pile of coats, hats, and scarves that had been resting on top; they plopped to the ground in a poof of dust. She unlatched the lock with a key she kept taped to the inside of the frame of the closet.

Hazel opened the trunk. On top lay Flora's tattered bear. Below, neatly folded in separate piles, were Harry's sketches, newspaper articles, and photos. And at the very bottom, buried beneath all of it, rested a pile of letters from Harry that had been gathered together in twine. Even now, she didn't bring them out, leaving the letters in the musty corner of the trunk.

Hazel had never told her mother she still had Berry. In fact, Mum had never even asked about it. This seemed as damning to Hazel as the fact that her mum had remarried and had another child: now a teenage son named the ridiculous faux-royal name of Barclay—nicknamed Tenny, for his last name, Tennyson. Hazel's eyes rolled each time Mum said it, and Mum had asked her to stop. "It's a family name, Hazel. Don't be disrespectful. He's your brother."

Under the bear's left arm, the seams were coming undone. She carried the battered stuffed animal to the kitchen. Sifting through the junk drawer, she found a needle and thread and sewed the torn area. She pulled the final stitch, tied it, and bit off the end. She rested Berry on the kitchen table next to the parcel. He looked at Hazel with a certain expectancy.

Hazel thought about the shimmering door to Whisperwood and the birds and lions and fish she and Flora had become all those years ago. She thought of the river, and Berry found on its muddy banks. She thought of tiny Flora, floundering in the Thames.

*Stop!*

This is when the panic always arrived: a flood of adrenaline mixed with the aroma of grass and mud. Then came memories of Harry, along with the guilt about how she'd forgotten to watch over her sister because she'd been alone with him, because the thrill of early desire made her forget what was truly important: her sister.

Hazel shook off the feeling and picked up the phone to dial numbers she knew by heart.

"Hallo," Kelty's singsong voice answered.

"Can you come over? I have something to tell you."

Thirty minutes later, Kelty burst through the door without knocking. She wore a new minidress covered in geometric patterns of yellow and blue. How she managed to look chic all the bloody time would usually annoy Hazel, but she had other things on her mind just now.

Hazel looked behind Kelty. "Where's Midge?"

"The museum is closed today. Fergus is home watching her." Kelty dropped her bag on the bench by the door. "As it is, she prefers him."

"I doubt that." Hazel loved Kelty's husband, the director of the Victoria and Albert Museum, but everyone, no matter who they were, preferred Kelty. Leading her friend down the dim hallway, Hazel flicked on the overhead light as they neared the closet, its door propped open by the trunk.

"Did you find treasure?" Kelty asked, and plopped down on the floor, daintily folding her legs into a *V* to her left, as if posing for a photo.

"Not hardly," Hazel said, taking a seat beside her.

Kelty peeked inside the trunk and looked up, eyes wide. "Those are the newspaper articles from when Flora disappeared." She looked again. "And Harry's sketches!"

"Yes."

"What's happening?"

Hazel settled back on her bottom, already feeling better with Kelty near. The open trunk looked accusatory, its contents huddled for so long in its dark cave. Hazel lifted a yellowing *Oxford Times* newspaper. "They never put Flora on the front page. They treated her disappearance like it was just a bother."

"Can we take it all out? To the kitchen table?" Kelty asked softly.

They made a few trips back and forth with piles until Harry's sketches were spread across the table along with *Oxford Times* articles, yellowed and curled at their edges. A photo of Flora at her sixth birthday in July of 1940 was the size of a postage stamp in the upper left corner of page four, the story of her disappearance summarized in a few sentences below.

"The Blitz took up all the news in the nation," Hazel said.

Kelty sifted through the pages. "Yes. Children dead on the streets of London, and Flora lost in the mayhem."

GERMAN BOMB KILLS 64 AT BALHAM STATION IN THE LONDON UN-DERGROUND.

CHURCHILL SUCCEEDS CHAMBERLAIN AS LEADER OF THE CONSER-VATIVE PARTY.

PRINCESS ELIZABETH DELIVERS HER FIRST PUBLIC SPEECH ON THE BBC: SHE IS FOURTEEN YEARS OLD.

Flora was a footnote among great historical events.

Hazel picked up Harry's sketches, some as small as the palm of a child's hand, and others filling sheets of paper torn from the back of schoolbooks. Occasionally, when Bridie could afford it, she bought Harry a real sketch pad.

Hazel's eyes watered a bit as she gazed at young Harry's intricately drawn sketch of a three-mast ship on a sea of stars and clouds. "He drew this the day after we read *Peter Pan* to Flora. He left it for us the next morning." Another of his sketches was of a shattered tree lying on limp grass. "This was the day lightning felled an oak in the field."

There was a drawing of Hazel running across the woodlands. "He drew this on the summer solstice."

"Why have you kept all of these?" Kelty asked quietly.

"I've kept everything," Hazel admitted, "thinking someday I'd spot an overlooked clue."

"I think of Flora all the time. Still—" Kelty said.

"How could we not?" Hazel glanced down, then back up at her friend. "She's everywhere and nowhere all at once. When the police saw Harry's sketches, they were just awful, accusing him of being obsessed with both of us and having done something horrible to Flora. They questioned him to no end."

"Oh no. I never knew that."

Hazel looked to Kelty. An aura surrounded her friend, as it had that long-ago afternoon they'd met. A vivid intensity drew others to her flame. Kelty's beauty wasn't false like some women with perfect makeup and tailored clothes and pearl strands. Her beauty was wilder. She always looked, as she did now, as if she'd just come in from a hike or swim.

"Kelty," she said. "I want to tell you about Whisperwood."

"Whisperwood?" Kelty sat at the table and tapped her fingers on the wood in a staccato rhythm. "Wait, I know this . . . Whisperwood."

"What do you mean?" Hazel asked.

"I forgot. I did forget until right now. Do you remember the first day I came over to the Aberdeens'? I was scared out of my mind and that woman—"

"Mrs. Marchman," Hazel said. "The hag."

"Yes, God, I had blocked out her name." Kelty shuddered in exaggeration. "Anyway, when we went back to the bedroom, for a few minutes it was just me and Flora. I was crying like a two-year-old, and she was calm as a bird in a nest. She told me not to worry because you would take us to Whisperwood."

"You remember this?" Hazel leaned forward.

"Yes. Then you came in and told me the story of Frideswide. And I thought that's what she'd been talking about."

"That's all she told you?"

"She was what? Five years old? Yes, that's all she said. But I remember it because it was such a pretty name. I wondered about it for a while but forgot until right now."

"So if Flora said something to you, she might have said something to Harry or Bridie or Mum or—"

"The nurses. Or Father Fenelly."

Kelty picked up the book, with its whimsical blue-and-green cover brightly displaying two girls with their hair streaming behind them. "But why didn't you tell me about Whisperwood?"

"This was the land I created for me and for Flora when we needed something of our own. As lovely and kind as Bridie was, she was Harry's mum, not ours. The house, too—we were guests. But this, Whisperwood, was *all* ours. The day Flora disappeared, she went looking for it, I'm sure of it."

"You don't know that." Kelty held up the book. "So, you made up this exact place?"

"Not exact. Mine was more of an imaginary land. In the book, it's more a full-on fairy tale, and she's added other fairy-tale characters."

Hazel went to the kitchen window, cracked it a bit to let in the spring air. "In this book, there are other differences. The American author took our safe Whisperwood and made it a place where battles are fought and a queen must be saved. Peggy Andrews made Whisperwood a scary place of adventure for two girls. It's still *our* place, yet the woodlands have been invaded by dark forces and the girls—they're the ones to save the land. None of that was my idea. I never meant for our story to be any sort of morality tale—Whisperwood was a wonderful place where magical things happened, a refuge for us while the world was burning around us."

Kelty patted the top of the book and then flipped it over. "Who is this Peggy Andrews?"

"I intend to find out. What if she is . . ."

"Flora." Kelty sat back and crossed her arms. "Adventure lies ahead."

Her freckled cheeks rose with her smile. "So this book is our first clue in twenty years. Where do we go first? America to track down this author? We can, you know, Fergus would buy us passage."

"Of course he would." Hazel gazed up at the phone. "Well, I did phone her."

"*What?*" Kelty said. "Did you fall into a money pit?"

"Just burying myself in debt, but it's for Flora."

Kelty nodded. "A damn fine reason. What did she say?"

"Not much, and she hung up on me, so for now, I have to talk to Bridie Aberdeen. I can think of better things to do than facing her. You know I haven't spoken to her or Harry since I left. I have to find out if Bridie ever knew about Whisperwood or told anyone else about it."

"And Harry."

"Not yet."

"Hazel, you cannot ignore him forever."

"I can for as long as possible." She thought of the childhood vow she'd made in that damp church. She thought of her last moments with Harry. She thought of their kiss in the woodlands. She remembered screaming at Bridie and Harry that she never, not ever, wanted to see them again.

"Have you *ever* been back to Binsey?" Kelty asked.

"No, not once." Hazel shivered although her kitchen was warm. "What a cruel thing I did—abandoning a family who'd loved me. But, Kelty, it was all too awful, and then time passed and then more time, and what was I to say? Or do? I was frozen with grief, and when I finally thawed, years later, I didn't know how to approach them, or what to say. And it's not like they ever came looking to find me, either." A defensive bristle of anger filled her next words. "It seemed best to let it stay in the past. Too much hurt to bring it all back for any of us. There was and is nothing I can do to fix it."

Kelty placed her arm on Hazel's shoulder, and they stared at the blue-and-green book with the countryside and the sisters and the castle in the background, a trail winding through trees to the river of stars. Hazel wondered if it was too late, if the path to Flora was long overgrown.

# CHAPTER 15

## September 1939

Hazel and Flora took turns in the washroom before their first dinner in Binsey. Hazel scrubbed her sister's face and hands, washing off grime from the trip, and the smoke and the dust of the station. Staring into the wavy mirror at herself looking back at her, the one with tangled hair and a flushed face, Hazel told herself to be brave.

In the bedroom, they changed into their matching favorite cornflower blue dresses with the white Peter Pan collars and took out a pair of neatly folded-by-Mum socks. Hazel plaited Flora's hair like Mum had taught her and asked, "You ready?"

"Not yet," Flora said.

"What is it?" Hazel leaned down and tapped Flora's nose.

Her sister looked up at her shyly. "This isn't Whisperwood, is it? We're still in the real world, aren't we?"

Hazel thought of all the times they'd visited Whisperwood in the past days and smiled. "Of course *this* is real. We're at a house in Binsey, where we'll stay until the bombs stop dropping. It isn't home, but it isn't *our* land, either, Flora."

"Right now, it feels like I can turn into anything I want."

Did she need to explain everything? Well, perhaps she did. Just like Mum would do. The sisters spoke in hushed voices, their foreheads nearly touching as they bent their heads together. From outside the door

95

came the *cling-clang* of pots and pans and the muffled voices of Harry and Mrs. Aberdeen.

"Right now, we can only be us," said Hazel. "And you can't disappear. We are to go out there and have dinner with Mrs. Aberdeen and her son. Then we wait."

"Wait for what?"

"For Mum to come get us."

The sisters took each other's hands and walked into the kitchen.

Mrs. Aberdeen stood at the stove, wooden spoon in hand, stirring a pot bubbling with what smelled like lamb stew. "Girls! Have a seat."

Four mismatched wooden chairs crowded a table that had been set with cream-colored china plates with green and yellow flowers about their edges. The green linen napkins with crisp edges had obviously been ironed. Four milk-colored glasses circled the table, and Harry was placing the silverware.

The past few months had been so chaotic in their own home in Bloomsbury that Hazel couldn't remember the last time Mum had set the table with the fine Arthur Price silverware that she kept in their pine hutch. Sometimes they even ate from their laps while the evening news droned on from the staticky wireless, with Chamberlain giving them the latest grim updates from the war. Mum sat mute, listening while the girls silently ate.

Harry set the last fork down, then looked up. He waited for them to sit before taking his seat. His curls looked as if he'd just come in from a wild windstorm and his grin made it appear he'd just won something. He echoed his mum: "Sit!"

He set the bowl of steaming stew in front of Hazel. Carrots and potatoes, sprigs of thyme floating in gravy. Mrs. Aberdeen opened the oven and pulled out a tray of puffy biscuits, tossed them into a ceramic bowl, and set them on the table. After she and Harry sat, Mrs. Aberdeen closed her hands in prayer, and they all did the same.

"Lord God, Heavenly Father, bless us and these, thy gifts that we receive from the bountiful goodness—"

Hazel opened her left eye, glancing around the table as Mrs. Aberdeen blessed the food. Sure enough, Harry was staring back at her when both of them were to have their eyes shut. He smiled at her and closed his eyes. Her secret was safe with him.

"—through Jesus Christ, our Lord, amen."

Mrs. Aberdeen sat up straighter and looked at the girls. "I think you'll love our hamlet. It's as lovely as any can be. I have lived here for all my life. It's not really a town and not a city at all. There's only one road in and one road out."

"Where's your papa?" Flora asked, looking at Harry with adoration.

"He's . . . gone." Harry looked at his mum, who nodded.

Hazel sat quietly thinking that the word *gone* hid a story she wanted to know. If someone left, if they disappeared or drove off or were simply called away, there was usually a reason. She loved knowing why things happened, because if she did, it was quite possible she could keep them from happening again.

Mrs. Aberdeen turned her attention to Hazel. "My first name is Bridgette, and you can't go calling me Mrs. Aberdeen; it is too many syllables. And my name is a tongue twister, so you must call me Mum Bridie—Bridie was my nickname as a child."

"But we have a mum," Hazel said.

Instead of tossing her the derisive look that Hazel was accustomed to from adults, Mrs. Aberdeen nodded. "Quite right, Hazel Linden. Then how about . . . Aunt Bridie?"

"You aren't our aunt." Hazel's voice sounded harsher than she'd meant it to be.

"Then you will call me . . ."

Mrs. Aberdeen paused long enough in her uncertainty that Flora proclaimed, "Just Bridie!"

Mrs. Aberdeen lifted her arm like a queen holding a scepter. "It is proclaimed: I am just Bridie." She smiled. "Tomorrow we'll go into Oxford and mail the card to let your mum know you are well. And we'll invite her to come visit us out here." Bridie dipped her biscuit into the stew. "I must go into the market as it is, so I will take the mail. The autumn equinox is in two weeks, and we need supplies."

"What's an equinox?" Flora drew out the long, melodic word, stumbling over its end sounds.

Mrs. Aberdeen cleared her throat and spoke in the most beautiful singsong voice. "Once, long ago—"

"Just like our story!" Flora exclaimed.

Hazel reached under the table and squeezed her sister's knee to be quiet.

Bridie continued as if she'd never been interrupted. "There was a goddess named Persephone, and during the summer she lived above the earth with her mother, but every year when the day of the equinox arrives, she must return to the underworld, to her husband, Hades."

"Mum!" Harry exclaimed. "Don't go scaring them. They've been here for but a minute."

"That's not scary," Flora said.

Hazel observed Bridie with curiosity. Who was this woman who told stories about goddesses? Their mum had never told a story that wasn't in a book, something she read to them. Hazel couldn't help it. Curiosity bubbled to the surface. "Why live in the underworld? Why can't Hades just come up to summertime with her?"

"Good question, Hazel. You see, as ruler of the underworld, Hades must stay there."

Hazel thought about this. "So he can't leave, but she can?"

"She can leave for six months of the year where she joins her mum on the spring equinox and then . . ." Mrs. Aberdeen trailed off as if the words on a page had run out. "That's a story for another day."

Harry twirled the stew with his spoon. "Mum likes stories," he said.

"So do we!" Flora pronounced, and because she lisped *so* sounded like a *though*, and she came across as formal and sweet.

Bridie and Harry gazed at Flora with smiles. Hazel noticed the look, and something mean inside her made her want to holler that she, Hazel Mersey Linden, was the one who created all their stories, and they were meant for just Flora.

Bridie didn't need to know everything about everything.

But Hazel also knew that stories didn't belong to anyone. They were everywhere. She should be happy they'd found themselves in a place where a mum told such tales. And yet Hazel resisted feeling happy; it wasn't fair to Mum, who was without a doubt sitting at home worrying.

Just the thought of Mum brought a flash of tears to her eyes, unnoticed by Bridie and Harry, who were devoting all their attention to Flora. And why wouldn't they? She was the cute one, the one with the singsong voice and the blond curls and button nose. Flora was the one worth loving. Flora was the one, Hazel knew, they all adored.

# CHAPTER 16

## September 1939

That first night in Binsey, the sisters curled up tightly in bed together. Flora whispered to Hazel, "Bridie's nice."

"Yes, she is," Hazel answered. "And we must be just as lovely, like Mum said. This will all be over soon enough. England will win the war, and we'll go home. We must be patient."

Flora lay still and quiet, as if she'd just heard the first Hazel-story she didn't altogether believe.

"Take me to Whisperwood," Flora said, her tone demanding.

"Okay." Hazel paused dramatically, taking a big breath before starting. "I see a shimmering door right there." Hazel waved her hand through the air, and they snuggled closer as she found the words awaiting her.

"Not that long ago and not so far away, in a land that is right here," Hazel whispered into the dark, "there was a place where anything could happen, where we might become anything we wish, where a river of stars runs through its woodlands. Keep your eyes open for hidden doorways! They're everywhere, but visible only to those who are worthy. And we are worthy."

"Yes," Flora said, her voice soaked with sleepiness.

"The forest is thick with the sweet smell of pine and something like ..."

"Candy," Flora interjected.

Hazel said, "Yes, like melting caramel."

"What are we?" Flora asked, snuggling closer, her eyes shut tight.

"Hold on. It's coming. I feel it in the wind blowing through the trees. Follow me down the crooked path to the river. Keep up now, Flora."

"I'm coming!"

"I think I have a paw . . . do you?"

"Oh, yes, it's big," Flora exclaimed. "What kind is it?"

"I think we are—"

"Lions! We are lions!" Flora cried out.

"Headed to the river to drink stars," Hazel said. "Stars make lions stronger."

Hazel's voice took them through the forest, past a talking hawk, over a bridge made of glass, under a canopy of trees that sang songs, and to the river with an owl flying behind them keeping watch. And off, far off, the tiptop of a castle rose above; it was a wonderful place they might someday reach if they never gave up.

Flora was asleep before they reached the castle and Hazel stopped the story, thinking she too was just about to fall asleep, her eyelids heavy and thick. But then she didn't. Instead, she thought of Mum and their empty bedrooms at home.

She slipped out of the bed and flicked on the small bedside lamp. On the dresser rested the postcard they would send Mum tomorrow. With the pencil from her knapsack, she sat on the edge of the bed to write with the postcard balanced on her knees.

She imagined her mum checking the postbox every hour looking for the note. What would she want to hear?

*Dear Mum,*

*We are in a cozy cottage in Binsey with the Aberdeen family—a mum named Bridgette and boy named Harry, who chose us to come live with them. Please come visit. We are safe. We already miss you so much. Your loving daughters, Hazel and Flora.*

She set the postcard on the dresser and crawled into bed next to her sister, wondering what kind of story they'd found themselves in the middle of—wondrous or horrifying, she couldn't yet know.

—

Hazel dreamed of a postcard flying over London, then fluttering to the ground before it reached its destination, washing away down the gutter, rushing, rushing toward the sewers below Bloomsbury.

She woke to rain pattering on the rooftop and tinkling against the windowpanes. The dream wasn't a premonition—she hoped—it was just the outside world entering the dream world. Hazel shook off a feeling of dread and rose quickly, enticed by the aroma of something rich and tasty.

Hazel had placed her hand on the brass doorknob when she realized a piece of paper had been slipped under the door. She picked it up.

In the soft morning light, Hazel looked at a pencil drawing of Berry. It was remarkably realistic, like a blurry photo, the stuffed animal's fur thick and even worn thin on his paws where Flora held and rubbed him against her cheek. Berry sat up, his head flopped slightly to the left, face and fur soft in the pencil marks.

This drawing was obviously for Flora, and it was sweet. The kindness erased Hazel's disturbing dream. She placed the paper on the wooden bedside table before heading to the kitchen, where Bridie was making porridge and sausage.

"Good morning," Hazel said, unsure of her own voice in this quiet place.

Bridie turned. "Good morning, sweet pea."

Hazel had never been called *sweet pea* before. She kind of liked it.

"You ready for some breakfast and tea?"

"I am. Flora is still sleeping. Should I wake her?"

"Let her be. This has all been quite the shock. Now have a seat, my dear."

Hazel sat, crossing her legs at the ankles like the queen for she so wanted Bridie to know she had chosen well, that she had taken in polite and good girls. Bridie set the porridge in a creamware bowl, and a plate of mashed sausage smelled so divine that Hazel wanted to dive for it without asking.

The porridge was thick and lumpy, just the way Hazel liked it; a lake of cream floated on top, and Hazel dipped her spoon to watch the cream river through the porridge. She took her first bite. Though she'd never say such a thing out loud, it was so much better than Mum's. What an awful thing to think.

"You like it?" Bridie said.

"Oh, yes, very much! The cream—"

"—is from our cow."

"It's not from the market?" It took Hazel a minute to think through this, never having given too much thought to where things came from, only that Mum bought milk in the market and that rationing had kept so much from them.

Bridie sat beside Hazel. "Yes, at first light Harry goes to milk our cow. We're lucky. Not everyone can get such things right now."

"I wish you had a cow that made sugar. It's been so long."

Bridie laughed softly. "You, my dear, are going to be just fine here in the Aberdeen home. Harry was right to choose you."

Choose her.

Harry had chosen her.

Nothing could be done to suppress Hazel's smile.

"And here he comes," Bridie said, and pointed out the window. Harry appeared as a form of brown coat and red knit cap, jogging down the hill toward the house. In an instant, the rain stopped and the sun burst through a low flat cloud, ripping it apart like a piece of paper. Rays of light, filtered hazy in the mist, fell upon Harry as he paused at the field's edge. He lifted his face to the warmth and smiled before running toward the front door.

What a place this was, Hazel thought. All the wide green space to run; the rippling of the sky that touched a horizon of trees unobscured by a cathedral or tall building. It was as if by taking a simple train ride the world had unfolded, presenting itself in long stretches of rolling hills and heather fields. Look, it said to Hazel, there is so much more than you ever knew. The feeling of little minnows swimming in her stomach—a thrill that this world would change her forever.

*"Hathel!"* A distressed cry rang out, and Hazel jumped from the table, tripping over Bridie's foot in a rush to the bedroom, only steps away.

She hugged her sister close and told her they were safe and that there was a lovely breakfast waiting.

"I thought you left me!" said Flora.

"Never. I would never leave you."

# CHAPTER 17

## March 1960

Hazel walked the towpath beside the River Thames toward Binsey and Bridie, the words she had uttered long ago still echoing down the winding river: *"I would never leave you."*

She'd broken that promise.

The spring grass grew so green it looked painted with emerald hues, and shadows sketched lacy patterns on the ground. At the river's edge, alder and aspen rose high, green buds on their branches. Wildflowers were bursting, white as snow, raspberry red, and blue as sky.

She'd come to see Bridie for the first time in twenty years, and now she wished that Barnaby or Kelty had accompanied her. Early that morning she'd made the impulsive decision to come; Bridie was the first person on her list.

Hazel had grabbed her rain slicker and wellies and had taken the train on the Piccadilly line toward Oxford. A cabbie who smelled of cabbage had dropped her off at the edge of Port Meadow. Hazel had walked slowly into Binsey, taking it all in as she went over the bridge and into the hamlet.

Hazel stopped at the edge of the dirt path, touched the soft part of a purple thistle while avoiding the prickles at its edge: Bridie's favorites. A jackrabbit with one ear shorter than the other bounded from the grasses, paused to stare, and was off again. Hazel smiled sadly thinking of all the times Flora had wanted to be a rabbit and all the times she'd said no. Why? She had no idea.

Wandering down the path she thought maybe she should have brought flowers or a cake, or at least phoned before showing up on the doorstep. After twenty years, a bit of decorum might be called for.

Midmorning bloomed so warm that Hazel slipped off her rain jacket and tossed it over her arm as she passed the pub, The Perch. Mr. Nolan stood on the front stoop just as his father had done before him. He wore that amiable smile and energetic wave, still had that dark wavy hair and the denim button-down shirt. He didn't recognize Hazel, and for that she was grateful. The hamlet was accustomed to walkers from Oxford, to those making a pilgrimage to the church and sacred well.

This morning she and Barnaby had gone about their morning routine of *The Times*, two soft boiled eggs, and tea with toast. Neither said a word about Whisperwood or the illustrations until he finally asked, "Have you decided what to do about the . . . parcel? I worry, my love."

"Yesterday afternoon I tried to return them and now I own them."

He'd sat back in his chair with one raised eyebrow. "Own them?"

After she'd finished explaining all that had happened, he'd shaken his head. "Wow. That's a lucky break."

"Lucky break? Barnaby, they're worth a fortune. I have no idea how I'll ever pay Edwin back. But I intend to find a way."

He'd smiled. "Well, since I ruined two of them I'll help . . ."

"No," she'd interrupted.

"Well, all I know is this: Paris is in"—he counted fingers, exaggerating the movement—"ten days." Then he'd kissed her before asking, "What are your plans today? A free woman without a job? Coffee shop with Kelty? Shopping on Carnaby? Packing for Paris?"

She hadn't answered, as Binsey was foremost in her thoughts. Barnaby had kissed her goodbye and grabbed his coat from the peg by the front door.

Now, Hazel stopped at the end of Bridie's cottage's drive. Tire marks were worn into the dirt like tattoos, rainwater filling the divots and reflecting the high sun. A few steps ahead the cottage stood, as if waiting in a timeless pause.

Hazel hung back for a moment, looking at this place that had sheltered her for a year. The stones many shades of gray—dove, cloud, and nearly white—layered upon each other, solid and worn. The bright blue front door now had a brass knocker. The garden bloomed with emerald leaves and grass, the white narcissi stared with their yellow eyes.

A woman opened the door, holding her palm over her brow to block the afternoon sun. The tilt of her head was familiar.

*Bridie.*

Her hair was silver, pulled back into a knot that was coming loose. A breeze lifted her flowered dress by the hem, swirling the fabric around her. "You're here!" she called out. "Halllooo."

Did Bridie know it was her?

"Hazel!" Bridie broke into a run. "Is that you? My God, is it you?"

"It is," Hazel called out. Her heart leapt as the woman ran toward her, and yet she stood still; expectant and yet also timid. The last time she'd stood where she now was, she'd called out, loud and clear—*I never, ever want to see you again.*

Then Bridie's arms were around her, along with the aroma of rosemary, and she heard the sound of her name in that soothing voice.

"Hazel."

Hazel wrapped her arms around Bridie, holding her close.

"Bridie," Hazel said quietly, feeling the comfort and love she'd not felt for twenty years now.

Bridie let go, placed her hands on Hazel's shoulders, and met her gaze with a mother's tenderness.

"Now let me look at you. Just as beautiful and full of light as I remember. You are finally here. I have waited."

"Waited?"

"I knew one day you'd come. I knew that whether it was the fates or the furies, you would find your way to my door. Tell me why you're here." Bridie laughed, high and clear. "Oh, it doesn't matter why. Not one bit. You are . . . finally here." Her voice choked with emotion and her eyes were wet with tears. "Come in. Come in. There is so very much to catch up on, isn't there?"

The cottage's interior wrapped around Hazel like Bridie's hug. Hazel glanced around to see the table where she'd done schoolwork with Harry; the plaid throw on the couch; the logs piled in a crisscross pattern in the brick fireplace. The scent of wood smoke, strong tea, and rosemary hung in the air. The wooden doorframes were honey-hued in the sunlight streaming through diamond-shaped windows. There was nothing here to accuse Hazel.

"Oh." Hazel exhaled as the door shut behind her.

They entered the kitchen and Hazel glanced around; the door to her and Flora's little end room off the kitchen was shut. She walked toward it, touched the egg-shaped brass knob, and then turned to Bridie, the tears she'd tamped down threatening now.

"You can go in," Bridie said softly. "If you'd like. I sew in there now, and there's a desk, but I can feel both of you when I enter; I can feel your bright lights and beautiful energy. I can feel you both."

Hazel turned away from the room. "Not yet," she said.

Then, as if feeling Hazel's unspoken question lingering below the years: "It had to be you who came to me, Hazel. I could not come find you even if I'd wanted to."

"Why?" Hazel asked.

"I tried once, years ago, and your sweet mum made it clear that you needed to heal, that you didn't need to revisit that time over and over. I understood even as it broke my heart. But I have waited."

To be waited for, what a wonder, Hazel thought, to have someone expectantly bide their time for *her* was absolutely glorious.

Hazel noticed a man's tweed jacket was flung over a kitchen chair and a pair of large and very muddy boots stood to the right of the back door. Bridie smiled when she saw Hazel looking. "Yes, I married."

"Oh, Bridie! Did your . . . did your ex show up?"

Bridie shook her head. "No," she said.

"Who is it? Your husband? Do I know him?"

Bridie smiled shyly and gave an almost imperceptible nod. "It's Johnny Nolan."

"Mr. Nolan?" Hazel asked. "I saw him on my way here! I would have sat here through a thousand guesses before that one."

"The town's church outcast marries the pub owner," she said with a grin.

"Well, I think it's lovely," Hazel said.

"But that's not why you came here today. What at long last brings you back to me?"

"I am sorry." Hazel said it before she knew what was falling out of her mouth. Maybe she should have spent the walk here deciding what to say.

Bridie looked over her shoulder from where she stood filling the kettle at the kitchen sink. "Whatever for, darling?"

"Everything. I ruined everything. Your life. Harry's. Everyone. My mum's."

Bridie set the kettle on the burner and twisted the flame on high. She turned and set her palms on the counter behind her, tilted her head in that little-bird way, and shook her head slightly. "Whatever do you mean? I don't understand."

"When it happened." Hazel slumped into a kitchen chair. "When Flora disappeared, I heard they blamed you. I read the papers. I know. Harry, too."

"That is what police do." Bridie came to Hazel and sat next to her.

"I wasn't brave enough to tell them the truth. But I am here to tell it to you now."

"You came here to tell me something?" Bridie asked.

"I did."

"We'll talk over tea." Bridie set out teacups, sugar cubes, and cream. After the kettle sang, she poured the tea. She didn't say another word, just gazed at Hazel with that look that had melted her heart and fear on the first day they'd arrived here from Bloomsbury.

"Bridie, did you know about the stories I told Flora?"

"The ones you read to her?" Bridie looked up as if the memory rested on the ceiling. "How that little girl loved *Winnie-the-Pooh*—Tigger the most. And *Peter Pan*."

"No. Not those stories. The one I made up."

"You made up a story? How grand!"

Hazel felt a flood of relief because if Bridie hadn't known about Whisperwood, then maybe Flora was the one who told the story; maybe Flora was alive and the one carrying on the tale. Hazel told Bridie all about it, how she'd made up the land for Flora.

Bridie sipped her tea and leaned forward, placing her elbows on the table. "You were always such an enchanting child, seeing magic all around you." Bridie smiled. "It would make sense that you'd know the secret worlds hidden inside our own."

"Oh. No." Hazel shook her head. "It wasn't like that. This was a simple place where we went together and had adventures, then came home."

"But for being there, you were better and braver upon your return?" Bridie asked.

"Yes, better and braver. That was true." Hazel bit her bottom lip. "Until it wasn't true."

"Go on."

"I believe that on the day she disappeared, Flora went looking for our land without me."

"You *believe* she went looking for the land or you *know* this?"

"I believe."

"The name of this place?" Bridie asked.

"Whisperwood," Hazel said.

"Whisperwood," Bridie repeated, closing her eyes.

Hazel reached into her bag and withdrew Peggy Andrews's book, dropped it onto the table. "Now there is this."

Bridie didn't pick it up but instead just touched its surface. "Did you write this? You were always such a beautiful writer."

"No. An author in America wrote it. Someone is using our land for their own stories."

Bridie paused. "Could this author be Flora?" Her voice held such hope as she said out loud all that Hazel wanted to believe.

"No. I thought so for a brief moment, but she's the wrong age. That's all I really know about her."

"Could Flora have told this author her story?"

"That's what I am trying to figure out."

Bridie nodded. "So you feel like your secret place, your beautiful world, your fairy land as it were, took Flora from you."

"Yes. I know it did."

"You must let go of such ideas, Hazel." Bridie slid her chair forward and placed her hands on either side of Hazel's face, just as she had done when Hazel had been a child. "Despair leads us to stories, of course. We invent them so we can live in a world with meaning. I told you stories. We danced to stories. I spun them over fires and over this very kitchen table. What you did—making up a land for Flora and for yourself—gave you both comfort during a very scary time. Dearest Hazel, bad things don't *always* have a blaming place to land." She paused. "Did you or Flora ever tell Harry?"

"I didn't, but that's what I need to find out. Perhaps Flora told him and he told someone else? Or she is . . . alive?"

Bridie's brows rose. "Oh, if that were to be true." She held her hand over her heart.

"What happened after I left?" Hazel asked so quietly that Bridie had to lean forward and ask her to repeat the question.

"It doesn't matter now," Bridie said. "The investigators were doing their job."

"Tell me, please. I did hear them asking Harry about his sketches, and I took some with me."

Bridie leaned back in her chair, finding Hazel's gaze with her own. "Everyone in town was a suspect, Hazel. We weren't singled out."

"Yes, you were," Hazel said. "I know you don't want me to know, but you were. I read the papers. I have the articles." Just saying it out loud—what she knew, what she heard during those days she wandered the streets of Oxford with her mum, who hung photos of Flora on every lamppost and shop window she could.

The Aberdeen family had been under suspicion. Bridie first had a missing husband, and years later a missing child. The story was too delicious for the press to ignore.

"They did not accuse me because of you, Hazel. They questioned me because they said I had already lost one person."

"Your husband," Hazel said.

Bridie looked at Hazel. "Yes, but, I didn't actually lose him. He was never my husband. He was . . . my lover. A visiting Oxford professor. Unbeknownst to me, he had his own wife and child in Scotland." She lifted her chin. "It wasn't something to talk about. He returned to his family and I never heard from him again. I have no idea what happened to him. For a long time, I wanted to know where he went and why. I dreamed of him returning. Harry and I found our way together. I know you heard the gossip about it, but listen, Hazel, people need explanations. They need meaning and reasons. Even if that reason turns an ordinary woman into one who can make people disappear into thin air."

"Oh, Bridie. I didn't know about Harry's father."

She nodded. "Why would you? I told Harry when he was ten years old, but he's never sought him out."

"And they blamed Harry, too," said Hazel, feeling the familiar guilt and shame.

"They questioned him about his sketches. That's true. There's always a scapegoat, my love. Always. It is part of every story if you look closely enough."

"But this isn't a story," Hazel cried out. "This is your life. His life. Where did he go? Where's Harry now?"

"An artist colony."

A jolt of electricity hit her gut. "Where?"

Bridie stood and walked toward Hazel's old room off the kitchen. Hazel wanted to follow her in, look around to see if there was anything of their old and beautiful life to be found in there, but she waited. She heard a drawer opening, then Bridie returned with a folded newspaper article about St. Ives—an artist colony on the Cornish coast.

"I've heard of this place," Hazel said. "I went to an art show in Chelsea last month and it featured these artists. The pottery was extraordinary."

"Maybe his paintings were among the others," Bridie said. "He's quite good. As you know, he was always a drawer, but now he's expanded into oils."

"What does he paint?" Hazel asked.

"Why don't you go find out for yourself?"

"I don't think I can," Hazel said. "I don't know if I can face him."

"Well, dear, only Harry can answer the questions you have for him. Sometimes . . ." She leaned forward. "Sometimes we have to face our dragons."

"And there's no knight to save us," Hazel said, remembering when they sat around a bonfire on St. Brigid's Day. It had seemed such a fun thing to say, such a flippant idea that they didn't need a knight, but now it was raw and true: Hazel needed to slay her own dragons.

The cottage had changed little. The embers in the hearth might have been burning since Hazel left that October morning with her mum and without Flora. But just like that, Hazel was back here, in the kitchen, only steps from her old bedroom. She almost saw the girl she used to be, the one who believed in magic and hidden lands.

"Can you tell me the story of Whisperwood?" Bridie asked.

"Yes," Hazel said. "Not very long ago and not very far away . . ."

# CHAPTER 18

## March 1960

Hazel sat in the metal chair in front of Chief Inspector Aiden Davies's cluttered desk in the Thames Valley Police Department.

After their tea, Bridie had dropped Hazel off in Oxford's town center, late afternoon offering it a hazy magical glow. Hazel had walked straight to the Thames Valley Police Department across from the grand tawny pinnacles of Christ Church College. Now she stared at Aiden Davies's bald head. It had a shine that Hazel believed must be from the way he continually rubbed his broad hand over his head, back and forth, as he spoke, taking his time as if waiting for the right words to form under his palm.

This was the man who had given up on Flora's case years ago when a nameless body had been found in the bogs of Wallingford, the child they'd believed to be Flora.

"Good to see you, Hazel. So, you have new evidence, you say?" he asked.

"Yes." She quickly told Aiden about the fairy tale; she didn't use the name Whisperwood, or even the full tale, but told him just enough to let him know that there might be hope. "I've made a list of everyone who might have heard us tell the story, and the only people I am unable to locate are those four nurses who lived behind the parish."

"I remember 'em—one American, three British. One of them wept when Flora went missing like it was her own child. We sent a social worker to calm her down. But, believe me, we checked 'em out, Hazel. And the war did those volunteer nurses no good. Many were traumatized. They'd believed they would just wear white uniforms and wipe the brows of handsome soldiers. Most of us saw what was coming, if you paid any attention to the planes buzzing overhead, to the wireless addresses, but I don't think those nurses were ready. When your sister—"

"Disappeared," Hazel said.

"Yes, that was right at the beginning of the Blitz. It was bad days."

"Indeed." She leaned forward and placed her hands on the edge of the desk, gripping it. "Do you have the names? Their contact information?"

"We don't track 'em if they aren't suspects. But I do have their names, of course. In the files."

"Could you get that for me?"

He rubbed his head again and stared off, past Hazel, past the moment, and muttered, "It ain't gonna do you no good, digging around back there. You can't find what's gone. I tell that journalist the same bloody thing." He looked at Hazel and sadness shimmered about him. It was more than Flora's loss that affected him, Hazel knew that. It was what he'd seen in the twenty years since. War. Drugs in Oxford. Gangs. Death.

"But here's the new thing," she told him, wanting to relieve some of the deep sorrow. "If that story is alive, she might be, too."

"Oh?" His eyebrows lifted. "So that's what you're thinkin'."

"Yes."

He automatically tapped his fingers on the desk, a metronome of his thoughts. "I can find those files for you." Aiden stood up, placed his hands on the desk, and tilted toward her on their weight. "You be waitin' here. I'll be back in a moment."

It was longer than a moment that Hazel waited, standing, sitting, standing again, looking about his cramped office, but Aiden eventually returned with a piece of paper and gave it to her. "All of their names are right here. I will do some digging of my own and see if I can find out where these ladies are living."

Hazel glanced at the page.

1. Imogene Wright (UK)
2. Frances Arkland (US)
3. Maeve Muldoon (UK)
4. Lilly Carnigan (UK)

"I'll be giving these to that journalist, too. She's trying to write the story. And to be honest, I could use the help. A new pair of eyes. She's done a mighty fine job with the other stories."

"Please don't." Hazel shook her head. "What I just told you about the book is confidential. You cannot tell Dorothy Bellamy about this. Do you hear me? Aiden, she calls Flora the 'The River Child.' It's rubbish."

"Yes, I hear you."

"That woman writes to me and Mum nearly every three months. Please. Let me find this on my own." She paused. "Let's me and you find out what this means on our own."

"Well, I think her articles in the magazine are good. She sticks to the facts. As for Flora's case, she ain't doing a hit piece or even trying to solve the mystery; she just wants to tell what happened that day. She ain't investigating it. She's not gonna fly off on some whimsy. I promise ya."

"Sounds like she got to you. But you can't promise me anything about her, Aiden. And this is *ours*. Not hers. Please, I can't see Flora in yet another magazine. It would bring it all back for Mum."

"I hear ya." Aiden took a breath so deep that his nostrils flared. "But if I missed something back then I will never forgive myself."

"Don't think like that," she said. "We all have to forgive ourselves."

*We all have to forgive ourselves.*

The words were bitter and false on her tongue as Hazel walked out of the police station and onto the high street. It was advice she knew was impossible for herself to take, cold comfort to be uttered carelessly to a man who spent his life solving mysteries and seeing the worst of humanity.

⁓

Day rolled toward night out the train's window. Returning to London from Oxford, Hazel watched the sky shift from pale to inky blue, the greening trees transformed to darker shades. By the time she stepped onto the railway station's platform at Oxford Circus Station, she was as bone tired as if she'd run from Binsey to Bloomsbury. But she'd promised Barnaby she'd meet him for dinner at Simpson's in the Strand.

It was time to plan Paris, he'd said.

But if she were honest with herself, all that—Hogan's and Paris and Sotheby's—seemed like someone else's life. Her past had tumbled into the present, blurring the lines.

She'd gotten off the train one station early, clearly not thinking straight. She glanced at her watch to see she had fifteen minutes to hustle to the restaurant. She'd be late; it was over a mile to walk.

Already a mess, she was also not dressed for the restaurant in her beige slacks and simple white poplin shirt. Her hair was flying about untamed, but at least this time she'd show up. She couldn't disappoint Barnaby again.

Passing Liberty London's brightly colored store windows, then weaving through the crowds and onto Carnaby Street, she felt she was in a peculiar netherworld. Music poured out the doors of jazz venues that would be open all night. Mannequins wearing short skirts gazed from windows with painted-on unblinking eyes that seemed like hallucinations. Passing more clothing stores, she dully wondered what she'd wear to see Harry if she went to St. Ives, then chided herself for the foolishness of caring when she was on her way to see Barnaby.

Walking as fast as she could without breaking into a run, she turned onto Beak Street to find an art display. A sapling-thin artist, tall with a grimy top hat and a mustache so bushy it seemed false, displayed his wares as tinny carnival music played from a transistor radio. His bright and garish paintings were of clowns, jugglers, circus tents, and acrobats. And among them, spotlighted below a streetlamp, glared the Pied Piper, who wore a bright red cap, strutting along playing a flute, leading little boys and girls to their doom.

Hazel stopped midstep, tripped on the edge of the granite curb, and fell. She felt a shock of pain in her right knee and left wrist as she hit the pavement. The artist reached out his hand to help her up, but she didn't take it, instead standing on her own, brushing dirt off her pants, and staring at his painting. "This," she said.

"It's a copy of the famous Maxfield Parrish," he said in a deep voice with a thick Cockney accent. "If you ask me, mine's better than the original."

She was too steeped in messages from the invisible world to see this painting as something as simple as a reproduction. It was a sign to keep going. She was on the right path.

She looked to the man, someone out of a strange mirage. "It's lovely," she lied as she walked away, not looking back.

Ahead of her on the pavement stood her brother with a group of friends; Tenny. She knew him from a block away by his floppy hair and tweed jacket. He and his mates were smoking, passing around a bottle of wine that looked mighty fine, even from where she stood. It was most likely from the wine cellar of Mr. Alastair Tennyson. She moved to cross the street, hoping to go unnoticed, but then changed her mind. She approached the group of four boys, all of them laughing about something Tenny had said.

His eyes met Hazel's and his face fell, the laughter gone. He dropped his cigarette and crushed it with the heel of his camel-colored Oxford shoe. She smiled at him and for a moment she thought he might run. Then he smiled in return. It was a moment of camaraderie without a single word spoken. The other boys saw the glance.

"Who's that dame?" a boy with hair so black it shimmered under the lamplight asked.

"My sister," Tenny said. "So shut your mouth."

"Damn," another in a felt cap said. "Nice."

Tenny shoved the boy, who held up his hands in surrender with a laugh. Tenny glanced at Hazel and she waved over her shoulder and continued walking.

Neither she nor Tenny had chosen their parents or their life, so why had she been so hard on him? On her mum? What she'd really have liked to do was grab that bottle from the blond boy with the plaid jacket and taken a swig of the wine herself.

Minutes later, she rushed under the restaurant's arched entryway and into the main room lit by the flash and sparkle of crystal chandeliers. Barnaby read the menu at a table near the paneled wall; a gold sconce cast light above his head.

Everywhere there were men in suits and ties, women in black dresses with pearls. Barnaby looked up as she approached the table. He smiled at first, then his eyebrows moved down. He tilted his head. "Love, are you all right?"

She sat, facing him across the white linen tablecloth and red short-cut roses in the silver vase. "It's been a hell of a day. I'll tell you all about it after I have a drink. But how are you?"

He lifted a highball, already nearly empty. He drank the remainder and set it down.

"I'm *really* sorry." Hazel glanced around for the waiter.

After ordering a bottle of wine and an appetizer of calamari, he asked, "Where have you been all day, my love?"

"Binsey."

A long pause before he repeated the name of the town. Leaning back, Barnaby sipped his whiskey. "Looks like the past didn't so much come back to haunt you as you went and hunted it down."

Hazel felt a deep tremor of an unsettling at the foundation of their life; he was annoyed by something that was as important to her as the next breath. The sounds of other patrons filled the room, laughter and overlapping conversations, a piano player in the far corner singing a Frank Sinatra song.

"I don't understand why this is happening to us," he said. "Just when we're about to start our new life."

———

In Hazel's bed, Barnaby pulled Hazel close, spooning around her. He was naked and she in a silk nightgown he'd once bought her as a birthday gift. He kissed her earlobe and whispered, "I want you to know that I will pay for the illustrations and the book. Please stop worrying about it."

"No, love." She turned to face him, so tired that the right words were hard to find. She couldn't tell him what at that moment twisted and tumbled in her gut—not worries over money, for that she would find a way. Uneasiness about seeing Harry again made her feel unsettled; thoughts she could usually avoid were bubbling to consciousness. "I will pay for them," she said softly, kissing him.

"You don't always have to be so independent," he said, running his hand along her thigh. "It's like you don't want me to take care of you. It's like you want to prove that you're not your mother, and I am not your stepfather."

"You may be right," she said, "but some things must be mine alone to take care of."

He pulled her even closer, as if to prove the opposite with his touch.

# CHAPTER 19

## March 1960

Dinner was light that night for Peggy and her mother, Linda: roasted chicken and asparagus. Peggy had been too preoccupied to cook much more. While Mother had typed, Peggy felt her mind jumping about like a grasshopper in tall grass, never settling. This was at least in part because her Whisperwood sisters had become grasshoppers in the last story.

Her distraction had started with that strange phone call. She'd spent two days pondering it. Her story? Where did it come from?

Peggy's education had been focused on mythology and fairy tales, which most people didn't know are *not* the same thing, and yet they are connected, part of a larger universe. She'd studied everything from Greek gods to Indian deities, from Celtic myths to Grimm's fairy tales. She could unravel a story with its multilayered meanings and Jungian archetypes. And yet when it came to her own life story, she was at a loss. She knew the motivations of the characters in her novels better than she understood what she herself wanted—or *why*.

Knowing why was always important; *why* the orphaned sisters chose certain transformations or adventures. And always, it returned to this: an escape from the orphanage of cruel Madame Bullynose, becoming who they were meant to be. But Peggy's desires, whatever they might be, seemed to shift with the hours. Poor character motivation was the death knell to any story.

She thought of Wren's question: *Why are you so frightened of the answer?*

A storm flared outside the windows, rattling the frame of the house, as lightning traveled across the ocean waves.

Peggy carried their empty dishes to the sink. "Mother, remind me how Whisperwood came to exist."

"Why are you asking?" Linda's voice was tight as a wire strung across the yard for laundry.

"It's one of the questions in the publicity kit. They want to know its origins. They want me to write about my inspiration." Peggy kept her back turned, so her mother wouldn't see the lie that slipped so easily from her lips. Writing fiction had made her an adept liar, quick to the story, but she usually didn't employ these skills with her mother.

"Your aunt Maria and I made it all up when you were a little girl. You wanted your daddy so badly you wouldn't stop crying. God rest his soul. And I wanted to give you a safe place to escape." A sigh. "I've told you this."

"Yes, my daddy." Peggy wished above so many other wishes that she remembered him, but he'd died when she was five years old during the invasion of Pearl Harbor, his body sent home in a coffin with an American flag over it.

In his photograph, he was elegant in the way of soldiers: hat straight, a stern expression on a chiseled face over a uniform with emblems she didn't understand. Garrett Witherspoon Andrews, a name as handsome as his face. There were a few pictures of him. In one, he held Peggy as a baby. She could see the profile of his smile as he stared at her adoringly, at the bundle of baby she once was but had no memory of being.

Peggy asked her mother, "But did you hear it somewhere else first or did it come straight from your imagination?"

Linda laughed, a gay sound that signaled the fun mother was coming near, the one who played gin rummy and drew hopscotch on the sidewalk in chalk and ran into the waves with Peggy until they both collapsed on the sand. "It's *our* story, my love." She paused.

The troubled water inside Peggy settled. The woman calling from England was daft, as they say. But one more question waited impatiently.

"The name, Whisperwood: Was that mine or yours or Maria's?"

Mother rose from the table and came to Peggy's side at the sink, taking her hands and kissing them each on the palm. "There is no mine or yours. There is only ours."

"But the name—" Peggy said, looking up from the sink.

"I don't rightly remember, my sweet girl. The name arose from the tellings. Maybe it was partly mine and partly yours or even Maria's, combining just as our stories do."

"Yes," Peggy said. "As our stories do."

———

After their nightly reading of the day's pages, and a conversation about what had worked and what hadn't, Peggy laid awake in bed for hours, thrumming with energy like the lightning outside. Her bedroom was decorated for a princess: pink and frothy, with a four-poster bed and a gossamer white canopy, which was now in shadow.

The room hadn't changed in the eighteen years they'd lived in Cape Cod. Her memories of California were blurred and ragged: crashing waves on another coast, green fields in the countryside of Napa where they'd once lived.

*Why are you so frightened of the answer?*

Her defenses rose: She wasn't frightened. It was just that her story's origin had never mattered until now. Origin myths were the most important tales ever told: They were used to explain the creation of the world.

And yet not once had Peggy given a thought to how her world, Whisperwood, began. She'd been told a simple story: Mother and her sister, Aunt Maria, made up stories to comfort Peggy after Daddy died.

Outside her window, somewhere in the distance, lightning struck a tree with a splintering and explosive sound, and Peggy jumped out of bed. There was no use trying to sleep. She wandered into the kitchen, but she didn't turn on the light; that would wake Mother. She reached in the lower kitchen cabinet and slipped her hand into the trash, past slippery asparagus to the crumpled paper with Hazel Linden's phone number. She carried it back to her bedroom. Like the *Teen Magazine* she'd often hidden from her mother, who thought them vapid and ridiculous, Peggy hid the scrap of paper beneath her mattress, then she slipped under her pink covers again.

She closed her eyes and thought of the fairy tale of the princess and the pea; the small and imperceptible pea beneath a pile of mattresses had been a sensitivity test, to see if the princess was worthy of the prince. No one needed to prove Peggy's sensitivity, but she swore she could feel the crumpled piece of paper beneath her mattress.

# CHAPTER 20

## March 1960

The black cab pulled in front of the Palladian Georgian house with its symmetrical brick façade and ornate woodwork. The gravel drive crunched beneath the tires as the red-nosed cabbie wrapped up his chatter about the decline of London with Prime Minister Macmillan at the helm, about the budding protests against nuclear weapons, about America possibly entering the Vietnam War, and weren't they all just tired enough of war?

Hazel paid the cabbie with, "Yes, aren't we all tired enough of war." And she climbed out to stand at the end of a bluestone walkway. She gazed up at her mum's grand house. Its façade whispered old London stories of family heirlooms in the attic and genteel afternoon teas. Alastair Tennyson was descended from some duke or viscount or some such thing that Hazel gave no importance to, but obviously Mum had. And now there was their son, a fourteen-year-old dubbed Tenny.

He was, Hazel realized with a jolt, the exact same age she was when they'd been sent to the country. Tenny had the better life; he'd never know the exile and fear. He'd never know what it meant to be sent away from comfort, familiarity, and love.

Hazel walked up the path, stepping from stone to stone until reaching a large wooden door carved with a family emblem of a lion and castle. She hesitated. This was her mum's house and rightly so she should just walk in, but it was also the house of her stepfather (she hated that term).

She couldn't fully reconcile the mum she knew in Bloomsbury with the mum who lived here. Hazel and Mum talked often, and they loved each other, but a long shadow had fallen over them both after Flora disappeared, and lingered still with its cold gray shade.

One day, in 1945, on an autumn afternoon two weeks after the church bells had announced that the war was over, Hazel had returned home from the bookstore. Mum was waiting on the flowered couch, patting the cushions for her to sit. "I need to talk to you," Mum had told her. "I am marrying Tennyson next month. A small affair in his back garden with only family. A heart," she told Hazel, "can hold much joy and great sorrow at the same time. It's a mystery and it's also true."

Hazel felt that Mum's joy was a betrayal. Flora had been gone for five years by then, and it felt like she'd been gone for but a day and also forever. Sometimes Hazel would calculate Flora's age and she had at that moment: eleven years old to Hazel's age twenty. And Father, five years older than Mum, would have been forty-five years old. It was an alternate family, Hazel knew that. A completely imaginary family still intact and whole in her heart, alive and thriving. Hazel needed to believe Flora *was* actually alive and eleven years old. If Mum married and moved forward with her life, if she vacated this flat and moved somewhere else, how would Flora find them?

It was an irrational and absurd thought and Hazel knew it even as she thought it. But absurdity didn't change her deep-settled belief that Mum needed to be in their family home for Flora to return to it.

Hazel had blurted out, both incredulous and surprised, "Marrying him? Are you serious, Mum?"

"I am." She'd fluffed the pillow next to her, rested her arm on it to display the large rectangle-cut sapphire engagement ring sparkling on her left ring finger.

Hazel hadn't wanted to see the proof in a large stone and she turned away. "Do you love him?" Hazel had popped off the couch in her indignation, pacing the living room. She slammed her hand on the mantel and turned to face her mum. "Do. You. Love. Him?"

"I do, my dear. I know that's hard for you to understand, but there is room in me for this love without taking away other loves."

"No," Hazel had shouted.

"I want you to have this flat if that's what you're worried about. I want you to stay here. Live here. It's yours now."

"I don't want your leftovers." Hazel hadn't meant it; of course she wanted the flat, but it seemed the hurtful thing to say. Now she'd be left alone with the ghosts of her family.

"Then consider it a gift from your papa."

"Mum," Hazel had said. "Please don't marry him."

"Why?" Mum had twisted the ring with her other hand, fiddling with it. "It doesn't change what happened."

Hazel had shut her eyes and known that this was the crux of it all: her childish wish that if they stayed right here and changed very little Flora might return.

*Grow up, Hazel,* she thought.

Mum had stood, walked to Hazel, and faced her with a sad smile. "It's not possible, my dear daughter, to change what already happened. If I could, I would. I'd give up anything and everything."

"Even Tennyson?"

"Even Tennyson," Mum had agreed. "But giving him up now doesn't fulfill that wish."

It had been the right time, Hazel had thought. Right now she could tell Mum about Whisperwood and how Flora had gone to look for it, how Hazel had kissed Harry in the hollow tree and forgotten about her sister just long enough to lose her, how love and desire and storytelling had altered their lives so that they arrived at this moment. She could tell her mum that loving someone new would mean moving on from Papa and from Flora, and that there was no way that Hazel could do the same.

But the confession lodged in her tight throat like a cork, and she said not one word.

Now on Mum's front stoop, that shadow remained, long and dark and cold. It was time to remove it.

Hazel pushed the large ceramic button and rang the bell, which echoed inside like a church tower calling the hour.

Moments later the door opened and Hazel faced Tenny. "Happy birthday!" she said cheerily.

"Thank you, sister."

She walked past him into the dark and cavernous entryway. Oil paintings of Tennyson ancestors hung on every red-damask wallpapered space. The large iron base on the round oak table in the hallway held enough roses to fill their childhood garden. However, they did smell heavenly.

"Where's Mum?" she asked.

"In the sunroom." Tenny looked about, as if checking for someone. "All she's talked about this morning is you coming to visit. So be nice."

"I'm always nice."

Tenny stared at her, his brown eyes like shiny stones in a river, alert and aware. His blond hair tousled just right and his thin chiseled nose telling a story of his ancestry. "No, you're not." Then he was up the stairs, taking them two at a time.

Hazel wandered to the back of the house down a hallway that led to the sunny room where Mum sat at a glass table, eating her breakfast and reading *The Observer*, a bold headline about Macmillan and De Gaulle's "tête-à-tête."

"Hello, Mum," Hazel said.

Mrs. Alastair Tennyson looked up with a wide smile. "Darling!" She put down the paper and held out her hand for Hazel to come to her. She tapped the front page. "Look, it's coat week at Rodex. We should plan an afternoon of shopping."

Hazel kissed her mum's cheek. "Sure, Mum."

Mum was free of pretense this morning: no makeup and her still dark hair falling over her shoulders. She was radiant at fifty-five years old, a vital force as always.

Hazel sat next to her mum and shifted her chair so they looked at each other. She set her bag on the floor.

Mum tilted her head at Hazel. "You look peaked. Oh, dear, are you pregnant? I do love Barnaby Yardley." Mum smiled, hope rising.

"Sorry to disappoint you, Mum. No."

"I could have the most glorious engagement party here. We could string lights and hire a quartet and my florist, oh, she could make the most divine arrangements—"

"Mum, I am not engaged and I am not pregnant. Maybe someday, but not today. I'm sorry to disappoint you."

Mum leaned forward. "You never disappoint me. I just want happiness for you."

"Marriage and a baby don't always equal happiness."

Mum cringed and closed her eyes for a moment before opening them. "I know that, Hazel. So what is it then?" She lifted her teacup and sipped.

"I think I may need some tea and some of what you're eating, if I may?"

While her mum went off to the kitchen to tell the cook to make another plate of eggs and hash, Hazel gazed around a room slathered in sunlight, like butter on toast. Her mum had made a quiet and lovely life for herself. Photos in silver frames stood on the side banquet: Hazel at five years old in the backyard, Hazel and Flora with Papa in a rowboat on the lake in Victoria Park on Hazel's thirteenth birthday, Mum and Alastair's wedding, Tenny at his birth. Flora might have disappeared from the world, or Oxfordshire, but she'd never disappeared from Mum's life.

At the far end of the table, a mirrored frame glittered. Hazel went to it and picked up the photo: Hazel and Flora stood hand in hand in front of their childhood Mecklenburgh flat, the one she still lived in. The photograph was taken the day they'd left London for the countryside. It was early morning, Hazel remembered. Their knapsacks slung over their shoulders with the gas masks bobbing, grotesque with their wild-eyed goggles. Hazel's smile was forced while Flora grinned sincerely, holding Berry under her arm, smothering his face.

All in one fell swoop Mum had been left alone in Bloomsbury to face what might come.

When Mum returned with the plate of breakfast and set it on the table, she turned to see Hazel crying.

"Hazel, Hazel." Mum rushed to her and threw her arms around her. "What is it?"

Hazel held the photo.

"Oh, darling." Mum's shoulders slumped and her mouth, now surrounded by thin lines, turned downward. "Sit, dear."

Hazel put down the photo and sat across from her mum.

"Hazel, I couldn't go to Binsey with you back then, my dear girl. You know that, don't you? Not only did I have to work but they would not billet an adult." She handed Hazel a linen napkin to wipe her tears. "God, I was so young. I had you when I was twenty years old. I did the best . . . I did . . ."

"Mum! Stop. I know."

"I don't regret it, but I wouldn't do it again," she said firmly.

"I don't blame you, Mum. I never did."

"Deep down you may still wonder why I deserted you both."

"I don't, Mum."

"If I could go back in time and change that decision, I would. The government was telling us how to keep you safe. If I'd abandoned my work, I was slacking off, not doing my duty for the crown, and for the family. I thought you'd be back quickly. I had no idea . . ."

". . . what would happen. I know." Hazel wiped away proof of her tears.

Hazel hesitated. Today was her mum's son's fourteenth birthday and guests were coming over tonight. There were caterers and florists even now arriving at the back service entrance. "I want you to enjoy Tenny's birthday."

"If this is about Flora, you tell me now. What is it?"

Like diving into a cold lake, it was best to just jump, so Hazel jumped. "You know how Flora and I used to make up stories?"

"You always whispered them, darling. There was a river, that much I knew. And a castle. But the rest was vague and belonged to you and Flora."

"We gave our place a name."

"What was it?"

"Whisperwood," she said.

Mum closed her eyes, and her cheeks rose with the squeeze of her eyes, a sound near a cry but softer. "It's beautiful: Whisperwood," she said and opened her eyes. "And it belonged to just the two of you?"

"Until now." Hazel reached down and slipped the book from her bag, handed it to her mum. "Someone else knew."

"Who?" The word came like a bullet, fast and quick at Hazel.

"I don't know. That's what I'm trying to find out."

"Harry? Perhaps Bridie?"

"No, it wasn't Bridie."

"So you've already asked her?" Mum paused, leaned back in her chair. "You told her about this before you told me?"

Hazel saw the hurt in this. "I'm sorry, Mum. I needed to know if she told anyone before I even came to you."

"You love them both so much."

"Yes, I do." Hazel shook her head. "I did. But you always think I love them more. It's not true."

Mum smiled with her lips slightly closed and nodded toward the rest of the house. "Just like you, Hazel. You think I love them more . . ." She swept her hand across the sunroom. "And that is also not true. We can miss our Flora, still grieve, but we cannot let that keep us from loving."

"Mum . . . that might be true for you but great, mad love for someone or something ruins me and them. Every single time."

"Oh, my Hazel." Mum's mouth quivered. "I have wanted to find a way for you to heal for so long. I loathe the fact that you believe love ruins. I've watched you destroy relationships and shut off your heart. I've tried and tried to help, but I don't know how to do it for you." Mum leaned forward and kissed Hazel's forehead. "I love you so much." Then she picked up the book. She read the back cover copy and opened the inside, scanned it for a moment before looking to Hazel again. "A coincidence?"

"Not a chance."

"Okay, then. Who told the story to this author?"

"I am praying, Mum, I am praying it was Flora who told the story."

Mum's hand flew to her chest, where she let it rest for a moment, a face contorted by a hope she'd thought gone.

"Delia, honey, where are you?" a deep voice called out, clear and echoing.

Mum answered, "In here with Hazel."

Hazel despised the way that Alastair had cut her mum's name short from Camellia to Delia, the way he'd taken ownership over her by giving her a new name, one shorter, less melodic than her real one.

He burst into the room the same way he always did, with glee and as if he were expected. He was a tall man, and when Hazel first met him, she'd thought he looked like a coatrack with a crooked hat hanging at its top—an image that never left her. He gave the impression of man who was born knowing his rightful place in the order of things.

"Hazel!" His voice filled every crevice, blotting out the music. Then he was at her side, reaching his hand down to shake hers. "We are so glad you arrived for the party. Welcome."

"Thank you, Alastair," she said, wanting to be the crueler Hazel and call him "Stair" and see how he liked it.

"What are we talking about in here so seriously?"

Hazel couldn't get the book off the glass table fast enough. He gave her congealed and uneaten eggs and hash a cursory glance. "This looks good."

"Yes," Mum said. "It does."

Hazel knew then that her story was safe with her mum, protected. Her heart rate slowed and she greeted Alastair with a smile he'd never know was false.

"I must go pick up the champagne," he said. "Do you need anything else, my love?"

"Everything is set and ready," Mum said. "I have my beauty parlor appointment in an hour but Lorraine has everything else on a smooth schedule."

Alastair nodded, gave her a kind kiss, and squeezed her shoulder, gazing at his wife as if Hazel weren't in the room. "Our son is fourteen. Can you quite believe it?"

"No." She smiled and kissed him again. "I cannot."

He rushed off to his errands. Mum gazed at Hazel and nothing else needed to be said right now.

# CHAPTER 21

### September 1939

Just after breakfast on their first day in Binsey, Bridie shooed Harry, Hazel, and Flora out of the house. "Now go! Harry will show you about. I have work to do, and I will pop into town to send your postcard. We must figure out your schooling, but today is Saturday, so off you go." But before they left she tucked a sprig of rosemary into their coat pockets. "For protection," she said with a wink.

"What work must she do?" Hazel asked Harry, while slipping on her mackintosh and wellies.

"Mum does accounting for businesses in Oxford."

Outside, Hazel took a deep breath. This world smelled of grass, possibly dirt, and perhaps the crushed flowers or decomposing leaves scattered about. Whatever it was it was glorious and fresh. Walking a few steps behind Harry and Hazel, Flora jumped, tripped over an enamel milking can, and cried out as she fell to the ground.

Harry turned, hands reaching out for her, but Flora was already on her bum in the middle of the field. "Are you all right?" he asked.

"That?" Flora lifted her wellie and there, on the boot's bottom, was a dark brown glob, its aroma rich and dank.

Harry offered her his hand, which Flora grabbed, getting back on her feet. "You've stepped on Daisy's dung," said Harry with a laugh.

133

"I'm assuming you don't have many cow patties in London?" He smiled. "Welcome to the country."

Flora seemed to grow four inches, lifting her chin, and smiling at Harry as if he'd saved her life.

"Come now, let me show you the river," said Harry. "If you know where the river is, you can never get lost. The river is our guide to the edge of our land."

Flora looked at Hazel and smiled. Harry could be as charming as a prince, but Hazel and Flora had their secrets and their own land. Only they knew what the river meant, and it was more than a guide, it tethered them each to the other.

They followed Harry down a well-worn dirt path that cut through the grass. Stones were set at the trail's edge where the ground dipped, and muddy puddles dented the earth.

Hazel lost track of time as they wandered past thatched-roof houses on quiet lanes. It was one of the most beautiful walks Hazel had ever taken. Past browning horn bush hedges, with leaves falling from the trees like rain. The sun seemed to hang in the sky, unmoving, waiting for them to reach the river's edge.

The three of them ran down the path with green fields on either side and Hazel spied the blue-and-gray ribbon of river sparkling, and beyond the waters, another but larger pasture. She stopped short and Flora did, too. "Oh, it's beautiful," Hazel said. In London the river was often dirty, and there were large boats coming and going, the call and cry of seagulls and horns. But this river, the same one in name, the same one that flowed to London, glittered and winked as ducks waddled toward its silty edge and swans floated serenely by the tree branches that bowed over the waters, worshipping it.

Harry waved his arm in a "come on" gesture and took off. Hazel and Flora ran to catch up. At the river's edge, hand in hand, Flora and Hazel stood next to Harry as a punting boat rowed past with three women, laughing and trying not to tip over. Across the river on the flat green pasture, black-and-white cows grazed, nosing into the grasses and chewing lazily. White clouds reflected in the water. Hazel said, "It looks like another world, an upside-down world inside the river."

Harry shook his head with a grin. "Wouldn't it be brilliant if true?"

Flora pulled at Hazel's coat. "Is this ours? Are there stars?"

Hazel shot Flora a look with her eyes wide and a small shake of her head.

"Stars?" Harry asked.

"It just looks sparkly, that's all," Hazel said.

But Harry looked directly at Flora. "You can never go in there. It looks pretty but it will take you . . ." He stopped and looked at Hazel as if for backup.

"Yes," Hazel said. "You cannot, ever, go into it without us."

Flora nodded, looking near tears.

"All right," Harry said. "I have more. Let's go . . ." And he was off and they followed him. Although Hazel wanted to stay and stand at the edge of that river where the willow trees bent in submission to create hidden hollows, where the green reeds swayed to water's music. She wanted to stare at the cows who nuzzled grass in Port Meadow across the flowing waters, wonder at the reflected sky. It all seemed as mysterious as the land she imagined, a world so ancient it might tell its own tales.

"Those roofs you see beyond are from the towns of Gadstow and Wolvercote." He turned in the opposite direction and pointed. "And that way is where the river splits around a little island and there is a boat house, and then the bridge across to walk through the meadow to Jericho and Oxford." He smiled. "Now on with us."

They followed Harry until he led them down a long path and they approached a stone chapel blinking in the sunlight. As they walked, Flora gathered fallen leaves in the hem of her dress until they arrived at the wide lawn in front of St. Margaret's Church. Gravestones, white and gray, slanted and straight, were scattered about the church graveyard.

"We're walking on the dead," Harry said with a mischievous smile.

"*Ohhhh*," Flora said, looking down with curiosity.

"Stop it," Hazel said. "You'll scare her."

"No, he won't." Flora's voice rang high into the trees.

Hazel stopped and Flora with her. In the quiet, Hazel heard the high trilling call of birds, even the rustle of insects scurrying beneath fallen leaves. Flora pulled on the hem of Hazel's raincoat, allowing her collected leaves to fall to the ground. Harry was a dozen feet in front of them now, walking and kicking leaves into the still air.

"I see a door," Flora whispered.

Hazel smiled. "Where is it?"

"Right there, under that twee."

"I see it, too," Hazel said, "but we must come back later for it. Okay? We mustn't tell Harry about our doors."

Flora nodded, her curls bounced, and her smile widened.

Ahead Harry stopped and turned, motioning them onward. Hazel thought he was undoubtedly handsome. But it wasn't just his looks that gave her an odd feeling. It was Harry's way in the world that made her stomach feel funny. He was nothing like the wisecracking boys who slicked their hair and sauntered through Bloomsbury. Instead, it was as if the sunlight followed him. Hazel felt flipped inside-out, a sensation she couldn't name. It was a bit like fear, but that wasn't quite right.

She noticed a gray, shingled cottage behind the parish church. Smoke curled from its chimney, and on its front porch was a table with four chairs around it and candlesticks with burned-down candles, as if there'd been a party.

"Who lives there?" Hazel asked.

"It's usually the rector's home, but he lets the nurses who came to help at hospital live there while he stays in a guest room at the Baldwins' house. We all must help somehow." He paused. "Come on, I want to show you something."

They followed him until he stopped short before a rectangular stone wall surrounding an opening in the earth. Brick steps led steeply down to a flat gravel area in front of a triangular opening, a wellhead of water hidden in shadow. Hazel felt a chill. This was as old as time, or so it seemed.

Harry leaned forward, planting his hands on the stone wall. "This is the well in *Alice in Wonderland.*"

"*Ooohhh!*" Flora let go of Hazel's hand and stepped closer.

Hazel grabbed her shoulder, pulling her sister back from the dark hole of water that led underground to who-knows-where.

Harry clapped his hands, and they both jumped. He stepped closer. Hazel felt the warmth of him with an earthy scent. "Remember the part in Wonderland where the Dormouse tells the story of three daughters who live at the bottom of a treacle well?" he asked.

"During the mad tea party," Hazel said.

"Yes!" He lifted a fist in the air like she'd won a prize. "This is *that* well." He pointed to three brick stairs, which led down to where dark water glistened like ink.

"What's a treacle?" Flora asked, mangling the word.

"It means healing," Harry said.

"No!" Hazel stomped her foot, for if he was to tell stories he must at the least use the right words. "Treacle is molasses; it is sweets and sugar."

"You're right, too," he said, so amiable and kind that Hazel's thorny words seemed cruel. "It also means healing; its roots are Latin." He rolled his eyes in great exaggeration. "Just you wait, you won't escape Latin lessons in Mum's house."

Hazel stared at him and Flora stepped closer, touching the edge of the well's stones with her fingers, gently.

"There is another story about this well, even older than *Alice in Wonderland*."

"Tell me!" Hazel said with a startling forcefulness.

Harry patted the top of the worn stones where there were engraved words. "It says Saint Margaret's well, but another saint came here first: Saint Frideswide."

"That's not a story!" Flora said as she drew closer to Harry than Hazel.

"No. It's the *beginning* of a story."

"But that's not how to start a story!" Flora said.

"Okay, so how should it start?"

"Not very long ago and not very far away . . ." She looked to Hazel for confirmation.

"Fine." He nodded. "Not very long ago and not very far away there was an Oxford princess named Frideswide."

"Are you making up that name?" Hazel asked.

"No! That was her name. Let me tell the story!" He grinned. "Frideswide grew up in an Oxford priory, and she wanted to become a nun. But her beauty attracted men from all over the kingdom who begged to marry her." Harry deepened his voice. "One day the King of Mercia, named Algar, arrived in Oxford and asked Frideswide's father for his daughter to become his bride. Frideswide would then be the Queen of Mercia."

"I want to be a queen!" Flora threw her hands out wide.

Harry lowered his voice. "Perhaps you do, but you see, Princess Frideswide did *not* want to be Algar's queen. So she ran away. She jumped onto a boat and sailed up the River Thames and arrived at . . ." He paused dramatically.

"Where?" Hazel asked, her mind and heart leaning into the story.

"Binsey!" he said.

"She came here?" Hazel asked. "So the king couldn't marry her?"

"Yes!"

Hazel paused to think about what this meant. "She didn't want to be a queen?"

"No, she wanted to be a nun and heal people, which she did with these waters."

"If the king loved her and wanted to marry her, why did he just let her run away or did he go looking for her?" Hazel asked. This seemed important to her. Wasn't it worthwhile going after someone you loved?

"Yes," said Harry. "Algar searched for her, and one time he was near to finding her when . . ." Harry paused dramatically, wiggling his eyebrows.

"What?" Flora asked. *"What?"*

*"BOOM!"*

Both girls jumped back, then laughed at their silliness.

"King Algar was struck by lightning. It blinded him, so he would never ever, ever find Frideswide."

*"Ohhhh."* Flora's eyes widened.

Hazel wondered out loud at a story she'd never heard before. "A princess who didn't want to be found and didn't want to be a queen."

"Strange, isn't it?" Harry said. "And now she's a saint. Her shrine is in Oxford at Christ Church. Even Catherine of Aragon visited the shrine when she could not have children; she thought Frideswide would heal her."

"Is being a saint preferable to being a queen?" asked Hazel.

Harry shrugged. "That would depend on the person, I'd think. Frideswide also has a stained glass window with her shrine."

"What are all of these?" Hazel asked, pointing to a small pile of stones and feathers, jagged pieces of glass and links of a tarnished gold chain, a cracked piece of blue china.

"People bring offerings and pray to Frideswide. They believe that if they leave something and pray, the well will heal them." He paused before grinning. "Now, follow me!"

He walked off while Hazel and Flora lingered, gazing into the hole of dark water. Its healing powers turned a princess into a saint, a princess determined to live her own life.

"Does Whisperwood have a well?" Flora whispered to Hazel.

"I bet it does. We'll look for it next time."

They ran to catch Harry, who wasn't even looking behind. He was onto the next adventure even before they were done with this one.

The three children scampered down the hill, browning grass bending beneath their feet until they reached a dirt road. Harry stopped and turned to check. In front of them was another ancient stone building with a sign on a wooden post swinging in the wind: The Perch.

Harry pointed. "They say Lewis Carroll wrote pages and pages of *Alice in Wonderland* here," said Harry. "And"—he lowered his voice and looked about as if frightened—"a sailor haunts this place."

"There's a ghost?" Flora asked in a whisper.

Harry shrugged. "I've lived here all my life, and I've never seen him."

Walking off, he halted just a few yards later in front of a wooden building. "Binsey School," he said.

"School?" Hazel hadn't considered a return to something as normal as school. They were in a more magical place: in the middle of a hamlet near a river where a boy told stories about saints and kings and princesses who ran away.

"Yes," Harry said with a laugh. "Did you think kids only go to school in London?"

"No." Hazel blushed hot with embarrassment. "It's . . . small."

"Only two rooms," he said. "Now you've seen everything there is to see. Binsey is nice, but not a very big place."

"Stop!" a high voice called out.

All three turned to see a girl, auburn braids flying behind her, her dress's hem in hand, the better to run faster, bounding straight for them down the hill. With something like awe, Hazel wondered why the girl didn't rise and fly, for she looked as if she might. It was Kelty, the crying girl from the hall, the one taken away by the hag.

Gasping, Kelty came to a stop in front of Hazel, Flora, and Harry. "They're chasing me." She pointed up the hill. Two boys with ruddy cheeks—obviously twins—ran toward them.

"They're the Baldwin twins," said Harry. "They're harmless."

The boys halted in front of them all. "You think they're vaccies?" the right side asked the left side.

"They're dirty vaccies," the other replied.

"*Whoa!*" Harry stepped forward and clapped the right-side boy on the shoulder. "Ethan, these young ladies are visitors in our town."

Harry glanced at the girls with a grin and tried to make light. "You're evacuees, did you know that?"

Flora vehemently shook her head and was on the verge of tears. She buried her face in Hazel's skirt.

"That's not what we are," Hazel stated, acting braver than she felt as she moved closer to the two bratty boys. "We are from Bloomsbury, and we are here to help the war effort by staying safe and out of harm's way."

"So, you're scaredy-cats," said the right-side twin.

"What is a vaccie?" Hazel asked Harry, taking a few steps back.

"It's a stupid name for an evacuee," Harry told her.

"So what if we are!" The girl with the red braids—Kelty—pushed the second boy to the pavement. "Evacuee is not a bad name!"

The twin still standing formed his hand into a fist as if to punch Kelty, then thought better of it. His brother stood and brushed himself off, dirt on his knees and palms, and a growling noise came from deep in his throat. He said, "You're lucky you're a girl or I'd beat you until you begged me to stop."

"Adam, no." Harry stepped in front of the girls. "Stop, okay? It's not fun anymore. Go find something else to kick around—not girls."

The twins scurried back up the hill and disappeared, and above them a flock of starlings swooped into a cloud of wings. A priest rode by on his bike, tinkling his bell and waving at them. Behind him, walking, was a group of four women with blue capes fluttering in the wind, white caps like swans perched on their heads. They were laughing, jostling each other, and the shortest one, with dark curls, waved at the children before linking her arm through another woman's and saying, "Do you think he'll be at the pub tonight?"

Hazel looked away and stared with admiration at the astonishing red-haired girl. "I'm Hazel," she said. "I like the way you knocked that mean boy down."

"I'm Kelty," the girl answered. "I'd knock him down for you, too, you know."

Hazel wanted to hug Kelty. "No need. Did you billet with that mean-looking lady?"

Kelty nodded. "Her name is Mrs. Marchman."

Hazel lowered her voice, leaned forward. "I think she's a hag from a bad fairy tale. I saw you in the Oxford Town Hall."

Kelty bit her bottom lip. "Will you let me come home with you for a while?" she asked.

Hazel thought of Frideswide fleeing King Algar and finding a home in Binsey. She thought of Algar being struck blind and she wished the same for the hag. It was as if Harry had brought Frideswide into this world from another, and Frideswide had red braids and a wild spirit.

Harry piped up. "Yes, let's go home."

# CHAPTER 22

## September 1939

A blazing fire warmed the Aberdeens' cottage. The phonograph played Bing Crosby. This—Hazel thought as she walked through the front door with Harry, Flora, and Kelty—is what Harry means when he fondly utters the word *home*.

They shed their coats and hung them on the pegs, lined their wellies in a neat row under the pine bench as Bridie emerged from the kitchen and greeted them with a warm "Hallo! How was your traipse about our hamlet?"

Flora bounced on her toes and held up her hands. "We found a well where a princess ran away . . ." It sounded like *printheth*, but Bridie knew what she meant.

"Oh yes, indeed. Our local Frideswide." Bridie wiped her hands on her apron. "Who wants a cuppa and shortbread?"

"I do!" Harry said, and then, "Mum, meet Kelty."

Bridie smiled warmly. "Welcome, darling."

"Thank you." Kelty's voice shook.

Bridie moved closer. "Dear, are you quite all right?"

Kelty pushed back her shoulders and truth tumbled out. "I am not. The lady who chose to billet me is mean and dirty. I can*not* stay there. I must beg you to let me stay here with you."

"I am not permitted to take more children without another bed. But it can't be all that bad, can it?"

"I will sleep there." Kelty pointed at the flowered and saggy couch where Hazel had left a Peter Pan book open and facedown on the cushions. Kelty's lips trembled. "I would give you my rations, but Mrs. Marchman took them and put them in a locked drawer. And she wants to teach me to mend clothes, which is how she makes money. She drinks from a dark bottle at night and falls asleep in a big chair without making dinner." Kelty shuddered, and her words came fast. "I found some carrots to eat last night. Then she snores with her head all the way back and talks and yells in her sleep! You should hear some of the things she says!"

Bridie looked near to tears, but stood straighter. "Kelty, for now come have a cuppa and biscuit." She motioned to the back of the cottage. "And then you can use our bathtub to clean up. I have some rosemary soap with the most delicious aroma."

Kelty's eyes filled with tears, and she threw her arms around Bridie, a drowning child finding a life raft. "I know everyone gets money for taking us in. I heard. You get ten shillings and six pence each child."

Harry's shoulders straightened. "My mum makes her own money. She does the books for nearly every business in town. We didn't do it for money!"

Bridie reached for her son's shoulder, squeezed it. "It's okay."

Kelty's face seemed to crumble even more so now for she'd insulted Harry. "I know; I'm sorry. I meant to insult the hag, not you," she said.

Hazel and Harry looked at each other and Hazel felt a longing for something unnamed. But the feeling passed as quickly as it had come, and the five of them sat around the tiny kitchen table, dipping crumbly shortbread into warm tea.

Hazel saw the expectant look in Bridie's eyes and told her, "We love Binsey."

"Indeed." Bridie smiled. Hazel had pleased her. "Magic is everywhere here."

Hazel knew this wasn't true, but the saying of it made it seem possible while a war raged and Mum sat home alone, awaiting her postcard.

———

Slowly evening descended, and the fire in the living room hearth blazed again. Harry worked on his math sums and Hazel read *Peter Pan* out loud to Flora. Bridie cooked in the kitchen with Kelty watching, the warm aroma of lamb and rosemary filling the house, when a series of loud knocks at the door surprised them all.

Hazel jumped up. Had Mum received her postcard in just one day? And then she'd boarded a train and found them, lickety-split? Hazel ran in stocking feet to the door and opened it to find the disheveled and awful hag staring at her with dull eyes.

Not her mum at all.

Mrs. Marchman, with the sour smell of a London back alley, pushed past Hazel to see Kelty cowering on the couch. "I suspected Mrs. Aberdeen was at the bottom of this. She's the reason for many disappearances."

Harry jumped and his chair fell to the ground. "Do not speak to or about my mother ever again."

Bridie appeared, seeming to float into the room, her floral apron falling in soft folds from her waist. In every way, she stood in stark contrast to the hag. "Hello, Glynnis, may I help you?"

"You took the child meant to billet with me. Send her back right now or I will tell the police you kidnapped her."

"Do calm down. I didn't take anyone."

"Give me back the girl." The hag moved fast, standing so close to Bridie that their noses nearly touched.

Bridie didn't budge. "Hazel," she said without turning her head, "will you please take both girls to your bedroom?"

Hazel didn't budge as Flora and Kelty fled. "Please," Hazel said to Bridie. "Let Kelty stay with us."

Bridie nodded. "Hazel, I need you to go back to the bedroom and let me take care of this."

Hazel retreated to the bedroom, where she found Flora and Kelty sitting on the edge of the bed. "That lady is awful," Flora said. "Like the witch in the hidey hole."

Hazel sat next to Flora and squeezed her leg so tightly, hoping her message was clear. Do. Not. Talk. About. Our. Story.

"She's more than awful. She's"—Kelty played with the frayed edges of her braid—"she's *bloody* awful."

They laughed, but there was no joy in it.

Hazel considered telling Kelty about Whisperwood to comfort her, but then she didn't. It was too sacred. Instead, she told Kelty about Frideswide, the princess who didn't want to be a queen of Mercia, how she ran away and how God protected her by striking King Algar blind.

"Nice story," said Kelty, "but I'm not counting on God striking Mrs. Marchman blind."

The girls played jacks on the bedroom floor while Kelty told the sisters about herself. She was from North London, her father was at war, and her mum would come get her if she knew about the hag. She had a dog named Jack, and a kitty called Silver. Her best friend was Lila, and her purple bedroom at home had lacy curtains. Kelty chatted nonstop as if it might mute the hag's craggy voice slipping beneath the door.

They heard another knock on the front door, but Kelty continued on with a story about her mum taking her to the seaside just last year when none of them could have imagined where they were now.

The bedroom door opened. "Girls," Bridie said. "I need you to come out here."

They dutifully obeyed even as Hazel felt the rock of dread in her gut. In the living room stood a tall man, a bobby with his blue hat in his hand. A scar ran like a crooked road across his forehead and had turned whiter than the skin on his face.

He spoke sternly. "Bridgette, you must let the girl go back with Mrs. Marchman. She's been billeted with her; the paperwork has been done and—"

"Paperwork means nothing to me, Aiden," Bridie said. "Mrs. Marchman is cruel to this child. She doesn't give her enough to eat! Kelty stays here."

The hag let out a sound that could never be called a laugh but was meant to be one. "Cruel? Because I expect obedience and cooperation? Cruel? Because I don't dance around fires and play in the river like a child?"

Hazel looked at Bridie, her face as beautiful as Mrs. Marchman's was ugly. Dance around fires? Play in the river?

Bridie clapped her hands together like a magic spell about to be cast. "Get. Out. Of. My. House."

"Not without the girl," Mrs. Marchman said.

Bridie exhaled through her lips, her freckled cheeks puckering in. "Can we please talk about this outside?"

The adults left the house, and the four children huddled together around the kitchen table.

It didn't take long until Constable Aiden Davies returned with the devastating news that Kelty must return to Mrs. Marchman where she had been legally billeted.

———

Hazel was already awake the next morning when Harry's sketch slipped under the door. She'd been sitting with her back against the pine headboard of the four-poster bed, wondering about Kelty. The girl had been swept away by Mrs. Marchman and Aiden, tears pouring down her freckled cheeks. Hazel rose and picked up the sketch, held it to the morning light streaming through the bedroom window to see a drawing of a cow's downy face and wide brown eyes; one from the pasture next to the dirt path that led to the river. It was so realistic that Hazel wanted to run her fingers along its little comma-shaped ears.

After Flora woke, they ate breakfast silently. Harry did schoolwork at the table. Flora and Hazel went for a walk in the woodlands until soon enough they found themselves huddled together in a hollow opening of an oak tree on damp-soft soil. The nearly naked boughs arched over the forest floor, roots rose from the earth in humps of thick and shiny rope. The wind whispered a secret language between trees.

The open space in the tree trunk was just the right size for two girls to slip inside its cavern, and close their eyes and escape.

They traipsed through Whisperwood.

"Tell me," Flora said. "What are we today?"

"You decide," Hazel said.

"Fairies."

"Yes, we are," Hazel said. "Our mission is to save the faerie queen and return her to her castle beneath the alder tree."

The sisters flew above Whisperwood, where it was springtime, not the cold of autumn. In this land, flowers bloomed white and red. The paths twisted and tricked them on their search for the ogre who had stolen the fairy and hidden her beneath the branches of a dead hazelnut bush. As always, the castle beckoned far beyond the mountains while the land before them came alive. The trees transformed to helpful women, their leaves turning to small mice, the sky lifting them higher, and the grass waves pushed them onward—everything in Whisperwood was there for the sisters, to help them, to ease the way. A witch slept in a hidey-hole of a large fallen tree, and they snuck right past her. The girls finally reached the castle, and the queen, who looked nearly exactly like their mum in London, sat safe on her throne when they were jolted from the throne room by Kelty's voice calling their names.

"*Hazellll! Flora!*"

The sisters' eyes popped open, and they shivered. Dusky evening had fallen outside the tree, and they were hidden in the cavernous damp space.

"Over here!" Hazel called, climbing out, tugging Flora with her.

Kelty burst through the trees and stopped in front of them.

Hazel felt unsteady, for surely they had brought a fairy out of Whisperwood and into the forest.

Kelty stomped her foot and placed her hands on her hips. "What are you doing?" she demanded, her high-pitched voice both urgent and frightened.

"We were just playing, that's all," Hazel said. So much time had gone by. How long had they been in Whisperwood?

"It's past dinnertime and the nice lady you live with is frantic with worry and the boy is looking everywhere. He thought you'd be at the magic well."

"Oh no. We didn't mean to scare them. We were just trying to stay out of the way." Hazel's voice faded.

"I don't rightly believe Mrs. Aberdeen wants you out of the way—not like the witch I live with. She'd boil me for dinner if she thought she could get away with it."

Flora stood and stepped toward Kelty. "You live with a witch?"

Kelty touched the top of Flora's head. "Who is filling your head with stories so you believe everything you hear?"

Flora looked over her shoulder to Hazel and smiled the conspiratorial smile of a secret keeper.

"Mrs. Aberdeen is frightfully worried," Kelty said.

The three of them jogged as fast as they could, out of the glade and up the pathway toward the stone cottage. Almost there, Hazel stopped and gazed at the home. Smoke curled from the chimney pot on the sloped slate roof, and the ivy crawling up the left side of the cottage shone red and gold. The home looked nearly like the one she had created; she had told the story of a cottage in the woods and now they found themselves in it.

Hazel caught Flora and Kelty. Bridie stood in the front yard, waiting. Kelty called out, "I found them!"

Bridie shook her head. "Well, now, where did you two go?"

"Just to the woods, ma'am. It wasn't far," Hazel said.

Just then, as if answering Hazel, an owl hooted close by. They all stopped, lifted their faces to the sound. Had the bird followed them from Whisperwood?

"Ah," Bridie said dreamily. "An owl visit."

"What does that mean?" Kelty swiveled around, looking for the owl calling from the darkness.

"It means someone here can see what is hidden."

"Hazel!" Flora said. "*We* have an owl, don't we?"

Hazel squeezed Flora's hand and looked to Bridie. "I'm sorry. We lost track of time."

Bridie motioned for them to come inside, then shut the door behind her. She stared at the girls with an intensity they hadn't yet seen. "I want you to listen carefully. It is quite lovely to run about the woodlands and the river is one mighty beautiful thing. But you must tell me where you go and you must come home before dark. I am now responsible for you."

Flora sidled closer to Hazel, hid behind her, and buried her head into the folds of her dress.

"I don't mean to scare you, Flora," Bridie said, "but you girls gave me quite a fright." She turned her attention to Kelty. "And thank you, dear. Please do stay for dinner with us?"

"Yes, please." Kelty switched from foot to foot. "Can I . . . stay for longer?"

"Longer?" Bridie asked.

"Yes."

She was cut short by Harry bursting in with the cold air. He spied the group and slammed shut the door. "Where were you?"

"In our thory," Flora said.

"Story," Hazel corrected.

"What does that mean?" Hazel could smell his sweat mixed with the woodsy air of the outdoors.

"It means nothing," Hazel said. Her neck was warm, and her face felt like it didn't know what to do with itself, smile or frown or what. And she had an odd feeling that her hips wouldn't hold her steady.

Hazel turned away from him and Bridie returned to the kitchen with Flora following her. Kelty and Hazel walked to the opening of the fireplace and held their hands to the warmth. Harry followed, standing too close.

"You don't have to worry about me!" Hazel said in a voice that sounded sharper than she'd meant it to. It was hard to tell what all her feelings were lately. They came too fast and without names.

"But I do have to worry about you. Mum and I have already lost someone."

"Your father," she said.

"I don't remember him at all," Harry said with hard words, as if he spat them.

"What happened?" Hazel asked, no longer content with vague information.

Harry's face turned red and Hazel realized he was fighting to keep from crying.

"People don't just disappear," Hazel said.

"Yes," Harry said, now meeting her gaze. "Yes, they do."

# CHAPTER 23

### March 1960

The birthday party at the Tennyson house overflowed from room to room on the main level. On the stone veranda, almost every face was lit by the glow of a cigarette while a string quartet performed on the grass under the eaves where butter-yellow primrose grew. Lanterns flickered with candles that had been lit just before the first guest's arrival.

After her mum's appointment, Hazel had spent the day helping her arrange flowers, deciding where to put the wineglasses, lighting candles. Now that the bash was in full swing, Barnaby stood at her side, winding his fingers in and out of hers as if to knit them together. If she was truthful, this was the way she'd always wanted him: attentive, absolutely hers, asking if she was okay, bringing her glasses of champagne, exclaiming how beautiful she was in her new green silk dress with the skirt that swung with her every move.

Hazel looked to Barnaby, who was at that moment looking at her, and she kissed him. "I love you," she said. His face lit, and he kissed her in return.

"As I do you."

Tenny appeared at their side. "Are you enjoying yourself?" he asked. He'd always wanted Hazel to like him more than she was willing to show. But here, now, she gave in just a bit. "I am. I am having the very best time! Happy birthday!"

"Thank you." He grinned, a charming smile no less radiant than his father's.

A girl, Tenny's age of fourteen or so, sidled near to him, her red dress so short that Hazel wondered if she'd cut off inches of it. "Tenny," she said in a flirty voice. "Happy birthday." She leaned in to kiss him, but he artfully dodged her lips.

Hazel smiled and nodded for Barnaby to follow her. In the hallway, they heard Kelty's voice. "Finally!" Hazel said.

Kelty spied them across the parlor and rushed to their side. Her blue embroidered dress was covered in tiny white flowers and seemed to dance around her as she hugged them. "What a glorious party."

"It always is with Mrs. Tennyson," Barnaby said, and gave Hazel a nudge of companionship. Fergus wound his way through the crowd and greeted Hazel and Barnaby with a strong handshake. He was a wild-looking man with blond hair that had never faded, springing in every direction. He wore a green jacket with a yellow hankie in its pocket, ever so dapper, and held a martini with two olives, both with one bite out of them.

Kelty looped her arm through Hazel's. "Let's go find Tenny so I can say happy birthday and get the formalities out of the way."

"Good excuse," Fergus said, and shook his head at Barnaby. "These two."

Hazel led Kelty to the empty sunroom, shut the door. "Are you free for the next two days?" she asked. "I need to go to St. Ives."

Kelty nearly bounced on her toes. "In Cornwall? I'm all yours," Kelty said. "But before you tell me what this is about, I have to confess something."

Hazel slipped off her high heels, which were pinching her toes to near death. "Do I need to get the rosary beads?"

"Quite possibly." Kelty walked to the window and then turned. "I took that address from the Hogan's receipt, and I sent a telegram."

Hazel pressed her hand to her heart. "You can't just run off and do that . . . you can't."

"I know. It was presumptuous and I'm sorry. I did it for love and then realized it might have been best if I'd talked to you." She scrunched her face. "I tend to rush into things without thinking. Forgive me?"

"What did the telegram say?"

"Where did you find this story. Stop. It is life and death. Stop."

"Oh, Kelty . . ."

"I gave her your address. If she ignores this, we go to America."

Hazel went to her friend, hugged her. "I forgive you and I love you so. It's what I should have done."

"Now," Kelty said. "What's in Cornwall?"

The door to the sunroom burst open and in walked Fergus and Barnaby. "Told you they'd be sequestered away," Fergus said with a smile.

"Plotting world domination," Barnaby said as he came to Hazel and kissed her.

"Something like that," Kelty said.

Hazel slipped on her shoes and the four of them walked out, the couples arm in arm. Kelty looked over her shoulder with the question—"What's in Cornwall?"—lingering between them. She raised her eyebrows at Hazel meaningfully.

"Harry," Hazel mouthed silently.

# CHAPTER 24

## September 1939

On the fourth day in Binsey, finally, a letter from Mum arrived, tattered and dirty as if it had been through a great and terrible journey. Mum would visit in three weeks' time. But in between she would write letters and Hazel and Flora must do the same.

As the days passed, Hazel and Flora created a calendar with Harry's art paper, drawing a heart in red on the day Mum would arrive. Every night they drew tiny stars from their imaginary river into the calendar square of the passed day.

Hazel loved so many things about being there that it was hard to wish for Bloomsbury, even though Bridie didn't quite know how to plait her hair, and the mean Baldwin twins teased her at school for being an evacuee. School was horrible: She felt lonely among the children who had been friends all their lives, and the schoolwork was boring. But Hazel didn't want to complain; she didn't want to be sent somewhere else. Bridie had a warm kitchen and sweet cream porridge, there were books everywhere, and they could get more on Saturday trips to Oxford. There was also Harry and his daily sketches and the adventures he took them on every afternoon in the woodlands.

Kelty sometimes joined Harry, Hazel, and Flora on their adventures when Mrs. Marchman fell asleep or sent her on an errand; Kelty was one of them even if she couldn't spend the night. They built a fort made of logs and moss beneath a larger alder tree, and threw rocks into the green reedy-edged river until Harry taught both Hazel and Kelty how to make them skip. Kelty talked little of the horror of living with Mrs. Marchman, but they all knew it was bad.

Every few days Bridie insisted that Hazel write to Mum, and Hazel told Mum these stories. She practiced her neat cursive writing and tried to sound cheery and bright. They drew pictures of the country-side and Daisy the cow. It was all they knew to do and it didn't feel enough.

One afternoon, Flora called out from the bedroom, but her voice now sounded muffled, panicked.

Hazel rushed to find that Flora sat cross-legged on the bed, her red-and-blue gas mask over her face, her eyes large behind the plastic eyepieces and the reptilian snout with the perforated holes poking out. The buckles were snapped crooked. Flora squeezed Berry tightly in her arms.

"Flora!" Hazel sat next to her sister, the bed dipping, and reached to undo the black straps. "What are you doing?"

"I heard a siren," Flora said. Her voice and breathing from behind the mask caused her to sound like she was underwater.

Hazel undid the buckles and slid her fingers under the rubber, remov-ing it from Flora's face. Hazel saw the dents of the tight mask on Flora's pale skin. "That wasn't *that* kind of siren. That was just a police car far down the road."

Flora buried her face in Hazel's chest. "They said to put on the mask when the sirens came . . ."

"Oh, Flora." Hazel held her sister and rubbed her back; she made the clucking noises their own mum made when something had gone awry. Hazel imitated and practiced being an adult without feeling like one at all.

One cold afternoon with a fire blazing in the hearth, Hazel sat at the round table in the living room with Harry where they did their school-work. Numbers on her sheet blurred in her sight. Harry could add long rows of them without seeming to try at all, while she counted on her fingers under the table.

"I hate math. I hate it." Hazel slammed and dragged her pencil along the paper, the lead point breaking and the paper ripping.

Bridie called from the kitchen, "Everything okay in there?"

Flora looked up from where she sat on the wool rug sorting colored buttons into different jars. "It's just numbers," she said.

"You can't even count without missing the numbers seven and twelve, so how do you know anything?" Hazel asked, feeling her cheeks redden, embarrassed in front of Harry for looking stupid. She stood to leave, frustrated and wanting to be at the river.

"I can help you," Harry said.

Hazel looked down at him. He needed a haircut, Bridie had just told him that morning at breakfast; they'd go into town tomorrow. His dark curls were tucked behind his ears. His long eyelashes and dark eyes were so beautiful. She looked away. "I don't want your help," she said.

"Why ever not?" he asked, and twirled his pencil between his hands. "I'm not good at a lot of things, but I'm very good at math. I can help you."

"I don't want your help," she said again.

"Why?"

Because, she wanted to scream at him, if you help me I will like you even more than I already do and if I like you even more than I already do, you might not like me back. And that could ruin everything. If Harry didn't feel about her the way she felt about him, she'd have to go live with another family or go back to London. And of all the terrible things in the world, losing Harry seemed among the worst.

It was a dilemma she didn't understand: needing him to like her and pushing him away at the same time. Terrified they would have to leave Binsey and wanting to run away. Dreaming of him and seeing him across the breakfast table mussy with hay and morning dew. "It doesn't matter why," she finally said. "I just don't."

"She's not making sense," Flora said from the floor. "She does that sometimes." Flora resumed her button sorting and started counting again. "One, two, three, four, five, six, eight . . ."

"See?" Hazel said as she stomped out of the room. "You always skip number seven!"

Later that night, a day before Mum was to arrive at the Aberdeen cottage, Hazel held Flora close. "I'm sorry. Sometimes I don't act like the grown-up I want to be."

"That's okay," Flora said, and snuggled closer, forgiveness so easy for her sweet spirit while Hazel felt the ache of regret.

They finally fell asleep when a *tip-tap* started in Hazel's dreams, then brought her awake. Another knock on the window resonated through the bedroom. From the bed, with Flora's left leg tossed over hers, Hazel saw in the window the outline of a girl's face with two braids.

Kelty.

Hazel stumbled from the bed and cracked open the window. A low and curved moon settled as a bowl in the inky sky behind Kelty. "What are you doing?" Hazel whispered.

"I came to tell you that I'm running away. I took the money from the hag's jar and I'm walking to the station through Jericho; it's an easy walk across Port Meadow and then a train to Paddington. I'd rather be killed by a bomb than live with that horrible lady."

"It's the middle of the night. It's dark."

"Of course. That's the best time to run away. All secret things happen in the dark," Kelty said. "But I wanted you to know that you will forever be my best friend because you're the one who told me about Frideswide. Sometimes we can't wait around for someone to save us."

"That was just a story," Hazel said, a trill of fear rising in her. The night was dangerous.

"No," Kelty said. "It wasn't just a story. It is never *just* a story."

"Kelty, don't go."

"Promise me you won't tell anyone until I get home to Mum. You can't tell anyone. Promise you'll give me time to make it to London."

"I promise," Hazel said into the night, under a crescent moon. Surely that was the kind of promise that could never be broken.

And with that, Kelty was gone.

By morning, Hazel thought she'd dreamed about Kelty running away, and another sketch slipped under the door—this one of the fort they'd built before it had been washed away by the rain. Hazel set it on the dresser before she went into the warm kitchen.

Bridie looked from the pot she stirred and her smile fell. "Sweet pea, what is wrong this morning?"

The way Bridie asked in such a sweet voice showed she cared, and Hazel told the truth. "I want to do school here, like Harry does. I don't hate real school—I love it in Bloomsbury. But here, I always have to eat lunch alone on the hill because no one will talk to me or play with me."

"But why?"

"Because I'm not from here. And I always finish my work early and have to just sit there—the teacher won't even let me read. And they say . . ." Hazel froze, and Bridie squeezed her hand to go on. "They say you made your husband . . . disappear."

"Gossip is something awful in a hamlet this small."

The porridge on the stove popped, a siren wailed far off, and Flora called out for Hazel, but neither Bridie nor Hazel moved.

"You will do school with Harry, here at home."

A warm sensation of relief spread from her stomach to her throat, where she let out a sigh. Bridie reached down and hugged Hazel so tightly that Hazel wondered why others didn't hug the same all the time.

Bridie stood and picked up the wooden spoon from the floor. "I know what they say about me, Hazel. Don't let it bother you. It doesn't bother me one bit. They are ignorant and you can't change that."

Bridie turned and walked back to the AGA, her back straight and wisps of her curly hair falling from the hairpins. Hazel wanted to stand and put her arms around her, hold her tightly while she stirred their bubbling breakfast, fix for her what Bridie had just fixed for Hazel.

If Bridie was trusting her, she must trust Bridie, too. "Bridie, I have to tell you something."

Bridie turned around, her smile wavering. She was about to break a promise. But what if Kelty got lost in the woods? Or fell in the river? Knifed on the streets of Oxford? "Kelty ran away . . . she took the hag's money and she's taking the train to her mum in North London." The words tumbled over each other.

"Oh, Hazel! When?"

"In the middle of the night."

"Darling girl." Bridie closed her eyes. "I will make sure she is safe; I'll use Father Fenelly's phone to ring around and find out where she is. Hazel. I wish I could save everyone." She opened her eyes. "I am sure she is with her mum now. Don't you worry about her. Please."

———

The rain blew sideways, turning the view of the pasture into blurry watercolors. Hazel and Flora stood at the front windows of Bridie's cottage watching for a cab to drive down the rutted driveway and bring Mum to them. It had been three weeks. They'd never, until now, been away from her for one day. Flora clung to Hazel's hand and silence rested uneasy between them.

Flora whispered, "I think I see a shimmering door." But it was a weak declaration.

"No," Hazel said. "We can't go anywhere. We have to be right here when Mum comes."

From the kitchen the wireless played softly. Harry sat at the round table where he concentrated on his schoolwork and his head was bent over a sheet of paper with a long equation Hazel would never be able to figure out even if they forced her.

"There!" Hazel cried out and pointed at a mud-splattered cab pulling into the drive. It came to a stop and Mum climbed out of the backseat without an umbrella. She wore a long green raincoat and her hair was pulled back. She carried a canvas bag over her shoulder and she futilely lifted her hand to the pelting rain and ran for the front door.

Hazel flung the door open and Mum nearly fell into the cottage, laughing and gathering her girls into her arms. Mum smelled of wet wool and home and comfort. She trembled beneath the girls and tears joined the rain on her cheeks. "My girls. My girls. My girls."

Finally they all let go. Mum lifted Flora to her hip and gazed at Hazel. Dark colors bloomed beneath Mum's eyes and her lips were chapped and dry, her cheeks red. But she was the same otherwise and a fear Hazel hadn't realized she carried as an arrow in her chest calmed down. Mum was here and it was all okay. They would be just fine. A little time in the country and they'd all be together again.

Mum kissed both of them. "I've missed you so much."

Flora placed her palm on Mum's cheek and patted it as if checking if she was real. "You're here," Flora declared.

"And I brought you some surprises," she said.

Bridie's sweet voice interrupted. "Welcome, Mrs. Linden!"

Mum looked to Bridie and smiled. "Camellia, please. And how do I thank you for taking care of my girls?"

"They have brought great joy to our home," Bridie said. "Now who would like some tea and shortbread?"

"Oh, I would," Mum said with a laugh. "Indeed."

The afternoon passed so quickly that Hazel thought it was possible it had folded in on itself. Mum had brought bright blue ribbons for their hair, a spinning top that had seen better days with a dent on the left side, and new wellies for both of them: green for Flora and blue for Hazel. Bridie and Mum got on so well it was as if they'd already known each other and Mum had called ahead and told her to choose Hazel and Flora. Harry was quiet no matter how much Mum tried to get him to talk.

Hazel and Flora chattered away like the squirrels of Whisperwood— telling Mum about the magic well and the mean twins, about Kelty and how she ran away and was back in North London. They told her about the river and the town and Father Fenelly and Daisy the cow.

Mum wasn't the same and Hazel didn't know how to define it, but the before-war Mum was gone. The pearls and high heels; the singsong voice of happy adventure; the cakes she made that tipped over with thick icing; the picnics in the backyard pretending they were on holiday. That mum seemed asleep, as if an evil witch had put a spell on her. Now she spoke softly, startled easily, and her body seemed tense. She rarely laughed and when she did it sounded forced and false. When the war was over, maybe the before-mum would return.

By the time Mum left, although the rain hadn't stopped for even a minute and they hadn't been able to show her about the land, Hazel believed that she'd been wrong to worry and believe that the war would ruin everything. And as she fell asleep, and although it made her feel the littlest bit guilty, Hazel didn't want to return to Bloomsbury. Not yet.

When Mum hugged them goodbye, there weren't tears this time. Only later did Hazel discover that Mum cried the whole way home, but for Hazel and Flora all was well.

# CHAPTER 25

## March 1960

"All the best love stories are doomed love stories. Romeo and Juliet. Tristan and Isolde. They all end in heartbreak," Hazel said, pointing to Kelty's book on the kitchen table: *Wuthering Heights.*

Kelty made a face of amusement. "We are going to St. Ives to see Harry, and you're talking of doomed love."

"I'm talking about that book you're reading."

Early morning light softened the kitchen as Kelty rinsed egg cups and Hazel packed a lunch for their trip to Cornwall. "It's not my book that's bothering you. It's Harry. You're afraid of seeing him, aren't you?"

"I am not afraid of Harry. It's Barnaby." Hazel folded parchment around the ham and cheese sandwiches and faced Kelty. "We leave for Paris in a week. If I do anything to muck that up, he will never forgive me."

"So seeing Harry isn't on the top of his desires for you?"

"I don't think he's quite keen on us finding him. No."

"I think you're afraid of Harry not living up to the man you imagined he'd become. Perhaps he's unworthy of comparison to every other man you've dated."

"Kelty, stop. I am not seeing Harry to undo some doomed love story. I've never compared other men to him. All of this is *only* for Flora. For Whisperwood. To find out if Flora survived to tell the story."

Kelty nodded but Hazel knew she didn't buy it, not one bit. But before they could say another word, the phone rang. Hazel picked up.

"Miss Linden?"

"Speaking," she said, and cradled the receiver between her shoulder and ear as she slipped the sandwiches into a basket.

"This is Lord Arthur Dickson from Sotheby's."

"Oh, hello, Lord Dickson." She cheered her voice and stood straighter, placed the receiver in her hand. A man who needed to remind her that he was in the House of Lords was a man who needed an ego boost. "I'm so looking forward to my first day."

"Well, yes. That's why I'm ringing you. We here at Sotheby's receive any and all police reports and blotters about art or book heists. Your name has appeared in our last report from London. I am just making sure there is another Hazel Linden in London who might have done such a thing as take valuable prints and a signed first edition." He paused, and Hazel tasted the bile rise in her throat, the metallic taste of fear.

His voice, rising in question. "Is there another Hazel Linden?"

"No, sir. That was me. It was a dreadful mistake and all has been set right."

"Well, well, that was some kind of mistake, Miss Linden."

"Yes, it was on my last day of fifteen years of impeccable work at Hogan's."

"Indeed. Yet, before the board decides what to do with this information, I wanted to confirm the facts with you. Thank you for your honesty."

"My record until that moment has been unblemished. If you let me, I am sure I can explain."

"This places your employment at risk, Miss Linden. We will get back with you."

And he, like Peggy Andrews and the man at the publishing house, hung up without a goodbye. She was rightly tired of people hanging up on her. She slammed the receiver back in the cradle and faced Kelty.

Kelty grimaced. "Oh . . . no."

"This bloody well better be worth it," Hazel said. "If I lose my job, *and* lose Barnaby . . ."

Kelty held up her hand, as if talking to her little daughter. "Stop. Do not go down that trail of mad thinking. Let's just concentrate on what's ahead today. Just for now . . . today."

So, the time had come for Hazel to see Harry Aberdeen. He'd receive no warning. No call. All these years of wondering if and when she would see him; today was the day. And what Hazel had meant to tell Kelty, what she had not found the words to say, stayed stuck inside her.

Although this would be the first time she'd seen him since Binsey, it would not be the first time they'd communicated.

# CHAPTER 26

### November 1946

At twenty-one, Hazel had been in her third year at university and living in rooms at Newnham Hall of Cambridge. As she entered the building one autumn day, the porter handed her the mail, damp from that November's incessant rain. She entered her room and tossed her mail onto a round coffee table in the center of the seating area. Preoccupied with the coming Michaelmas exams and distracted by too-loud music coming from two doors down where a freshman girl from Lancashire cared little for anything but pubs and the boys from Hughes Hall, Hazel didn't notice the letter for a bit.

The war was over now, Germany was defeated, but rationing of items like sugar and chocolate continued, and in the cobblestone streets of Cambridge were the ghosts of boys who hadn't returned, and the hollowed-eye looks of those who did. Her papa was gone and not even enough of his body to bury, and Flora remained a mystery that even the best of Oxford's detectives couldn't solve. They'd given up, even as every few months Hazel took the two-and-a-half-hour train ride to Oxford and stopped by Aiden Davies's office and asked for updates.

There never were any.

Meanwhile, Hazel had disappeared into the books and stories she studied. She walked the green paths of Cambridge, past glorious and ancient buildings, yet she barely noticed the scenery. There were boys to be sure, but her heart was unavailable to them—also to herself. She would never tell or write stories again, that was clear. Making stories brought misery but reading and studying them provided comfort. In the stories of others, there were endings without loose ends, those who were missing were found, and the world made sense.

Tonight there was a visiting lecture by the professor J. R. R. Tolkien from Oxford—she planned to be early and find a seat near the front. Tossing her knapsack on the floor, she sat on an overstuffed chair with tea stains from generations of students, sifting through the envelopes to see if Mum had written from London.

No.

But there was a letter from Scotland, the red stamp damp where she'd touched it. No return address. She ripped it open, knowing before she read the signature that this was the letter she'd been waiting for. All this time, she'd been waiting to hear from Harry Aberdeen. The rest of the world faded away, time and Tolkien forgotten as rain struck iron-paned windows and the autumn night descended.

*Dear Hazel,*

*I hope this letter finds you. I have wanted to write to you for many years now but haven't known what to say or where to find you. Ethan told me he saw you in Cambridge and that you are now a student at Newnham. So if this reaches you—bravo to Ethan!*

Hazel let the name Ethan run past her. Ethan Baldwin was the boy she'd pinned to the ground at school with her boot. The boy who'd called her a "vaccie" but then had helped them search for Flora. The boy who'd wept when he realized they could not find her.

She read as quickly as possible, then read again slower this time, then another time, shifting her mind from how she'd imagined Harry's last six years to the man he might be today.

She read that Bridie had sent Harry to boarding school at the same time Hazel had returned to Bloomsbury with her mum. Bridie had wanted to protect him from gossip and innuendo. He'd graduated, and now attended University of Edinburgh, studying mathematics. He had never stopped thinking about Hazel. Not ever. And he wondered if she might tell him how she herself was doing in the world.

She closed her eyes, fell backward in time, remembering the vow in the stone church when, crying in her delirium, blood on the altar, she'd promised to never see Harry Aberdeen again.

But a letter was not the same as *seeing* him. The promise would not be broken if she wrote back to him, would it?

It was a week before she penned a letter, as the remembrances of his kindness returned with the ache of missing him, joining the yearning that had never gone away. What to write to him consumed her thoughts, her schoolwork neglected.

Their correspondence continued for three years. They told each other of their lives, Hazel found herself jotting down things she noticed each day to share with Harry: a speckled thrush rising from the river's edge, a blooming rosemary bush that made her think of Bridie and how she'd tucked bundles of it in their pockets, a new Agatha Christie just out, the burst of blue cornflowers, ones that Bridie once told them healed Achilles.

And Harry told Hazel of his life: his studies and his journey to America to visit Princeton, where he studied a semester under James Waddell Alexander, the world-famous mathematician. He wrote of adventures with Ethan Baldwin, hiking in Scotland and learning to hunt the Monarch of the Glen, even attempting to sneak onto Balmoral's hunting fields to catch a sight of King George! But not once did either Harry or Hazel write about Flora or that awful day that ripped their idyllic world to pieces.

Hazel graduated in 1948, moving into a flat above a dry cleaner in London City Centre. She took a job at a pub called The Crown, drawing Guinness and pouring whiskey.

Over the course of that year above the dry cleaner, she told Harry about all of it—the odor of chemicals rising through the floorboards, the books she read. She asked him questions, which he always answered. Do you still sketch? (Yes, he did.) Do you still look for walking sticks when you hike? (Yes, he did.) What she didn't ask: Do your lips still move while you read? Do you hike at the edge of the river and think of Flora?

Do you miss me?

He asked her questions about her life, and she began answering with stories, taking the dullest detail of her day and turning it into a sensational tale, exaggerating for the fun of it and describing every color, aroma, and sound.

She felt a bit more like herself when she wrote to Harry.

One of his letters to her read, "You make life magical, Hazel Linden. Did you know that?"

The thrill of reading this compliment brought back the afternoon in the riven tree, his lips on hers, his body . . .

Finally, he wrote, "May I visit you in London?"

She almost wrote back. She tried to answer. If she said yes, she'd break her own blood vow. If she said no, she would always regret it. In the end, she never answered him, and he stopped writing to her. Just like that, he quit. When she wanted to mourn him, she just tapped into the anger like she'd tap into a draft of beer, reminding herself that he just up and quit when she didn't answer him. He didn't fight for her.

And her vow in a church on St. Frideswide's Day of 1940 remained unbroken.

So, she made a new promise: to be the Hazel who Harry knew in letters, a person who could make life magical. She was determined that—without Harry and without his letters—she would change. It was then she took her mum's offer of the flat and applied for a job at Hogan's. Possibly, in the end, that's all the communication was meant to do: push Hazel toward the right direction in her life.

Or so she told herself.

# CHAPTER 27

## March 1960

Three hours into the drive, Hazel pulled into a station for more petrol. Kelty stretched and opened the passenger door to unfold her long legs. She sighed. "How much longer?"

"Two hours. We can picnic in the gardens at Rougemont Castle."

"How far is that?"

"Around the corner. We're in Exeter already."

"How grand to sleep through all of the dullest scenery! Without Midge around to call my name every two and half seconds." She smiled at the name of her child, even within her bit of joy at their brief separation.

"But you missed so much," Hazel said. "It's such gorgeous countryside in the spring. The baby lambs, all wobbly on their feet, trying to keep up with the others. The thatch roofs with the whitewashed houses. Chapels with steeples reaching for something they'll never reach. The—"

"You are a natural born storyteller, my friend."

"That's not a story. It's just what I saw on the way."

"It's both."

Within a few minutes, Hazel found a parking spot at the edge of the road near Rougemont Castle, at the visitor's parking lot at Northernhay Gardens. They climbed out with the basket they'd packed in Hazel's kitchen that morning and ambled down a dusty lane where an alley of Dutch elms rolled out their sleepy leaves. Into the gardens they went with the grass soft under their boots, past the iron Deer Stalker statue turning green with age to find a picnic table and wooden bench nearby.

"Does that castle resemble yours in Whisperwood?" Kelty asked as they spread the picnic across the table beneath a sycamore.

"No, those are red stones. Ours was . . ." Hazel closed her eyes and lifted her face to the sun, let it warm her. She allowed her thoughts to meander down a woodland path she'd avoided for years. "It was made of white and gray stone. Even before we saw Bridie's house, it was made of the same. Flora thought I'd imagined Bridie's house into being." She opened her eyes. "Maybe I shouldn't have allowed her to think that way, to think that I had that kind of power. But it seemed harmless."

"It was harmless but not without effect. In those awful times, Flora needed an escape, fairy tales and magical lands." Kelty picked a piece of cubed cheese and popped it into her mouth.

"I'd try to find different words for white and gray each time we approached the castle. It looked like a pearl in a shell. The wing of a dove. The edges of the sky before rain. The pure white of a summer cloud." Hazel shook off the old dreams and glanced at the red stones of Rougemont. "The Devon witches were tried here, the last to be executed for being witches in England."

"How do you know such things?"

"1680," Hazel said. "I read, and these little facts get stuck in my head."

Kelty opened her mouth as if to speak and then stopped.

"*What?* What were you going to say?" Hazel asked, nudging Kelty's boot with hers.

"I wonder what Harry looks like now—that's all."

Hazel didn't want to admit to wondering the same. "Who cares?" Hazel said. "We get there; we ask him if he knew the name of Whisperwood, and we get out."

"I remember him so well, and I knew him for what? A week? He was so full of—"

"Adventure, I know."

"And so—"

"Cute, I know."

They smiled their best-mates smiles, finished their picnic, and got back on the winding road to St. Ives. They passed sun-bleached wheat fields that echoed the tawny sand beaches in color, drove through a patchwork of green fields and between unforgiving hedgerows that scraped the side of the car, all in friendly silence wondering what might happen when they arrived.

———

They arrived as the afternoon sun rolled toward the thrashing sea, which bashed against the gray stone walls of the Cornish town bookended by concrete piers. St. Ives curled like a lazy cat around the bay. The peaks of gray-roofed houses rose and fell on green hills. Hazel heard the high squeal of seagulls, spied the jetty with the white lighthouse and a tower with four peaks. The tide was low and a long stretch of sand glowed the color of buttered toast. Boats rested, waiting for the water to rise.

Hazel parked the car in front of the Sloop Inn on the corner of Fore Street. FOUNDED IN 1312, the sign read in red letters. In front, caned chairs and marble café tables sat on the pavement facing the sea. Hazel and Kelty were silent in all this beauty until Kelty asked, "How are we to find him?"

"We can ask around." Hazel turned off the ignition and they climbed out. Their bags in tow from the boot of the car, they walked toward the Sloop Inn. Couples and singles gathered at the tables, sipping wine and staring out to sea. A spring seaside holiday for those in their bright sweaters and colorful hats, in their love gazes and soft afternoon buzz.

When they reached the wooden front door, Hazel said, "Let's check in, unpack, have a pint, then find Harry."

Kelty shifted her bag to her other hand. "Always, with the lists! It must be exhausting."

"If I didn't love you . . ." Hazel shook her head. "Or if I didn't know you loved me, I'd take that as an insult rather than the intended compliment."

"Of course. Everything about you is lovable."

———

An hour later, dressed in her favorite shift dress with swirling patterns of green leaves, her hair tamed back in a matching headband, Hazel waited for Kelty at one of the café tables on the sidewalk. The padded light of midafternoon filled the air with a haze, a softening of the world that brought with it a kind of luminescent focus, an easing of the hard edges.

"You look marvelous!" Kelty plopped into a chair and took a long swig of the amber pint awaiting her.

"As do you." And it was true. Hugging her body was a simple cerulean shift dress with pockets and a Peter Pan collar.

"I know you, my friend," Kelty said. "You are sitting here, fast forwarding through the day, wondering who what where—"

"I was actually thinking about how sublime the light is here, how this is definitely an artist's light. No wonder there are all these studios."

Kelty settled back in her chair and stared out to the sea, crossing and uncrossing her legs. "*Hmmm . . .*" She tapped the top of her pint glass with a finger. "Okay, so I asked the waitress where I would find the artists of St. Ives. It turns out there a few schools: pottery, painting, sculpture. But no need to go house by house because she knows Harry Aberdeen. She said his studio is on Fore Street, number 6123."

"Wow, that was easy." *Too easy*, Hazel thought. She'd imagined wandering through St. Ives and maybe they wouldn't find him at all.

"It's a small village, and the artist colony is both loved and hated. 'Those Bohemians' the manager called them. 'The true artists', Silvie the waitress called them. 'Smelly vagabonds' the manager called them, 'darling' Silvie called them."

Hazel's laugh bubbled. "I doubt Harry smells."

"Let's go find out."

# CHAPTER 28

## March 1960

Light rained down on Harry, surrounding him. He stood in front of an easel near the high iron-mullioned window, his left hand in midair, holding a paintbrush, his head tilted to the right, his right hand tapping a rhythm on lion-colored pants. His hair was long enough to touch his shoulders, tucked behind the shells of his ears.

Hazel and Kelty stood at the open door. Three other artists were at work; two men, one at a pottery wheel and another staring blankly at a block of marble with only a few chips gone, and a woman wearing slim black pants and a gray T-shirt stained with splashes of red paint in front of another easel, a cigarette dripping lazily from her left hand.

From the radio came Bobby Darin singing "Dream Lover." The back door, Hazel now realized, was open, and a fresh sea breeze blew through.

The woman was the first to notice Kelty and Hazel, offering them a slow smile that felt both lazy and seductive. She sauntered over to a cardboard table where the wireless sat peppered in paint and dried clay and turned down the music. "Hallo! Sorry to be so rude. Welcome to 6123."

Hazel's throat closed, full of so many words that they seemed clogged and useless. But not Kelty; she burst out with "Harry!"

He turned so suddenly that he dropped the brush, orange paint splattering his already-stained pants and the tarp below. His recognition came slowly, wave upon wave on his face, then his eyes.

It was only a second, maybe two, but time elongated in the room, stretched out with Hazel noticing Harry's each twitch and move. The spark in his brown eyes, the raised eyebrows, and Hazel having enough time to wonder if he would smile or frown, if he would nod in dismissal or . . .

Then he rushed toward them, taking them both in his arms, one on each side, pulling them close. "Hazel! And am I right, this is Kelty?"

Kelty laughed gloriously and said, "I can't breathe." Hazel felt his arms around her and marveled how he'd become a man, this man.

Time swooped back in, turning itself right side up and moving along its regular rhythms. Harry stepped back, yet kept one hand on each of their shoulders. Damn, he was handsome. Probably always had been but it had been hidden beneath the puppy-ness of an adolescent, nothing quite matching yet, each part waiting to grow into the other parts.

"What are you doing here?" He shook his head and his curly hair fell from behind his ears. "No, let me start again. I am so glad you're here! How did you find me?"

"Your mum," Hazel said.

"Well, good on her. You saw Mum?" He directed the question to Hazel with a familiar eagerness.

"I did," Hazel said.

"She's well, isn't she." It wasn't a question at all.

"She most certainly is. And Mr. Nolan?" she asked. "I didn't see that coming."

"Seems I was blind, too." Harry shook his head. "Love is strange."

"Indeed," Kelty said, and took in the room. "This is amazing. What a life."

Harry seemed to realize they weren't the only ones in the room. "Oh, Ethan! Look who is here. Marvin and Dawn, meet my childhood friends Hazel and Kelty."

The man at the marble sculpture stood, his stork-like legs surprisingly long. He walked a few steps toward them, but that's all it took before both Ethan's name, the young twin boy from Binsey and his grin full of shenanigans, and the shy blue eyes registered with Hazel.

Ethan Baldwin.

"Jesus, Mary, and Joseph, if it isn't the beauty and grace of Hazel Linden come to visit upon us?" he declared.

Everyone in the room burst out laughing. Voices overlapped and there were hugs and cheek kisses before Harry suggested they settle in and reminisce at the pub a block away—the same one Hazel and Kelty had just left.

But that wasn't the purpose of their visit, Hazel wanted to tell him. And it wasn't to see his art or drink pints. She was there to ask a single question, but the surge of their energy had them winding through the secreted cobblestone alleys and back to the Sloop Inn pub within minutes, leaving Marvin and Dawn behind, with pints all around. Hazel sat next to Harry and on her other side was Ethan. Crowded four at a table for two, their knees touched. The table was soon filled with fish and chips, with grease soaking into its parchment paper. Awkwardness replaced the initial unfettered happiness at the studio.

Kelty, as she did, filled the silence with a warm burst of energy. "An artist colony," she said to the men. "I guess we should have known all along."

Harry shrugged and set his elbows on the table. "I didn't know all along. I tried a few other things."

"Like?" Hazel was immediately and shockingly ravenous, starving for information about his last years. For all the times and days she'd looked away from her curiosity, now she was leaning into it. Was he married? Kids. His art? His other jobs?

He draped his arm on the back of her metal café chair. He looked up. "Banking, financial advising, newspaper printing . . ." He met Hazel's gaze. "None of it interesting to me at all. I've been here for ten years, painting in all kinds of mediums and waiting, like everyone else, for my big break, for the right person to notice my genius." He laughed.

"If there's a place to wait out a big break, I can't think of a better one," Hazel said, her palm up as she swept her hand across the table to the sea.

"It is an extraordinary place," Harry said. "The light here is sometimes otherworldly. You can spend your whole life trying to capture it, to find it, to take the miraculous air of Cornwall and put it on a canvas. I might never achieve it, but I will damn sure not stop trying."

Hazel smiled at the boy and the man whose exuberance was still pup-like and free, even if tempered.

Kelty pointed at both men. "Kids? Wife?"

They both shook their heads. Ethan companionably slapped Harry's shoulder. "Although Dawn back at the studio is most likely waiting for a proposal from this one." Ethan pointed back at Kelty. "And you?"

"Married to a wild man, Fergus, with an astounding girl named Midge."

"That's mighty fine," Ethan said. "At the moment, this lug and I don't make the best prospects for husbands and fathers—what with living in a house with four people and trying to bust out in the art world." He nodded at Hazel. "You?"

"Yes, there's a man. Barnaby. He's a professor." She stopped; it seemed the wrong place to talk about him. She glanced between Harry and Ethan. "You made a choice," Hazel said, knowing she'd made a choice, too, but a different one. "Art over safety and—"

"Over what some might call normalcy," Ethan said, and took a swallow of his pint, wiping foam from his beard. "But if you aren't living *your* life, whose life are you living?"

"Damn fine question," said Kelty.

"You know," Harry said. "If you'd waited two days, we have an art show in London, in Hampstead Heath, and we'd have come to you."

Hazel and Kelty looked at each other and laughed.

"Where's your twin . . . ?" Hazel blanked on the name of Ethan's brother, another thing lost in the dingy basement of those days.

"Adam is living in America. Met a girl who came to Oxford for a semester. Then he up and moved to New York." Ethan rolled his eyes. "And now he works at her parents' garment warehouse. Or should I say, runs it. He's becoming the garment king of Manhattan's Lower East Side."

Adam moved to America.

The information hummed across the table like Ethan had plucked a guitar string. This was it—this, right here—possibly all the answers in a single moment. Harry had told Ethan of Whisperwood, Ethan told Adam, Adam told a girl, now his wife . . . in America.

"When did Adam move to America?" Hazel asked casually, her hands clasped together.

"Oh, ten years or so ago. He has two monsters I adore, a boy and a girl. But I don't get to see them often, as you'd imagine."

Kelty narrowed her eyes at Hazel, and Hazel knew what she was saying with that one glance.

Ask now.

But she couldn't, not in front of Ethan. "Harry, can you walk down to the water with me for just a minute?" They all heard the tremble in her voice.

"I'm all yours," he said, and stood, brushed his palms on his paint-stained pants, and pushed back his chair. "Low tide. Good time for it."

Getting to her feet, Hazel felt the leftover winter hiding in the spring breeze, a chill that had her grab her cream wool jersey and slip it on as they silently walked across the street and toward a wide stretch of tawny beach. She thought of their long walks in Port Meadow toward the river, of quiet mornings and of sketches slipped under the door, of the way the soft edges of the pathway went from brown to green to bursting with color, and how she'd seen it all with Harry at her side.

They climbed down concrete stairs and reached the wet strip of sand, darker brown and soft. A bright blue rowboat rested on its side, a red buoy dangling from a barnacle-covered rope, which was tied to a metal ring on the beach's stone wall. Harry sat on the edge of the boat and crossed one foot over the other, tilted his head in his mother's move, and smiled. "Damn good to see you, Hazel. I've wondered about you for so long. I've asked around . . . so to be honest, I know you work at Hogan's. I've thought about stopping in, but I knew you didn't want to see me."

She shifted her feet in the sand, feeling it give way beneath her. She couldn't find a word to say now that they were alone.

He looked down and switched one foot for the other; the boat rocked back a bit, then settled again. "You never answered my last letter."

"I know. I can explain," she said. But could she? Could she truly tell him of the blood vow she'd made in a cold stone church with her sister gone? Even now she felt as if she were betraying her sister, breaking a promise, even now with her adult eyes and mind, the child within her screamed "*betrayal.*"

He interrupted her thoughts. "You don't have to explain. I know you blame me. There's nothing I can do about it and although I hate it, it's true."

"Why ever would I blame you?"

He tilted his head. "For losing her . . . for losing Flora."

"Losing her?" An electric shock shot through Hazel's chest.

"When I went to find you, I thought Flora was sound asleep. I left her alone by the river—for five minutes? Ten? I think back and back and try to remember how many seconds or minutes it took to find you and then—"

"Stop. It was never your fault. Never. I'm not here to fish for an apology."

"Then why are you here?"

As she stood there on a wet strip of Cornwall sand, as the seagulls squawked, and a dog ran past covered in a fine crust of sand, she knew there was more than one reason for being there: She missed him. She wanted to see him again and know he was well. She wanted absolution. She wanted to touch him. She wanted . . . so much.

His hair was burnished with the evening sun, hay-flecked, his eyes so fixed on her she thought it possible that he had missed her just as she had missed him.

"Harry, I need to ask you something."

"Anything."

"Did you know the name of our land? Of the made-up land that I told Flora about?"

"Isn't that why you got so mad at me that day? Because I asked?"

"Yes."

"Then how could I know?"

"Did you ever hear me speak it or did you tell our story to anyone? To Ethan, who maybe told it to Adam or . . ."

Harry stood. He came so close to her that Hazel smelled his warm breath of beer. "Hazel Mersey Linden, I have never repeated your story. I wouldn't know it to tell it, to be honest. And I never told anyone what we fought about that day at the edge of the river. What is this about?"

"Whisperwood," she said.

"Wytham Woods? Above Binsey?"

"No."

Then in what felt like one long exhale, Hazel told Harry the entire story, from the day less than a week ago when she'd found the book *Whisperwood* to this moment on the beach.

He listened without moving, barely blinking. She made herself stand fast, not run from his gaze. When she finished, he pulled her into him, held her against his chest without a word. She felt his heart through his T-shirt, the rolling of it with hers. She lifted her arms and wound them around him, holding fast.

She'd wanted him to hold her like this when she was fifteen years old, yet she'd done everything to push him away. Now silence until he loosened his hold, and she stepped back. He was crying without regard for how he looked or who would see him on a wide-open beach in Cornwall.

"Harry."

"So if I didn't know the story, and Mum didn't know, that means Flora might have lived? She didn't die or drown that day; she lived to tell your story?"

"You see," she said. "I thought she disappeared looking for Whisperwood."

"No." Harry shook his head. "I left her alone."

My God, they'd been carrying the same burden. The same bloody weight of guilt. They could have, she realized, been carrying it together all this time.

# CHAPTER 29

## February 1, 1940

Hazel had never heard of St. Brigid's Day or Imbolc, but it arrived at the beginning of February and most of the townspeople joined Bridie to celebrate.

The bonfire, set a distance away from the Aberdeen cottage in the wide pasture, lifted high, its sparks rising to reach the unseen stars they resembled. Bridie set out colored wool blankets about the lawn and upon each was a small pile of green rush. Harry dragged out an old barn table, scarred and lopsided where one leg had been chewed by some sharp-toothed animal. He set it nearby and placed a log beneath the left back leg to level it. On top were cheeses and fruits from the market, fresh baked bread, and a large jug of red wine.

Late afternoon rippled across the sky, the clouds torn scraps of gilt-edged fabric. A man in a dark coat played the fiddle and drank wine from a mug at his side.

Also present were the four nurses who lived behind the parish chapel: Frances was from America while Maeve, Imogene, and Lilly were from villages around England. They were young and eager to help heal the boys who arrived at hospital with war wounds that nothing could truly heal. Frances was shy and guarded, Imogene had a frenetic playful energy, while Maeve and Lilly seemed like twins to Hazel, both blond and quiet. Bridie had Imogene babysit Flora now and again when she took Hazel and Harry alone into town to shop and run her errands.

That day, the nurses all played with Flora more than they talked to the townspeople, as if their job was to guard the smallest of them.

Father Fenelly and Mr. Nolan stood together, laughing about something Mr. Nolan said. The twins, Ethan and Adam, kicked about a leather ball with Harry and another boy from town, whose name Hazel kept forgetting, a wild-eyed boy with greasy hair who'd come to Hazel and Flora and had quietly asked, "Are you orphans?"

"No," Hazel had declared. "No, we are not!"

When he'd walked away, Flora had snuggled closer to Hazel, grasped Berry tighter, and asked with a tremor in her voice, "What is an orphan?"

"Don't listen to him. Don't listen to anyone but me and Bridie and Harry."

"And Mum."

"And Mum," Hazel had said as she crouched down to hug her sister. "We are not orphans."

But Hazel wondered, with a piercing pain—what would become of them if they suddenly became parentless? It happened in war.

Now the party grew as two of Bridie's girlfriends from Oxford arrived without husbands, wearing flowered dresses under their thick coats and wool scarves.

The cold bit everyone's exposed faces, and most noses were red as cardinals.

Hazel and Flora had been living with the Aberdeens for four months now, through Christmas and New Year's when Mum came to visit with her gifts. Father Fenelly sometimes visited and Harry drew sketches that he slipped under the door every morning. Hazel learned Latin when Bridie noticed she was finishing her schoolwork too quickly with nothing to do. Time moved so softly in Binsey that Hazel took little note of its passage, but Bridie marked the seasons with rituals and candles and scented sticks.

Kelty was gone and Hazel missed her, but Kelty had made it safely to Piccadilly by train with money she'd taken from the jar on the hag's kitchen counter. Kelty's mum had taken her back in and decided that billeting her daughter with another possibly cruel stranger was worse than the threat of bombs.

Kelty's letters arrived one a week and Hazel wrote back the same, telling her everything about Binsey: Mr. Nolan and his dog, Mackey, who they visited when they were done with their schoolwork, of the town festival for Christmas Eve when Mum came to visit, and of how the Baldwin twins were nicer now. She wrote how the countryside looked so different from morning to night with the dew and then the frost, with the rising sun and the rising moon. She wrote about Bridie and her sweetness.

"Why is it safer here?" Hazel had once asked Bridie when they were sitting at an outside table at an ice-cream shop in Oxford proper. They'd just been to visit Frideswide's shrine in Christ Church and Hazel was still thinking of the glorious stained-glass window that told the story of a princess who became a saint. Flora was licking the edges of her cone, trying to catch the melting bits of her vanilla.

Bridie had her own way of speaking, and she never said Hitler's name. "It's said the terrible man wants to keep Oxford as his very own, so he won't bomb here—dreadful, yes, but it's keeping us safe." When she said "the terrible man," it sounded to Hazel as if they lived in the fairy tales that she created for Flora, and Hitler was a dragon or an ogre they must defeat to reach the castle.

Hazel and Flora whispered in the night. "Can we take Mum to Whisperwood?" Flora had asked.

"Maybe she can come next time," Hazel told her.

But they never took Mum to Whisperwood and even if they had, it wouldn't change a thing to come.

Mum had come to visit for the holidays, as well as every few weeks, yet only once had she stayed the night on Bridie's flowered couch. She brought small gifts at first—a hair bow or new dress—but as money grew scarcer, she stopped. Bridie always saved the best butter and cream for when Mum visited, knowing of the rationing in London.

One winter day, when the sky was woolly with clouds, Mum had come to spend the whole day and even the night. Hazel and Flora had plaited their hair, washed their faces until they were pink, and waited on the front steps. The cab pulled up, and as always, Mum jumped from the passenger side and swooped her girls into her arms, crying out how very much she missed them.

Hazel noticed her mum grew thinner each visit. They'd tried to cheer her, bringing her into their everyday world: playing jacks on the living room's hardwood floor, the ball bouncing into Mum's hand, showing off Flora's newfound knowledge, sifting through schoolwork pages and Harry showing off how he did math in his head like he could see things none of them could see. After a warm dinner, it was off to bed.

It wasn't until Mum had tucked them in that night, after they'd said their prayers and she'd kissed them like the old days, the Bloomsbury days, that Hazel learned the truth of her mum's life.

Hazel had tried to go to sleep, she really had, but she couldn't. She'd snuck out quietly to sit in the hallway between the kitchen and living room. On her bum with her legs curled to her chest, she listened to the rise and fall of Mum and Bridie's talk.

Hazel only caught snippets, but her mum spoke of hiding in subway tunnels when the bomb sirens went off, of others who had husbands and sons missing. Hazel heard Bridie insist the girls were safe and that she loved them so very much. Hazel heard the soft sounds of crying.

When she could no longer strain to listen and the heaviness of Mum's sorrow felt too much, she ran into the living room and threw herself onto the couch between Bridie and Mum. "You stay with us, Mum. Live here with us!"

Mum took Hazel in her arms and pressed her face to her chest, held her there with brave words. "I can't, my love, but one day we shall all be together again."

Hazel put that promise close to her heart. *We shall all be together again.*

Now she wished Mum was there to see the St. Brigid party. She huddled beneath her coat and blanket, watching as Bridie demonstrated how everyone could make their own St. Brigid's cross with the rush branches she'd placed on the blankets.

"St. Brigid is the saint of Imbolc, the coming of creativity, of spring and new growth, new things," Bridie said as her hands deftly wove the rush branches into the signature cross. "And," she said, looking up, "she wants us to ask—what do you want to bring forth into this world in this next year?"

Voices overlapped, laughing and answering each other, what was new in their life? They fumbled with the rushes, some making a lopsided cross while others gave up and wandered over to the cheeses and wine.

Mr. Nolan piped up, his gloved hands wrapped round his wine mug. "She's a Christian saint, isn't she?"

Bridie smiled. "She is."

This satisfied Mr. Nolan as he clumsily tried to make a cross, to honor the saint who signaled the arrival of spring, of new light.

Bridie leaned over to Hazel and whispered, "But first she was a Celtic goddess."

"First, a goddess," Hazel said, and smiled, tucking that bit of glorious story away for a time she might need it.

"Why do you have these parties?" Hazel asked, teeth chattering.

"To honor the seasons, curious one. To honor each other. To gather. To remember that we are part of something much bigger than the petty things of today, bigger than gossip and—"

"War."

"Yes, we are part of something even bigger than war. Something that goes on and on and was celebrated before us and will be celebrated after us."

"After us," Hazel said, wondering for the first time what that meant. A life without her inside of it, without people she loved.

Hazel moved closer to the nurses, but they barely noticed her. They were puckered together in a circle. The nurse named Imogene was crying and the quiet one, Maeve, had her arm around Imogene. "It's all right."

Imogene lifted her face to Maeve and shook her head. "You didn't see it, Maeve. You weren't there. They assigned me a shift at St. Hugh's and there was a soldier, and I swear he was no more than nineteen years old, and the whole left side of his skull was missing; I could see his . . . the inside of his head. I couldn't do anything to save him."

"I know." Maeve handed Imogene a cup of wine and Imogene drank it in three big gulps.

Hazel let out a small cry; it sounded too horrid to be true.

The nurses turned at her sound and Imogene held out her hand. "I'm so sorry, dear one. You weren't meant to hear that. You are here to be protected. I'm so sorry."

Hazel ran off to Bridie and Flora, warming herself by the fire and swearing to never tell Flora what she'd heard. This was the horror they were hiding from, but it was out there, dark and sinister.

Later, when the warmth of wine and fire had filled Imogene, Hazel watched her take Flora by the hand, dancing around and around until they collapsed on the cold ground, laughing.

"Do you think she's a witch?" Imogene asked Maeve, cradling her wine and nodding back at Bridie.

"And why ever would you say such a thing?" Maeve shook her head. "Bridie?"

"Well, isn't this a pagan ritual? And I heard she never goes to the church." Imogene's lips were blue with the cold and Hazel thought if anyone was a witch, it was her for saying such things.

"This isn't pagan," Lilly said, gently. "It's *Saint* Brigid, isn't it?"

"Not to her," Frances whispered, but loud enough for Hazel to hear. "To her"—she waved her hand toward Bridie, who was showing a young boy how to fold the rushes to make a cross. "To her Brigid is a goddess."

Hazel didn't want to hear any more of this; she wanted to scream at them, "She is the best of us all!"

*Pagan.*

How could anyone believe anything of Bridie but goodness and love?

There was a pop of fire and a hiss, and they all glanced up to see that the fat clouds above had gathered into a low ceiling of gray, rendering the afternoon sun weak and pale. Those clouds released fat flakes of snow that dropped lazily in swirls, first landing alone, then gathering and turning the ground white.

"We must head home," Mr. Nolan finally said.

"Indeed," Father Fenelly said, with such sadness soaked into it that Hazel wondered if the word meant something different than she'd thought it did.

"So much for coming spring," Frances said, her voice cold as the ground Hazel sat upon.

Imogene placed her arm over Frances's shoulder. "Just try to have a bit of fun."

Frances shook her head. "It's dangerous playing around with things as this."

Bridie spoke with a laugh. "You can barely tell the season is changing, but it is," she said. "Energy comes in subtly and then all of a sudden there will be a shift. It can feel like we are stuck in winter but we aren't. Brigid's archetype is the alchemist."

"See?" Frances said to Imogene. "Wicked. Unchristian."

Bridie smiled and moved away, nearing the fire and Mr. Nolan, who never shied away from her and her beautiful stories. Everyone gathered for last goodbyes as Bridie thanked those who had come and raised her voice to everyone. "As well as you are now, may you be seven times better this time next year."

Everyone raised their mug and cheered. Father Fenelly held up his right hand and said, "In darkness and in light, in trouble and in joy, help us, Heavenly Father, to trust your love, to serve your purpose, and to praise your name, through Jesus Christ our Lord."

Hazel thought of how Bridie should have lifted her hand with her proclamation. Why did only the men in the black coats get to do such things?

The crowd slowly left, with kisses on red cheeks and hollers across the wide pasture. Flora had fallen asleep in Imogene's arms and Harry jostled her awake.

"Harry?" Flora asked, wobbly with sleep. "Is magic real?"

"Yes, it is." He held out his hand to take her inside.

Bridie's face broke into the widest smile; her son had given the same answer she would have given. Bridie kissed her son and Flora, issuing instructions that Flora brush her teeth before getting tucked into bed. Hazel watched Bridie's every expression and word, as if she might learn the secrets of being a woman like her.

While gathering the wool blankets, Hazel told her, "They call you a pagan."

Bridie laughed. "Who, my dear?"

"Imogene and Frances."

Bridie poked at the fire with a long, gnarled branch, covering the blinking eyes of the dying embers with soil. "Oh, my sweet Hazel, I consider that the finest of all compliments. A pagan," Bridie said, "is nothing more than someone who still believes in the very animation of nature and uses the old stories to build new ones." She turned to Hazel. "Don't let others take away good stories so they can feel better about themselves."

"Okay," Hazel said, thinking of Whisperwood and the kind queen. "Can we make our own pagan stories?"

Bridie set the blankets on the cart and came to Hazel, taking her in her arms, holding her so close that Hazel was warmed by her. "Telling stories is one of the greatest powers we possess. It's like a dream you can fill with what you want. And the knight doesn't always have to save the princess; sometimes she saves herself."

Hazel nodded, her heart lifting for whatever Bridie was to say, for she knew it was important.

"The best stories are soul-making. But stories we tell about ourselves, and even the harrowing ones told by others about us, can also be soul-destroying. We have to choose what is good and true, not what will destroy."

"Yes," Hazel said.

"Now, let's go inside," said Bridie, "and make sure Harry has tucked Flora into bed and isn't doing that lion puzzle for the hundredth time."

Hazel folded the last plaid wool blanket, set it in the rolling cart, and walked back to the house with Bridie under a low and dark sky. Bridie opened the door to the house and Hazel entered, a warmth settling deep inside of her.

# CHAPTER 30

## March 1960

The St. Ives pub's honey-wood paneled walls glowed with the low lighting. A short woman with a wide smile played Irish jigs on the fiddle. Some of the crowd bellied to the bar while others danced on the wooden floors in the small area where tables had been pushed back. Kelty watched from the round table where they'd been sitting since a dinner of shepherd's pie. Kelty was laughing with Ethan.

Hazel was dizzy from dancing with Harry. He dipped and twisted, and she with him, her dress swirling about her. She needed air; she needed stable ground. She let go of his hand and ran out the door, the music and Harry following her.

"Are you all right?" he asked, catching up to her on the sidewalk outside.

"Fresh air?" she asked, and pointed down the street where the beach they'd walked that afternoon shimmered in moonlight, a block away.

He nodded and took her hand. Harry's hand in hers, knit together, was natural yet overwhelming. Whiskey in her veins, night surrounding them, they reached the beach and stood at the edge at high tide. The lighthouse light swept across the sand and his face.

There was nothing but this—Harry, stars above, sand below, and desire. But she could have none of it, and she let go of his hand, backed away as he watched her. She reminded herself it was just old feelings rising, nothing real.

The lighthouse shine swept past them again, illuminating his face. "Hazel . . . are you all right?"

With the utterance of her name, she came back to herself, awoke from the dream of being with him. It was wrong. If she let him touch her, it would destroy her. It would drown Flora again.

"Being alone with you," she said. "It's dangerous."

"How is it dangerous?" he asked. "We are just standing on a beach . . ."

"But are we? What are we doing, Harry? You have a girl; I have Barnaby and to feel this way . . . it ruins things."

"What will it ruin?" he asked.

"My life," she said, knowing it made no sense and also knowing it was true.

"Then, Hazel, just stay here with me for a little while. Don't leave. I promise we won't ruin anything."

———

"My head." Kelty's voice echoed through the inn's room, waking Hazel from a fitful sleep. The red plaid curtains were open, and morning appeared in lemony light.

Hazel sat and looked at Kelty in the next bed. "I get it."

But Hazel's hangover was of a different sort. Hers was one of the heart. She'd said too much; laughed too much; opened up too much. She'd come for a single answer and ended in a pub with Ethan, Harry, and Kelty singing silly ditties with the band, then sitting on the beach with Harry as the moon rolled up and the stars pierced a dark sky one by one.

She and Harry had stayed on the beach for hours, telling stories of their lives over the past twenty years. Not all of it, of course. There wasn't time for that. For one night, the past had faded away instead of lurking in the corner. Last night's hours with Harry were a time Hazel knew she couldn't have again. One night had to be enough. There was no way to change what happened and now their lives were on separate trajectories. They had other obligations, jobs, loves, and families. She'd come here to find out if he knew about Whisperwood, and he hadn't.

"We need to go home," Hazel said.

"But we told them we'd stop by and see their paintings and sculptures today." Kelty stretched. "Fergus said not to rush back, so we needn't hurry on account of me." Kelty swung her legs over the side of the bed and ran her hands through her hair, pulling at the tangles. "Didn't it feel like no time had passed at all? I know you felt the same—like we still knew them."

"No. I felt like a million years had passed." Hazel stood. "Listen, I got what I came for. We need to go."

As Hazel walked toward the bathroom, Kelty called out, "Did you even think about Barnaby last night? Did you miss him at all?"

Hazel spun around and looked at her friend. "Yes, of course I did," she said. "And we have to go." And yet, the truth was she had thought about Barnaby, but only with guilt because if he'd seen her on the beach with Harry, if he'd seen them on the sand talking until the moon sailed across the night and the stars blanketed the sky, he would have been both hurt and angry. But she'd done nothing wrong.

Kelty flopped back on the pillow. "Fantastic, now I can be both car-sick and hungover. Jolly good."

They were in the car soon after the early morning tea and croissants had been put out in the inn restaurant. They'd put tea in their thermos and biscuits in their purses. Outside, as they tossed their bags into the boot of the car, Kelty paused to stare at the sea, the boats bobbing on the water and the fishermen pushing to sea with their nets flung out, and their caps low on their heads, hollering words lost in the breeze.

The road wound through the countryside as they retraced the route they'd taken only the day before. "I can see why they want to live here," Kelty said. "It's extraordinary. I can't paint a straight line and this light and this place make me want to be an artist."

Hazel nodded. She agreed, but everything was coming at her too fast. It was two hours before Kelty gently said, "Tell me what Harry said."

This was the crux of it all, and Kelty had waited long enough.

"He never knew the story or the name of the land."

Kelty let out a whoosh of air. "How do you feel about that?"

"I feel everything, Kelty. Everything all at once."

"Then what's next?" Kelty asked.

"I don't know . . ." She fought tears of hopelessness as she stared out the windshield to see a blurry view of the velvet-nosed cows at the fence's edges, the lazy sheep dotting the fields like gardenia blooms, and the road winding back to Bloomsbury.

———

"He was never suspected of foul play," Hazel said, fire in her words.

Barnaby paced Hazel's living room. He poured another finger of whiskey in his glass, and he rolled it between his palms. It was late, and he'd just returned from an outing with his cousin in town from Winchester. He was already well into his drink when he poured himself another. "Yes, Hazel. Harry Aberdeen was a suspect. I read it in the newspapers you left out on the kitchen table. He and his crazy mum. And there's never been a father? She made him disappear?"

"It's not like that, Barnaby." She was tired to death of explaining how things weren't the way they looked.

"Like what? It wasn't like what?"

"It's not how you're making it sound. Like they were suspects or had the ability to make people disappear. Stop."

Barnaby had arrived at her flat late that night after she'd returned from St. Ives. She'd been awake on the couch reading Peggy Andrews's *Whisperwood* one more time, hoping to find a hint, a clue, a hidden phrase that might lead her to the truth. She'd forced the thoughts of Harry far from her mind but he returned again and again.

Barnaby now stepped closer. It was possible his anger had little to do with her being gone for two days and more to do with being able to see right through her.

"Hazel, you've never lied to me. So tell me the truth. Have you seen Harry since the day you left Binsey twenty years ago? Until you went to St. Ives with Kelty yesterday, had you *ever* seen him?"

"No."

He pointed to the hall table where Hazel usually placed the mail, and Hazel spied the letters she hadn't seen, the letters she'd left in the dusty corner of the trunk in the hall closet, the letters no longer wrapped in twine.

"You went through my things?" Her voice rose with each word.

"The trunk was open. It was open with all the articles and photos. I didn't break into it or even go looking. It was right there."

"Barnaby, I can explain, of course."

He lifted one letter and then tossed it back onto the pile. "These are the melancholy letters of two people in love. It's not hard to read between the lines."

"They are old, and I never saw him again." She held her hands in surrender. "And obviously I haven't looked at those in years and years."

"But you saved them. Tell me, do you still love him?"

Hazel thought about the truth and what it might mean to them both, about the honesty it would take to get to the other side. "Yes, and I always will. But not like that, not like us. It was childhood. And it was over the day Flora disappeared."

"No." Barnaby pointed at the letters with his lit cigarette. "It wasn't over. For God's sake, Hazel, he says life is more magical with you."

"Barnaby, I'm sorry you saw and read those old letters, but this quest I am on isn't about Harry."

"I love you so much, Hazel." His eyes softened. "And you're worrying me, becoming obsessed with that book. You're worrying me, running off to see an old love when a phone call would do perfectly fine, and believing your sister can rise from the dead like this . . ."

A surge rose through Hazel's body, electric and fiery. "Don't say that. Do *not* say she is dead. What is wrong with you?"

"Hazel, please calm down."

She nearly laughed but it came out as an indignant sound of disgust. "Calm down? Seriously?"

He lowered his voice, softer now. "I know this is the biggest wound of your past, and I am so sorry. I wish it had never happened to you, but you can't go chasing wild geese all over England and America, looking for your own fairy tale."

"I already found a fairy tale, Barnaby. It's in a book written by an American author. I am looking for the *truth*: How did this author know this story and is Flora still—"

"All right. If it's important to you, it's important to me. To lose a child is . . . beyond awful."

"I'm so sorry, Barnaby." She touched his unshaven cheeks. "We both lost someone."

Barnaby's baby daughter was gone, and he'd watched it happen. Hazel hadn't seen Flora leave the world, but their losses were entangled, and he could not imagine anything different for Hazel, could not imagine that her story might be altered by a book that she just happened upon.

# CHAPTER 31

## March 1960

Peggy Andrews couldn't sit alone with a telegram that said "Where did you find this story. It is life and death." Now it flapped in her hand as she ran toward Wren's house.

Wren answered the door and, after seeing her face, slipped on his worn blue corduroy jacket and cupped his hand under her elbow as he led her toward the beach. Their feet slipped in the sand. She gave him the thin paper to read.

"What's happening, Pegs?"

"I don't know what to think or believe. Isn't this nuts? Do you think she's insane?"

"Hard to accurately diagnose psychosis from a telegram." He grinned, and she punched his arm. "But let me ask you this—why are these woman's questions so important to you?"

She stared at him as they stood on the far side of the sand dunes, mid-morning sun warm on their backs even as the breeze carried a coolness that made her shiver. "Do you know who Oscar Wilde is?"

"Yes. Of course. Irish poet. Playwright. *The Importance of Being Earnest.*"

She smiled at him. "Well, he once said that telling 'beautiful untrue things' was the aim of art. I like that a lot."

"So do I," he said. "Beautiful untrue things. We all know when we read about Narnia or Middle Earth or Wonderland—we know it's not true but it's so beautiful, so damn beautiful that we believe it while we're there."

"And beautiful untrue things carry the truth," she said.

"He said that, too?"

"No," she said. "I say that. It feels like I am telling you—or not you, since you don't read such things—but I am telling the reader . . . I'm reporting back from an invisible land."

"And what's there?" he asks. "Tell me."

Peggy closed her eyes and saw her river of stars, her forest glade, and the dunce-hat towers against an inky sky with a crescent bowl of moon. "They are like dreams. In a fairy tale, words and curses and spells have power. There is magic. Everything is animated, from a grass blade to a talking owl, from a table carved of hazelwood to a fish that warns you not to drink the river water." She opened her eyes and looked at him, wanting him to understand. "Magic is the point of it all."

He nodded and reached up, touched her cheek. "You are something special."

"And my stories usually, but not always, have happy endings. Grimm's original fairy tales are quite awful, and that's why I sometimes have the girls run across an ancient fairy-tale character to alter their destiny."

"Well then, it's no wonder this woman wants her story back, or wants to know how you found it, wants to . . . find her sister."

"But that's the thing, it seems her sister is gone. But the story somehow ended up with my aunt and mother. How is that *my* problem?"

"It's not your problem one bit. But I also think—and don't be mad at me, I know your mother already despises me—but maybe it's a gift to send you on a greater adventure."

"What's that supposed to mean?"

"For a smart girl, sometimes you are very obtuse."

Peggy felt the flicker of anger rise. He was smiling, not accusing. "What do you mean?"

"Maybe this inside world of yours is now sending you on adventures in the real world. A quest, to find out where it came from, to help this woman in England settle her own story."

"I don't follow." She regretted telling him now, his answers were impossible. "What are you saying, Wren?"

"We go to England, Pegs. We go to London and find this woman and talk to her and try to help her. Instead of having adventures in your pages, let's have one in the world. Me and you."

"To England?"

"Yes, to London. I've been and I'll take you. You won't believe the beauty of it."

"I can't . . ."

"You can." He paused. "Do you have a passport?"

She nodded. "Yes, from that trip to Canada my senior year."

He took her hands.

Peggy had, since the first time he'd touched her arm in a game of tag in fifth grade, wanted him to touch her again. She'd been with two other boys in college, fumbling in the dark, sloppy and unsatisfying endeavors. But now, here, she knew it could be otherwise. She didn't know what to do next.

She wrote adventures. Could she have them?

"Do you want to find out where this story came from? Or do you want to stay stuck here, always believing what you're told?"

She stepped toward him. They were so close that if he chose, and she hoped he would, he could tilt his head an inch and they'd kiss.

"Peggy Maria Andrews!" Mother's voice cut through the breeze.

Peggy spun around to see Mother stalking toward them, her black coat flapping behind her like the wings of a giant crow.

"And the witch returns to take the princess back to her tower," Wren said with a bitter tone.

"Wren—" Peggy said.

"It's true." He shoved the telegram into his back pocket, hidden away.

Before Mother reached them, he leaned close, his lips touching her ear. "Whisperwood. Whisperwood. Whisperwood," he chanted her incantation. "Meet me here at midnight. Bring a packed bag; we're going on a quest."

Mother arrived at their sides. "Whatever are you doing?" she asked.

"Lovely to see you, too, Mrs. Andrews," Wren said, taking a step away from them both. "Pegs, I'll bid you adieu." He bowed in an exaggerated move.

Mother stepped toward him, and he backed up. She said, "Her name is Peggy."

"Mother, stop it," Peggy said, a flame of anger filling the middle of her belly. "What's wrong with you?"

"Did you know he's been arrested?" She lifted her chin to Wren. "That he has a police record? That he was almost kicked out of Harvard?"

Peggy turned to Wren, who looked as if Mother had just slapped him. "It's all true," he said, "but it's not like you think."

Mother spat out her words: "What a ridiculous thing to say."

Wren looked to Peggy, and she saw pain in his eyes, not defensiveness, not a fight to prove himself right, but shame. She wanted to throw her arms about him, pull him close, soothe him. But she'd bide her time.

He must have read her eyes for he smiled and departed, his shadow following him, elongated.

Peggy spun around to her mother. "You are so cruel sometimes."

"I am only protecting you."

"Mother, I don't need protecting." For the first time in her life, Peggy turned her back on her mother and walked home.

Peggy felt the pages of her life flipping forward, faster than she'd imagined they could, and moving toward something dangerous or wonderful, she didn't know, she couldn't know, but something was afoot in a fairy-tale way.

The beach at midnight with a suitcase.

———

Peggy barely ate the bland dinner of spaghetti with sauce from a can. She didn't rise like the good girl she was every single night to wash the dishes while Mother read the pages aloud. Instead Peggy placed her elbows on the table, forbidden, of course, and said, "Could Whisperwood have belonged to someone else before us?"

Mother's voice softened, singsong but tired. "It's ours. It doesn't matter so much how it started, only that we made it fully our own."

"Mother, it matters to me how it started. Now tell me who made the land's name? Who called it Whisperwood?"

"Why all these questions? What *is* going on with you?" Mother rose from the table, and in slow motion she reached into the pocket of her dress, a ballooning of the checkered fabric. She pulled out the crumpled phone number Peggy thought had remained hidden below her mattress. "Could this be why you're asking?"

Peggy stared at the piece of paper, then looked to her mother. "Yes, that's why. Why is this woman claiming this story as her own?"

Mother smiled at the admission and softened just enough to speak without a bitter voice. "Oh, darling girl, I've warned you about crazy people, about those who will try to take what's yours and steal that which is wonderful and true. Like the Lindbergh baby who—"

"Stop with that already. I want to know why this woman called me." Should she tell her mother about the telegram? No, she would not tell her mother about the missing sister or the telegram, at least not until she decided whether to meet Wren at midnight.

Peggy stood and went to her mother. "I know it is our story, but if this woman has questions, why not answer them?"

"No. We ignore this insanity and continue the next book—which has a looming deadline, as if I need to remind you. If this story belonged to this woman, why doesn't she have this book out in the world for others to read? If it belonged to her, why would she hide it?"

These were good questions. She had no answers, not yet, but she planned on finding them.

———

There had been no need to set her bedside alarm for 11:45 p.m. Peggy was wide awake. After years of writing adventures, she was ready for her own. Especially with Wren. She was tired to death of dreaming and imagining and making things up. She wanted to do more than write about journeys—she wanted to have one.

She pulled her small circular suitcase, the one with the orange and green daisies on it, from beneath her bed. She wished for a more grown-up bag, but this was all she owned; she and Mother never traveled.

In the dark, she folded the silk matching sets of underwear Mother had bought at J.C. Penney for Christmas last year, two flowered dresses she wore for special occasions, a pair of dark blue trousers, and a cashmere blue sweater, still in its box.

As in a dream, she tiptoed down the hallway and out the back door, finding herself on the beach walk, feeling as if she had not merely left her own home, but had walked through a shimmering door.

# CHAPTER 32

## March 1960

Framed artwork, sketches, oils, and photography hung on the white walls of the Lamplighter, a Hampstead studio on the high street. Hampstead Heath was one of Hazel's favorite areas in London. Its subtle charm was made of narrowed cobbled alleys, bright yellow and pale blue doors shaded by crawling vines, hedges hiding verdant gardens, old stone stairs leading to pubs and homes. Tiny churches were hidden here and there. It was Barnaby's childhood neighborhood.

The party had been swinging for an hour now, and the room was loud with chatter, not a single word rising above the rest. A man wearing all black played music from a phonograph in the back of the room. The crowd wore their artsy best clothing. Replacing postwar dreary were bright dresses on the women who held martinis with floating olives and lipstick-smeared rims.

A white table perched catty-corner to the left of the front door, and a young woman stood behind it, pouring wine and tossing a shaker to make drinks for those waiting. Hazel ordered a glass of chardonnay. She cradled the lukewarm wine in her hands and moved to the art hanging on the wall.

There, in a silver frame, surrounded by a mat of dark charcoal, was a pencil sketch of a young girl running through the woods. Her curls shone and her arms were akimbo with movement. If a piece of art could laugh, this one would do so. The full-leafed trees bowed over her as if to protect her, and in the distance, a river.

The glass, with only a sip gone, fell to the floor and shattered, the sound a mere tinkling beneath the roar of conversation and music, not even loud enough to cause too many people to turn.

Below the sketch a small framed square label: *Flora in the woodlands.*

The young woman behind the bar rushed out with white towels and cleaned the spilled wine before Hazel could fully register what she'd done. Hazel looked down at the woman squatting in her minidress, wiping up the liquid on the hardwood floors.

"I'm sorry," Hazel said, leaning down to help. "How clumsy of me."

"Happens every night, ma'am. Do not worry one bit. Would you like another?"

"Yes, please."

Hazel stood again and let her eyes wander to the next framed sketch: A well—St. Margaret's well, to be exact. The next was of the parish church, then a river with a bridge that reached into the mist.

Harry's art mirrored her unconscious. Her nightmares. Her hidden secrets. All was here, plain as day, with brass lights hung over them to illuminate the truth: The past was alive and well in both of them.

With a new drink in her hand, Hazel walked further into the room to a profile in simple sketch, a face she knew well, a rendering of an innocence and a simple joy. A face she saw in the mirror.

Her own.

"Hazel." Kelty was at her side and kissed her friend's cheek. "You made it!"

"Auntie Hazel." Midge came running full speed, slamming into Hazel and wrapping her arms around Hazel's waist. She lifted her face.

"My girl," Hazel said, and kissed Midge's forehead, tearing her gaze from the lines and curves of her own childhood face.

Kelty then saw the drawings. "Oh!"

"His art," Hazel said. "Some of it is about us."

"Maybe he wanted to surprise you?"

"Surprise me? With drawings of Flora in the woodlands?"

Midge stomped her foot. "Stop talking about things I don't know."

They both laughed. "Go find your daddy," Kelty said, and pointed across the room. "We'll join you in a minute."

"I hate grown-up conversations," Midge said, and ran off.

"Both of you," Kelty said. "Have this thing—this wound—this old devastation. You can't pretend it's not there. Yours comes *out* in some ways. And his in art. Or so it seems."

"You analyzing us on this very spot?"

"No. I am telling you not to wig out." Kelty moved closer to the charcoal portrait. "Looks like you aren't the only one who thinks about the one who got away."

"Stop with that." Hazel turned away from the sketch of her. "When he slipped drawings under the door every morning, they were never of me, always of the day or the fields or his mum or Flora, and once you. But never of me."

"Looks like he saved those."

"Do you like them?" Hazel turned to see Harry, his fingers brushing through his hair.

"I do. It's just taking me a minute to . . . I don't know . . . absorb this."

He cleared his throat. "Hazel, I've thought a million times about what you would say or do if you saw these. And look at us." He tried to laugh but it sounded more like a cough, a sputter. "Here we are."

"Yes."

Kelty slipped away.

"They really are beautiful," Hazel said, gripping her drink so tightly she was surprised the glass didn't shatter. How many glasses could she break in one night? "The one of Flora is lovely."

"On that wall"—he pointed across the room—"there are some of St. Ives and boats and landscapes. Not everything is . . ."

"About that terrible time." She reached out and touched his arm, clad in a dark shirt. He stood so still, as if waiting for what else she might touch.

"Don't let it frighten you. They're from memory. They aren't from those days. I drew them over the years."

"Why?"

"When I can't shake something, I draw. I paint. I sketch. I let it out."

"Like I once did with stories." She stared again at the extraordinary art. "But you kept going and I quit."

He nodded his head toward the door. "It's bloody loud in here. Outside?"

She followed him.

Outside on the high street, he faced her, rubbing his hands up and down his arms to warm himself in the night's chill. Rising and falling voices fell through the doorway onto the street, a river of sound, and they stepped to the right of the door where it was quieter.

"I wonder if you know . . . ," he said.

"Know what?"

"Your mum never let us near you during that horrible time. We tried to visit you in Oxford. I came alone to try to find you, and Mum had to come get me and bring me home. We didn't desert you. I was always afraid you thought so."

"I didn't think that. I thought you . . . hated me." A nightingale sang out, sang out, high and clear. Together they cocked their heads toward the sound and then Harry took her hand and ran his thumb along her wrist.

"I could never hate you."

His hand on hers in the woodlands; his hand on hers here and now. "But why all the drawings of that horrible time, Harry?"

"Much of it was *not* horrible, and sometimes life breaks your heart to give you the best art. I don't know why that's true, but that's as true as anything I know. If you let it be, anyway."

"I assumed you forgot about me," she said, knowing it was impossible but wanting to hear why it was not.

"It's not that I forgot you, Hazel. It's that I *needed* to forget you. You didn't answer my last letter when I asked to see you. What was I meant to do? Track you down? Run after you?"

"Yes," she said with a smile.

He shook his head and laughed. "No. If you don't remember, in Binsey, you told me you never wanted to see me again."

"I was fifteen years old and in complete shock. How could you take that seriously?"

"I always took you seriously." He paused as if he could remember that morning, that cursed morning when she'd said those very words to him. *I never, ever want to see you again.* "It was your mum, too. She told my mum to make sure I stayed away."

"She was trying to protect me, I assume," Hazel said. "And in doing so, she kept me from what I loved the most."

He grinned, sly and sweet. "Ah, so you loved me."

She thought to laugh it off, but what did it matter now? "Yes, I did."

He looked near to tears and yet he said the sweetest words in a steady voice. "So did I," he said. "I loved you, too, Hazel."

"We were lucky," she told him, "to have each other as a first love. We were lucky until we weren't."

He stepped closer and dropped his forehead to hers.

She was silent, waiting.

"You are the first girl I ever loved. I didn't know what it was then, but now I do." He kept on. "I forever regret listening to my mum or yours. I should have found you. I was a coward. I know it changes nothing today but it is true all the same."

His words released something in her, something held as tight as a boxer's fist when the starting bell rang. She let go. "Harry, I was sick with that love. I felt guilty for missing you when Flora was truly gone."

He lifted his forehead and looked at her, a kiss so near.

"Hazel?" Hazel spun around to see Barnaby's mother, Eleanor, and his father, Meldon, standing ten feet away. Eleanor wore a champagne-colored dress that fit so well it might have been sewn onto her, and her silver hair was in a tight chignon. Meldon had his hands stuffed deep in the pockets of his long black coat.

Hazel and Harry separated, no easy task when Hazel's body was moving for something different. Her face prickled with adrenaline. Her tongue felt thick with excuses and lies.

"So lovely to see you! Whatever are you doing here?" She was stunned by her calm voice as her heart rose into her throat.

She'd been caught.

Eleanor stared at Harry, her lips hard and straight. "We're here for the art show. And you?"

"Aren't you the lucky ones then?" said Hazel. "This is Harry Aberdeen, one of the artists!" Her voice shook, but she did her best, holding steady. "Harry, meet Eleanor and Meldon Yardley."

Eleanor's face turned to stone and her eyes ice as she stared at Hazel. She'd seen her; she knew. "Where is my son?" she asked.

"He had a faculty dinner." Hazel felt she might be sick on the pavement. "We leave for Paris in a couple days."

"Oh, do you?" Eleanor looked up to Meldon, who stared at Harry.

What had she been thinking? She was immature, foolish, and impulsive. Now she would pay.

Meldon looped his arm through Eleanor's and turned her around, so she nearly tripped in her dainty high heels. Moving in the opposite direction of the art gallery, back down the street from where they'd come, with Eleanor crying out, "Meldon, darling . . . the art show!"

Harry watched them and turned back to Hazel, his hand over his stomach on his pale gray sweater. "Who are they?"

"Barnaby . . . my boyfriend Barnaby's parents. He's one of the most famous art and artifact collectors in England."

Harry nodded. "They seem none too pleased."

"I am sure they're not." Hazel stared after Barnaby's parents, whom she was quite sure were on their way to call their son.

# CHAPTER 33

## March 1960

Hazel's flat lights were off and once inside she removed her raincoat and shook out the umbrella before closing the front door. Small puddles formed on the entryway rug, and Hazel shivered in her damp dress. Stalking through the flat, she flicked on every lamp.

But in the kitchen, a low light already burned, a shadow form leaning against the counter with a lit cigarette glowing.

She let out a small yelp, then, "Barnaby, you scared the wits out of me, lurking in the darkness." She turned on the side lamp, and he squinted. He walked slowly toward her.

"Hazel, honey, where have you been?"

"I told you, an art show in Hampstead with Kelty and Fergus. Midge, too."

"My mother called me."

"Yes." Hazel tried to hold calm, not give away a thing.

"Who were you with, Hazel?"

"This isn't like you, Barnaby. Quizzing me like I did something wrong."

He smashed his cigarette into the ashtray although it was only half-smoked. "You were with the boy from Binsey."

"Yes, Harry Aberdeen was one of the artists." She would hold on to truth as long as she could. But she would not let a stupid mistake—to fall into her childish desires for Harry—ruin the life she had made with Barnaby.

"Do you love the man you stood on the sidewalk with tonight?" Barnaby asked. "Looking like you were lovers, according to my mother."

"That's ridiculous."

He leaned forward. "They also asked about the stolen book and illustrations."

"Stolen? You damn well know I didn't steal them . . . it was . . ."

"A mistake. I know."

"Wait, how the bloody hell do they know about that? You told them?" Her mouth went dry, arid.

"No. I didn't tell them." His voice was fading with fatigue. "My father helped you with that job at Sotheby's, and they called him."

Hazel heard what Barnaby said. The words were clear and yet she was baffled. She opened her mouth to speak and then shook her head.

"Are you all right?" he asked.

"No. I'm . . . confused?" A crack appeared, sure and jagged, beneath Hazel's understanding of her life. "Your *father* helped me with that job? What are you talking about? I earned that job."

"He made a few calls. That's all."

"So many calls that they felt they had to tell him about Hogan's and the illustrations?"

"Yes, I suppose so. And Mother, overreacting as usual, saying you had betrayed us." He fished another cigarette from his pocket and stuck it between his lips without lighting it.

"I'm betraying all of you?"

Hazel put her fingers to her temples, massaged. She couldn't answer his questions, for she had too many of her own. "Barnaby, Harry and I are not lovers."

"Hazel, my love, we leave for Paris in two days. If there is anything you need to tell me, please tell me now."

"Barnaby, I went to an art show with Kelty and as I stood outside talking to Harry, I ran into your parents on the street. Your mother misconstrued what she saw. I love you. We leave for Paris in two days. That's all I know to tell you."

He stared while weighing her words, her past, and their future. Then he pulled her toward him and kissed her. Hazel felt as if she were watching herself being kissed, as if she stood outside the window peeking in on two lovers she didn't know.

———

Barnaby snored on, and Hazel glanced at the clock: six a.m. She couldn't sleep so she might as well rise. Slipping from bed, she went into the kitchen to boil water for tea. She needed to get her feet under her, to find her way back into the real world.

On her way through the living room, her gaze landed on the new *Vanity Fair* magazine that Barnaby had taken out of the trash and tossed onto the side table. She picked it up and stared at the text on the cover again. *The Lost Children of Pied Piper* by Dorothy Bellamy.

Maybe Hazel was wrong. Maybe the journalist could help. It was entirely possible that Dorothy Bellamy had sources Hazel didn't have. She took the magazine to the kitchen and after making tea, she sat at the table and read. Bellamy's article told of a young girl from Hillingdon, a member of the Mickey Mouse Club, on her way to Canada during the evacuation to live with her cousins. But poor Beryl Myatt had died at age nine when the ship she was on had been bombed on September 17, 1940. Ninety children evacuees were on board, and seventy-seven perished.

Hazel's heart rolled. She couldn't read another word. So much heartache. Children sent from home to be safe, only to then be lost.

She could not allow Flora to be one more of Dorothy Bellamy's melodramatic stories, something for a "*younger, smarter woman*" to read about in horror. She again tossed the magazine into the bin and looked to the untouched mail on the table. She sipped her tea and shuffled through the bills until she saw the letterhead of the Thames Valley Oxford Police Department.

She ripped open the envelope and read the names of the four nurses in a typed line; their names dented the paper and every "e" was crooked. A note paperclipped to the list was in Aiden's block handwriting.

*In September of 1940, they were all interviewed and easily cleared of suspicion of foul play related to Flora.*

*Imogene Wright, now Mulroney, in Henley-on-Thames. She is married with one daughter named Iris Taber, also of Henley-on-Thames.*

*Frances Arkwright passed away a year after the war.*

*Maeve Muldoon is married with six children and lives in Glasgow.*

*Lilly Carnigan is a spinster and lives in Birmingham.*

*Sincerely,*
*Aiden*

Attached were their addresses and phone numbers. Hazel's heartbeat raced.

"What's that?" Barnaby's voice surprised her, and she dropped the letter. It fluttered to the floor, where he picked it up.

"Good morning," she said, kissing his rough cheek. "Did you sleep all right?"

"Good morning, love." He squinted at the note. "What's this about?"

"The four nurses from Binsey. Remember I told you I visited Aiden, that police inspector I know?"

He looked at her, his eyes shaded. "You will never let this go, will you? For your whole life you will endlessly chase this loss."

"That's unfair, Barnaby. How could anyone *not* pursue this?"

He set the note on the table and readied to leave. "I have morning office hours. Must head out."

"This early?" So much doubt now between them. And he looked hurt by the question.

"Yes, I have to go, love." He kissed her. "See you tonight."

"Barnaby—" she said as he walked out.

He looked over his shoulder, but he was already moving away. "Yes?"

"I love you," she said. She didn't know how to make this better. Or anything else, for that matter.

"I love you, too." But his response rang hollow as the door opened and shut.

*Imogene's daughter.*

*An only child.*

*Iris.*

# CHAPTER 34

### February 1940

It was after the Imbolc that Hazel started writing down the Whisperwood stories in school notebooks. She hid them in the bottom dresser drawer beneath folded shirts and pants, beneath a silk drawer liner Bridie had sewn for them. They nestled right next to the daily sketches from Harry.

Even though Imbolc was to be the start of spring, winter had its last say that late February. A snowstorm raged for two days, covering the land in a veil of white that shut them in the house with a roaring fire, their schoolwork, and piles of books. They would go outside to play in the snow and return with numb toes or fingers, then warm themselves by the fire as feeling returned with electric tingles. Bridie made steaming cocoa and they all wished for sugar to sweeten it.

All the while, Hazel kept writing.

*If you were born knowing, and to be honest we all are, you will know how to find your way through the woodlands to the shimmering doors that are meant for you. They lead to the land made for you.*

It became her routine every night to add to these stories in their tiny bedroom off the kitchen. With Bridie's wireless music playing low, Flora closed her eyes to sleep as Hazel scribbled in notebooks until she couldn't keep her own eyes from fluttering shut. She wrote of the day's activities, yet it was more than a list; she added magical elements, as if Whisperwood had ceased being imaginary and entered their world. That owl slipped from the bonds of the imaginary and watched them at the riverside with Harry. These worlds braided together as she wrote and months passed.

On the twentieth of May, Flora and Hazel raced to the meadow and found it transformed into a noisy, chaotic land of bell-shaped tents and soldiers. Terrified that the evil man had arrived in Oxford, they ran home to Bridie, who explained they needed to stay clear—it was an operation to help the British Expeditionary Force and allied troops who'd been saved from a French seaport called Dunkirk; the men gathered there had been rescued. They were Belgian and French and British and had been brought here before being sent to their next assignment.

The morning after the soldiers' arrival, Harry, Flora, and Hazel ran out the door just after breakfast. The morning sun rose across a silver sky as Bridie headed into town on errands. Flora was waddling, imitating a mama duck leading her ducklings to the river. Harry laughed and picked her up to swing her around just as they reached the river's edge.

At the same time, they all saw the men and encampment. They stopped perfectly still to gaze across the river to the tents perched on the green carpet of Port Meadow's pasture. Men in British Expeditionary Troop uniforms—brown as earth and green as olives, buttons and bars and medals pinned on the fabric—were marching into the area. Others walked around, looking dazed, as if they'd just woken.

"They're from Dunkirk," Harry said in a low voice, as if it were a secret, which it wasn't. Hazel had read all about it in the *Oxford Mail,* and Bridie had already explained. But Hazel let Harry go on, allowing him to feel smart. "They were evacuated because Hitler invaded France and we had to get them *all* out of there."

We, he'd said. By "we," he'd meant Britain, and he was proud.

"When I can, I will join them," he added.

Hazel faced Harry. "No, you will not."

"Of course I will," he said in a louder voice, as if trying to convince himself. "I only have three more years, and I can join. I'd go now, but Mum would rat me out for lying about my age."

"Don't do it," Hazel said, thinking of her papa and the day of his leaving. She looked away from Harry, for fear she'd cry at the very idea of him leaving and never returning.

A mist hung over the meadow, rising from the flowing river like a ghost. The pinnacles of an Oxford church loomed in the distance watching over the rescued people. Flora held to Berry, and Hazel sidled closer to Harry, an instinct that grew every day. "You cannot go where you might be killed. Your mum wouldn't bear it."

Harry moved just enough to meet her gaze and she saw the question—could you bear it? But she wouldn't answer the unasked question, not even with her eyes.

"Hazel?" Flora pulled at the edges of Hazel's flowered dress, the one that had just in the past month become at least an inch shorter.

Hazel crouched down. "Yes?"

"Is Papa over there?"

Hazel understood Flora's confusion. The last time Flora had seen her papa, he'd been wearing one of those uniforms. A sob grew in Hazel's throat and she swallowed it. "No. He's gone, Flora. You know that."

"How do you know?" Flora swatted at Hazel, hitting her thigh with a helpless cry. "He could be there right now. Maybe he didn't die. Maybe he's one of them . . ." She pointed across the river and broke free, running toward the water.

Hazel chased her sister and caught her by the arm before she reached the soft, muddy edge. Startled, ducks and geese launched into the river, and an early morning rower floated by in a punt. "Flora. Stop it now."

"I want to find Papa. I want to find him. I want . . ." She buried her face in Hazel's dress. "We have to find him."

"Oh, Flora." Hazel dropped to the grass, feeling the mud seep into the thin fabric of her dress, staining her bum.

The sight of the bewildered and bedraggled soldiers, their uniforms torn, rust-stained bandages evident on arms and faces, made the war very real. It made Papa's loss very real.

Hazel felt it; she'd gone too far with her imaginary land. Flora had lost track of what was real and what was not. She was doing her sister no good with these fairy tales.

"Please just go over there and look," said Flora.

Hazel took Flora in her arms and then Harry was there, sitting right beside them on the muddy soft grass, putting his arms around both of them.

Flora buried her face in Harry's neck. "Can you bring him back?"

Harry rested his head upon Flora's and looked to Hazel. They locked gazes over Flora's downy hair, and Hazel allowed her silent tears to fall. Harry wiped Hazel's cheek with one finger, a feather of a touch.

Then he reached down and from the ground plucked a ragwort flower; its downy yellow center and lemony petals were delicate. He pulled so hard the roots came out, white tendrils trickling dark soil. He broke off the stem and then tucked the flower behind Hazel's ear, Flora's face buried between them as she shook with her helpless crying. There was nothing for Hazel to do but what she did—she leaned forward and kissed Harry on the cheek. Or that's where she meant to kiss, but he turned and their lips met, softly and quickly.

"Children!" A woman's voice echoed across the meadow, caught in the morning mist.

Flora lifted her head so fast it cracked against Hazel's chin. They both cried out, and Flora broke free. Hazel touched her chin, felt warmth, and withdrew her hand to see a crescent of blood on her middle finger. Flora rubbed at her head, yet didn't cry.

They turned to see the approach of the four nurses—blue capes sailing behind them, white uniforms wrinkled and stained with the rust of iodine and the red of blood. Which one of them had called out, they weren't sure.

Frances reached them first. "What are you doing down here? Where's Bridie? Are you unattended?"

Harry stood, wiping his muddy hands across his brown pants. "We were watching the soldiers. Not doing anything wrong, ma'am. Flora's upset so we were . . ."

Frances's face pinched together as if something rancid and dank had crossed the river and she shook her head. "Looked to me like you were sneaking a little sugar over an innocent girl's head."

"No!" Hazel jumped up.

The other three women arrived at Frances's side, and they all stood at the river's edge. Their faces were drawn and exhausted. Bruised circles bloomed under their eyes. Beneath Maeve's chin, just below the soft space of her throat, a blotch of dried blood was in an oval crust. Hazel longed to reach out and clean it for her.

Flora stood, too, drawing Berry to her chest and looking from one nurse to the next. "Is my papa over there?" she asked.

Imogene, the one with the raven-dark hair who often babysat, answered, "No, darling."

"How do you know? Did you look for him?"

Imogene crouched, set her hands on her knees, then kissed the top of Flora's head. "He's not there, darling girl."

---

By summer the tents and men were gone. Awareness that war raged on again receded. Hazel and Flora ran through the woodlands, behind the stone church, past the nurses' cottage, and alongside the treacle well. They threw rocks into the river and watched them plunk, creating a dimpled dent that disappeared and scattered the ducks and swans. The days seemed suspended in time, endless and made for just their pleasure as they visited Whisperwood.

Bridie knitted thick socks for the soldiers, made pickled cucumbers and onions, and had the girls label the jars and store them in a cold cellar room. Bridie taught the girls to make rabbit and lamb pies, to roll out dough with just enough flour to make it flake in the oven. While other children had to tolerate long Sundays of formal clothes and stiff services, Flora, Hazel, and Harry hiked the woods with Bridie. They learned the difference between the rare lime green stonewort submerged just below the river's edge and the delicate violet. They found the meadow mushrooms growing in what were called fairy circles. Bridie taught them to watch for the green leafy hogweed that would burn their skin, and they discovered the difference between the call of a willow tit and a nightingale. Flora could name flowers like the ox-eye daisy, meadowsweet, and adder's-tongue fern.

It seemed impossible, or maybe unfair, that they lived this idyllic life while elsewhere bombs dropped and people died and soldiers arrived at hospitals, torn apart. The days were filled with innocent adventure. Hazel and Harry walked the dirt path along the river as far as they could go before they knew they'd have to turn around. They chased the cows in Port Meadow. In the summer, when Flora was with Imogene or with Bridie in town, they swam in the river. Every morning Hazel would look for Harry's sketch and wonder what they would all do together that day. Sometimes, she and Flora sat on the grass and watched Harry with the other Binsey boys play cricket with bats made of spare wood and balls that had seen better days. The boys teased Harry about living with two girls and he laughed it off, tossing Hazel and Flora a look of "what do they know?" Hazel was jealous when he ran off with the boys and didn't let her come with them.

When she thought of returning to London she couldn't see it in her imagination. She could imagine the entire land of Whisperwood and yet not see herself in a city that already existed. In London there were no wide open pastures and the river was choked with ships and litter. In London there were no daily sketches under the door and no schoolwork at a round table in the living room where a fire often blazed in the hearth. In London there was no Harry, and that felt impossible for now he was . . . what was he? Not a brother. No. A best friend? She didn't know and for now it didn't matter so much as long as she woke in the same house as him.

On the July day that Flora turned six, she and Hazel were in the woodlands. Sunlight flashed in bright swords through the canopy of summer-rich trees, along the dew-dimpled grass. They ran between thicketed oaks and alders until Flora pointed—Hazel always let her find the door—and exclaimed, "There it is!"

"I see it," Hazel said, and ran with Flora.

They'd found the shimmering door to Whisperwood so many times that Hazel could almost believe that they both saw the same door at the same time. She knew where Flora was pointing, where they would rush and enter, falling to the grass to close their eyes and take off on a new adventure. They'd slip into the riven tree's opening and whisper their incantation.

The ground was spongy with last night's rain. Hazel rested her hand next to Flora's and they pushed against the tree, feeling the sharp edges of its skin bite into their palms.

Once they slid into the hollow, Hazel began as she always did: "There was once and still is an invisible place that is right here with us. In the land of Whisperwood, we can become anything we desire to reach the castle that waits."

"Owls," Flora said.

She was losing her lisp, and somehow it made Hazel a bit sad, losing Flora's babyhood.

"Yes! Owls," Hazel said. "The starry river runs fast today, and the sun is bright. Look at the wild stags on the far side. They're looking at us!"

"*Hoot hooooot,*" Flora said.

They flew toward the castle, past fairies in bright blue and green surrounding them like rainbows, whispering words of encouragement, telling them of secret paths to the castle. "We're here," Flora said as she snuggled closer to Hazel. "See the gates?"

"I do," Hazel said. "Who will open them?"

"We will."

They flapped their owl wings until the gates opened, and they flew into the courtyard, heading to the throne room where the queen sat, as she always did. She was a beauty, fierce and wild, with red hair and a starry crown.

"Greetings," the queen said with glee. She enjoyed their visits, whatever form they took.

"I have a question," said Flora.

"Is everyone worthy?" Hazel asked.

"Yes, but not everyone knows they are, so they act as if they are not. They haven't discovered their own shimmering doors."

Flora laughed at Hazel using two voices.

Then another voice interrupted: Harry's, calling their names.

Immediately they returned to the real woodlands of Binsey, the sun casting longer shadows, a pattern of intricate lace.

They crawled out of the hollow, a smile at the ready.

"Happy birthday, Flora," Hazel said, hugging her sister.

"That was the best one yet," Flora said. "If we can be anything, maybe someday we can be the river."

Hazel stopped, crouched, and gently spoke. "If you turn into a river, you cannot come back to be here with me. Remember Harry said you can never go into the river."

"I don't want to come back," Flora said. "I love Whisperwood the best."

Hazel thought how to answer this, how to keep her sister safe. "If you stay there you can never see me or Harry or Bridie or Mum ever again. You don't want that."

Flora's lip quivered, and she buried her face in Hazel's dress.

Hazel didn't care if she'd scared her sister. She led her to where Harry stood at the edge of the wildflower field, gooseberries green and veined drooping over a stone wall next to him, Angus cattle plaintively mooing in a field beyond, and sunlight surrounding him like a cloud.

Harry wore his summer khaki-colored pants and a white linen short-sleeved shirt that Bridie had sewn new buttons on only last night. He spotted them coming and waved. "Mum says it's birthday party time, little girl. The cake is done, and your mum is almost here."

Flora broke into a full run, but Hazel held back. "I'll be right there," she called out. "You go on."

She wanted to walk back to the cottage slowly. She'd never used the queen's voice as her own before. It was something to think about, to wonder. How could there be two voices inside of her? One who asks questions and one who answers?

This was new, a plot twist. And it made Hazel smile; she could grow the story. This newfound power, this bright light of knowing that she could expand an entire universe, had her tingling.

Hazel reached the cottage just as a taxi pulled into the gravel drive, and Mum climbed out of the backseat. She stood, looking around, not seeing anyone, and lifted her palm to her forehead to shield the sun. Without her knowing, Hazel watched her mum.

Something was wrong.

It wasn't just the way her clothes hung looser, or that her hair was uncombed. It reminded Hazel of the day when Mum had walked into the back garden of Mecklenburgh Square and held out the note of evacuation. Her face was now devoid of makeup and lacking her characteristic bright red lipstick. Her mouth was quivering.

Hazel ran to her, skirting bales of hay and an upturned cart to call out, "Mum!"

Mum turned and didn't smile, merely held out her arms as Hazel ran into them. Now she felt it, the thing that made Mum look not quite right—she was crying.

"What is it?" Hazel asked into her mum's pink dress. "What, Mum?"

"Everything we have is safe, so let me begin there, my love. I am safe, but three nights ago, the McWhorter's son was killed in a battle in Belgium." She paused and puddles of tears pooled in the corner of her eyes, and then spilled over and ran down her cheeks unnoticed. "Hazel, he is gone."

Hazel closed her eyes, and tried to imagine the young neighbor killed in a field of battle. It was impossible. "No!" Hazel shot backward, took two steps, and held up both palms as if to ward off the truth.

"I'm not trying to scare you. I'm only telling you this to show you that you can't come home. Not now. Not for a long while."

Bridie appeared at the doorway and Flora burst out from behind her, straight to Mum, raising her arms to be lifted and held. "Mum!"

Hazel didn't want Flora to know about the McWhorters, didn't want her sister to feel the unsteady world in which they actually lived, to feel the fear. Hazel ran. She ran through the fields, over the dirt road, and past the raspberry bushes and snagging brambles, barely noticing the nettles biting into her ankles. Up the hill to the church and the treacle well, where she fell to her knees and dug her fingers into the dirt.

Hazel gazed down at the dark water: a hole in the land where water sprang from below the earth, an opening she had imagined was magical.

There was no magic here or anywhere. This was just water rising from the earth.

—

The next night, the stars were bright enough to light the pasture and Hazel lay down on the plaid blanket they always took to the river with

Flora. Everyone else in the house was asleep but she could *not* find rest; she imagined bombs dropping on her neighborhood. The horror had finally reached Hazel's neighborhood. How could it not? How could she have thought that making little stories could keep them safe?

Hazel cried softly for she didn't want to wake anyone. The grass was wet and soaking through the blanket to her flannel nightgown. She shivered and stared at the sky. The crescent moon was waning, and Hazel knew this for Bridie always told them the phases of the moon.

The ground shook and Hazel turned her head to see Harry walking toward her. He plopped down next to her and then he, too, lay down, staring at the sky in silence until finally he asked, "What are you doing?"

"What are *you* doing?" she asked.

"I heard you sneak out. I was worried."

"You don't have to worry about me, Harry. So stop. I'm not some little girl you need to take care of." Anger was better than sorrow.

"I know you can take care of yourself. I just like to do it, too." His voice was so soft that it made the longing she'd come to feel over the past months flood her body. For all the times she'd needed to touch him, she did so now. She reached over and took his hand.

Harry wound his fingers through hers. "Are you sad?"

"Very," she said. "Sometimes the stars make me feel better, but not tonight."

"How?" he asked. "How do they make you feel better?"

Hazel thought about this for a silent minute. "Maybe because they tell me that there is something more I can't see. Or if I can see it, I can only see the littlest bit of it when there is much, much more."

"I like that," he said, and rolled over. He let go of her hand and propped on his elbow, his chin in his palm. He faced Hazel, staring at her so intently she had to look away.

"Or maybe they make me feel better because even though they hide all day, they always come out at night; they don't go away." She paused and looked at him looking at her. "Where do you think stars come from?"

"There are people smarter than me who are trying to figure that out," he told her.

"Do you think that's where we go?" she asked. "Somewhere up there?"

"If you're asking me if I think that's where your father went when he died, I think it's possible."

She tried to hold back the tears but they came anyway. She didn't want to be weak; she didn't want Harry to see anything she felt. It was all too much.

He came closer, his elbow bending until his lips touched where the tears wet her cheek. He kissed her so gently that she might have imagined it. "I'm sorry," he said. "It's sad not having a dad."

She turned her face just ever so slightly, just enough that his lips brushed hers. He could have pulled away, but he didn't. This was what she'd ached for for so long and yet she didn't know what to do now.

He kissed her once, and then twice, lingering long enough that she found herself kissing him in return, her lips moving against his, her body loosening, sorrow seeming to rise from her and into the starry sky. His arms were around her and then he stopped kissing her. He pulled her close enough that her head rested on his shoulder and his arm supported her neck.

"I feel better," she said.

"That's what I hoped."

Her body tingled and if she'd been brave enough she would have begged for another kiss. "Did you take some of it?" she asked.

"Take what?"

"The sadness."

He brushed his hand through her hair. "I hope so."

# CHAPTER 35

## March 1960

Hazel's early morning decision to take the train to Henley-on-Thames was as impulsive as taking the book from Hogan's. It was almost as if something inside her, a separate piece of her, was making decisions, and she was on the way. She'd called all three nurses that morning: Maeve had no idea about anything as frivolous as a fairy tale and was sorry for Hazel's loss as she had six children of her own and wouldn't survive their loss; Lilly had never heard the word *Whisperwood* and her hard voice informed Hazel that she never wanted to talk about those horrid days again. It was Imogene Wright who never answered the phone no matter how many times Hazel had called this morning.

Now she grabbed her coat from the peg and was on her way to Piccadilly train station. She should tell Barnaby or her mum, who was calling every few hours checking on her, asking if there was news about the source of Peggy Andrews's story, worried and strung tight.

Hazel rushed out the door and toward the park, morning rising with a soft mist. A squirrel scuttered up a tree, chirping at Hazel for disturbing her. A man on an iron bench chomped down a croissant, a wool hat pulled low on his head.

"Hazel."

She jumped, turned around.

"Harry."

He was walking toward her with a paper bag. "I brought you a croissant."

"What are you doing here?" She slipped the croissant out of the bag, grateful. She hadn't eaten anything before running out on what was most likely another fool's errand. She took a warm buttery bite.

"I wanted to talk to you," he said. "You ran off last night and . . ."

"Yes, I'm sorry about that." She smiled at him; damn, she was so happy to see him waiting in the park for her.

"Where you headed?"

"Are you stalking me?" she asked with a grin. "Hanging out in the park waiting to follow me? Seems unlike you."

He laughed. "No. I don't have your number and I was afraid to knock on your door in case I disturbed . . . something." He shrugged. "This seemed the best option but by the look on your face it wasn't a very good choice."

"It's a good choice and I'm happy for it." She smiled. "I'm headed to Henley-on-Thames."

"Whatever for?"

"It's a story."

"I want to hear it," he said. They stood under the unfurling leaves of an oak as a mum pushing a pram rolled past.

She began to walk and he fell into stride with her.

"I was—" She shook her head. "I *am* going to Henley-on-Thames to talk to one of those nurses who lived in Binsey. Do you remember them?"

He nodded. "I do. Let me come with you?"

"That's a terrible idea."

"I'm sure it is," he said. "We seem to be good at those lately."

———

"Like Flora, her name is a flower," Hazel said as they settled into their train seats, flipped down their trays, and sipped tea. "Iris Taber."

"That seems a coincidence."

"And as your mum might say . . ." Hazel slid closer to the window to twist and face Harry next to her. "There is no such thing as coincidence."

Their gazes met. Hazel felt a familiar flop in her stomach.

"But if a nurse stole her," Harry said, "and brought her out here to raise her, wouldn't Aiden have found out?"

"Not if she hid her, right? Maybe she's a criminal mastermind—or just lucky, I don't know," Hazel said. "I swear it's like I've been struck blind like the king of Algar you told us about all those years ago. Flora is Frideswide, and I'm never meant to find her."

She thought of Barnaby's talk of lost causes as the train started up. The station house disappeared, and not long after the landscape shifted from city to country, just as it had when she and Flora had left London all those years ago.

She looked to Harry. "So I thought this was at least worth a try, but... I am ruining things in this quest."

"How so?"

"I might lose my new job. Barnaby's upset." She stared out the window at the passing town, the thatch roofs and steeple of a small church, the graveyard too close to the tracks. She turned to Harry in wonder. There he was, after all these years, sitting right beside her.

"I have to tell you something," he said. "I should have told you when I first saw you."

Hazel's breath puddled in her chest. Was it about Flora? An answer she'd been looking for?

"I *did* come to find you. Once."

"What?" Her hand went to her throat.

"It was a year after my last letter, and I went to the flat that you'd been writing from. The dry cleaner gave me your new address and I came to see you."

"I'm so confused. What happened? Why didn't ..."

"I waited in the same place you saw me this morning. Same bench. Same park. It was dusk, and you were coming home, walking arm in arm with some tall man. You looked so happy. He was kissing you and I thought—I can't do this. I can't bring her past into her future. I can't bring it all back to her. She's doing so very well and quite obviously in love."

"So you just left? You just walked away?"

"Yes."

"My God, Harry, I don't even remember the name of the man you saw me with. I'd have to go back and try to bring back that year—what was it? 1946?"

"I think so, yes."

"Whoever it was, it wasn't love."

He cringed. "I'm sorry. I saw you and knew I couldn't ruin whatever new and good life you'd built."

Hazel wanted to rush backward in time, look up from the tall man whose name she couldn't recall, see Harry sitting on a park bench just as she found him this morning. She exhaled. "I wish I'd seen you."

"Me too," he said. "Me too."

"Okay, let's talk about something else?" she asked. "Tell me about St. Ives. It's so beautiful. Tell me about your art." She squeezed his hand. "Tell me about you."

———

Hazel had learned that Henley-on-Thames was almost equidistant between London and Oxford, said to be in existence since the second century. The stone, brick, and red-roofed village was folded into the undulating hills around it, reached by crossing a four-arched stone bridge. Hazel and Harry walked past white-plaster homes, then stood at a crossroads by the market and bakery. The Thames, said to have taken Flora from them, flowed past silver-gray, moving with swift assurance toward London. Docked boats covered in blue and white tarps bobbed side by side at the edge of the river.

A brutal thought shot through Hazel's mind: If Flora had drowned, her body could have been carried this far and through the town of Henley-on-Thames. She shuddered and turned away from the river.

"You all right?" Harry asked.

"Yes," she answered quick enough for him to know it was a lie.

He took her hand and kissed her palm in such a tender gesture that she wanted to wrap her arms around him, allow him to hold her until the image of Flora's body at the bottom of the river, carried by a current, vanished forever. They were jostled by an older gentleman walking by, a cigarette smoldering in one hand and a leash in the other. A small white dog pranced and preened ahead of him.

"Excuse me," Harry said.

The man stopped and smiled, tipped his gray wool cap. "Yes?"

"We are a bit lost. We are looking for 17 Allington Way."

"Ah, Iris Muldoon?"

"Yes." Harry's eyes opened wider. "Do you know her? Or her mother, Imogene?"

"I do," he said. "Everyone does. Is it a dog you'd be wanting?"

"A dog? No . . ." Hazel stared at him in confusion.

"Imogene saves every wounded animal in town, every stray, and every abandoned animal from birds to dogs to cats. Most who come here looking for her are wanting a pet."

"And her daughter?" Hazel asked.

"Twenty steps that way"—he pointed east—"and then the second right past the gallery and the fourth house on the right. White with flowers at the window." He ambled off without a goodbye, and Harry looked to Hazel.

"Well, that was mighty specific."

"Seems to be a well-known family."

Hazel averted her gaze from the river as they passed the red brick town hall dominating the view at the end of the main village. Soon they found the house with a walkway made of pebbles and brick that led to a dark wood front door with an iron Celtic cross knocker. Two windows on either side of the front door had window boxes beneath them, overflowing with spring madness.

Hazel and Harry stood on the pavement outside a low white fence with an iron scrolled gate. Ivy crawled up the west wall of the house, winding its way around the corner to the front.

"This looks like a place Snow White would live," said Hazel. "Like the dwarfs are nearly set to run out."

Harry pulled her close, kissed her cheek. "Okay, let's do this."

Hazel's hands shook in the pockets of her lightweight wool coat. The afternoon sun cast their shadows long on the ground: two stick people stretched across the cobbled lane.

"Would you know Flora right away if you saw her?" Harry asked.

"I think so. I look for her everywhere; sometimes I don't even know I'm looking for her. I just glance about a full room or a crowd at a pub or market and realize I'm looking for a six-year-old girl with blond curls and remind myself that she is now twenty-five years old. She could be tall or short or chubby or thin. How do we know?"

"We don't know, but Hazel, I do hope we find out."

Hazel lifted the latch on the gate. They walked up the pathway, and she was just set to rap with the knuckles of her other hand when the door opened.

Lamplight from inside the house formed an edge of yellow around a woman's silhouette. "Hallo?" Iris Taber's voice was friendly, but with a bit of caution. "May I help you?"

Behind her came the cry of a child, then the yappy bark of a small dog. The woman stepped onto the stoop and shut the door to whatever was inside that she might need to protect.

Iris was a tiny woman, younger than they were—by how much Hazel couldn't say. Her hair was blond turning custard-hued, and her eyes brown, or maybe green.

"My name's Hazel Linden and a long time ago I knew a woman named Imogene Wright in Binsey." The rest of it came out in a torrent. "I knew her when I was a child. She was a nurse in the village during the war with Operation Pied Piper and . . ." She paused. "I lived with the Aberdeen family."

"Oh how lovely!" The woman clapped her hands together and held them to her chest. "Mum will be thrilled to know you're here. She told me about your family and the mum . . . Bird or . . ."

"Bridie," Hazel said. "And this is Harry Aberdeen."

Iris smiled at Harry. "Let me ring her! She lives just down the lane. She would very much love to see you."

"Before you do," Harry said, stepping forward, "may I ask a strange question: How old are you?"

Hazel was shocked at his boldness and feared the answer. It seemed like it was happening too fast.

Hazel took apart the woman's face in small bits and pieces. The nose, a button. Clear white skin without freckles. High cheekbones. Did these pieces add up to Flora, twenty years later?

Iris bit her lower lip. "Twenty."

Five years off. It was impossible. Iris Taber was *not* Flora.

The ground beneath Hazel's feet turned spongy and unstable.

"Do you have a sister?" Harry asked.

"May I inquire why you're asking me so many questions?"

"We are so sorry to disturb you." Harry's smile, smooth voice, and amiable aura allowed the woman to relax again. "When your mum lived in Binsey, there was a young girl . . ." He looked back for Hazel's nod before finishing the sentence.

Iris chimed in, "Yes, a girl disappeared. Mum told me. She never forgot her."

Hazel spoke up, "That was my sister, Flora."

"Can we talk to your mum?" Harry asked.

Iris opened the door and motioned inside. "Come in. I'll put a kettle on and we'll have a cuppa."

# CHAPTER 36

## September 8, 1940

Harry's sketch slid under the bedroom door that morning of September 8 and it was one of her favorites so far: Flora running toward something blurry in the foreground. Her hair flew behind her, her arms akimbo. Her unclear destination consisted of rounded objects and pointed tips. It could, Hazel thought staring at it, be anything she wanted it to be: a castle, a mountain, a cathedral.

Before waking, Hazel had been deep within a fuzzy dream. Father Fenelly had been in her house in Bloomsbury, and he'd been laughing and talking to Mum, who flitted around him in a long gown of gossamer and bright blue ribbons. Her hair was so long it swept along the ground. Mum paid no mind to Hazel and Flora, even as they called out for her.

Hazel shook off the odd dream, the last of the night's shadows, and dropped Harry's drawing on the dresser for Flora to look at when she awoke. Later, she'd place it into a folder where all the other sketches had gathered—352 of them so far, kept in the same drawer as her stories.

Hazel put on her fuzzy slippers that had by now formed to her feet and entered the sun-drenched kitchen, surprised to find it empty. Even when Bridie had such a bad cold that her nose turned cherry red, she'd been there, stirring porridge, frying sausage, and brewing tea, which she now let Hazel drink each morning from her own flowered china cup they'd found in a thrift store in Oxford on one of their adventures.

That was the thing with Bridie—nothing was an errand or a market run—it was an adventure.

The room was empty.

Something was wrong.

Hazel walked to the sink and stood higher on the balls of her feet to look out the window. The beat-up Flying Nine that always surprised Bridie when it started was gone. Frost licked the window's edges, beginning to melt with the rising sun. Morning shadows distorted the grass and garden so that, like Harry's drawing that morning, she could, if she was in the mood, make the shapes become anything she pleased. But she wasn't in the mood. She wanted to know what was happening, what wasn't right, what niggled at the edge of the morning.

Hazel turned on the wireless by the kitchen sink.

The announcer's voice filled the kitchen. "London has been bombed."

Hazel dropped to a kitchen chair. Even as they all knew it was coming—for why else was she in Binsey?—the truth slammed into her chest. She turned off the radio so Flora would not hear. She waited for Bridie or Mum or anyone to come tell her what was happening. These were the bombs they'd been waiting for, the anticipated explosions that sent them to Binsey a year ago.

Not long after, Flora woke and Hazel toasted some bread for them both. Then came the sound of the car chugging into the drive. Bridie and Harry had driven into town for a newspaper.

Bridie sat them around the fire's hearth and told Hazel and Flora that at 4 p.m. yesterday the first bombs had whistled from the sky to shatter the streets, homes, cathedrals, and beauty of London. Father Fenelly's voice had *not* been a dream—he'd come by the cottage in the morning hours to tell Bridie of the devastation.

Bridie continued with a wavering voice. "Your mum called and sent a message through Father Fenelly to tell us that she is okay, and your home is safe. But I have terribly sad news."

"Kelty," Hazel said, knowing it was Kelty. She never should have run off that night to return to her family.

"Well, yes, Kelty is in hospital. She and her mum were walking home from visiting a friend in hospital when a bomb dropped near

Willowbridge Road where they were walking, shattering two homes and . . ." Bridie shuddered. "And igniting a busload of people."

"And her mum's okay?" Hazel asked with a clenched feeling in her throat.

"No."

Ice filled Hazel's chest, a chill moving down her arms and up her spine making her dizzy.

"Is she hurt?" Hazel hoped for a terrible thing rather than its alternative.

"She was killed." Bridie's voice broke and tears fell from her eyes and down the sides of her nose to the creases at the edge of her mouth. She didn't even wipe them away as if she didn't know they had fallen.

"Like Papa," Flora said, so matter-of-fact it cracked Hazel's heart. Death should never be matter-of-fact. Not one bit.

"I am so sorry," Bridie said, and took both girls' hands in her own. "Kelty is in hospital, injured but alive. Nothing life-threatening. From there, she'll go to her aunt in Lancashire. I'll try to find out more."

"She has an aunt?" Hazel asked as if this was what mattered. "I didn't know. Why didn't she take Kelty instead of her mum sending her here, to the hag?"

"I don't think her aunt, her father's sister, wanted her. But now, she must."

"Oh, poor Kelty." Hazel pressed her fingers to her eyes. "Her father, where is he?"

"Right now they say he's missing in action; last seen in Luxembourg."

The various names of the places across the warfront meant little to Hazel. She heard them rattled off from her own mum and in the newspapers; foreign names where men were fighting with guns and knives and bombs, places where people died while she sat in a cozy cottage in the countryside of Oxfordshire and made stories of a magical land.

It wasn't fair or right. She shouldn't be allowed this life when others suffered so much. "It could have been our mum. It could have been . . ." Hazel choked on the words and the knowing.

"Bring Kelty here!" Flora said, jumping from the couch.

"Darling, I wish I could, but I can't. When this is over, we'll all be together again."

Hazel cried out, "Mum. I need Mum."

———

Three days later, their mum arrived in Binsey, her red-rimmed eyes telling them all they needed to know about London's horrors. Sixty-three miles away was a whole different world, and Mum didn't want to talk about it.

Instead she asked about the news in Binsey, oohing and aahing over their schoolwork, the garden Flora had helped Bridie plant for winter vegetables, the stew Hazel made for them all from the recipe Bridie had taught her. Mum said their home was safe and so was she: She rode her bicycle to and from her job at the war offices, and she ran to the air raid shelter in the Tube whenever the sirens whirled through the night air.

Rain fell steadily that evening, drumming on the roof, and soon the last train for London was leaving. Bridie convinced Mum to spend the night on the soft couch, instead departing early the next morning.

In the middle of the night, Hazel was unsure of the time, but the moon wasn't in her window and the house was silent but for the creaks and whispers in the floors and walls. She crawled next to Mum on the couch and allowed herself to be held the same way she held Flora every night.

Hazel thought of poor Kelty without a mum. Finally she slept, and in the morning, Mum slipped from the couch without waking her. She woke to the sounds of Mum bustling about with Bridie, in preparation to leave and catch the first train.

Hazel knew what she must do. While Mum said goodbye to Flora and finished her tea, Hazel ran into her bedroom and hastily packed her knapsack, attached the rubber mask, and slipped the name tag that hung on a nail next to the dresser mirror over her neck. It was the same tag she'd worn the day she arrived here in Binsey.

When she ran outside, rain pelted her rain jacket. Her wellies sloshed through the wet grass until she reached Mum's side at the open passenger door of Bridie's car.

"Take me with you. I need to see Kelty," Hazel said, her bottom lip trembling in a giveaway that she might cry. They huddled under a bright red umbrella Mum held. Flora and Harry were inside, watching from the cottage's front door, Harry holding Flora's hand as she strained against him to join Hazel and their mum.

"It's too dangerous," Mum said. "If anything happened to you . . ." She swallowed and shook her head. "You need to be here for Flora. Be my big girl."

"Just for the day, Mum. That is all. Take me with you on the train, and I'm grown-up enough to come back alone."

"No."

Hazel stomped her wellies; mud splashed, staining the hem of her dress and the edge of the car door. "If you don't take me, I'll come anyway. I know the way to Great Ormond Street to the hospital where Kelty is." She sounded much braver than she felt, her voice strong but her insides jiggling like aspic. She wasn't actually sure she knew how to get there, despite everything she'd just said. "I need to see Kelty."

Mum stared at Hazel, Bridie already in the driver's seat turning on the ignition, once, twice, until it caught. "Okay, but you're returning to Bridie this afternoon. I will not allow you to spend the night." Her voice was stern, almost cold. "I'm taking no chances with you."

"All right, Mum, I promise."

Hazel opened the back door and crawled into Bridie's car.

# CHAPTER 37

## March 1960

In Henley-on-Thames, Imogene Mulroney sat across from Hazel and Harry at her daughter Iris's oval wooden kitchen table, upon which were scattered coloring books, pencil boxes, and toy cars. She was a slight woman with bright blue eyes who looked older than her fifty years, with muddy-colored curls sprouting every which way. To Hazel, she did not appear to be a person who would steal a child, even if Hazel actually wanted Imogene to be a person who'd steal a child.

They'd sipped their tea to the bottoms of their cups. They talked of Bridie and of war, of how the world seemed to have moved on but inside they all still felt that any moment everything could tip down.

"Such willful forgetting is necessary," said Imogene. "We can't wallow now, can we?"

At last, Hazel gingerly asked, "Do you remember Flora?"

"Of course! She was a sprite, that one. I think of her often. I can't imagine what you and your family went through. I pray the rosary for her every October nineteenth and remember her on St. Frideswide's feast."

"And you have no idea what happened to her?" Hazel asked.

"Oh, if I did, I would be the most blessed. I would certainly shout it to the world, or run and find her, to bring her back to you."

"I would like to bring her back also," Harry said and lifted his empty teacup. He stared into the bottom and set it back down.

Imogene glanced between Harry and Hazel. "I remember the both of you. Thick as thieves. Two peas in a pod. Climbing trees, running through the woodlands. When I'd babysit dear Flora, you two were gone fast like grasshoppers through the woods. I rightly knew you two would end up together. It was as if no one else existed."

"Excuse me?" Hazel leaned forward. "We aren't together and . . . Flora existed."

"Of course she did. And excuse my presumption. You just seem—"

"Mum, stop," Iris said. "It isn't any of your business."

"My daughter says I'm too nosy, and I talk too much."

Iris brought a pan of shortbread from the oven, which she cut into careful small squares while they talked more and her toddler, a boy two years old, ran about the house, looking for an imaginary rabbit.

Imogene continued softly. "So you were askin'. Well, the police did come to talk to all of us. No one saw or knew anything. We were all crying and all feeling so helpless when we heard the news. I think he was quite annoyed with us." Imogene's brows drew downward and she tilted her head. "How did you come to find me?"

Hazel dove into the truth. "Aiden, the police inspector, gave me the name and address of all the nurses. I hope that was all right."

"Oh, yes. But maybe you'd be more interested in the American nurse from the Red Cross—Frances, I believe?" Imogene stared off. "She was from . . . I don't remember, to be sure. An odd but nice girl. The war wasn't what any of us expected, for her least of all. She came over here, expecting to meet a nice British boy and fall in love. She had romantic dreams, that one, fancied herself Florence Nightingale who'd wipe the brows of the fallen boys, as if one day there might be a statue in her honor. She left straight away when things got really bad." Imogene shook her head. "The Blitz . . ." Her voice trailed off. "Those poor boys. Especially the RAF ones, given those flimsy planes that fell from the sky, tearing to bits when they landed."

"Yes, it was awful," Hazel said.

Imogene's face shifted, as if she was set to cry or scream, Hazel couldn't yet tell. "I couldn't save them. You know I tried. I tried my bloody best. We all did. Sometimes you can't save them. Even when you want to, even when you try and don't sleep for ages and hold your hand against their wound with blood spurting . . ."

"Mum!" Iris called out, and then took her mum's hand. "It's okay."

"Yes," Hazel said, flinching and reaching for Harry's hand. "You all tried your very best."

Imogene seemed to come back to the room, a smile now. Hazel knew she'd seen things that had been hidden from her and from Flora and Harry, from all the children. She tried again to reach the truth with Imogene, find a kernel of something that would lead her to Flora. "When you babysat, did Flora ever tell you a story about a magical land?"

Imogene looked off toward the window. "Not that I remember. I'm sorry I can't help you more than that." She nodded toward Iris. "During that St. Brigid's Day bonfire, I was with this child. And scared witless, my man off at war. We hadn't married before he left."

"Mum," Iris said, "they don't need to know any of this."

"So old-fashioned, this daughter of mine," Imogene said, a twinkle in her eye. She patted Iris's hand. "That's why I was so enamored of Flora. I had just found out about my own baby, and I was imagining life with a little one."

"Did Iris's father make it back?" Harry asked, taking his second piece of shortbread, wiping crumbs from his lips.

"He did—missing one of his legs, but what do I care of a missing leg? I loved him madly. Still do."

Iris sat next to Hazel. "Father is wonderful. He's working in the marketplace today," Iris said. "My husband, Martin, and Father work together. We have the only market in town."

The talk continued until baby Toby tumbled onto the slate floor with a cry. Then they stood to say their goodbyes.

On the front stoop of the house, Iris jiggled Toby on her hip as Imogene bustled about cleaning the kitchen. "I'm sorry Mum couldn't be of much help. Those days were awful for her. Now she tries to save everything in sight, from dead plants to wounded animals. But nothing can make up for what happened with those poor boys who arrived at hospital. Nothing."

"I'm sorry for her," Hazel said. "And thank you for welcoming us into your home. I'm sorry for everything that happened in those days."

———

Once again on the train, Hazel spoke the words that bubbled below her disappointment. "It was a long shot among the millions of long shots. It's like . . . a sickness. I have to let it go, but how can I?"

"Hazel," he said.

"I have to be careful now, Harry. I'm about to lose everything to find an answer that can't be found."

He settled back on the window. "Define *everything* for me, Hazel."

"My new job. Barnaby. Love. I am about to lose all of it. Flora must have told someone who told someone. I *must* let this go."

"And how do you propose doing that?" Harry asked. "How, bloody how, do you let it go? Now you know about the book called Whisperwood, and . . . there's me. There's us."

"Harry, stop. There is *no* us."

"You can't un-know things, Hazel. You can't un-see them. You cannot look away from everything that you've been shown. You just can't."

She slapped her hand on her leg. "That is a lot of things you're telling me I *can't* do. And yes, I can. I can move on from things that make no sense in an attempt to save my life."

"Save what life, Hazel? What kind of life are you saving?"

"Harry, what are you doing?"

"Trying to tell you that you are not losing anything."

"But I am. I wanted something to be true, and I broke things trying to make it true. I hurt Barnaby. I hurt my boss at the bookshop, Edwin Hogan, who I love like a father. No more."

"Breaking free isn't always graceful or painless, you know that better than anyone."

Hazel slumped back onto the seat, exasperated. "Harry, whether it was stupid conjugated Latin verbs or a row of multiplication tables or learning to skip a flat river stone, you never let me give up." She pushed at him. "It's a very annoying trait."

He laughed and leaned back in his seat. "I've always adored annoying you." He winked. "It means you care."

"What are you, fourteen years old?"

He suddenly turned serious. "I wish, Hazel. If I was, we could change everything."

"I know," she said. "I know."

~

In the early dark of evening, Harry stood at the entry of Hazel's flat, and she didn't unlock the door. "Harry, you can't come in."

He stepped down once as he held on to the iron gate.

"I cannot do this with you even as part of me wants to invite you in. We lost our chance, Harry. You know that. I know that."

"I don't know that. I heard what you said about the American author. About how she changed the middle of the story. We can do the same thing."

"No," Hazel said as she dug out her key and unlocked the door. "We can't. I can't." She placed her hand on the brass knob.

"You're just going to walk away?"

"I'm not going to destroy anything else in my life. I'm not going to betray Barnaby. Please, let me go inside alone, because if you don't, I'll make another mistake with you, and that is something I can't afford to do." With that she unlocked the door, entered, and closed it without looking behind.

Inside, Hazel dropped her bag on the bench and hung her hat on the peg. She stood alone. This Bloomsbury flat had seen loss before: of a pair of sisters sent to the countryside, of other men Hazel had sent walking out the door, of war and demolition and heartbreak, of a father who never returned.

She walked bleary and on the verge of tears to the kitchen. How could she possibly let Harry Aberdeen walk away? How could she possibly allow him to stay?

Then she noticed, there on the pine table, in the open notebook was her handwritten list—anyone or everyone who might have heard about her magical land.

She stared at the names, trying to find a connection when fragments of Harry's words returned to her.

Harry: *Sometimes life breaks your heart to give you the best art.*

Bridie at the Imbolc fire: *Stories are soul-making.*

Hazel sat.

What if, before Paris, what if she just allowed the extraordinary to imbue the ordinary one more time. What if she allowed the owl to hoot long into the night?

One. More. Time.

*If you were born knowing . . .*

# CHAPTER 38

## September 1940

After traveling from Binsey to the Russell Square Station, Hazel thought she and Mum had disembarked at the wrong place: The landscape was altered just enough to be at once familiar and not. They walked past a tattered British flag, flapping in the wind from a pole poking out of a pile of rubble, bricks and concrete, charred wood, and fragments of furniture: a drawer, a turned leg of a missing table, a bedpost.

In front of Hazel was a house with its front missing. There was a clear view into the living room where a couch sat under a crystal chandelier. It was a life-size dollhouse, nothing disturbed inside, but glass glittered on the ground outside, and concrete and bricks were in piles like a child's tumbled game of blocks. They passed a mum in a tattered khaki dress, with three small children. They stood outside a home with their arms wrapped around each other, staring at a pile of rubble and wood, the boy pointing at something Hazel couldn't see. The youngest was crying about a lost cat named Sandy and the oldest, maybe ten years old, was stoic but trembling.

"They lost their home," Hazel said.

"Yes," Mum said. "So many have. We've been lucky so far."

*So far.*

Dust was everywhere, covering lampposts and cars parked at the edge of the street, on the sills of storefronts with blown-out windows, and black

239

curtains fluttering in the shattered spaces. Then there was an undamaged butcher shop next to a destroyed café. It was all randomness. Intact houses sat next to destroyed ones; undisturbed pavement would drop off into a crater big enough to crawl into, where earth and concrete crumbled.

The Number 77 red double-decker bus with KINGS CROSS emblazoned on its rear, an advertisement for *Picture Post* on its side, was perched nose-up from a giant crater. The vehicle's back end had been swallowed.

"This area was hit two nights ago, Hazel. So you know I'm not fooling with you when I say it is dangerous."

"I don't think you are fooling. I didn't . . . I thought . . ."

Mum stopped midstep and turned to Hazel. They were the same height now, and Mum took Hazel's face in her hands. "If you think you want to be here, if you think coming here or running away like Kelty is something you want to do—I want you to know the truth."

Hazel nodded as a woman walked past carrying a suitcase, dirt on her face.

Mum's voice was clear and loud. "The bombers fly up the river, Hazel. They use our beloved Thames as a map into the city. You can hear the grind of their engines, then the high whistle of a bomb being dropped, then the thump of it hitting the earth, exploding homes, setting afire cathedrals and libraries and museums. They come just after dark." She shuddered. "You never know when the next one will arrive. The sky trembles like a thunderstorm. Far away or close, you see a bright white light, then a yellow flame."

Hazel felt the fear of it happening right then wash over her. How did Mum go to sleep at night, knowing they were coming again and again?

"We're jammed into underground platforms. I've witnessed people digging their way out of an air raid shelter, all thank God alive, but next time—"

"Mum, stop!" Hazel couldn't breathe. The words her mum was saying were like bombs themselves. "Come live with us in Binsey."

"I cannot, Hazel. But this will end, and you and Flora are staying away so that one day you can come back. Kelty might have been spared, but if anything happened to you . . ."

"You don't have to protect me."

"Yes, I do. That is my job. That is all that matters. It matters little if I am happy or I am content. My job is to take care of you." She kept her gaze on Hazel's. "We are lucky Bridie chose my girls. You must stay safe. They think they can destroy us. Well, they can destroy our houses and buildings and boats and cars but they can't destroy the British, not the morale. Not us. Not you, Hazel. Not me."

"I understand, Mum. I will go back to Binsey, I promise. Just let me see Kelty and my home. I will go right back to Bridie."

Mum put her arms around Hazel and pulled her close. "I cannot lose you, my darling Hazel. I will not take that chance."

———

Everyone wore white. That was Hazel's first thought as Mum led them through the wooden front door of the Great Ormond Street Hospital. Hazel followed Mum to the front desk where a nurse in a white cap, a white apron over a white dress, gave Mum directions to Kelty's room.

"Down the hall to the right, Ward C." The nurse looked as tired as the nurses behind the parish church. Her low bun tucked under her hat was coming loose, and greasy strands of hair fell onto her shoulder. The phone rang with a broken jangle, and the nurse lifted her chin, indicating the hallway they should take, before answering. "Great Ormond Street."

The ward where Kelty was supposed to be had floor-to-ceiling iron-framed rectangular windows that were smudged and dirty. The room was crowded with rows of white iron beds and cribs. A boy sat as a nurse read to him. A petite woman wore a lace nurse's cap different from the rest of the nurses' caps, and she leaned over a child asleep in a crib, patting its back.

White lamps dripped puddles of bright light, circled by shadow, on the bedside tables where vases held wilted flowers and scattered papers with scribbled notes. Colored ribbons hung from some beds, fluttering as a nurse walked by. One girl ran her fingers through the ribbons even as her eyes were closed.

Hazel scanned the room for Kelty, locating her on the far side of the room. Her bed rails on either side were up, as if imprisoning her. As she approached, Hazel saw that Kelty's eyes were closed, and a bandage covered her arm and forehead.

Hazel let out a cry and ran to her side. "Kelty!"

Her friend opened her eyes and smiled. "I told them you would come and they didn't believe me."

"Oh, Kelty . . ." Hazel reached to take her friend's hand but a tube ran into a vein, a large bandage with a single spot of dried blood covering it. "I'm so sorry about everything that happened."

"Mum is dead." Kelty's left cheek was distorted with a yellow-green bruise beneath the bandage on her forehead, but her eyes were dry. "She was right next to me. And then she wasn't." Kelty's voice was clogged with emotion and she squeezed shut her eyes. "They are going to send me to my aunt Bernice in Lancashire. I've only met her a few times, Hazel. Let me come back to Binsey with you. Please."

"Mum, can I?"

Mum didn't answer, and Hazel's gaze wandered to the fluttering ribbons. "What are those?" she asked.

Kelty looked sideways, and her face fell. "Some of the girls trade ribbons. Their parents bring them, and they trade them to have every color. The mums braid them into their hair and then they bring even more of them."

"Mum!" Hazel cried out. "You have to bring Kelty some ribbons."

"I will, darling."

"Kelty must come back with me," Hazel said. She lifted her gaze to her mum, who now stood on the other side of the bed, stroking Kelty's arm.

"She isn't going anywhere," said a stern voice from behind. The nurse with the lace cap had arrived at the bedside of the child next to Hazel. The girl, her eyes closed, was no older than Flora, and there were black letters written on her forehead: M ¼. The nurse was short enough that she would look like a child if not for her graying hair and uniform. Obviously in charge, she read the chart at the end of the child's bed, then turned to Hazel and Mum.

"I am Matron Lane, and this young lady isn't going anywhere yet."

Hazel stared at the little girl in the other bed. "Why is there writing on her head?"

The nurse stared at Hazel as if deciding what to say, then softly told her, "In an emergency, it is the best way we have to quickly communicate. The notation means she's had a fourth dose of morphine." Matron Lane placed her hand on Kelty's bedside rails. "Kelty, is your headache better?"

"Much better," Kelty said. "Nothing hurts. Can I please go now?"

"Not yet." The nurse looked to Mum. "Are you kin?"

"Yes," Hazel answered, "we are kin."

Matron Lane offered a weary half smile at Hazel, then repeated the question to Mum. "You are kin?"

Mum shook her head.

Matron Lane gently touched the bandage on Kelty's forehead. "She will be just fine. One more day to make sure she is nourished, and her aunt has time to come here and retrieve her. These are terrible days, to be sure."

"She's like my sister," Hazel said. "Please let her come home with me."

Tears filled Kelty's eyes as she looked up. She tried to be brave and said, "Hazel, we will find each other again."

———

Flora curled into the curve of Hazel's body, her back resting against Hazel's tummy. Bridie had told Hazel that Flora hadn't left their bedroom in the cottage all day, that she'd waited there, clinging to Berry, until Hazel returned. It was a moonless night.

"Tell me," Flora said.

"I'm too tired to make anything up," Hazel said, already near sleep, feeling the comforting soft edges of oblivion.

"No, tell me about Kelty."

Hazel decided not to tell Flora of the hospital or the bandages or the ribbons or the child with writing on her forehead. "Kelty is all right. Her aunt Bernice will take her home tomorrow." Hazel took a deep breath. It was hard to say but she must. "We cannot leave here. This is our real home, and we have to stay safe. Until this is over, we can't go anywhere else."

"Not even Whisperwood?" Flora's voice cracked.

"No."

Only then did Flora cry, pulling away from Hazel and curling into herself, Berry grasped tight. Hazel reached over and rubbed her sister's back. After the horrible things she'd seen that day, she knew their land had been an illusion. Whisperwood and its sparkling river made of stars—of course none of it was real and true. Child's play. There were no stars in the rushing river; it was just muddy water running to the sea as it always had and always would. She was fifteen years old, and the war was real. No more fairy tales or fake queens or shimmering doors. She had to protect her sister, help Bridie, and keep them safe.

The end of Whisperwood wasn't Hazel's fault; the bombs and the war and the evil man with the mustache had ended their story.

# CHAPTER 39

## October 19, 1940
## St. Frideswide's Day

The temperature was unusually high for October. Bridie told Hazel it would probably be the last warm day in Binsey before winter set its roots into the hard cold ground. She had trimmed the garden to its nub, and the trees outside the cottage had shed their leaves.

Bridie's music didn't play quite so often these days as Churchill's voice echoed in the house with news, the BBC giving updates while Harry and Hazel did their best to focus on their schoolwork, to do as both Bridie and Churchill pleaded: "Never surrender."

As the months had passed, Harry and Hazel never spoke of the kiss and their night under the stars, and yet the silence hadn't made it matter less, for whenever her mind wandered she thought about Harry's touch. She remembered her head on his shoulder, and the way his arm rested under her neck, the way he smelled like wood smoke and soap. The desire for him consumed her in the oddest hours: eating dinner, running through the woods, taking Flora into town with Bridie for errands. His touch. His lips. She didn't understand what had happened and yet she wanted it to happen again.

And again.

She found that the more she wanted him, the more brusque and short she became with him. She snapped at Harry when he asked her a

245

question; she ignored him when he asked her how she liked the new hat his mum had knitted her; she took the last bite of cake and didn't share. The anger was a shield to keep her from begging him to touch her one more time.

Meanwhile, Flora was learning her letters, sounding them out one by one. A hand-painted alphabet hung in squares of paper strung across the back wall of the living room next to the table where their schoolwork was done each day. Harry had drawn the letters in varying colors, each with an image below that started with the letter. A is for arrow, B is for balloon. He didn't choose the regular nursery school words like *apple*; he chose his own or ones that Flora chose with him. R was for river. S was for star. W was for whisper. O was for owl. These words were hints of their secret land and yet Whisperwood was gone.

They now had blackout curtains that Bridie had sewn herself on the Singer machine in the corner of her bedroom, and the new rations had Bridie waiting in line for enough meat for the four of them. Newspapers trumpeted headlines of death and destruction.

But on St. Frideswide's Day, Bridie packed a picnic basket with cheese and slabs of ham. She sang a song about a tisket and a tasket while folding napkins, slipped in three white china plates with the emblem of Oxford University stamped at its center. On top she placed a neatly folded red wool blanket that they had spread at the river's banks more times than Hazel could now count. The repeated rituals made the children feel safe.

"I must go into Oxford today," Bridie said that October morning as she patted the red blanket and folded the wicker top over all of it. "I am going to get us a telephone. We need one now in case there is . . . news." She kept her gaze on the basket so as not to give away any fear in her eyes.

But Hazel knew what she meant: news of Mum's injury or death, or something else that was awful. Bridie was taking her wheezing car into Oxford to pay for a new phone and have the lines brought across her sweeping field for only one kind of news: bad.

She gave the basket one more pat, then looked up with that bright smile, crinkling her cheeks into folds. Bridie lifted her black purse with the silver clasp, kissed Harry, Hazel, and Flora on top of their foreheads, and walked out the front door, calling out behind her, "Now go enjoy the day, and watch out for each other."

*Watch out for each other.*

———

Heather swayed in the breeze as Hazel and Flora ran, their feet trampling through a path they'd taken many times before. Harry ran behind them, carrying the picnic lunch Bridie had packed.

The river ran hard that day, rushing as if late for its destiny.

The children reached the river's banks and stopped, Flora bumping into Hazel and nearly sending her into the rushing water.

"Flora!"

"Sorry."

When Harry reached them, he dropped the wicker basket to the grass. His cheeks were red from running. Hazel tried not to notice that the muscles in his arms were bigger than they were even a month ago. It was like a man within was pushing out of the boy he was. Hazel spread the red blanket on the grass and the three of them sat cross-legged.

Over the past months, Hazel did whatever she could to have some part of her body touch Harry's. An elbow during schoolwork as he read, his lips moving silently to the words, a knee as they sat there at the river, a hand during prayer. It was a strangely vivid feeling when their skin met, even through jerseys and gloves and stockings. She felt she could both breathe deeper and could not breathe at the same time. She watched his face for even the smallest recognition that he felt the same.

In her dreams at night, he'd take her hand or touch her cheek or hold her close while a storm howled outside. She even made stories about them in her head, nothing she'd ever write down for fear that he or Bridie might find them. But in her stories, she and Harry lived in the house, just the two of them. They wandered not only through the woodlands but through life. He kissed her good morning and kissed her goodnight. They shared a bedroom—what went on in that bedroom was unclear, but the door closed with them inside.

In place of the Whisperwood stories, as if Hazel's heart and mind could not bear being absent of tales, in rushed new ones about her and Harry.

At the riverside, with him beside them, Flora was beginning to doze off for her afternoon nap. "Just one more of our stories . . ."

"*Shh,*" Hazel told her, feeling the heat of their secret while Harry unpacked the basket.

She rubbed Flora's back until she fell into a soft sleep. Harry leaned back on his elbows and smiled. "So, then tell *me* one of your stories."

"How can you know . . . how?" Her voice was sharp.

He looked confused, as if she'd slapped him across the face.

"Did I say something wrong?" he asked, shifting on the blanket and looking at her, his eyelashes long, glinting in the sunlight.

Hazel stood, calculating how he could have possibly heard them speak of Whisperwood. "Have you been spying on us?" Her heart pounded crazily, like one of the hammers Bridie used on the fences.

"No. I would never!" He blushed beneath his freckles.

He stood, and they were face-to-face. "Then how do you know about our stories?" she asked.

Flora lay curled on her side, her teddy close. Her flowered dress with the pink and blue cornflowers surrounded her like a cloud.

Harry's and Hazel's gazes locked. Hazel was flooded with embarrassment, as if in hearing her talk about her imagined land Harry had seen her naked.

"I don't spy," he said. "We live in a small cottage, you know."

Hazel took two steps toward him, placed her hands on his chest, and pushed him away. He stumbled backward.

"Don't listen to us!" she said. "It's private."

"Why are you so mad?" he asked, coming closer, just as she always wished he would.

"That story is ours. It's our secret place. Even Mum doesn't know."

It was quiet suddenly. The two of them stood there in the autumn afternoon.

Harry cleared his throat and pulled his wool cap lower. "You have a secret place?"

"I will never tell you," Hazel said.

"Aw, come on, tell me." He grinned with that look that made Hazel wish he'd only look at her and never anyone else.

But he had so many of his own things—a mum who sang songs and took them on adventures, a cottage in the middle of a grand field of heather, friends who sought him out and adored him. Hazel would not hand over to him the single possession shared by her and Flora.

Hazel moved closer to him. "Never! It's ours and not yours!"

She ran, as she often did when she didn't know what else to do, without knowing where she'd go or why. The path to the riven tree and the cavernous space of Whisperwood was well worn. She reached the grove and slipped inside, nudging to the edge of the dark space so the inside of the tree rested against her back, as it had done so many times.

How long was she there with her eyes closed, with confusion and tears and frustration flowing through her blood? She would, for the rest of her days, wonder this. Her body thrummed, everything rushing in at once: anger and desire, need and fear, loss. Her dead father. Her battered mum; Kelty's mum; bombs and war and fear.

And how she'd killed Whisperwood, taken it away from Flora.

And then a longing for Harry, his touch, something more than what she had, something that kept her awake at night.

Eventually a rustling came from outside, and her name was called.

It was Harry and she answered him. "In here."

His face appeared at the slit-opening of the tree; he bent down and crawled in with Hazel. "Look what you found," he said. "This is so magical."

Hazel didn't answer him.

"I didn't mean to make you so mad." Harry reached over and touched her cheek so gently it could have been the wind; she closed her eyes. She was falling, sinking, falling . . . and it was like she'd wished for. His arms were around her, pulling her close. She rested her head on his shoulder, and it fit as if made for her.

He felt like home.

He ran his fingers through her tangles and the sheer joy of the tingles in her scalp calmed her. She lifted her face for whatever came next.

He placed his forehead against hers; she smelled morning tea. He kissed her, and the rest of her roaring thoughts faded away. The kiss was gentle at first, then their arms and legs tangled, and the ache of longing transformed into something she had less control over: desire.

He nibbled the edge of her ear, murmuring, "Mum said to watch out for each other. I won't stop now."

"Watch out for each other."

A ringing keened in Hazel's ears, a high-pitched sound that had her pushing Harry away and sent her feet moving again, toward the river, toward Flora, toward the red blanket on the cold ground.

Harry's footsteps followed behind her, the ground shaking. They reached the river's edge together. There was the blanket with the basket and a piece of cheese; an empty stillness.

Flora was gone.

# CHAPTER 40

## March 1960

"Pegs, tell me the difference between fairy tales and, say, *The Tale of Peter Rabbit* or *Gulliver's Travels,*" said Wren.

They were tangled together in a canopied bed in London's Savoy Hotel, and even as Wren's hand ran down her leg and scooped her closer, Peggy had a hard time believing it was real. Everything had happened so fast: a meeting at midnight in the garden behind his house, the rushed drive to the airport, a day in Boston and its airport, a sleepy all-night plane ride, and soon after a cabbie chattering away in a British accent.

She answered Wren as best she could with the disconnected feel of someone suspecting they might be dreaming.

"Aesop's are beast tales," she told him. "And *Gulliver* is a traveler's tale and another one . . . *Alice's Adventures in Wonderland* is a dream tale."

"Someone has divided up these tales?" he said. "Does it matter what the stories are called?"

"Only to academics who need to finish their doctorate." She trailed her fingers along his chest. "I've always loved Alice the best. I never thought of hers as a dream story, not until I heard it described that way. I've had dreams about her dream, which sounds a bit nutty, I know."

This discussion about fairy tales and stories was one they'd been having since the plane lifted off, since her head rested on his shoulder, and they rose above the clouds to eventually descend into a new land. It was an ongoing conversation punctuated by touch and kiss and a sense of becoming someone else, like a transformation of Proteus the shape-shifting god.

High in the sky, she'd asked, "Wren, can you tell me why you were kicked out of Harvard?"

He'd pulled away from her. She shouldn't have asked.

"There was a cheating incident in our chemistry class," he said calmly. "I refused to rat out my pal, and they suspended us all. Eventually, what your mother didn't tell you was my pal confessed and we were all exonerated. Suspension lifted. I have no idea how she knows anything about it. She's . . . wow."

"Yes, she is." Peggy had snuggled closer, astounded that she could.

And now in bed in a luxurious hotel as far away from her mother as she'd ever been, she stretched out her arms languorously as Wren said, "Dreams about dreams." He reached over and gently pulled her to his side. She nodded into his chest, a soft place with downy seagrass-colored hair.

"What a fairy tale is meant to do," she said, "if it's meant to do anything at all, Tolkien says, is give us new perspective in our world, the consolation of a happy ending. A recovery of sorts. Like we leave that world to see ours anew. Does that make sense?"

"Like when I leave you, and everything is different; or when I'm with you, and it feels like the world and everything in it is alive and for me?"

Heat rushed through her; his words were as water to parched earth. "*I* give you new perspective?" she asked, nudging her hip closer to him as he wrapped his leg around hers, their bodies coming together again.

"You are my fairy tale. You always have been," he said.

# CHAPTER 41

### October 19, 1940

"When was the last time you saw Flora?" Standing at the river's edge, Aiden Davies asked Hazel, then Harry, and then Bridie, with such a calm expression on his face that Hazel felt a scream building within, spiraling up and up.

"For me, it was late this morning," Bridie told him. "When I left the children to drive into Oxford to register for a telephone."

"She was right here sleeping like she does every afternoon, just fine as could be." Hazel stomped her feet on the blanket just a few yards from the muddy river. Her wellies dented the earth, divots the size of her feet.

Harry's face was so pale that Hazel thought he might faint. "I went to find Hazel," he said. "I didn't want to wake Flora."

Aiden Davies wrote in a notebook he'd pulled from his pocket. His cheeks were rough with a beard just starting to grow in.

When Hazel and Harry had seen Flora was gone, Harry had bolted back to the house to tell Bridie while Hazel ran up and down the riverbank, screaming "Flora Lea!" so many times now her throat was raw and burning.

In a few minutes, Harry had returned, calling Flora's name, too. Bridie went to Father Fenelly's to summon the police, and then together they'd all searched the riverside. They spread out along the banks of the river and into the woodlands all around, up to Wytham Woods and beyond.

Some ran to the boathouse where the river split before joining itself again on the other side.

*Flora Lea!*

The police arrived fast and loud, with sirens screeching along Binsey Lane. Hazel, Bridie, and Harry covered as much ground as they could while Bridie asked Hazel questions. She wasn't accusing; she was too kind for that.

Where did you go? Why was she alone? How long? What was she doing?

Harry was the one who told his mum, "Hazel was upset because I said something dumb, and she ran away, but just right to the glade. I ran after her. We weren't gone five minutes."

"How far can a little girl go in five minutes?" Bridie asked, her face contorted with fear.

Hazel wasn't so sure it was only five minutes. She wanted to reach backward to the moment she ran away from Harry. She'd never leave her sister. Not ever. What had she done?

Thoughts bounced and tangled; all of them coming too fast, accompanied by a metallic taste at the back of her tongue.

At the river's edge, Hazel's foot skidded. The water was muddy, churned-up, and angry in its run, its edges soft with shadows falling in dark stains, the water moving faster with the previous night's rainstorm filling its banks.

Hazel spotted the muddy fur and screamed. Berry's head and right arm were in the shallows of the river, his body and legs in the soft silt, almost swallowed by the brown rush and green reeds. She grabbed at the teddy bear's arm.

"Here!" Hazel called out. Everyone ran to join her; the two policemen and Bridie and Harry, staring down at the river as if expecting Flora to be bobbing atop it, waving at them.

Aiden Davies let out a groan and looked to Hazel.

"Is this hers?"

"Yes. She never goes anywhere without Berry."

Word spread fast, and Mr. Nolan and Miss Slife, the Baldwin twins, and some schoolchildren with their parents arrived. The crowd was rushing to the riverbanks when Aiden called out, "Do not go near there. We have to look for footprints."

The group halted as Aiden methodically moved along the edge, slogging through the reeds, peeking inside the watery hollows under bent tree branches. "I don't see any footprints," he said, as if this was good news. But Hazel knew what it meant: Flora had gone into the river and hadn't stepped out.

She knew what she had to do: Hazel sat on the earth, soft and cold, yanking off her wellies and thick woolen socks, tossing them to the ground. Before anyone could notice or stop her, she jumped into the river, ignoring the cold and how swiftly and murkily it moved.

These were the shallows, and Hazel had entered them in the summer with Harry, when Imogene babysat Flora. They'd jumped in to cool off, the water a slap of wonder and luxury as they dug their feet in the silt below and let the river rush past them like smooth hands.

The river was frigid and higher than when she'd swum with Harry, and she sank to her waist and found purchase in the slippery, unstable silt below. With a deep breath that ran across her raw throat, she ducked under the surface, opening her eyes and letting her palms travel along the sifting ground. She found nothing but rocks. She rose and dove under again.

She ignored them hollering her name, telling her to stop, to get out, Harry's voice above them all. Then came a pain in her shoulder— someone was dragging her, pulling her by her arm. She fought back, but it was useless. Aiden Davies was bigger, stronger—made of steel, it seemed. "Stop it, Hazel," he said. "We'll find her. Stop!"

The policeman had his fingers around her numb arm in a grip that dented her skin and would leave a bruise. The gathered townspeople stared at her. Hazel only knew she was cold because her body was shivering, her teeth slamming into each other, but she didn't *feel* cold, not the way she understood feeling cold. She felt only a great yawning despair, similar but even larger than when she'd heard her papa was gone.

"Where's the hag?" she screamed. She yanked her arm from the policeman but he wouldn't release her. She slapped at him, hit him. "Don't you see? Mrs. Marchman is the only one not here. She took Flora, I know it. She took Flora to replace Kelty."

Aiden released Hazel and picked up the blanket, the last place Flora had been, and he wrapped it around Hazel. "Go home. Get warm. Let us do our job."

Hazel looked at him, didn't nod with agreement, but instead ran away at full speed. They would assume she'd be headed home, but she remembered the way to Mrs. Marchman. Her bare feet smacked against the soft ground, then along the dirt road. She passed The Perch, its door left open as Mr. Nolan had run to the river to help. She passed the low-slung thatch-roofed schoolhouse, past the American nurse riding her bike with wild Queen's Anne lace filling her basket, waving in the wind with their clusters of white.

Hazel *must* save Flora.

This was not a magical tale; this was her sister.

This was real life.

She heard Harry running behind her. He didn't call her name, but he was there. Together they'd free Flora from the clutches of the hag. Mrs. Marchman, with her wiry hair and yellow nails and the stench of liquor and sweat, who must have been watching and waiting in the woods until she could steal Flora to replace Kelty.

Aiden Davies might believe that Flora had fallen into the river and drowned, but Hazel would prove him wrong.

The yard in front of Mrs. Marchman's house was a slipshod array of a shattered world: a deflated tire on its side with grass sprouting from its middle, a busted hoe with bent and rusted teeth, a defeated white fence flattened over a dead garden. The front door's green paint was peeling and blistered with age, and when Hazel reached it, she banged on it with her fist. Harry arrived behind her, gasping.

Mrs. Marchman opened the door wearing the same dreary dress she always did. Her long hair was pulled back into a braid. Blinking into the sunlight, she lifted a wrinkled hand to shade her eyes. "What do you want?" she asked.

Hazel could smell a yeasty aroma waft from the interior of her squalid home, the stench of a basement or a cement storage cellar.

"Give Flora back!" Hazel screamed.

Mrs. Marchman stared at them and narrowed her eyes in confusion, and Hazel immediately knew that she'd been wrong. This wretched woman didn't have the ability to steal away anyone. She was addled, confused, and completely unaware of the great drama taking place beside the nearby River Thames.

Hazel's legs gave way beneath her, but Harry caught her as she fell. He lowered her to the ground and held her while Mrs. Marchman regarded them coldly.

Harry ignored the hag and pulled Hazel in close. "We'll find her."

Hazel closed her eyes, wanting it all to disappear. Instead, she recalled a nightmare she'd had of Flora falling through Frideswide's treacle well at the edge of a cemetery.

The well.

*Alice's treacle well.*

Hazel's teeth chattered. She grabbed the collar of Harry's sweater. "The well," she said.

If Hazel had not allowed Flora to enter the shimmering door in the woodlands, she might instead go to her spot at the well, where the Dormouse told Alice three sisters lived at its bottom.

Harry pulled Hazel to her feet. He looked to Mrs. Marchman. "If you have a phone, please call the police and tell them to meet us at the chapel."

She nodded and slammed the door as Hazel and Harry ran toward the church. Harry knew a shortcut through the Oxfordshire fields. Heather swiped his corduroys and Hazel's bare legs, the nettles catching the edges of her feet with the ground soft and giving. The day was sinking toward evening, and ahead she saw the chapel steeple, piercing the setting sun like a needle in a pink balloon. Slanted and cracked, the gravestones in the cemetery glistened in waning sunlight.

Hazel was terrified this day would end without Flora beside her, that darkness would cover this land. Flora had never been alone at dark, always curled tightly to Hazel's side.

When they arrived at the well, Aiden Davies was already there with Father Fenelly and a smattering of the townspeople. Ethan Baldwin was peering into the dark hole, too narrow for a child to enter, but the lure of it fascinating even to him.

"Today's the feast of St. Frideswide," Father Fenelly said, his voice soft. "It's the day Oxford celebrates the day of her death."

Hazel, sick and dizzy, turned on Father. "I don't care. I don't care about the stupid princess. Where is Flora?"

"You called us here?" Aiden asked Hazel so gently, pressing his palms together in a prayer gesture and holding them against his chest.

"Yes. If Flora ran away, she would come here. She thought it was magical . . ."

"Magical?" Another policeman, a new one she had never seen before, spat out the word with contempt, spinning around to face Hazel and Harry. His face was pockmarked with an old illness and his eyes so hidden beneath the folds of his lids that they looked pressed into dough. The man shifted his hat on his head and glared at Aiden. "Coming here was a waste of time. It's obvious she's in the river."

Aiden took off his coat, a dark blue wool one with fat brass buttons, and threw it over Hazel's shoulders. "You're going to get sick if you do not go home and get warm."

The running, the fear, the knowledge that this was all her fault swamped Hazel with dizziness. Haloes of sunlight flickered around all the faces at the well, the glistening water at the edge of the dark rock like diamonds of the treacle—it all swam before her, melting. She was the one in the river, drowning, gasping for breath, going under.

# CHAPTER 42

## March 1960

The night before leaving for Paris with Barnaby, Hazel dreamed of Harry. He was standing at the edge of the river surrounded by wildflowers growing so fast he was watching them thrust through the earth. He laughed as the red and yellow and orange flowers opened their petaled faces to the cerulean sky. Hazel was calling his name and he didn't hear her, over and over she called his name until she awoke. Her neck was cramped and her face smashed against the kitchen table where she'd fallen asleep.

Barnaby was gently shaking her. "Hazel."

She sat, groaned.

Barnaby stood over her, dressed in his suit and a tie, the university logo on his pocket. "Are you all right?" He grimaced. "You were calling out . . . that boy's name."

She rubbed her face and rotated her head, cranked her neck left and right before gazing at Barnaby. "It was a nightmare and no one could hear me. I was at the river and . . ."

He lifted her notebook, scanned the pages, and his eyebrows rose. "You're writing your story? That's why—you're reliving it all? Why?"

She stood with a shooting pain in her hip. She'd rested her head on the table somewhere in the middle of the night, in the middle of the writing. What time had that been?

"I need tea," she said.

She felt him watching as she moved to the kettle and the stove, rubbing her head and trying to wake. She turned to him. "I wanted to finish the story, but I didn't."

"Our stories are never finished." He smiled weakly.

"But I want this one to be done." Her voice cracked with the truth. "I desperately want those days to be over and in our past. I intended to write down all that happened until now, but I fell asleep writing the day Flora disappeared." She rubbed at the fatigue. "I'm so sorry about the past two weeks. I've been so distracted and distant and . . ."

"Come here, love." He held out his arms and she went to him. He rubbed her back and whispered, "It's all going to be okay."

"I just wanted to get it out. It's like those days have been stuck inside of me." She shuddered against him. "They've been living inside me without my permission."

"Get it out of your system. Get *him* out of your system." He kissed her neck.

She lifted her head and gazed into his eyes with a question.

"Harry," he said. "Get him out of your system, please."

She moved toward the kettle as it steamed, making a cup of tea without another word. "*He's* not the problem. It's everything else."

"It's all right," he said. "I smoothed everything over with my parents. I explained who Harry was and why you were there. They understood."

"Thank you," she said robotically. "But honestly, your parents are the last thing I'm worried about."

"You realize we leave tonight"—he glanced at his watch—"in ten hours, don't you?"

She turned to him with a forced smile. "The *Night Ferry*. I've been thinking about it for so long. Moving across the English Channel in the night, in a train on a ferry! How amazing and posh is that?"

From the inside pocket of his coat, Barnaby produced two tickets. "We'll take Charing Cross to Victoria and board the sleeping car. They have catering onboard. When the train arrives in Dover, it uncouples from the tracks and the entire car drives onto the ship. We'll wake in Paris!"

"Imagine that." She kissed him.

"Yes," he added. "Then to the Le Meurice hotel, followed by maca-roons and the Louvre and red wine and . . ." He swept her backward as if they were dancing, and she wished she felt as free and light as she feigned. He brought her upright and kissed her. "But for now I must work and you, my dear, must pack—although I hope you won't be wearing clothes all the time." He kissed her one more time and winked before leaving.

———

Charing Cross Station's black clock above the ticker tape of train sched-ules read six p.m. Barnaby pushed the trolley with one hand and used his other to steady the stacked-up luggage threatening to tip. He and Hazel hustled toward Platform 7. With each step forward, she felt something tugging her backward, a rope pulling at her that she would cut if she knew how, but the best she could do was ignore it.

She walked beside Barnaby in her smartest traveling suit: a red tweed skirt and matching jacket with big black buttons. Her outfit was com-pleted by black ballet shoes and a pillbox hat. She would not arrive in Paris looking anything less than chic.

The evening's mellowing sky was visible above the open latticework arching over the station. Posters announced Moss Bros. clothing and Guinness beer, red and white British Union Jack flags fluttered from the roof, porters in black hats pushed carts of tipping luggage, and children trailed behind their frazzled parents amid the grind, puff, and screech of arriving trains.

Hazel's two suitcases were filled with the best of her wardrobe, from silk dresses with matching hats to lingerie she'd bought just for the trip—there were still tags on the straps of nightgowns and demi cup bras with lace.

Barnaby juggled the suitcases off the trolley, cursing as her smaller black one landed on his foot.

Maybe she should just jump on a plane to America, track down the author, and demand an explanation. *Tell me now! Who are you? Where did you find this story? Are you hiding my sister?* She'd gone as far as she could here in England, tracked down every source she could think of, and hit her head on dead ends as dense as brick walls.

What if she grabbed his arm right now and told him, Barnaby, love, I think we should change our plans and instead of a trip to Paris we should fly to Boston. It'll be grand!

How absurd. How mad. If she wanted to blow up their life and their relationship, if she wanted to end it all as she had every other relationship before him, that would be the perfect plan. But that *wasn't* what she wanted. She wanted to stick it out; she wanted love that lasted; she wanted to walk through life with someone who loved her and whom she loved in return.

If she kept running backward, she would never quite be able to run forward. Even if a miracle had occurred and Flora had survived to tell the story and carry it across the sea, even then, six-year-old Flora was still gone. Even if Hazel found her sister, she would not find the sister she lost.

Her obsession with reasons and explanations, her desperate need to make meaning of the meaningless and sense of the senseless was destroying what she had right here, right now. She watched Barnaby move toward the train and she followed. The olive-colored train car rolled to the platform, smoke pouring from its stack as its brakes gave a high squeal. He smiled at her. "Off we go."

The door hissed open, and Hazel stepped after him onto the metal stair of the first-class sleeper car. Barnaby held out his hand to help her up. Above Hazel in the train stood a woman with an owl brooch on her blue suit jacket.

"Oh, pardon me," she said, moving sideways to make room for Hazel.

An owl.

Whisperwood.

"Hazel!" Kelty's voice, or was Hazel imagining it? Then again. "Hazel! Stop."

Barnaby turned, letting go of Hazel's hand, and she stumbled on the stair. Quickly regaining her footing, she stepped back to the platform and spotted Kelty bounding toward her, with Midge fast at her heels.

"What the bloody hell?" Barnaby said. He glared at Kelty.

"Midge!" Hazel bent down and hugged her goddaughter, who wore a bright blue jacket with a lace Peter Pan collar, beginning to look so grown-up and proper. "How's my girl?"

"I want to come to Paris with you, but Mum said that's impossible."

"Next time?" Hazel asked.

Midge nodded and looked to her mum, who was out of breath, sweat on her forehead, with her wild red hair dashed about her like fire. Kelty spoke so rapidly it was hard to understand, "I went to the flat to say goodbye, to tell you two to have the most lovely time in the whole world. Midge and I had a gift for you. We'd brought a box of chocolates for you to eat on the train."

"We left early to be sure," Barnaby said. "And you came to the station for chocolates?" His voice filled with hope even as Hazel felt that this was not about a box of sweets.

"No." Kelty held out a piece of paper. "And although I changed my mind ten times on the way here—"

"She did," Midge said. "We turned around twice."

"But I knew you wouldn't forgive me, Hazel," said Kelty. "Or I wouldn't forgive myself."

Hazel took the paper from Midge. Neat script stated: *I am here in London. I'd like to meet you at The Savoy lobby tomorrow morning at 9 a.m. if that is agreeable with you. Peggy Andrews.*

Hazel grabbed Barnaby's arm, held herself steady.

"What does it say?" he asked.

"Peggy. She's here. In London."

He grabbed the note and read it, his teeth gritted. "Hazel . . ." Barnaby set his hand on top of their pile of luggage, and she knew what the slight movement meant.

*Choose. Me or her? Me or the past? Me or the magical land of childhood?*
She couldn't have both.

# CHAPTER 43

## October 19, 1940

"Hazel!" Mum's voice pierced a long echoing tunnel padded with thick blankets.

For a few blessed moments, fifteen-year-old Hazel forgot the truth and thought herself soft and warm in bed with Flora. Mum had come to visit them in Binsey, bearing gifts: a new whirly toy, possibly a jump rope or, if they were truly lucky, a new cloth bag of marbles or a whip-top Flora could spin.

Hazel opened her eyes. Confused, she found herself lying in the back of a car, her head in Harry's lap. The car door was open at her feet, and she pushed Harry away in surprise and confusion. She sat and saw her mum outside the vehicle.

What was Mum doing here?

What kind of car was this?

Why was she barefoot?

The questions rolled over her in one foggy morass.

And then the answer in her own heart: She'd lost Flora.

Hazel stumbled out of the car; they were in front of Bridie's cottage. She threw herself into her mum's arms. Mum had worn her softest coat and camel-colored cashmere gloves, and she stroked Hazel's hair, but didn't say it was okay. The absence of soothing words was as good as confirmation that Flora was still and truly gone.

After warm broth that didn't warm and soft blankets that didn't comfort, Hazel was left alone in the bed in the little room off the kitchen. A hot water bottle sat on her tummy and blankets piled all about her, pinning her down, their warmth no replacement for her sister's. The others were doing the adults' work now: planning search parties and sending others to the neighboring villages to make calls, notifying the press so they could hang pictures of her around various villages and into Oxford proper.

Shivering, hot and cold at the same time, Hazel threw off the blankets. The hot water bottle fell to the floor in a thump, the bladder jiggling.

She deserved no comfort.

St. Frideswide's Day—today—was the day the princess died. Hazel would not allow Flora to share the day of Frideswide's death. Hazel rose from bed, her flannel pajamas like rough sand against her burning skin, her slippers moving silently along the hardwood floor. She opened the bottom dresser drawer. Her stories of Whisperwood were neatly piled, one on top of the other, right next to a pile of Harry's drawings. She lifted the pages she'd written, staring by moonlight at the words, the story that had taken Flora from Hazel.

Guilt and shame warred and stormed inside of her. She had led her sister into a rushing river, looking for something that didn't exist. No one must ever know about these pages or these words.

Fever sizzled behind her eyes and on her neck, yet nothing mattered more to her than destroying these stories. Gathered around the kitchen table just outside her door, the adults would see her if she walked out.

In the moonlit room, she filled her knapsack with the pages, shoving them to the bottom of the bag where just a year ago her mum had packed her jersey and ration book, her socks and sneakers. Hazel remembered it all with such clarity, it could be happening right then.

Hazel unlatched the window, its brass lock easily sliding up and away. She placed her chapped fingers under the lip of the sill and pulled up slowly and with all her might, creating an opening just big enough to slip through. Outside she landed softly on the earth with both feet, her white lamb's wool slippers absorbing the dampness.

The full moon cowered behind low flat clouds. Knowing her way, even in the dark, she reached the riverbank where she'd found Berry, where she'd lost Flora, where the world had caved in on itself.

Hazel dropped the knapsack to the ground and opened its buckles, her hands steady with purpose. She lifted the pages, then removed her slippers.

Her bare feet caught on nettles that stung, but Hazel didn't feel that until later when the welts rose, and a poultice was wrapped around her feet while her fever raged, and a nurse hovered over her with clucking sounds of sympathy.

But for now, she walked along the river without sliding in. In her mind, she saw horrible images of Flora tumbling into the water. Why hadn't she called out? Why hadn't Flora called Hazel's name? Or had she?

Hazel opened her hand and let the pages fly away, wings of white with her scribbled handwriting across the lines. The papers dropped and sank, one by one. She watched as the weight of their guilt, the shame of existing, dragged them to the bottom of the rushing river heading toward the sea.

Hazel prayed the same had not happened to Flora, but if it had, the stories must go with her.

When the pages were gone, she trudged through the night, a growing hollowness within, widening, spinning outward. The world without Flora was impossible.

Shivering and not caring one bit, she reached St. Margaret's church again. This time, instead of going to the well, Hazel pushed at its massive wooden doors and entered.

Even in the dark, Hazel knew her way to the altar, to the wooden kneeling step with the needlepoint images of the saints sewn by the women of the church. She stood and faced the crucifix above: Jesus, bleeding from the crown of thorns, blood flowing down his face.

She stared at Jesus and knelt. "Please send her back to me."

Hazel glanced about for something that might cut her skin and bring a swell of blood to the surface, for that was the only way now. She glanced about and spied nothing to injure herself with, but remembering her bare feet, she glanced down. There, her ankle bled with the scratches from her flight through the woodlands. She scratched at the wound, allowed the blood to become fresh and red. She swiped her finger across her skin and then rubbed the blood on the marble altar. "By my blood," she said. "I vow to never again tell an untrue, made-up story or escape to Whisperwood. Bring Flora back to me, and I will never see Harry Aberdeen again. I will never do any of these things. I swear upon my life."

Then the cries filled the church—were they hers or the owl's? The cries echoed and rang against the damp stones. She repeated the vow three times—the three times of magical incantations.

This was the unraveling Hazel had felt in her gut when Mum held the note of evacuation in the backyard in Bloomsbury. It hadn't been the war that threatened her life; it was Flora's disappearance. Somehow she had known that something terrible would happen, and that it would be her fault. A thread had been pulled; it was her undoing.

The only thing to do was to find Flora. And Hazel would. No matter how long it took, or what she lost along the way.

———

When Hazel arrived back at the cottage, she crawled again through the window and into the empty bed. In the early morning hours, she awoke as Mum shook her.

"Hazel, wake up. I can't carry you. We must get you to hospital."

She shivered with fever. Her tongue and face were on fire and her thoughts muddled as she obeyed her mum, stumbling from the bedroom in her flannel pajamas, through the living room and out the front door.

Just before she reached a waiting taxi, the previous day and night before exploded in a thunderous memory. Hazel turned to see Harry and Bridie on the front porch, bereft, leaning into each other for support. Aiden Davies stood next to them with a notebook and a lost expression.

Hazel remembered Harry asking about the story, then kiss in the hollowed tree, and her own promise at the chapel under the crucified Jesus to never, not ever see or talk to Harry again. This vow might bring back Flora. She broke free of Mum's grasp and screamed into the haze of fear and loss, "I never, ever want to see you again!"

# CHAPTER 44

## October 1940

When Hazel finally woke fully in hospital, Mum sat at her bedside.

"You're here," Hazel said.

"Yes, darling."

A glass bottle of clear fluid hung on a metal hook and was tethered to her arm with a tube. Hazel heard the rustle of stiff uniforms. There was the clang of rolling carts, hushed voices, and a holler of pain from down the hall. It smelled nauseating, of alcohol and urine mixed.

"How long have I been here?"

"Three days."

Hazel had succumbed to the quicksand of despair; even breathing hurt. There had been long warped dreams in Whisperwood, of talking owls and the silent queen on her throne, of drowning and of wells over-flowing.

Hazel groaned, her throat cracked and parched. "And Flora?"

"The Blitz is taking the world's attention," Mum said, her face thin, skin papery around her eyes. "The world is on fire. But Constable Davies says they are looking for her. I've placed signs and photos of her in every window in Oxford."

"I will find her," Hazel promised with a voice cracking on every word.

"Darling, at the moment you have pneumonia and cannot leave this bed. Not yet."

"When I do get up, I will find her." She pulled her thin blanket around herself. "I know you will hate me until I do."

"No!" Mum cried out so loudly the nurse came, then quietly closed the curtain that separated them from a woman unconscious in the next bed. Mum took Hazel in her arms. "It is not your fault. Don't you dare carry that with you. Promise me."

"I promise nothing," Hazel said, "only that I will find her. And I will never see Harry or Bridie Aberdeen again."

"Oh, Hazel. I should have never sent you two away. I should have kept you in Bloomsbury. I should have gone with you."

"Mum, you did what you were told was best. And we loved it there. This is not because of you. I didn't watch out."

"Oh, darling, you aren't making sense."

"Bridie and Harry must hate me, too." Hazel felt this loss as severe as an amputated limb, her left hand gone, her heart, which she thought could feel no more pain, collapsed.

"They absolutely do not hate you."

"That's a lie to make me feel better. Don't bother, Mum." A long stretch of silence followed that, then she asked, "What does Constable Davies say now?"

"He believes she drowned. He said someone would have seen her; so many are looking for her, and just her teddy bear at the side of the river."

"She didn't drown," Hazel said.

"I pray you are right, darling. I pray you are right."

———

The police sent search parties from Binsey to Oxford to Godstow, people gathering in groups to slowly scour the riverbanks, comb the woodlands of Shotover Hill. Nets were dragged along the river bottom.

For two months, Hazel and Mum stayed in Oxford in a one-room flat where they shared a bed and spent days wandering from shop to shop, door to door, hanging missing girl posters and bursting through the doors of the *Oxford Mail* to beg them to put a photo and story about Flora on the front page.

The Blitz was unrelenting for eight months. Newspapers and reporters and police were buried under an avalanche of disaster. What was one more child who had obviously been left alone to drown?

Some mornings Mum was unable to get out of bed. Other times, she stayed awake for days. Hazel didn't go to school and wandered the streets and woodlands of Oxfordshire, looking for her sister. Each carried her own grief, sometimes in opposing ways, and in other moments they found themselves on the same grief-stricken sea holding on to each other for breath and life. What surprised them both was the fear, and the casual way it would sneak up on them, grab them by the throat or the chest. There was the fear that she was alive and with someone else; the fear that she was dead; the fear that they'd have to live their entire lives without her; the fear that they, each, were to blame.

Mum fretted that she'd lose Hazel to the same fate as Flora and her husband, and finally in the new year, holidays ignored altogether, Mum took Hazel back to their home in Bloomsbury. Bombs and fear be damned; for there in London was a flat and a job and neighbors to help them.

Hazel searched desperately for someone to blame—from God to Bridie to the Pied Piper scheme of Britain, but always in the end she blamed herself. She knew gossips and the newspapers pointed their fingers at Bridie and at Harry. Hazel felt she could have changed that by telling the truth about her Whisperwood story, how Flora must have gone to find it, why she and Harry weren't watching Flora. But she didn't.

Hazel considered herself a coward.

Hazel and Mum settled in to dreary London, waiting in queues ages long for everything they needed from Spam to wilted vegetables.

Then at seventeen years old in 1942, Hazel left London for university, trying to also leave behind memories of events she couldn't change. With the war raging, Hazel took the entrance exams and found herself in a dorm room of Newnham College. She studied literature at Cambridge University. The dreams never stopped: the panic and scrabbling for something lost, the sickening drop of dread when she remembered. She made her way through the days carrying the memory like a boulder she refused to put down.

By May 7 of 1945, Hazel had graduated, and she was in London working at Hogan's as the church bells rang in September, announcing the end of the war. And yet she still kept her eyes peeled for a girl with blond curls, laughing in the woodlands of her imagination.

# CHAPTER 45

## March 19, 1960

Peggy Andrews rose quietly from the four-poster bed; the lamps with red fabric shades cast a sunrise glow. Wren slept soundly on his side with his legs stretched their full length, his toes poking from the end of the sheets. Staring at him, she realized she loved him.

My God, what had her mother kept her from all these years by telling her of the dangers of boys and sex? Of pregnancy, and the evils of Wren?

Peggy reached for anger and hate for her mother but found instead pity. What danger her mother had experienced, the ripping loss of Daddy downed in Pearl Harbor, moving across the country to be with her sister, whom she then lost. It was no wonder Mother savored safety.

Today Peggy would meet the woman who claimed that Whisperwood was *her* story, and that did not fall under the category of "safe" at all.

The first thing Peggy and Wren had done after they'd landed in London and checked into the hotel was take a cab to the British Library in North London and request access to the newspaper archives. They'd asked for the Oxford papers from late 1940 and in silence read the articles about Flora Lea Linden. Peggy had been overwhelmed by the sadness and mystery of this loss, of the unsolvable disappearance of someone who had been deeply loved by her family. She cried and tears dropped onto the curled and yellowed papers.

"How did they bear it?" Peggy asked Wren.

"I'm not sure it is something you bear. But it does explain the letters and calls and telegrams from her. I would never give up, either. Not for something like this. Never."

Fairy tales, and this one in particular had consumed her life and her education. Now she was living inside her own very *real* life story, living it out one breath at a time, lingering until Wren woke so she could slip on the flowered dress and meet Hazel Linden.

———

Hazel stood at her kitchen counter and sipped her tea while she waited for Mum and Kelty to arrive. She tried to empty her mind of expectations, but that was like trying to stop the sun from now rising outside the window, turning the day dusky gray to gold.

Eight-thirty a.m.

Right now Hazel was meant to be waking in a first-class sleeper car with Barnaby, the ship coasting into dock as they rose for tea and their first view of Paris. Guilt washed over her in a damp sweat. She'd left him on the platform, his angry face mottled. And she understood—if he had done the same to her, she'd have been just as enraged. Kelty had helped Hazel with the luggage while Midge just looked confused and wanted to know if they could now eat the chocolates.

Hazel had tried to apologize to Barnaby, to explain that she had no choice, but he'd stopped her. She tried to ask if they could delay the trip just one day and he glared at her. She'd left him there with his luggage. Had he gone on without her?

Hazel cracked the kitchen window and let in a damp spring breeze, full of a loamy smell that meant the ground was bursting with new life, an aroma of green. Birds chirped and sang and trilled. She'd thought she wouldn't sleep last night but she had, and deeply.

The idea, and it crept up on her slowly, that this author might be Flora had turned to hope.

———

Back in the hotel room, sustained by coffee, Peggy stood in front of the hotel room's full-length mirror and assessed herself, attempting to view herself as Hazel might do.

Behind her, Wren zipped his pants and ran his fingers through his hair before slipping his arms around her, pulling her close in that way that made all her thoughts disappear, fall fast down the drain of her never-ending sink of worries. Together in the mirror they gazed at each other's reflections.

"Just look at us," said Wren. "What a mighty fine pair we are."

"In England," she said with a smile she was learning to see and feel on her face more often.

"It's time," he said.

Peggy turned and threw her arms around Wren, as if this was the way they'd been all their lives, as if this was how they'd always touched and talked. "I still don't know what to say when I see her," said Peggy. "Even though I spent most of the night thinking about it."

Wren stepped back and tapped her forehead. "Always thinking, this one."

She laughed, and he kissed her, and they headed out the hotel room door and down the long green-carpeted hallway. She pushed the elevator button.

———

Hazel buttoned her thin pollen-yellow coat with the belt that tied into a neat bow. Mum and Kelty waited outside on the front stoop. Hazel shut the door and locked it. "Okay, let's go."

They climbed out from the back of the cab a block from the hotel and the sky domed over them, blue and curved, high and cheerful, cloudless.

Kelty asked them, "Do you think you'd know Flora if you saw her?"

Mum answered quickly, "I would know her the second I saw her. If she's mine."

Hazel felt a trill of love. Mum might have married and loved and had another child, but she would know her own daughter in less than a breath. Loss lived alongside them both, yet somehow Mum had loved again.

"I think I would, yes," Hazel said. "When I was looking at Iris, I was trying to find Flora in her, but just couldn't. Of course I could have just asked her to show me her wrist and looked for the bunny ears."

Camellia spoke up. "The butterfly wings."

"The angel wings," Kelty said.

And they smiled at each other, the old quip revived.

Then Kelty asked, "Do we have any idea at all what this Peggy Andrews looks like?"

"I know only her age—twenty-four. I have no clear idea what she might look like." She gazed at the entry. "She said she'd meet us in the lobby."

"I am dying to know what this woman might possibly have to tell us," Kelty said as they stood in front of the red-lettered façade of The Savoy, the roundabout full of cabbies coming and going, the doorman in a black top hat with a white rose at his lapel opening the door with a swish. "And this better be good because I'm not accepting any cockamamie stories about magic floating in the air."

Even through the worry burrowed in her bones, Hazel laughed at her best friend as they entered the shining and flower-filled lobby.

—

Peggy looked about her. The hotel restaurant yawned open to the lobby. A marble floor entryway with a round table and a flower arrangement of roses, daffodils, hydrangeas, ranunculus, greenery, and tulips spilled from a white porcelain urn. Peggy stopped to stare at the blooms, touching the edge of a yellow daffodil to make sure it was all real: the hotel, the day, the flowers. The petal fell off in her hand, and she closed her fingers around its silk and tucked it into her purse.

The restaurant filled quickly, a din of voices in which a sentence or two slipped Peggy's way for her to pick up. Peggy scanned the lobby. "I don't know what Hazel Linden looks like. How will she know who we are?" she asked Wren.

"I guess she'll ask at the front desk and be directed to us."

"But I used your last name, not mine."

"I don't think it's hard to find two Americans, one whose first name is Peggy. Let's just wait here in the lobby like you said in the note. If she doesn't arrive, I'll go ask the front desk if anyone has been asking after us."

"Thank you, Wren. Thank you for being here. Thank you for bringing me."

"You," he said. "Thank you for you."

Heat flowed to her cheeks, the warmth of him so near. Only a minute passed when the concierge in her bright red uniform approached. "Are you Peggy Andrews?"

"I am." Peggy placed her left hand over her heart as if that could keep it from banging out of her chest.

"There are some women looking for you."

"Women? As in more than one?" she asked.

"Yes, three of them." She pointed across the large lobby.

"She probably didn't want to do this alone," Wren said.

"What if she brought her mother? What if they make a scene? What if they brought police or an attorney?"

Wren smiled. "What if none of that is true?"

Peggy took Wren's hand and they walked across the foyer.

———

Hazel and Kelty stood in the middle of the lobby, glancing back and forth between the elevators and the restaurant. A nervous Camellia had gone to powder her nose. The blooms from the wild bouquet on the round table emitted such a lush fragrance it nearly made Hazel dizzy.

A man and a woman approached them. The woman's brown hair was wound into a knot at the base of her neck. She wore a green dress and matching cardigan with pearls, which made her appear like a child playing dress-up.

Hazel searched the woman's face, looking for evidence of Flora in the way she walked and clung to the man's arm. He was tall with blond hair still damp at the edges, wearing a pair of tweedy trousers and a cream-colored sweater, looking like he'd just jumped off a fishing boat.

Their gazes met. "Are you Miss Linden?" asked the woman.

"I am." For all her wondering about what to say, Hazel merely held out her hand and said, "Hallo, I'm Hazel Linden."

When they shook hands, Hazel waited for the tremor, the knowing, the tingle that would tell her if this was her sister.

It could be. It was possible. The upturned nose, the tiny frame, the brown eyes a bit more golden. And yet something essential was missing. Something . . . Flora.

"It's nice to meet you," Peggy said quietly.

Camellia emerged from around the corner and reached Hazel's side. She gazed at Peggy Andrews, then in a strong, sure voice said, "It's not her."

"No, it's not," Hazel said.

Peggy looked to Wren. "What is she talking about?"

Wren smiled sadly. "I think Miss Linden was hoping you'd be her sister. The lost sister."

# CHAPTER 46

## March 19, 1960

They all stood outside at the back of the hotel in the Victorian Embankment Gardens, which faced the rushing River Thames, where most of the world assumed Flora had gone. Looming beyond, Big Ben kept the time, the pinnacles of Parliament pierced the sky, and Waterloo Bridge arched over the river. All five of them—Hazel and Kelty flanking Camellia and standing across from Wren and Peggy, behind them the iron statue of Robert Burns seated and staring off.

"I *am* sorry about your sister," Peggy said. "I really am." She fiddled with the buttons on her cardigan. "I want to help. That's part of why I came here. I also want to find out why my mother isn't telling me the entire truth about Whisperwood."

"Your mother must know," Hazel said. "Someone told her, and she told you. Your mother is the key."

"She didn't write the book." Peggy stood taller, slid back her shoulders. "I did."

"I know, and it's amazing. I'm not accusing you of stealing something I've written. That's not what this is about. You took a simple land I created, and you made it into an entire enchanting and beautiful series of stories that I am *not* trying to claim. I just need to know how you came upon it, because it might mean . . . it might mean my sister is alive. I don't want your stories. I want to know where they came from."

"The only one who can tell us the truth—" Peggy stopped abruptly, her gaze over Hazel's shoulder. "Mother?"

Something about Peggy's exhaled breath, the fear quivering in the word *mother*, and they all turned. Striding toward them across the wide green grass, anger emanating like a shimmering gray aura, was a woman with long ebony hair flowing behind her like a dark veil.

"This is Mother," Peggy said to all of them.

The woman's unbuttoned black coat flapped until she reached the group gathered in the gardens. The clouds moved quickly to cover the sun, sending long shadows on the grass.

Before reaching them, the woman shouted, "Peggy Maria Andrews, what have you done?"

Peggy stepped forward and asked, "Mother, how did you . . . what are you doing here?"

"I always know when you're in danger." She pointed at Wren. "And it's usually with him."

As her voice echoed across the park, a group of tourists with maps and cameras stopped to stare, yet Linda Andrews paid no mind to them, focused solely on her daughter.

"You flew on a plane? I can't believe it." Peggy's voice small now, tinny. "I don't understand how you knew where I was."

"A letter arrived after you snuck out of our house in the middle of the night. It was a letter from a crazy woman named Hazel Linden; it came from the publishing house. Didn't take much to find you after that. I went to Wren's mother; somehow *he* told *her* where you were staying, even if you didn't tell me."

Hazel stared at the woman. Oh, God, yes, the letter she'd sent two weeks ago had arrived in America, summoning this woman. Hazel struggled to see if there was anything familiar in her chiseled face.

Linda Andrews set her hands on Peggy's shoulders. "I'd do anything for you, even fly on a contraption that might kill me. Anything." Linda looked at the rest of the group and shook her head. "Which one of you is Hazel?"

"I am," Hazel said, and stepped forward. "I wrote to your daughter."

"You stalked and tracked down my daughter and seduced her to come to England?" Linda looked as if she might break into tears.

"No," Hazel said. "It appears you sold a first edition of her book with original illustrations and they ended up in my hands."

"Mother!" Peggy found her voice. "You sold the illustrations?"

"For us, sweetie. For us and for our future. It was a grand amount of money." She turned to Hazel now. "You lost your sister? That's what the letter said."

Peggy interrupted. "Mother, it's true. I read the articles and it's horrific," Peggy said. "Time for you to tell the truth." Her voice was calm and steady. "Tell them what happened. They've suffered. You must tell them what you know. Or what you did."

"I didn't do anything." The woman turned to face Hazel, Kelty, and Camellia, repeating, "I didn't do *anything*."

Camellia took a step toward Peggy's mother. "Imagine, just for a moment, that your six-year-old daughter disappeared. And imagine that all your life you looked for your daughter, always keeping your ears out for her laugh or your eyes peeled for your little girl."

Linda Andrews let out a cry. "No!"

Camellia continued, stepping closer. "That is what has happened to us, so please forgive us for wanting to know, desperately wanting to know, where you heard this story, in the chance that my daughter Flora, who is Hazel's sister, survived when everyone thought she had not."

After wiping at her face with both hands, Linda collapsed onto the black iron bench behind her. "I didn't *do* anything, I swear."

Camellia sat next to Linda. This was now between mother and mother. "I'm sorry your daughter ran here to England and didn't tell you. I would be upset if mine had done the same."

"It's that boy." Linda pointed at Wren. "He leads her astray."

"I'm sorry about that," Camellia said softly. "I've had to watch my daughter wander astray looking for her sister, grieving, and blaming herself. It's been dreadful. It has defined our life. If there is anything you can tell us. Anything at all."

Linda looked to her daughter, and her eyes filled with tears. "Everything I've ever done or said has been for your own good."

Peggy dropped into a crouch in front of her. "It's okay, just tell us now so we can help these people."

"Your aunt Maria . . ."

"The one who made the story?"

"Yes, but she didn't make it up. She brought it to us. For a year . . ." Linda looked around to the crowd of them, to Wren and to Hazel and Kelty.

"Mother, go on."

"During the war, my sister, Maria, wanted to be part of the solution, a meaningful part of the victory, so she volunteered for an organization that sent women overseas to help with the children of war widows. Maria was sent to Newcastle, England, where for a while she took care of a girl who used this story as what Maria called a pacifier. The little girl used it to calm herself."

Having drawn closer with each word, Hazel now stood over Linda and Camellia, listening.

Linda continued, "When Maria came home after that year, your darling father had been shot down by those savages in Pearl Harbor. I didn't know how to calm you, how to keep you safe. We moved to Cape Cod to be near Maria, and she told you this story . . . We then . . ." Linda stopped and sat straighter. "We grew it together as our own story."

"Oh, Mother. Why didn't you just tell me that?"

"Maria never gave me the little girl's name and it didn't matter to me." Her voice rose. "Why did it matter if a little girl in England told Maria? She told us and we made it ours." Linda slapped her hand on her leg for emphasis. "Ours."

Hazel interrupted, her voice louder than she'd meant for it to be, a breeze off the Thames carrying her words. "No! You wanted to make it yours."

Linda shook her head. "That's not true." She twisted on the bench to face her daughter. "It's ours now. It's been ours for all our lives. My little girl and I had nothing, absolutely nothing. My sister gone. My husband gone. Maria left us one thing—this story. What did it matter where it came from?"

Peggy stood now, shaking her head. "Mother, stop saying it's ours. Stop. What if that little girl from Newcastle who told the story is their lost daughter? Their lost sister?"

Linda Andrews placed her hand over her mouth but couldn't stop the cry that erupted. "Oh, God." She grabbed her daughter's arm, squeezed.

"Do you know any names?" Camellia asked. "Any names at all? The family? The little girl?"

Linda pressed her middle fingers to her eyelids and shook her head. "Maria never said." She opened her eyes to look at Camellia. "I'm telling the truth. Maria helped many families, but this story stuck with her. She felt it . . . saved this girl. And then shortly after she came back, we lost Maria—three years, to be exact. This story is as much a part of our family's past as it is yours."

"Mother!" Peggy cried out.

Linda shook her head. "I'm sorry. All I mean is that I lost Maria and this story came from her. That's all I can tell you. She never said a word about a missing child. Nothing like that." She paused. "It was just a story."

Hazel almost laughed. "It is never just a story."

Peggy nodded. "Yes, I know."

Camellia was the one to stand now. "Do you know the name of the organization that sent your sister to volunteer?"

Linda grimaced. "Maybe somewhere in my files at home? I don't know."

Camellia faced her daughter. "I know you don't want to, Hazel, but maybe it's time to talk to Dorothy Bellamy. Maybe if we let her write this story, someone will recognize this family or the young girl from Newcastle."

"Mum, I could just go to Newcastle and ask around."

"Twenty years now gone. Do you really think they'd still be there? A magazine will reach thousands, not just a few locals."

Hazel hadn't heard that kind of desperation in her mother's voice in so long; it was an echo of the years after Flora disappeared. "Mum, Dorothy Bellamy will tell the whole story of that awful day in a magazine. And people will blame Bridie and Harry and me all over again. She will dredge up—"

"But what if that means we find the girl who told the story? An article about a little girl from Newcastle might get someone to step forward and say they knew her."

Mum was right. It was time to talk to the reporter who wrote for *"younger smarter women."*

———

Only a half hour later, Hazel burst through her front door and dug out the crumpled letter still in the waste bin. Beneath a few days' of mail, she found it. She dialed the number quickly. "Dorothy Bellamy," the clipped voice said on the other side of the phone.

"Ms. Bellamy," Hazel said. "Hazel Linden here."

A sound of a brief intake of breath, of surprise. "Ms. Linden. I am so happy to hear from you."

She wasn't sure why she'd expected an older woman's voice, maybe one cracked with cigarette smoke and age. "Yes, well, I'm hoping you might meet me in Binsey. There is a pub there called The Perch. I can be there in two hours. I would like to talk to you."

"I am in North London and can be there in nearly the same time, yes. How will I know you?"

"I'm wearing a red coat." Hazel paused. "And you?" Hazel slowly shifted her expectations of Dorothy Bellamy from a stooped-shouldered journalist who had spent too much time bent over a typewriter to a woman who might be on the cover of the fancy magazine for which she wrote articles about lost children.

"I'll find you," Dorothy said, and hung up.

Hazel held the receiver, the cord stretched across her kitchen, and she wondered what the bloody hell she'd just done. What Pandora's box had she opened with a single small hope that this woman's article would bring someone forward with information about a little girl in Newcastle who talked of a magical land in the year of 1940?

But a little girl in that small northern village had told an American volunteer named Maria about Whisperwood and Maria had taken that tale to Cape Cod, Massachusetts, like a jewel in her hand, a gift for another young girl who lost her father, a consolation prize.

Hazel walked across the kitchen and replaced the phone in its cradle. She would be honest. If telling this reporter the whole story in all its brutal truth would bring her sister back, she would tell it.

Mum was back at her own home, Kelty, too. Peggy and Wren were with Linda Andrews somewhere in London, and Hazel wondered what their discussions were about now—forgiveness, blame, or possibly anger? But that was not her concern. Dorothy Bellamy was her concern now, a possible lifeline to the "little girl from Newcastle."

# CHAPTER 47

### March 19, 1960

Little had changed in twenty years. The Perch in Binsey nestled next to the River Thames glimmering blue and silver, steely under a low gray-cotton sky. An iron-scrolled table with two café cane chairs and a small glass vase with two red roses spilling petals onto a table sat under a weeping willow, its branches whispering in the breeze. Picnic tables were scattered about the grassy area outside The Perch; a small garden bloomed green between close-cut hedges.

Hazel sat and removed her red coat in the warming midday sun. She'd told her mum she would do this alone, but now she regretted it. She wanted Mum at her side.

Soon, she spied a woman entering the back garden. Hazel guessed it was Dorothy Bellamy by the pencil-thin skirt, wide-brimmed hat, and tailored jacket—all these in varying shades of olive but for a white crisp shirt with a neat bow at the neckline. She carried a black patent leather messenger bag as she glanced around.

The woman found Hazel's gaze and approached.

For all Hazel's evasion of the journalist, now this woman might be the link to Flora. Hazel would do anything, she'd come to realize. She'd left Barnaby at a train station and stolen from Edwin. And she'd do more than that if it was required. For she now understood that whatever her life purpose had been before Flora seemed to walk through the door of an invisible world and disappear, her purpose was now only this: Fix her mistake, find Flora, and bring the world to rights.

Hazel's heart quivered with expectancy. The road had led here and she would be honest and true.

Dorothy reached the table in long strides and Hazel stood to face her. "Hazel Linden?"

"Yes. Dorothy?"

"You can call me Dot." Dot glanced about the garden lawn, shadows from her wide-brimmed hat cast across her face so Hazel could not yet truly see what she looked like. "I thought I'd never been here before, but I think I have. Odd." She shook her head and unbuckled her messenger bag, slipped out a spiral-bound notebook, and placed it on the table. "Thank you so much for talking to me. This is a really important story and I can understand your hesitancy. I promise to treat your sister with the utmost respect."

Hazel watched Dot's red lips move as she spoke, the lilt of her voice giving Hazel tingles that shivered up and down her legs and arms, making her unsettled with an uncanny sense of the familiar. Her body knew something was true before she found the words, like when Mum held the evacuation notice in her hand in the backyard in Bloomsbury, or when she'd unwrapped the Whisperwood parcel in the back of Hogan's, or the hushed moment when Harry had kissed her, and she'd known to run for Flora, who'd disappeared from the river's edge.

A *knowing*. This was it; this was where Hazel had been headed all along: telling the truth to bring Flora home. The truth was all that had been required in the end.

Dot removed her coat, slung it over the back of the iron chair. She smiled, but it was shaky. "Do you mind if we sit and I can interview you?" She gestured toward the table and the sleeve of her white linen bell-shaped shirt fell back to expose her wrist.

Silver bracelets chimed against each other. And beneath them Hazel spied the birthmark. On Dot Bellamy's wrist, an inch above the bend, the shadow of two rabbit ears splayed east and west. Bunny ears, Mum had said. Angel wings, Hazel had declared.

Hazel felt the tremble of worlds colliding: real and imagined, seen and unseen, desired and denied. She reached for the possibility, the absolute and sheer against-the-odds chance. *Anything is possible now*, Hazel thought. *Anything at all.*

She said, "Not very long ago and not very far away, there once was and still is an invisible place right here with us."

Dot blinked into the sun, then locked gazes with Hazel. "And if you are born knowing . . ." She trailed off. "What is this?"

"And if you are born knowing," Hazel continued, her voice stronger with each word, "and to be honest we all are, you will find your way through the woodlands to the shimmering doors that lead to the land made just and exactly for you."

Hazel watched Dot Bellamy. Is this where hope met despair? Where the past rushed to the present? Where joy replaced the agony of the lost?

All this time Hazel had looked for Flora in the faces of the expected, and yet here she was in the unexpected journalist she'd spent a year avoiding.

"You," Hazel said, her hand flying to her mouth to stop the cry that came fast and full.

Dot backed away. "Me?"

"You are my sister," Hazel said, and gasped with the last word, tears spilling. "My God, you're here." Hazel longed to throw her arms around Dot, to pull her close and find every lost day in her face. But Dot Bellamy looked terrified, backing away from Hazel.

Dot removed her hat and then her sunglasses, slowly setting them on the table. "Are you quite all right?"

Hazel took Dot's hand, ran her thumb softly over the birthmark. Hazel felt her recoil, yet Dot did not pull away. "You are the child you are searching for. You are the River Child."

Hazel watched Dot's face. Hope, my God, it was such a strange word, so much larger than a wish. Hope had become life itself, for to discover the truth about Flora had been Hazel's life's wish and now that hope was flickering in the tentative eyes of a woman who had no idea who Hazel was. "Don't you *feel* who you are?"

"I am Dorothy May Bellamy," Dot said. "I know who I am."

The words pierced Hazel's soul, but she didn't let go of Dot's wrist. "Tell me it is not too late," Hazel said. "That time and lies have not replaced me. Look at me. See me."

Recognition was moving across Dot's face in waves. Her gaze seized on Hazel's intense stare, her hand trembled.

"For twenty years, I have been looking for you," Hazel said.

"Me?"

"You are my lost sister. I am yours."

Dot reached back with her free hand to grasp the edge of the café table. Hazel held tight to her sister's hand. She would not let go; not this time, not ever again.

It became more and more evident to Hazel that Flora was hidden in the movement of Dot's hands, the vulnerability of her unsteady fingers, the cast of her eyes. Hazel longed, no, more than longed, desperately desired, to throw her arms around Dot.

Dot cried out, her voice echoing and catching in the leaves above them. "You are not a dream. You . . . you're my sister." Dot reached for Hazel and they were in each other's arms.

All imaginings Hazel had ever possessed were nothing compared to this moment of pure and undeserved grace. Flora was in her arms. For all that had been stolen from them, here they now stood back in Binsey. Hazel held the body of her now grown sister.

Dot let go first and wiped at her tears with the back of her palm; black mascara smudged on her right cheek. She didn't break her gaze with Hazel, and it was desperate and searching. "I know about Flora Lea Linden. I know all of her childhood story; I have been obsessed with her. And I know you. How is this possible?"

"You never stopped looking for yourself and I never stopped looking for you," Hazel said.

Dot closed her eyes for a moment and then opened them. "What happened?"

Hazel nearly laughed through her tears. "I was hoping *you* could tell me."

Something inside Dot popped like a cork, a release, a door opening.

For two years, Dot had been trying to find Flora Lea Linden's story for her Pied Piper series and now here she was holding a woman she'd dreamed about as images in her mind unfolded like petals of a flower, one after the other.

A splashing river between two flat emerald fields.

A stone house with a soot-stained brick hearth in the kitchen.

A bonfire, sparks like stars on a cold night.

A well where magic might happen.

Dot shivered. Her head was dazed. There was gooseflesh on her arms and legs.

And both Dot and Hazel were in tears.

She could not fathom being anyone else but who she was: Dorothy May Bellamy, born in Newcastle, England, daughter to Claire and William Bellamy, sister to four brothers and cousin to numerous people. She was the wife of Russel McCallister, mother to a four-year-old son, a journalist. She was not a lost child.

But there *was* someone else inside of her. And that someone else, a little girl, was rising, carrying memories in her hand.

The images in Dot's mind merged into a long flower-strewn string like the kind she had made in the fields as a child, daisy after dandelion after daisy, until there were enough for three long necklaces. One for Hazel. One for the woman in a stone cottage. And one for herself, for Flora.

"I am Flora. I am the River Child." Dot swayed beneath the knowing. She felt light as a feather, floating in the wind. Dot looked toward the willow tree. "I think I see a shimmering door right there." Dot's voice changed now, softer, childlike, simple in its belief.

Other patrons at The Perch, with their frothy beers and greasy fish and chips, were staring at the two crying women.

For all the stories Dot had written about the lost children of Pied Piper, none of the children had been stolen to new lives. This outcome had never occurred to Dot. Like the police and newspapers, she'd always assumed that Flora Lea Linden had drowned in the River Thames. *That* was the story of the River Child.

"What are we today?" Dot asked.

"Whatever you want to be," Hazel said with a laugh of sheer delight.

"A rabbit," Dot said. "You never want us to be rabbits."

They faced each other, fourteen and five years old again, leaving London by train and then carried away by the river, eventually returning to each other in Binsey again.

Dot knew now: She *was* the River Child, the girl she'd been looking for all this time.

"I read that Flora's father had passed, but her mum . . . my mum is still alive?"

"Mum is very alive," Hazel said, "and Mum has never stopped looking for you, either."

"I don't understand."

Dot didn't know what to do now, how to act. Would she fall apart and allow the child inside to split her open and change everything she ever thought she knew about herself? "When I was a girl, I had vivid dreams of your voice and of a hollow tree, of woodlands and a well." She shook her head, her hair falling from the chignon and over her shoulders, curly. "Mother told me it was my imagination. Your wild creativity, she told me. And my dreams of drowning, she said they were nightmares left over from the war. I grew up in Newcastle. I lived there always."

"And yet I never stopped looking for you," Hazel said.

Dot placed her hands on either side of her head. "My God, I thought I was chasing the lost children but they were chasing me." She stopped and looked around as if she might find one. "I am one."

"We have a lifetime to figure this out," Hazel said. "But for now, we found each other."

"You told me the stories, didn't you? Of magical lands. It was you."

"Yes. We called it Whisperwood."

"Yes." Dot sat in the chair and Hazel opposite her. "That's it. Whisperwood. I'd forgotten its name. How did this happen?"

"I don't know," Hazel said, "but I do know this—you became who they told you to become. Your life may have been hidden from you, but it was always here, waiting. I was always here looking for and waiting for you."

Dot felt the memory as visceral and real as if right that minute she stood in a grassy field with Berry, so proud of her new green wellies, and she wanted to become a bunny. Then a river, a muddy incline, and she slipped and there was nothing to grab but wet grass and mud. "I fell in the river." Dot tried to shake the image but it rose and swallowed her. "I went under. I couldn't breathe." Dot reached her hand up as if looking for light and air above the surface of the water. She was not, in any essential way, who she thought she was. Not even close.

Hazel said, "This time, I am here. You won't go under."

# CHAPTER 48

## March 19, 1960

After Hazel asked The Perch's barmaid if she might use the house phone, she called Mum and told her to meet her in Binsey.

Now.

"Why? I'm on my way out with Tenny," Mum said in a rush, the shuffle of paper and someone's voice calling in the background.

"Mum," Hazel said in the most serious voice she could muster. "Come here now."

A pause and then a quick short cry. "Hazel, did you find Flora?"

"Just come, Mum."

"Tell me now. Is she alive?"

"Yes," Hazel said. "Hurry."

Hazel returned to Dot—to Flora—waiting at the table under the weeping willow. Dot sat staring out at the river, dazed. Hazel would be patient, for Flora Lea Linden was hidden inside Dot's memories, reaching slowly above the surface.

Hazel sat across from the miracle of her sister. "Ask me anything."

Dot didn't look at Hazel but only at the river. "How long did we live here? In Binsey?"

"A year. A lifetime."

The women talked, leaning toward each other. They drank cold white wine, and Hazel tread carefully along the path of old stories: when Bridie chose them in a crowded dusty town hall, their beautiful mum and the loss of their papa, of the train to Oxfordshire, the woodlands and of the well, of Harry and learning to read, of the nurses behind the rectory and trips to the library in Oxford.

Dot shook her head. "I don't remember any of this. And I do. I can't make sense of it. Do we even have memories from when we were six years old?"

"We do. But yours are hidden. But I promise you they're there, and true."

"Aside from my articles, how are we finding each other now?" Dot asked.

"A book arrived at the shop where I worked," Hazel said.

"What kind of book?"

"It is called *Whisperwood and the River of Stars*."

Dot leaned back in the cane chair and shook her head. "Who wrote it?"

"I thought you might have."

"I didn't."

"I know that now." Hazel told Dot the story of the Peggy Andrews book and the Pauline Baynes illustrations. Dot listened without uttering a word, sipping her wine and ordering more.

"That's a hell of a barmy story," Dot said with a shaky laugh, lifting her glass of wine for another sip. "You know, my aunt warned me to stay away from these stories of the lost children."

"Your aunt?"

"Yes, my aunt Imogene."

Hazel gasped and sat back in her chair. "Dear God, your aunt is Imogene? The nurse?"

Dot narrowed her eyes. "How did you know that?"

"She is the one who took you. God Almighty, it was Imogene all along."

"I don't understand."

"She was a nurse in Binsey when we lived here. She babysat you. She watched you, and it appears she took you."

"That is not possible," Dot said. "I don't know how I ended up in Newcastle but there is no way it was my aunt."

They were interrupted by the sound of a woman calling out and they turned to see Mum run, wobbling in her kitten heels, into the back garden of The Perch.

Dot stood and Mum reached her side, hesitated, and then touched her daughter's face, placed her palm lovingly on her right cheek. "My beloved daughter."

Hazel watched as Dot absorbed this moment, doubt still flickering from her like sparks. She didn't remember Mum—not yet, and Hazel could see Dot's hesitancy. But Mum was weeping and a halo of sunlight surrounded them. Mum reached out and hugged her lost daughter.

"I never surrendered hope, not ever," Mum said.

Dot allowed the hug but then stepped back with a sad smile. "It's nice to meet you."

Mum let out a cry. "Meet me? Oh, God, you don't remember."

"I do. Partially, I do, but this is a lot for me to understand. I did not expect this. At all. I am lost."

"No, my darling, you are found." Mum folded her hands in front of her as if her next words were a prayer. "We are here when you're ready. There is so much to tell you. So much love saved over the years I surely don't want to overwhelm you with it in the first few minutes."

Dot smiled sweetly. "I need to see my family. I need to find out what has happened to me. I don't understand any of this."

Mum nodded and looked to Hazel, her eyes pleading with Hazel to make this woman understand.

"Dot." Hazel stood and joined her mum and sister under the shadow of the willow. "How can we help?"

"I realize you might be my family, but for the past twenty years, I've had another. I need to know . . . more. I need to talk to Imogene."

"Don't leave," Mum said, her voice that of a child begging a loved one to stay. "Not yet."

From the table, Dot lifted her hat and placed it back on her head, shifted it so shadow covered her eyes. She placed her sunglasses in her satchel and squared her shoulders. "I know you must tell the police inspector what has happened today, but please give me this afternoon to talk to Imogene, if you will."

"I will," Hazel said. "I won't call Aiden Davies until tomorrow. Anything you need."

Dot smiled at them both but Hazel saw it: the doubt and the fear while trying to reconcile being two different people. Which one was true and how could she know? How could another girl live inside of her? Was she also a child who had another sister and another mum?

As Dot walked across the lawn, unsteady and not looking back as her bag bounced against her hip, Mum collapsed onto the café chair. "I can't lose her twice, Hazel. I can't."

"We won't," Hazel said. "We won't."

"How can you know that?"

"Whisperwood, Mum. It brought her back and it will show us the way. I believe that."

# CHAPTER 49

## March 1960

It was two a.m. Under the flickering yellow lamppost gaslights, Peggy and Wren walked back to the hotel from Ronnie Scott's Jazz Club in the West End. Fog had rolled in from the river while they'd been listening to live music, drinking gin fizzes, and dancing so close to each other that they moved as one. There'd been a five-piece band. Black men glistening with sweat as they blew into their saxophones, a platinum-haired woman singing with her mouth so close to the microphone that Peggy couldn't stop staring at her. Songs of longing and desire, songs of loss and of love. Peggy had been consumed with all of it, with Wren's touch, with how very much of the world she'd missed in the little yellow house on the spit of sand.

Loving Wren had been a low hum at the center of her being since they were children. He'd represented adventure and goodness and yet for all of their days next door to each other, no matter the attention he'd given to her, love between them had never seemed possible. But here they were in London, body to body. Even if he left tomorrow, even if his touch was as temporary as a wild sunset, she had this moment.

And all because of a story.

Before they'd left Mother at the hotel, crying into her tea about how she hadn't meant to do anything wrong, about how she hadn't meant to steal a story, about how everything she'd ever done in her life had been for her only child, her daughter, a message had come from the front desk for Peggy.

*We found her. Because you carried on our story, we found my sister. Thank you. Love, Hazel.* Hazel had left a phone number for her flat in Blooms-bury, an area of London that Peggy had studied in school. She'd learned about the Bloomsbury group and they had all sounded so romantic and artsy and frankly sexy. Now this was where the woman who started Whisperwood lived. How apt it all was. But then again, Peggy was prone to making everything a bit fantastical.

Now nearing The Savoy, Peggy asked him, "How do you think they found Flora? Where was she all this time?"

"I hope they tell us, but I bet it had something to do with that jour-nalist they were going to see."

"Well, that was mighty fast." Peggy thought about it for a minute. "Do you think the journalist was her sister?"

Wren shrugged. "I doubt it."

Peggy thought about what everyone might have done after they'd scattered from the Embankment Gardens that morning. At first, after she and Wren had left Mother in midafternoon, they'd wandered the streets: shopping without buying anything, sitting in a coffee shop sipping dark espresso so bitter that Peggy thought she'd never want another kind, and then to a beauty salon where Peggy had shown a slick-haired male hairdresser a photo of Jackie Kennedy from a magazine and said, "Cut my hair like that."

Mother would hate it and Peggy cared nothing for this fact, and it thrilled her that she could tolerate Mother's disappointment. What a new and wondrous way to be in the world! Turns out her dark wavy hair was perfect for the bob. A pearl barrette held back the left side. It made Peggy feel free, lighter, and a bit more brave. Which made little sense since it was just hair.

Peggy and Wren approached the doors of The Savoy and Peggy re-moved her hat, her new bob brushing against the upturned collar of the sky blue coat Wren had bought her the morning before they'd gone to the British Library. They walked through the turning door, warm air a blast on their faces. The gin fizzes she'd consumed in the jazz club made Peggy's head light and giddy.

In the lobby, a woman sat on a chair, her white gloved hands folded in her lap. It was Mother, sitting exactly where they'd left her almost eleven hours ago, wearing the same dress, her black coat over her legs. She stared at Wren and Peggy and tears fell.

Peggy walked to her mother. "Mother, are you all right? What are you doing?"

"I thought you were dead," Mother said without moving an inch, only her quivering face showing life.

"Why in the world would you think that?"

"The world is a dangerous place, Peggy."

Peggy held out her hand and her mother took it, standing stiffly. "Mother, it's also a wondrous place."

"I haven't seen that in a long, long time."

"Maybe," Peggy said. "Maybe, because you haven't been looking."

Mother slowly removed her white gloves and reached out to touch the edges of Peggy's hair. "You cut off your hair," she said.

"I did."

"It's absolutely lovely," Mother said.

The unexpected comment was a grace Peggy had wanted for so long—approval for what Peggy wanted instead of what Mother wanted.

Mother cried in earnest now, covering her face with her hands. "I am so sorry. I didn't mean to do anything wrong. Not one bit. All I've ever done is for you."

"Mother, maybe it's time to do something for you."

Mother looked to Wren. "I've been terrible to you."

Wren nodded and reached for Peggy's hand. "I love her, ma'am."

"I know you do."

"Mother." Peggy glanced about the lobby, empty but for one night concierge in a tall black hat, discreetly turning away from their conversation. "Have you been here, sitting right here, since this afternoon?"

"Yes."

"Why?"

"I thought if I just waited, if I didn't move an inch, you'd be okay. It's silly, I know. But here you are."

"Mother, I'm staying here, of course I'm here."

"Can I stay with you tonight?" Mother paused, fussing with the buttons on her cardigan. "Then I promise to go home."

The heat of a blush filled Peggy's cheeks, and she told the truth. "I don't have my own room. I'm sharing with Wren." She guarded her heart for the battle, a battle that didn't come.

"Okay, I will get my own room." Mother took a few tentative steps to the front desk and then stopped. "Will you ever forgive me?"

"I already did," Peggy said. "And guess what?"

Mother gripped the edges of her black purse dangling from her elbow, her back straight as the queen in the portrait behind them. "What?"

"They found Flora."

"Oh! Was she alive?"

"Very, but that's all I know. I can't wait to find out more. But I've been thinking about this all day and, Mother?"

"Yes?"

"No matter what you meant to do when you kept the origins of this story a secret, what you *did* do was keep it alive so that it could find its way to Hazel. You kept alive a story and a lost sister was found."

Mother almost laughed and then shook her head with something near delight. "So, I'm not all bad."

"No one is," Peggy said.

Mother took three long strides back toward Peggy and threw her arms around her, held her tight. "I love you, darling girl. I love you."

Peggy felt her mother's body tremble and she let go and looked into her brown eyes, at her mascara-stained tear tracks on her cheeks. "I love you, too."

# CHAPTER 50

## March 20, 1960

The morning after the great discovery of Dot Bellamy, the first day of spring, Hazel stood in her kitchen at dawn. The night before she'd dreamed of owls and thick-forested groves, of long paths and hollowed trees. She'd awakened with the searing and astonishing thought: *I found Flora.*

Last night after she'd returned home, Hazel had rung Kelty and told her everything. Kelty had cried over the phone, proclaiming she always knew they'd find her. She'd asked, "Now what?"

"I promised Dot I would give her the night to talk to the family. Then I call Aiden Davies. It's time to find out some answers."

Kelty let out a cry. "No! What if you gave Imogene time to get away?"

"She's a fifty-year-old woman, and do you really believe she will leave behind her daughter and grandson? I don't, but I am taking that chance to have Flora back."

"Imogene. She lied to your face."

"Of course she did. She stole my sister. What was she meant to say to me?"

Kelty had agreed. "I'm here when you need me. I can't wait to hug Flora. This," Kelty had said as Midge's voice called her name in the background, "this is better than any book I've ever read. Utter wonder."

"Yes," Hazel had said, and hung up.

Now in the morning light, Hazel imagined each of them holding on to the new and half-understood, unfamiliar story. Mum. Dot. Harry and Bridie. For surely almost everyone she'd ever loved would be changed by this.

And Barnaby? Was he in Paris? Had he gone without her?

Hazel set the kettle on the flame when she heard her front door open and close, and then Barnaby stood in the doorway of the kitchen.

He wore the same suit he'd had on at the train station, now wrinkled with the bottom of the jacket ripped. His face was crumpled in a look she recognized as exhaustion. He reeked of cigarettes and the sour smell of a late-night pub.

"Was it worth it?" he asked with a crack of anger. "Was it worth leaving me in a train station with two tickets in hand?"

She stood very still, as if he were a possibly dangerous animal in the wild that she'd never before seen. "Yes." Only the truth now. "We found Flora."

His hard-set mouth opened, and he let out a cry. "Oh, Hazel! Was it the American author?"

"No." She smiled at the irony. "It turns out she's the journalist I've been avoiding for the past year."

He came to her, but stopped short of putting his arms around her. "Oh my God, you have to tell me everything."

"You look like hell, Barnaby. Where have you been? Have you been wearing that suit for two days? . . . Did you get in a fight?"

He shook his head. "Doesn't matter. Tell me."

And she did. When she was finished, he said, "My God, Hazel, I am almost speechless. This is a mystery that keeps unfolding and never truly gives you answers."

"It's as if breadcrumbs lead me to only more breadcrumbs."

"In 'Hansel and Gretel' those breadcrumbs are . . ."

"I know—they are eaten by the birds so the children end up with a witch. Bad use of metaphor." She almost smiled.

He stood and stretched. "I want to talk about this with you. First, I am going to take a long hot shower before breakfast, if it's all right with you."

She nodded. "Yes, of course."

The water boiled, and she dropped two eggs into the pan, watching bubbles form on the white shells, watching them bob in the water. The phone rang and although Hazel wanted to ignore it, it could be her sister. She smiled at the possibility: her sister. She answered.

"Miss Linden?"

"Yes." She recognized the voice of Lord Arthur Dickson of Sotheby's.

"I am calling to assure you that your job is secure. We've spoken to Edwin Hogan and also to Meldon Yardley, and both expressed great confidence in your character. We look forward to having you join the Sotheby's family."

Hazel twisted the phone cord in her fingers, around her fingers and back again. She heard her heartbeat pounding fast in her ears. Confidence in her character? Who was this man to judge her? She thought of Poppy living on the streets and Edwin hiring her anyway. She thought of the warmth of Hogan's, and then of Barnaby's father making a call on her behalf to prove to Lord Dickson that she was worthy. In an exhale, she spoke the truth. "Thank you, sir," she said. "But I have decided to decline the job."

"Whatever do you mean?"

It had been almost two weeks since she opened that parcel in the back of Hogan's, yet it felt like a lifetime. "When I took that book and those illustrations it opened my eyes to what I want in my life and this, sir, is not part of what I want, I am sorry to say."

"I do believe you will regret this decision, Miss Linden, and I am sure Meldon Yardley will not be pleased. He went to bat for you."

"Yes, sir, I know." Yes, she was sure Meldon Yardley would not be pleased with her for many reasons. "I know you will find someone wonderful. Thank you for your time and generosity. Goodbye." Hazel dropped the phone into its cradle.

What the bloody hell had she just done? She'd told the truth, that's what she'd done. It wasn't so hard, was it?

She fished the eggs from the boiling water and set them into blue porcelain eggcups, lifted the bread from the toaster, and put all of it on her favorite green flower-edged plates. She spread butter on warm toast and plopped a dollop of raspberry jam on the edge of each plate, setting them on the kitchen table. This was her familiar and lovely life. In so many ways, she wanted to keep it.

Barnaby entered the kitchen dressed in a white T-shirt and gray trousers that he kept at Hazel's house. "Did I hear that right? Did you just turn down your dream job?" He stared at her, eyes wide, his pupils dilated with the combination of a hangover and the morning light flashing into the room. "You are going to throw away a good job? Everything you've worked for? Are you thinking straight?" He came to her and set his hands on her shoulders, gently shook her in a friendly way.

"Yes."

"Tell me what's going on . . ." His voice was equanimous but his eyes skirted about the room as if looking for danger.

Together they sat across from each other at the table. "I am both lost and found, Barnaby. I don't know which way to turn or what to do next."

He stared at his egg and toast without taking a bite. "I can't understand any of this. That book and drawings of childish imaginings and my whole life implodes?"

"Childish imaginings?"

"Isn't that what they were?" He set his palms on the table and leaned forward.

"Yes, I suppose, yet so much more. I am trying to figure it all out, too. Listen, I don't know why all of this is happening at the same time any more than you do."

"I heard you on the phone. I heard you tell Sotheby's that your eyes have been opened to what you want in life. What might that be, Hazel?"

"The truth, and the freedom that comes with it. I don't want to avoid things out of fear, or live only for things that look good, for pretense. Like that job. I liked my other job just fine—why did I feel like I had to go somewhere fancier or better? Why haven't I tried to write my own book? What am I so afraid of?"

"That's a lot of questions, Hazel."

"I know and I don't have all the answers, but I know I don't want a job that your father helped me get. I don't want to merely work around stories; I want to write them. I don't want to live on the outskirts of things, to shadow them." She closed her eyes and tried to find a center, but came up shaky. "I don't want to be scared anymore, but I also don't want to do things because they are safe."

"I don't understand at all. I love you so much, and it feels like you are saying you don't want me anymore?"

"That isn't what I said. I do *not* want to hurt you. I have kept you only so close, terrified of loving anything or anyone too much. I haven't let myself truly live the way I want, or love, and it has hurt you, the man I love; I am deeply sorry."

He softened now. "This is a lot to absorb. You know what happened?"

She lifted her eyebrows.

"You opened the door to Whisperwood," he said. "That's what happened."

She looked at him to see if there was malice or meanness in his words, but she only saw sorrow. "If returning to Whisperwood is about anything," she said, "it is about returning stronger, not weaker. It is about the courage that makes me a bit better, a person who knows more about herself. I'd stopped going there out of fear; I'd believed that the story lost Flora, that desire lost Flora, but in the meanwhile that means I left a large swath of who I am in those woodlands."

Barnaby nodded, his face fighting emotions. "Desire lost Flora?"

Would she tell the truth here? Would it set her free? She wasn't so sure. "I was with Harry when she was taken."

"With Harry?" If betrayal had a tone of voice, this was it and Hazel felt sick with the knowledge of what she'd kept from him. The truth wasn't so easy.

"Yes, he kissed me, but the problem is that I was happy being alone with him and for the briefest minute I forgot about my responsibilities. I haven't let myself . . . feel that way again."

"I need to get this straight. I need to understand because you are throwing a helluva lot at me right now. You were kissing Harry, at what, thirteen years old . . ."

"No! I was fifteen."

"Okay. You were kissing Harry, the boy you lived with, at fifteen years old and you forgot about your sister for a minute or two. And that has made you squelch wild desire? Which, if I am following the logic here, means you haven't desired me? This has been a façade?"

"No. That is *not* what I mean. Absolutely not. I have desired you; I love you. I can't fake that. I'm trying to tell you that I've been terrified of feeling *too* much, of feeling what I *really* want because at some point, on that October day in 1940, I lost what mattered because I wanted something so fiercely." She fussed with the linen napkin at the side of her plate, twisted it in her fingers before meeting Barnaby's intense gaze. "Whisperwood didn't leave me. I had convinced myself that the life we see is all that is real. Whisperwood didn't make sense anymore. It was just an illusion, a fantasy, my imagination run amok. But my imagination brought hints into the very real world that I ignored."

"Which," he said softly, sadly. "Which means I need to ask you: What do you *really* want, Hazel? I have a feeling it's not me."

"I want you," she said.

"Are you sure?"

"Yes, I am."

"Do you want me enough? Maybe that is the better question."

Hazel wanted to be careful here; to tread lightly on shifting sand. "What's enough? I don't know, do you?"

Tears were in his eyes. "Maybe you were never *really* free of who you loved before me, Hazel."

"Free?" she asked. "There are boxes and bags piled for three years now in your flat. Boxes and bags that belong to your ex-wife."

"I can't get rid of them until she comes to get them." His teeth clenched and unclenched, a quiver at his jawline.

"Can't or won't?" she asked, and folded the napkin into a neat square. He had no answer.

"Free, Barnaby? I don't know if we're free or caught in the past, but what I do know is what must be done right now. I must call Aiden Davies and tell him about Imogene Wright. I want to accompany him to her house. I won't give him an option. As for Dot, maybe she won't want to have anything to do with us. Maybe she will hate us for ruining the life she has now. But I have to follow this to its end." She paused. "Will you be here when I get back?"

"No, love. I won't." He stood and the shake in his voice had Hazel feeling unsteady. "You must come to me, Hazel. If you want us, come to me. You have a choice to make."

She faced him, feeling the urge to beg him to stay. But he turned away and walked off. She watched his backside, his dark shirt pressed against his shoulder blades, until he rounded the hallway's end. The front door opened and closed with a bang.

Maybe she should run after him, call after him, chase him down.

But instead, Hazel lifted the phone, dialing Aiden's number at the Thames Valley Police Station.

# CHAPTER 51

### March 20, 1960

"I wish you hadn't come, Hazel. This isn't safe," Aiden Davies said. "I have no idea what this Imogene Mulroney is capable of."

It was a cold day, as if spring were hesitant to arrive in Henley-on-Thames just yet. Hazel stood next to Aiden at the low white-picket gate where she'd been waiting for him. He would never have allowed her to come, so she'd arrived on her own before him. He wanted her to stay outside as he knocked on the door. That was not happening.

Hazel pulled her green wool scarf closer, burrowed her chin into its warmth. "Aiden, it might not be safe, but this is mine. I have lived this horror story for twenty years, and you won't keep me from this ending."

Aiden lifted his police cap and rubbed his head in that familiar motion before placing the hat on and nodding. Together they headed to the front door of a cream-colored stucco house with a thatch roof that curved around the front windows. There was no light in the windows or smoke from the chimney, as if the house were deserted. The door was painted bright green and after a quick knock, Dot Bellamy answered.

"Hello, Chief Inspector Davies," she said. She smiled a sad smile at Hazel before looking back to Aiden. "My aunt isn't here."

"Where is she, Dot?" he asked.

Dot grabbed a fleece-lined coat from the wall pegs by the door and slid her arms in lethargically, buttoning it in what seemed to be slow motion, as if she were just waking. From inside, the sound of at least three dogs barked in symphony. A calico cat tried to sneak out past Dot's legs and she shooed it inside. She walked onto the stoop and shut the door behind her. Her dusty brown shoes and loose hair tangled, she looked more the mum of a young boy than the sharp professional she'd been just yesterday. Her voice sounded exhausted. "She went to tell her daughter, Iris, just up the road. She says she will be home soon."

"Tell her?" Aiden asked.

"She told me that when Hazel arrived at her door last week, she understood her days were numbered. She's ready to face the consequences, and yet she wants to explain it all to her daughter."

"Where does her Iris live?" Aiden moved away, as if to run to a place that he didn't yet know.

"Please don't," Dot said, her voice choked. "There is no need to go and embarrass her."

Aiden shook his head. "I will give her a quarter hour and then I will go to her daughter's house."

Dot nodded, stoic. "Yes. Would you like to come in?"

Aiden and Hazel shook their heads and Aiden answered. "We will wait out here. Fifteen minutes. That is all."

"May I join you?" Dot asked. "May I sit with you?"

"Please do," Hazel said, watching the woman for the child within, looking for her sister. On a concrete bench in the backyard of Imogene Mulroney's house they sat next to each other, their heads bent together.

"How was your night?" Hazel asked. "I know this must be difficult."

Dot smiled sadly. "I'm confused. You have to understand, Hazel, I *am* seeing what they did to me, but they are also my family, ones I have loved dearly for what I thought was my whole life. I cannot just turn away, or walk away. I don't know how."

"I'm not asking . . . we aren't asking for any of that."

Dot leaned closer to Hazel. "My sister," she said. "I am remembering you. And yet Aunt Imogene will find herself arrested and in . . ." She turned away. "I can't bear to think of it."

Hazel sat quietly, sensing that Dot had more to say and not wanting to step on her words.

"You know," Dot said. "So many people I have interviewed barely remember their time as evacuees. They block it out. I've interviewed hundreds of them; some have even tried hypnotherapy. I was lucky. I lived in a small village outside Newcastle, called Wallsend, a place they sent children away to, not from. I can't imagine if they'd sent me away from my family."

Hazel held her breath, waiting for Dot to realize what she'd just said, and how very wrong it was.

It happened.

Dot took a sharp breath and her hand went to her mouth. "Oh, God. I *was* sent away. I'm the one who can't remember. Oh . . ."

Hazel nodded. "I know you can't remember, but I promise you will."

Dot's body seemed to freeze as she stared straight ahead, her breathing shallow. The minutes ticked by, closing the quarter hour until Aiden returned and bellowed, "Where is Iris's house?"

Hazel looked up and rattled off the address she had from the day she'd come here with Harry. Aiden headed over there, two streets away, as Dot and Hazel waited. Dot finally stood and looked down to Hazel. "The children who were sent away, they were forever changed. I've talked to them. I've listened to them. Some believe they completely lost their childhood. Others were so happy that they didn't even want to return home. Some couldn't wait to be reunited with their families. But no matter what, no matter the good or the bad, it altered them forever. The experience reshaped their life. How, my God, how could I have listened to all of them and not known I was one of them?"

"I don't know, Dot. But we'll find out."

Dot shook her head and paced the garden as Hazel's suspicion grew: Imogene was gone.

Then Aiden burst through the gate, his face red and mottled. "She is gone. Iris was inconsolable. Where the hell did your aunt go? Tell me now, Dot."

Dot let out a cry. "Oh no, no." She looked up. "I have no idea. I swear it. I truly thought she just wanted to tell her daughter the truth." Dot stood and faced Aiden. "I am not lying."

"You gave her time to get away?" Aiden's voice was angry and tight, his teeth clenched, forcing out the words.

"No. I didn't know. Until right now as the minutes ticked by, I didn't know she might run."

Hazel stood and Dot looked between Hazel and Aiden, her face fighting rising emotions. "What Aunt Imogene did was awful. Horrific. But we don't know the reasons yet. I had a birth certificate. I am Dorothy May Bellamy."

"I will find her," Aiden said. "She cannot just disappear."

Dot smiled at Aiden, so sad. "I did. I disappeared."

Then a voice behind them, rising in high-pitched anger: "Oh, look who it is, the ever-gallant bobby of Binsey who couldn't find a rabbit in a rabbit hole."

They all turned to see Imogene walking around the house to the back garden. Dot rushed to Imogene, hugged her. "Auntie! You're not gone. Thank God."

"No, I am *not* gone." She smiled at Dot and patted her arm, but Imogene's face hardened when she looked at Hazel. "I would never leave you like this one left you."

"Excuse me?" Hazel stepped forward, heat filling her face. Aiden caught her by the arm.

"Let her talk," he said in a low voice so only Hazel heard him.

Hazel knew what he meant—let her dig a hole of her own tellings. Let her anger and self-justified rage explode and possibly some of the truth with it.

"Mrs. Mulroney," Aiden said, his hand on his leather belt where handcuffs dangled off the left side, glinting silver in the sunlight. "We know you took the child known as Flora Lea Linden, who is now Dorothy May Bellamy."

"Took her? I *saved* her. I bloody well saved her. She would be dead but for me," Imogene shouted.

The woman Hazel had thought so sweet, the one at her daughter and grandson's table over tea and biscuits, angelic in her love, was now fierce and rage-filled. Her cream wool coat was open and yet she seemed to feel nothing of the cold. Her face was contorted.

"Saved her?" Aiden asked as he unclipped the handcuffs.

"You!" Imogene said, and pointed at Hazel. "Your mother was the one who let her beautiful and perfect child go to the country without her. Who gives away their child like that? Who just sends their children off on a train to live with strangers in a town they don't even know?"

"A mum trying to protect and save her children from war and bombs," Hazel said, her hands clenched in fists. This woman seemed mad as a cow, her eyes now rolling between Hazel and Dot.

"Auntie," Dot said. "What happened? Tell them what happened so they know you did nothing wrong."

"There you were, darling girl, only six years old." Imogene reached for Dot's hand, held it, and pressed it to her cheek. "Six years old and alone on a blanket by a raging river while this one"—she wagged her finger at Hazel—"she ran off into the woods with that boy to do God knows what at such a young age." She shuddered. "And left you alone." The woman dropped Dot's hands. "Then your teddy bear fell, that dirty thing they let you carry around."

"Berry," Dot said.

"You dropped it at the river's edge and bent over to get it and there you went, tail over tea kettle into that river. Into the water. You went under, my darling. You went under the water, only your blond curls bouncing above. I ran after you. I jumped into that freezing water, grabbed you, and then yes, I took you to Newcastle. I saved you."

"Then how was I Mother's child?"

"My sister, Claire, my poor and beautiful sister, had lost her child your age to consumption, and God gave you to us to replace her. Your name—Dorothy—it means gift from God."

A monstrous and unruly scream grew inside Hazel, and she let it out. "You used my sister to replace a dead child? You gave Flora to your sister like some consolation prize for her own dead daughter? Are you mad?"

"No, I am perfectly sane and I understood what God required of me. Do you? Do you know what God requires of you?" Imogene stepped forward and spat on the ground at Hazel's feet. "I very much doubt it."

Rage burned in Hazel's chest. She nearly reached forward to grab Imogene, to shake her for the pain and the loss and the lies.

"So you see," Imogene said. "I saved her, not stole her. She would have drowned if not for me." She gazed with such adoration at Dot that Hazel momentarily felt sorry for her. "You see, my Dot, you are the one good and saved thing. You."

"But then you took her," Hazel said. She needed to keep this woman talking, confessing, blathering in madness.

"Yes, I took her. You people who leave children and lose husbands were not to be trusted. You people who didn't worship at the parish but instead had your own ceremonies and didn't even attend school, I saved her from you all."

"Auntie," Dot said. "Thank you for saving my life. Thank you. But still and yet you should have told the police."

"The police? Are you serious? The inept Aiden Davies of our hamlet?" She shot him a cruel glance. "You, my darling, if not for you, I would not have been able to stand all the lives I lost, all the boys I could not rescue."

Aiden stepped up and unclipped the handcuffs, but Imogene was focused on Hazel.

Hazel couldn't keep quiet here—the nightmare night of Flora's loss coming back in dark images. "How did you hide her?" Hazel asked. "We searched and searched."

"You are all sods. She was in the church, with me."

"No," Hazel said. "That's not right. I went there. You're still lying."

"I don't lie," Imogene said.

"You don't lie? What the bloody hell? You kidnap but not lie? Absurd. And how did the other nurses not know?" Hazel asked.

Aiden spoke now, the handcuffs dangling in his hand. "We interviewed all of you. Flora was not there."

Dot said, "You hid me in a church?" She shivered, gazed off as if trying to find an image of such a thing, a memory that might be lurking near.

Imogene rubbed Dot's shoulder. "Oh, Dot, Dot, you weren't in that place long at all, darling. Not long at all. Just enough time for me to pack. I just wanted you safe until I was ready to take you to Newcastle, to your mother."

"I want to understand, Auntie. You saved me from the river, you then hid me in a church, and then you took me to Newcastle to replace a dead child of my mother's? I became that child? Am I hearing all of this correctly?"

"You make it sound awful when it was beautiful, Dot. Beautiful." She touched Dot's face again. "Think of your life and your parents and your family, of who you have become because of me. Of your brothers and aunts and uncles."

Aiden said, "Where is your mother now, Dot?"

"She passed of breast cancer three years ago." Dot looked to Aiden. "Pa years before that, even. They took this lie to the grave with them?" Dot shook her head. "What kind of insanity is this?"

"Yes." Imogene's face was deranged now as if it were crumbling, crust falling off. "You were my sister's gift for enduring suffering for good. You were and are our treasure found in hardship." She gazed to the sky. "Our beauty for ashes."

Aiden watched quietly but Hazel couldn't hold back. "She was not a gift; she was your . . . plunder. You believed her to be treasure? She belonged with her mum and sister. With me." Hazel bent over, placed her hands on her knees to catch her breath.

Imogene snorted. "Oh, that is where you are wrong. She always belonged with us. Look at the life we gave her."

It hit Hazel then, a fist to the chest. It hadn't been an owl or even her own imagination she'd heard crying in the night as she'd shivered in fever and wept at the church altar and vowed to never again see Harry or ever write another story. She'd heard Flora's cries. So close. Flora had been right there, only feet away.

"I heard you," Hazel said, energy rushing through her. "I was there. I thought it was an owl or my own cries, but I heard you. I went to the church in the middle of the night. I made a vow to find you. Oh, I could have saved you. I was . . . there."

Imogene laughed, crude and rough. "Now get out of my garden. Get off my land and leave us alone."

With that, Aiden was fast at Imogene's side, the handcuffs in his hand loose and chiming in the wind. "I have been waiting a long time to say this," Aiden said. "Imogene Mulroney, you are under arrest for the kidnapping of Flora Lea Linden on October 19, 1940. You do not have to say anything. But it may harm your defense if you do not mention when questioned something that you later rely on in court. Anything you do or say may be given in evidence."

"You're arresting the wrong person," Imogene screamed. "My niece would be dead but for me." She backed away, tripped, righted herself, and then ran toward her back door.

Aiden caught her in three strides and roughly took her hands behind her back and clicked on the handcuffs. Hazel watched in horror, a sliding sensation coming over her as if she were the one falling into the river.

Dot and Hazel watched Aiden Davies drag off Imogene. They heard the slam of the police car door and the siren as they took off.

Dot collapsed to the bench. "I couldn't have left well enough alone. She begged me *not* to write these stories. She told me they would dredge up old wounds. I didn't listen."

Hazel sat next to her sister and felt the child within Dot retreating, hiding behind the false stories that Imogene had spewed into the morning air. Hazel felt six-year-old Flora cowering beneath Imogene's lies so that Dot wouldn't know or become who she once was.

"I am so sorry," Hazel said. "This was terrible for you to watch. I know you love her, but you need to know that what she said about me, about Bridie and Harry and Mum—none of that is true. No one deserted you; no one was evil; no one abandoned you. You were—you are—deeply loved."

"I don't know what to believe," Dot said, sitting straighter now, brushing her hair from her face and biting her lower lip. "Why would she take me if she wasn't helping me?"

"Grief is a terrible gnawing passion that makes us do things we wouldn't do otherwise. She's obviously convinced herself that she'd done something true and right, when in fact . . ."

Dot held up her hand to interrupt Hazel. "Did you leave me alone?"

Hazel hesitated but she would not pile lies upon lies for she would collapse under the weight of them. "Yes," Hazel said. "We did. We left you alone."

"We?"

"Harry and I. The boy I told you about yesterday, the one who lived with us. We left you alone for a few minutes. You were asleep."

"Then maybe Auntie *should* have rescued me?"

"Possibly. Possibly, she saved you from the river, but she then took you, Flora. She took you to a new life and away from your mum and sister."

"My name is Dot."

"Yes," Hazel said.

"She took me out of love," Dot said. "She said it was *love*."

"Love?" Hazel asked, pushing down her own anger. "That is absolute bollocks."

Dot shook her head. "You have to understand, I had no idea. None. How could I, all this time, have been two people? And I can't even ask my parents for they're gone, too. They also hid this from me? My brothers are younger; they can't know. But Imogene and my parents? Other family who were alive before I arrived? They kept this."

"Families keep secrets. They all do," Hazel said. "But you have a mum right here in the world who has mourned you and hoped for your return for twenty years."

Dot bowed her head. "I don't know what to believe. I had a good life, Hazel. A very good life. I can't bear if it was all a lie."

"I hear you and I'm sure that much of it wasn't a lie. But the origins of it—the truth of where you came from—that was a lie. And it might have been a perfect life, but it wasn't *true*. Another life was always with you, running alongside you. I know you feel this." Hazel was desperate now, needing to make Dot understand that all Imogene had just spouted from her lying lips had been dirty and untrue, tainted with self-righteous madness.

Dot shivered and tucked her hands into her pockets, retreating again. "I need time with this. Auntie gave her sister what she thought God commanded—me. It was a horrible choice, and yet she has loved me and cared for me all my life. It is impossible to reconcile."

Hazel placed her hand on Dot's leg and Dot recoiled. The pain of Flora possibly disappearing again swamped Hazel with misery. She could not lose her sister twice. "Come with me, Dot. Right now just come with me to Binsey. To Bridie."

"No, I need to go home. I need to see Iris and try to undo what's been done."

"There is no undoing this. Trust me, I have been trying to undo the day you disappeared for twenty years. Please just come with me, even if it is for your article. Let's go see Bridie."

Dot shivered, buttoned her coat higher, pulling the gray wool around her neck as if protecting herself. She stood and Hazel stood with her. Dot took two steps away as Hazel said the only thing that rose to her panicked mind. "There once was and still is an invisible place right here with us."

Dot stopped and turned to face Hazel, wrapping her arms around herself and rubbing her hands up and down her arms. "All right. Take me to Binsey."

# CHAPTER 52

## March 20, 1960

The blue door to the stone cottage was open and Bridie stood on the front stoop watching Hazel and Dot walk up the path. Hazel opened the gate as Bridie stepped down onto the pathway. Her silver-and-chestnut hair hung free over her shoulders.

"Hallo there!" she called out as she walked from flagstone to flagstone, as if crossing a river rock by rock, meeting them halfway. "Hazel, what a lovely surprise!"

Then Bridie stopped short, stared at Dot Bellamy, and placed both her hands over her chest, took in a breath. When she exhaled it was with a cry, her face shining with recognition and relief. And instead of throwing her arms around Dot, as Hazel had thought she might do, she took Dot's hands, kissing the palm of each one. "Flora, of course you would arrive today, for today is the first day of spring."

Dot's face quivered, but she stood still and straight.

"I've dreamed of this twice in the past week," Bridie said, and she looked to Hazel. "I thought it was because Hazel had visited, but no, it was because you were on the way. I should have known. How are you here?"

"Now that's a story," Dot said, haltingly. "I was trying to write an article, an ongoing series about the lost children of Pied Piper," she said, never taking her gaze from Bridie. "I didn't know the truth of who I was, who I might be, until yesterday."

Bridie didn't try to cover her tears, just looked straight at Dot. "You found yourself," she said.

"I'm not sure yet," Dot said. "My memories are so muddled. I am confused but yes, I know I was once Flora. But I'm also *not* Flora because I *am* Dorothy May Bellamy." She laughed uncomfortably. "And actually I am Dorothy McCallister as I'm married, but I use my maiden name for my byline."

"It seems," Hazel said to Bridie, "that Imogene Wright kidnapped Flora that afternoon on the Feast of St. Frideswide."

Bridie closed her eyes and spread her arms wide, lifted her face to the sun. "Thank you for bringing her home. Now," she said to them all. "Come in. Let's all have a cuppa. Let the memories simmer for a bit."

The crunch of gravel, the low growl of a motor, and they all turned to see Harry's faded red VW van grinding too fast down the drive, dust and gravel rising like smoke. He slammed on the brakes with a loud squeal. Flying out of the driver's side door, he left it open as he bounded toward them.

"Harry," Dot said quietly, nodding at the man running toward them. "Yes, that's Harry."

In paint-splattered denim pants and a black T-shirt, a gray flat cap over his curls, he reached their sides and glanced at them with interest. He kissed his mum's cheek and then Hazel's. She felt the singular thrill of his touch, even fleeting. He looked to Dot. "Hello, I'm Harry Aberdeen." He held out his hand.

Dot smiled. "I know." She shook his hand. "I'm—" She hesitated and then forcefully said, "I'm Dorothy Bellamy with *Vanity Fair* magazine."

"Ah, the woman who's writing the articles." Harry looked to Hazel for answers.

"Yes," Dot said.

"Do you mean to interview us?" he asked.

Hazel smiled at Harry, lifted her chin toward Dot. "Harry, look. Really look."

Harry again glanced at Dot, and Hazel observed the recognition lighting his face, filling his mind, like watching a sunrise. "Flora."

"Yes," Dot said with a smile, the first real and full one Hazel had seen. Hope rose with it.

"You've returned," Harry said, his voice cracking. He took Dot in his arms. She stood rigid as a rod and then relaxed, hugged him in return with an uncomfortable laugh. "Well, you sure are the exuberant one."

*She's funny*, Hazel thought. So much to learn about a woman who was once a child whom Hazel knew as intimately as herself.

Harry stepped back. "It's the miracle we've all hoped and prayed for these twenty years. How?"

Hazel looked at Harry quizzically. "And why exactly are you here?"

"Mum phoned this morning, told me that she needed me."

Bridie shrugged. "I just didn't know *why* I needed him, not until now."

Harry shook his head, took off his cap, and held it. "I thought I was supposed to move the broken mower into the barn."

"Yes. I'd appreciate that, I did feel that there was something else coming." She kissed her son's cheek.

———

Dot Bellamy listened and watched as these people she was supposed to know spoke to one another with such joy about her return. She gazed at a stone cottage; a green pasture, a red barn, and a broken-down mower rusted on the lawn. She saw the ash tree and common gorse bush bursting with small yellow flowers at the edge of the flagstone path. There stood Hazel with the brown curls pulled back into a low bun, and golden brown eyes that at some level Dot recognized. Bridie was there with her warm smile and soft voice. And yes, she knew Harry; she felt it the minute he'd jumped out of the battered van with his bounce and his grin. What did that mean?

Last night she hadn't been able to tell Russel what she'd learned about her past or about her identity; not yet. With their four-year-old son, Connor, bouncing around them both, begging one of them to put together the dinosaur puzzle with him, Russel had absently asked Dot about the River Child interview with the woman from London. She'd told him she had a blistering headache and needed to go to bed early. It wasn't a lie.

She'd feigned sleep when Russel came to bed later that night, but she hadn't slept at all. Before dawn, she rose and snuck out of the house to travel to Henley-on-Thames to confront Aunt Imogene. How could Dot tell her husband and son she was someone else when she hadn't figured out how to understand it herself?

Yes, Aunt Imogene had always been a bit odd, gathering the wounded and the lost in her garden and home, from plants to animals, her husband often giving things away when her back was turned. But she'd never been actually mad, never insane. Or had she? Aunt Imogene had never screamed about saving children or rivers or churches. Dot had never seen, even out of the corner of her eye, anything like what happened yesterday with Aunt Imogene. Never had Dot imagined that the one secret thing Imogene had saved had been her. That she, Dot Bellamy, was the saved thing that kept Imogene from true insanity.

Now at Bridie's, she stepped back and placed her hand on the fence post. Yes, the place was familiar in the same fashion as the fragmented images that had come to her at The Perch yesterday, but her mind was disorganized. Her beloved Imogene had been arrested, her childhood stolen or saved—how was she to know?

Harry smiled at her. "Are you all right?"

"No." Dot looked for a place to sit and found one on a hay bale. Hazel sat next to her. But Dot needed air and space. She needed to try to remember the past without all of these people staring at her, these people who claimed they loved her and knew her. She stood again and paced. "I need . . . I don't know."

"Take your time," Bridie said. "Let me bring you something to drink?"

"Yes," Dot said. "Please."

Far off, or maybe it was close by, an owl uttered a long hoot, a mournful and seeking song. Bridie stopped and spun around. "A daytime call," she said. "How lovely."

Bridie's voice settled somewhere deep inside Dot and she stared across the pasture where the onyx burnt-wood remains of a spent bonfire glistened under the midday sun.

A bonfire.

Harry spoke into her confusion. "The river, it is just beyond, over that hill. We ran there nearly every day."

Dot nodded, but didn't look at him. The rolling, falling, heady sensation of sliding into another life was overwhelming her. Then the owl again, the call cracking the bedrock of lies, memories rising like smoke from the crevices.

Now she is six years old on a red blanket and someone is calling her name. Not the name she carries now but her first name: Flora.

"Flora!"

She is asleep in the afternoon sunlight, a plaid wool blanket over her and Berry tucked under her arm, his fur resting on her cheek, when the familiar voice wakes her from a deep nap.

Waking, rising to her feet, she moves toward the voice. But there is her starry river, the river her sister does not ever let her get too near. The river in her magical land of Whisperwood. She inches closer when she slips and Berry falls near the water.

That voice, it calls for her again, and she stumbles, her green wellies not catching the ground.

Cold! The splash of her body, the shock of October waters, the slap of the river against her chest. She is tumbling, rocks over rocks, smooth and rounded, underwater. She holds her breath until it burns and she thinks she just might take a breath, knowing that the water is made of stars.

Instead, she lifts her hand and another hand drags her up and out. She gulps the air, coughs and sputters, confused and so cold. She is on her back, staring at the sky.

Dot Bellamy gasped at the memory and spun to face Harry and Hazel, her hands clasped together so tightly it hurt. "She called me. She called my name. Imogene's voice startled me into the river."

Bridie was there now, offering Dot a cold glass of water with a sprig of rosemary in it. Dot took a long swallow.

They all watched, silent, allowing her to find her way. "I didn't *just* fall in. Aunt Imogene called me." Dot closed her eyes, swayed under the fevered dream of drowning. "Oh my God, the dreams I have of being trapped in a small room. Those images are not from fairy tales, those dreams are not from Blackbeard legends or nightmares or mythology like my mother and aunt told me, those dreams are from my life. My very real life."

"Let's go inside?" Harry asked with concern.

"No," Dot said. "The truth is out here, in the landscape, in the geography of this place."

"Yes," Bridie said.

Dot again sat on the hay bale. "My life has been a lie."

———

Hazel stood very still as Dot spoke, as all she'd believed was now upended.

She and Harry did *not* lose Flora. Their kiss had *not* made Flora disappear. Whisperwood had *not* taken Flora away in the river's current. The magical land Hazel had kept hidden away for all these years—the one she'd feared had destroyed her life, her mum's life, the Aberdeens' life—had *all along* been working its magic, bringing them ever closer, until this day when they stood in the pasture land of Bridie and Harry Aberdeen.

A heaviness Hazel had been carrying well over half her life lifted from between her shoulder blades, from the crevices of her heart.

Dot looked directly at Hazel, and as if she knew these were the words Hazel needed to hear she spoke slowly, carefully articulating every word: "She stole me. She woke me and called me toward the river. I know I was only six, but *that* memory is clear. Nothing else around it makes sense yet, but that night . . . I've always thought it was a recurring nightmare and now I see it was true."

Bridie sat next to Dot on the bale. "Back then, all the nurses carried codeine, aspirin, and Nembutal in their capes at all times. I believe you were . . ."

"You don't have to say it," Dot said. "Yes, she gave me the white pill that tastes bitter and biting. Yes."

Hazel and Harry looked at each other and in their secret language both knew: They did *not* lose her. Instead, Flora had been lured away as if Imogene Wright had played the flute and worn a red piper's hat. They looked at each other with compassion.

"She must have been stalking you," Harry said while still gazing at Hazel. "Following us."

Dot looked to Hazel. "Why did this American woman write about Whisperwood? Why not . . . you?"

"I'd turned away from the story," Hazel said. "I'd written much of it down, but the night Flora—the night you disappeared—I threw my pages into the river, asking the waters to take the story far from me and to bring you home."

"Home," Dot said as if trying the word on her tongue for the first time. A breeze through the air and a low cloud shifted; the sun was exposed, sending warmth and light to the pasture.

Bridie smiled at Hazel. "The invisible right here has become visible."

Hazel gazed at Bridie, needing her to understand. "I thought my imagination was what doomed us."

"It wasn't," Harry said.

Hazel felt the tears rising. "I see that now. It wasn't my love that lost her, and it wasn't my Whisperwood story that sent her away. All this time I'd believed both of those things to be at the bedrock of her disappearance."

"Love?" Harry asked.

"For you, for Whisperwood. For both," she said, and turned to Dot. "But it wasn't my love for Harry that had lost you, instead you were quite literally kidnapped by a nurse damaged from war, out of her mind, stalking and stealing a little girl."

"How?" Dot asked. "How could love and imagination lose me?"

"They didn't," Hazel said. "I only believed they had."

Dot stood and took a few steps closer to Hazel and gazed at her, eye to eye, face-to-face, and then did exactly what Hazel had desired, longed for, and dreamed of for over twenty years—Flora Lea Linden threw her arms around her sister and held her close.

———

Later, after Dot had walked through the cottage with tears pouring down her face, she stood in the entryway to their little bedroom off the kitchen and said, "There are other images, too, but I'm not sure how to piece them together. Honestly, after the river, there is nothing but Newcastle, and university and Russel and Connor, and then searching for the lost children of Pied Piper." Dot entered their childhood bedroom and ran her hand across the pine dresser. "She stole me, hid me in a church's dark room alone, then took me to Newcastle. I could not have imagined this narrative, despite all the stories I've written of lost children. My God, I am one. I'd been so secure in the knowledge of my family. Four brothers. A mum and pa now gone, but who loved me."

She turned to face Harry, Hazel, and Bridie. "I have a wide extended family, including Aunt Imogene. I am a Bellamy, so proud of my family that I wrote under my maiden name. What kind of insanity is this?" Dot asked, her voice rising and cracking. "I was not a gift from God. I was . . . what was I?"

"You were Flora Lea Linden," Hazel said.

"You never gave up. You kept your promise."

With the whistle of the kettle from the kitchen they all followed Bridie, taking seats around the table, the hearth flecked with the ash of a spent fire. The windows were open, birdsong filling the kitchen. They were crowded together, knees touching knees, leaning in closer at the arrival of cups of tea with rising steam and round sugar cakes with icing drizzled across the tops, just as when they were children.

Hazel was sitting next to Harry, dazed with the knowledge that her sister now sat across from her. All those years, Flora had been only a few hours away from London in a remote village with a different mum.

Dot looked around. "Part of me understands why she did what she did—but I don't excuse it. She was traumatized. I feel so sad for her. She lost so much, and she truly, and wrongly, believes she saved me. My poor aunt has been trying to save things for all her life."

"She didn't save you." Hazel gripped the edge of the table.

"I know, but she has convinced herself that she did. Now tell me more about our imaginary land," Dot said. "Whisperwood."

"Yes," Hazel said.

Dot closed her eyes. "Whisperwood. Whisperwood. Whisperwood." She opened her eyes. "You realize what the story did, don't you?" Dot paused. "The story brought me here, back to all of you."

"Yes," Hazel said, something in her moving around as if trying to find a new place to settle.

"All these years," said Dot, leaning forward, "I have been writing about the lost children of Pied Piper. A boy run over by a car during the evacuation. Others who ran away . . ."

"Like Kelty," Hazel interrupted. "She ran away."

"Kelty..." Dot shook her head. "I know her, right? At least the name?"

"You do," Hazel said. "You will."

"I wrote about the poor children on the ship that was torpedoed going to America. I wanted to write about Flora next. About—"

"Your own life," Bridie said. "About a lost child—now found."

Dot twisted in her chair to Bridie. "I dreamed about lost children. I was obsessed with writing about them. My husband, Russel, he says I care too much. He says it takes me away from him and our four-year-old son, Connor. Maybe he's right, I don't know. But something inside of me would not let me stop writing and looking for them."

"Deep down, you knew," said Hazel.

"You have a son?" Bridie asked.

"Yes. He's quite amazing."

"Your mum has a grandson," Bridie said to Hazel. "What wonder."

Dot lifted her tea, cradled it in her hand without taking a sip. "When Hazel started telling the opening to Whisperwood yesterday at The Perch, I recalled torn scraps of that day. I still don't understand it all, but I promise to get to the bottom of it." Dot turned to Hazel. "How did the story end up in America?"

"Do you remember a woman named Maria? Someone who helped your mum and other mums during the war? A woman who helped to babysit and teach?"

"There were a few American volunteers, yes, but I don't remember one named Maria."

"Well it seems that there was one, and you told her the story and used it to calm yourself, to settle yourself. That woman, Maria, took the story back to America and told her sister, Linda, about it to help calm her little girl, Peggy, who had also lost her father in the war."

"What a wonder," Dot said. "What an absolute wonder. A story you told me helped me when I was sad and confused, and then it traveled across the sea to bring us back together."

"Hazel, love," Bridie said. "You might have turned away from Whisperwood, but it found you—it was relentless in its pursuit of you, bringing us all home again."

Hazel nodded; no matter her love for stories, there were some things beyond words. They sat quietly as Bridie's kitchen glowed with afternoon light and outside spring burst from the ground, born again. All things made new.

After Dot left to take the train home, Harry and Hazel stood outside Bridie's home. The night was crisp and clear, the sky indigo with flecks of stars in their set patterns. A breeze floated, aromatic with Bridie's roses blooming on the climbing fence line.

Hazel sensed Harry's body next to her, the longing for him as strong as that afternoon of the October 19 Feast of St. Frideswide when his kiss had made her forget all reason and responsibility. And yet, this longing, as strong, was also different. For it had been forged through time and other men, through mistakes and grief and loss.

While Hazel searched in her heart for what to say, or how to say goodbye, Harry spoke first. "Today. It's a miracle, isn't it?"

"I think so," she said. "Although I'm not quite sure how to define a miracle. A young girl tells a story to an American volunteer. That woman carries the story across the sea for her niece, another child who has lost her father. That child grows to write the story and embellish it, to grow it to become more than it ever was before."

"And then," Harry said. "That story lands on a table in the very store you were leaving that day."

"Yes. Today is possibly a miracle. You're right."

"You didn't give up, Hazel. You never surrendered to anyone else's idea of who and what you should believe and do."

Hazel allowed the blessing of those words to fall over her. "Harry, I have given up on so much in my life. I really have. I have lost myself in many things that weren't good for me, but in this belief—that Flora could be found—I never gave up."

"And us?" he asked.

"Us?"

"Did you give up on us? Did you stop believing in us?"

She wasn't very sure what he meant. "How so?" she asked, and turned to him. "Believe? What is there to believe? We lost each other."

"We thought we didn't have a choice," he said. "We presumed we could never have each other, but we were wrong." His voice faltered. His gaze was so intent on hers as if searching for something he couldn't find. She wanted to give it to him; whatever he was looking for she desperately wanted to give it to him, but she didn't know yet what it was.

"A choice," she said, feeling the possibilities of them finally drawing near enough to be real.

"What do you want, Hazel? What is true for you?"

"I don't know, but I do know this—I believe I've always searched for the feeling I had with us." She would be honest, there was nothing left but that now.

"Yes," he said.

She met his gaze. "But you can't get something like we had back, Harry. We have Dot now, but she's not six-year-old Flora; we can't get *her* back."

"I'm not so sure it's about getting anything back." He looked to the sky and then back at Hazel. "It's about having what is right here, right now, and not squandering what remains."

Hazel heard the words like a song, the very essence of a truth she hadn't seen. Bridie came outside then, handing Hazel her coat. "Are you ready, dear? I'll take you to the station."

"Yes." She smiled at Bridie. "I'm ready to go."

Harry kissed Hazel on the cheek and she walked away with his mum.

A choice to make? Therein was freedom, she thought, the ability to make a choice she never thought she'd have the opportunity to make. But she had to be careful. Freedom, for all its claims of wonder, also had its price.

# CHAPTER 53

## March 1960

A week after Dot Bellamy discovered the truth of her past, she sat in the bookshelf-covered library of her home in North London; a brass goose-neck lamp sent a puddle of light onto the taupe-gray Underwood type-writer on a dark mahogany desk. Dot typed as fast as her fingers could fly. Russel and Connor were fast asleep and the mantel clock above the stone fireplace ticked past 2 a.m. But she wasn't tired, not one bit.

Aiden had sent a psychiatrist to visit Dot, a woman named Dr. Maisel who specialized in childhood trauma from the war. She'd told Dot how horrific memories were blocked, how a lie told over and over becomes the truth of the past, but also how the mind holds that truth and how Dot's subconscious had attempted to tell it to her over and over in dreams and hints and images until Dot would listen. The experts called it memory reframing, and Dot had been young enough for a lying adult to shift the cornerstone and bedrock of her early childhood.

If Dot's dreams of drowning and being trapped returned, she would know what they were: a message to remember, not a premonition of the future. She was realizing that her Bellamy family must have allowed her to tell the tale of Whisperwood for comfort and then they'd eventually let it fade; they'd allowed both her real family and the tale of Whisper-wood to disappear into a murky past.

Her life had been a good one in the quiet town outside Newcastle, an upbringing outside in nature with a raucous and fun family. But her life had *also* been a lie. She was still trying to figure out if deception negated the honest parts of her life.

Dot hadn't told Hazel and Camellia yet, but she'd been writing down whatever scattered memories she could find to build a cohesive story of the day of her disappearance. Writing was the only way to make sense of the mad world she now found herself navigating. Her husband and son were confused; her brothers were distraught; Aunt Imogene was in custody and a trial to come. When she imagined losing her own child, her beloved Connor, the grief was overwhelming and yet her mum had survived it. How?

There was one way she knew to get through this—write the article about the River Child. She would tell everything that had happened to her, everything that was done to the lost little girl of Binsey.

The article began—*Not very long ago and not very far away . . .*

Dot's *Vanity Fair* editor, Mia Hardingham, anxiously awaited the finished piece and every night Dot typed well into the dark hours. Dot sewed together the torn pieces of both Hazel's and Imogene's retellings to fashion a cloth of story. Imogene had given her the outline of what had happened to the small six-year-old girl at the river's edge, and Dot used her imagination to fill in the blank pieces. It was, after all, *her* story and she needed to find her way into it even if she filled in the unknowns with creative details.

Twice this week, she'd walked the paths of Binsey alone. She'd ambled past the whitewashed two-room school, the riverside pub called The Perch, and the stucco and stone homes scattered like white pebbles along the dirt road. She'd entered the moss-covered cemetery at St. Margaret's and knelt at the edge of the well. She'd run her fingers over the engraving on the well's interior wall: St. Margaret's Well. But Dot knew this well-head by another name: Frideswide's Well.

Just as the well carried two names, so did Dot. Dorothy May Bellamy had originally been Flora Lea Linden. The well belonged to both St. Margaret and St. Frideswide, but it was Frideswide who had arrived there first, Frideswide who'd built the Saxon church to heal others. Later, the Anglican Church had given the chapel another name. But the renaming had not changed the essential nature of the sanctuary and the well, just as changing Flora to Dorothy had not changed the essential truth of who she was. The church and then Imogene could rename anyone or anything they chose, but what came first remained. Someone always carried the first name, the first truth, the first story.

Dot had walked to the large wooden door of the church, pushed it open, and entered. She'd felt nearly floating as she'd walked up the aisle and knelt at the altar to find the small and hidden wooden door. She'd allowed the images and fear to rush over her, knowing they could not and would not drown her even as it felt they might.

Russel had asked if he might accompany her, and she knew both Hazel and Camellia would have done the same, but some journeys must be taken alone.

Between the drug and the hypothermia and the childhood shock, Dot might never *fully* remember, many evacuees never did, but she would take the faded scraps of her memory and tell the truth.

Writing at 2 a.m., Dot was now at the very part where the woman who went by many names—Aunt Imogene, the nurse, the babysitter— called her name, her original name, Flora, and then pulled her from the river.

Dot typed faster now, feeling the story rise like a full-moon's tide.

*"I'm cold," the River Child said, her body quivering so her teeth slammed on each other.*

*"Oh, my girl!" The nurse took off her gray coat, wrapped it around the child. Under her coat, she wore her white and starched uniform with blood on her sleeve, a rusty stain.*

*She picked Flora up, held her against her chest and cheek. The nurse, her babysitter named Imogene, smelled clean. Carrying Flora, Imogene ran, bolted across the field and away from Flora's sister, Hazel, and toward the church. Flora knew the way through the fields of gold grass back to the cottage and they were going the wrong way. Flora tried to point toward the cottage, toward home, but she was bundled tight in a thick coat.*

*"It's going to be all right," said Imogene. "Breathe. Breathe."*

"Berry," Flora cried out, as she was jostled in Imogene's arms.

Flora's sister, Hazel, had warned her: If you go into the river or try to become the river, you can never return to Bridie or Harry or even to me.

But Flora hadn't entered on purpose; the nurse had scared her and she'd slipped.

"Whisperwood, Whisperwood, Whisperwood," she mumbled, hoping the magical words would make Imogene turn and take Flora to Bridie, to Hazel and Harry.

But instead, they arrived at the cottage where the four nurses lived, and they were alone. Once inside, the room dark and cold, Imogene sat Flora on a kitchen chair and pulled off Flora's wellies and dumped the water into the sink. Imogene pulled huge wool socks, meant for a grown-up, onto Flora's ice-cold feet, and sat her by the dead fireplace where only black embers glistened.

"Take me home," Flora begged, shivering, cold, needing Bridie and Hazel and Harry, and the warm fire in their kitchen.

"They don't mind you well enough. You never have to return to the family who cares nothing for you."

"They love me," Flora said, knowing the truth of it.

"They don't, or they would have watched over you. You would have drowned without me. They left you alone."

Flora closed her eyes, whispering over and over, "Whisperwood. Whisperwood. Whisperwood." She needed to go back. She needed to find her sister. Weren't the words magic?

"What is Whisperwood?" the nurse asked softly.

Flora shook her head. Hazel said to never, not ever, tell anyone about Whisperwood. It was why Flora had been left alone. It was why Flora had found herself with Berry at the edge of the river—because she'd almost told Harry of their magical land. She would not tell Imogene, who smelled like soap yet had blood on her sleeve.

Imogene disappeared into a back room and returned with a woolen blanket. "I am going to get you clothes and food. But for now we need to hide you."

"Why?"

Without answering, Imogene reached into her pocket and slipped out a small white pill. "Open your mouth, sweet girl. This will make you feel better."

Flora shook her head, tightened her lips. Imogene tickled her under the arm, kissed her neck, and when Flora giggled, she slid the bitter pill beneath her tongue where it melted. She lifted Flora again, and Flora thought maybe she was finally going home to Hazel, who would take her to Whisperwood, to Bridie, who made warm porridge and hummed songs, to Harry, who was teaching her letters that made words.

Instead Flora was carried a few yards across the cemetery behind the house, past the slanted and mossy headstones, toward St. Margaret's church and the dark well where the princess Frideswide had once healed others.

Flora was overcome with fear and cold and helplessness. She needed something from Frideswide and from Whisperwood—she needed Hazel. She prayed to both but Imogene carried Flora into the dark church, a river of light falling through its windows. Flora felt she was underwater again and yet she could breathe.

Imogene stood with Flora in front of the altar. Then she took a few steps and Imogene opened a small hidden door, and they entered the tiniest room Flora had ever seen. There was a window so small that the light coming through seemed like a lit lantern. There was a single bench and a kneeling pad with a cover of green vines sewn into its cushion. A carved wooden crucifix of Jesus hung on the wall, his face contorted in pain, and blood dripping down his cheek.

Flora cried out. "Take me home!"

"I am your home. I saved you, just like Jesus saved me. Now stay quiet and still and I will be back to get you. Just tell me, my sweet child, what is Whisperwood?"

A flood of fear swept over Flora as the nurse set her on the small bench and leaned down to face her. And although Flora knew it betrayed her sister, she believed it would save her, send her back to Hazel. "It is our secret land."

The nurse smiled and she was so pretty that Flora believed she could do no harm. "Well, you shall get to keep your land, child. Shhh now, shhhh. Keep quiet and you shall keep your land. I'll be back with dry clothes and warm food. Rest."

Flora was alone again as the door shut and the lock engaged. She did her best to stay quiet but when she again turned cold and then hungry, she cried, calling for Bridie, for Hazel and Harry and even for soggy Berry. She curled into a tight ball inside the wool blanket and could no longer keep warm.

Imogene had said she'd come back with warm clothes and yet Flora grew more confused with each passing hour. Had she gone the wrong way through the shimmering door? Had she drowned and was now stuck somewhere on the other side? She shivered and she fell in and out of half delirium until she finally slipped into a fitful sleep, tumbling from the thin bench to the stone floor, painfully banging the side of her head.

Much later, after the lantern window went dark and light again, Imogene returned with warm soft clothes that were not Flora's. The nurse dressed Flora, fed her a cup of warm potato soup. At the room's doorway waited a flowered valise with leather handles.

"Where are we going?" Flora asked, realizing now that Hazel had been right; Flora could not return home because she'd entered the river; she'd betrayed her sister.

"To Whisperwood," the nurse said with a very sweet smile.

# CHAPTER 54

## April 1960

Hazel awoke in her flat two weeks after the revelations on the first day of spring when Imogene Mulroney was arrested.

During these past days, Hazel, Dot, and Mum had spent each afternoon together. Sometimes they walked the paths of Kensington Gardens and watched the ducklings splash at the edges of the silver pond; other times they sat in Mum's conservatory with strong tea and cream-filled cakes.

With constant chatter, they filled in memory gaps, building the lost structure of their lives: stories the bricks and love the mortar. Mum and Hazel showed Dot photographs of her childhood as Flora and tried to help Dot remember more than the day of her disappearance. Slowly, the child inside Dot rose in laughter and subdued her guarded heart's doubt. Her husband, Russel, and her little boy, Connor, spent those afternoons together so she could try to find her way into the truth of her past.

For as much as they found their lost sister as an adult, they'd lost Flora the child. They could never get her back.

One late afternoon as the sun filtered into Mum's conservatory and the three of them faced each other across the chintz-covered couch, Hazel had told Dot, "I can't forgive your aunt for all the years I've missed of you. For the days and hours of my own life that I mourned you, for the pain she caused us. I know you're sad for her, but I can't find any empathy for your aunt right now, for her or her ruined life as she leaves all she loves."

Dot, with her quiet elegance, had told them both, "I have to find a way to reconcile the memories and love into something new, to find a way to understand that for all the good of my childhood and life, underneath was the reeking rot of an immoral choice that I could not see or smell. I am sure it is a lifetime of work to understand."

Dot had finished her article for *Vanity Fair* and let both Hazel and Mum read it with tears in their eyes, for not only had they suffered Flora's loss, but Dot had been living with the repressed memories of nearly drowning and being drugged and stashed in a cold room for a full night. She, too, was rebuilding her life, relearning the cornerstones of her childhood long lost.

Being with Dot and finding their way to each other again had kept Hazel from dwelling too much on Barnaby. But she missed him, the loneliness a low hum, his absence in her flat a gaping hole. And yet she realized if she went to him or called him, there might be another letting go further down the line. She had to be sure.

It was clear: Hazel had spent so many years worrying about who loved her that she'd forgotten to consider who she loved. She'd been so damn troubled with whether the men she met wanted her she'd nearly forgotten to wonder if she desired them. And yet it wasn't fair of Barnaby to accuse her of never truly being free—he'd never been truly unencumbered, either; the boxes and detritus of his ex-wife kept Hazel from more than his flat. He said Hazel would have to come to him, and she knew it was true. She'd almost gone twice in the past week; a desperate need to fix what she'd broken, to tell him she loved him, which was true.

But love wasn't as simple as a word tossed from casual lips. When she thought of Barnaby, and of course of Harry, she couldn't find a gentle place to settle in her heart. It was possible to love two men, for she did. But right now, what wasn't possible was to see clearly through the murky fog of the past rolling in off the river. Was she confusing the warmth and comfort of childhood innocence for love?

*You have a choice to make,* Barnaby had said.

And he was right.

And Harry. She'd picked up the phone more than once to call him but had set it down. She wanted him near; she wanted to make up for lost time; she wanted to be fifteen years old again and never leave Flora asleep; she wanted to find her way back to innocence. But she could have none of that, and so what was there to say? She practiced lines that never rang true, lines that sounded like a cheap version of how she felt.

Hazel rose from bed and made her way to the kitchen: her tea, her toast, and her soft-boiled egg. She then set her notebook and Woolf pen on the kitchen table, turned on the baroque English wireless, and picked up where she left off that morning when she'd fallen asleep on the kitchen table, the morning before she'd been headed to Paris with Barnaby.

The morning of the day that changed everything.

She'd had a choice then, too—to leave for Paris or try one more time to discover the truth of the Whisperwood novel's origins. Now she knew—she'd set her own words to paper. She'd allow the story to break free from the sarcophagus of shame. She'd revisit each moment as best she knew how.

Of course the story could never be exact; no story ever retold was perfectly told. But it would be true.

Her pen moved across the paper, her heart opened, her breath evened out, and she returned to her first love, the love she'd once left in fear and guilt: story.

———

Late in the same afternoon, she set the pen aside and took a long walk alone through Kensington Gardens and past the enchanting statue of Peter Pan. She had gone nearly all the days she could without a job and a paycheck. Her accounting wasn't perfect but she knew she had no more than two months' of living expenses. She could ask her mum, but she wouldn't. It didn't take long to understand where she'd been headed all along on this walk, and it made her smile. Now she walked with purpose and within the half hour, she stepped onto the bluestone threshold of Hogan's Rare Book Shoppe and pushed open the door, the familiar bell above tinkling with greeting.

"Hallo," she called out. Tim and Poppy sat on stools behind the front desk, the store empty. They looked up from the books they were reading.

"Hazel! We missed you so much," Poppy said, and jumped to stand.

"So much," Tim agreed.

Poppy set down her Graham Greene novel. "And I have a feeling you have a lot to tell us. These two weeks you've been gone since The Great Book Robbery haven't been a holiday?"

Hazel laughed. "Not exactly," she said. "Is Edwin in the back?"

Tim nodded with a knowing smile.

Entering the room, Hazel spied Edwin sitting at his ink-stained desk across from a young woman in a smart pale blue tweed suit, her muddy-colored hair in a bun at the nape of her neck.

"And where did you last work?" Edwin gruffly demanded, stroking his beard in preoccupation.

"At Foyles, sir. But my degree in English literature makes this shop a better fit, I do believe."

Hazel cleared her throat and Edwin glanced up, a smile breaking. She took in the room: the logbook on the center pine table, the shelves overflowing with papers to be filed, a stack of unopened boxes that made her fingers itch to rip the tape from their cardboard. Not more than two weeks had passed, and it had all gone to pot without her.

"Hello, Edwin, I was wondering if I might have a word with you?"

He tapped the desk. "The only words I want to hear from you are 'This is my home.'"

"Then I guess I'm home," she said, heading straight for the unsteady pile of boxes and gathering the first one to set on the pine table. She opened the logbook.

The young woman stood and glanced between Edwin and Hazel. "I assume the job is no longer available?"

Edwin nodded and stood, grasping his cane. "Thank you for coming, though. Hazel's arrival is an unforeseen happenstance that has altered the status of the job opening."

Hazel swallowed her laugh but smiled at the woman. "I'm sorry. But from my experience, I know there is an opening at Sotheby's."

The woman grinned. "Really?"

"Yes."

The woman smiled before pushing at the swinging door and leaving.

"So, I'm an unforeseen happenstance?" Hazel asked with a laugh.

"Indeed," Edwin said. "By the by, you know I must dock your check each month until you pay me back for any ruined or stolen merchandise."

"Dock it," she said, and tried to keep from smiling.

"So, Hazel, what has brought you back to us?"

"Whisperwood."

"Ah, someday you must tell me more," he said with an even wider grin.

An hour later, back to work, Edwin's voice droned on a telephone call in the far corner while Hazel ripped the tape off another box. How had she thought it was a good idea to leave this place? Where else was she meant to be? There were more choices ahead for her, to be sure. But for now, this shop; Tim and Edwin and Poppy and rare books.

She wasn't going to be here forever, she knew that. She felt her life growing with every word she'd written that morning in her notebook, with every recounting of the awful, beautiful, terrible, enchanting days of Binsey. But what better place to bide her time than Hogan's?

Now, Edwin grasped his cane and hobbled over to the receiving table. She watched him move slowly, staring at her. He had something to say and he was going to take his time. He stood across from Hazel. "That was a certain illustrator on the telephone."

"Excuse me?" Hazel stared at Edwin, his rheumy eyes, were they filling with tears?

"A Miss Pauline Baynes."

"Oh?"

Edwin nodded and the loose skin under his neck did, too. "She read the article in the *Oxford Mail* about your story, about the stolen illustrations and how they led to the solved cold case of your lost sister, the River Child, as they call her."

"And?" Hazel's voice rose.

"She would like to draw two new original illustrations to replace the ruined ones, and then also one extra to make the package even more worthwhile for a buyer."

Hazel swallowed a large holler of happiness and merely smiled at

Edwin. "Well, well, looks like the parcel I own is worth far more than I'd anticipated."

"Yes, it does. Maybe there's someone at Sotheby's who might like to purchase it for auction." Edwin fought a smile. "Someone you might know?"

Hazel burst out laughing and shook her head. "I need you to trust me that a very specific Lord Arthur Dickson does not need or want to hear from me, no matter the treasure I hold." Hazel smiled at him.

Edwin offered a huge grin, and then, for the first time since she'd met him, he rounded the corner of the table and he hugged her. He held her for a moment or two, the aroma of dust and ink surrounded him. He let her go and patted her face, and although she thought he might speak, he did not. He turned and hobbled out of the room.

Hazel stood quietly and thought of the day she'd found the parcel, of all that had happened over the weeks and how something as simple as a story could shift the world. Whisperwood had returned to bring her back from a life shut off from imagination and beauty. Whisperwood had enriched her life even as she had turned her back on it.

But now what? What was next?

There was, she knew, no way to guess.

After logging in the last box's contents—a signed first edition *Screwtape Letters*—she reentered the bookstore's main room. There appeared to be no customers as Poppy and Tim stood behind the counter near the register. "Finished for the day?" Tim asked.

"I think so. Let's close early. Seems it's a slow day." Hazel glanced around the empty store. "Maybe a pint at The Plough?"

"I'm looking for something I can't seem to find." A voice came from behind the shelves of mysteries. Harry's voice. Hazel spun around.

Poppy didn't know him, of course, and she rose from her stool and walked toward Harry. "May I help you? What exactly are you looking for?"

"I'm looking for something rare," he said with that damn grin.

"I see," said Poppy. "You're surely in the right place."

Harry's eyes weren't on Poppy, and Poppy turned to see that he was gazing adoringly at Hazel. "Yes," he said. "I'm looking for something rare and true." He took the few steps toward Hazel.

"Ah," Poppy said. "You aren't exactly talking to me now, are you?" She returned to the counter.

Hazel moved closer, nothing in the room but Harry now. "That seems a bit nebulous. Can you tell me *exactly* what you seek?"

Harry smiled. "I seek imagination and goodness, woodlands and magical creatures, and a river where stars flow to the sea."

Since the day she'd found the parcel, Hazel believed that she'd only been on a quest to find Flora, but all along there had been a choice she would have to make. And now she understood—she'd already made it, for long ago she'd made her decision in the riven hollow of an oak tree where stories were told.

# CHAPTER 55

## Two Years Later

In March of 1962, exactly two years after the brown parchment package with the red frayed ribbon arrived at Hogan's Rare Book Shoppe, the Celtic Sea of St. Ives in Cornwall glitters flat and calm, a flinty mirror. A lamppost light hangs in the air like a fallen moon. They live here now in this place of myth and legend, of windswept cliffs and blue ribboned seas, of yellow lichen-covered roofs and long winding paths that whisper between stone cottages and whitewashed studios.

Hazel and Harry Aberdeen stand at the open window of their second-floor flat watching day transform to night, taking a moment alone before the chaos of the grand opening party in their gallery below. A briny breeze lifts the creamy gauze curtains and Hazel breathes in the smell of the sea. Harry holds Hazel close and his free hand rests on her stomach where, well into her seventh month, pregnancy blooms beneath her flowered-cotton dress.

"We did it," Harry says.

Hazel lifts her face to his and they kiss. "And what did we do?"

"We wrote a better ending."

"And so much more." She pauses and rests her head on his shoulder. "Do you know the first time I loved you?" she asks.

"No, tell me." His voice contains such joy in it.

"When you picked up the scatterings of my knapsack in the middle of the street."

"Well then, my love, we fell in love at the same moment."

From below lifts the sound of a guitarist tuning his instrument, testing a microphone. Then a call rises from outside the window. "Auntie, get down here and hug me right now."

Hazel and Harry lean forward to see Midge, now ten years old, with Fergus and Kelty standing on the pavement below. All three of them wave their hands like they're flagging down a ship.

"Coming!" Hazel calls out. She smooths her hands over her dress. "Do I look all right or do I look like a whale in a flowered sack?"

"You look like the radiant new owner of a rare book and illustration studio on the Cornish coast."

"Sounds fancy, doesn't it?" Hazel lifts her face for another kiss. "Very fancy."

But she knows it is all far from fancy. She lived with the dust and the grime and the long backbreaking hours it took to open the new gallery below their flat: H2: Art, Books, and Original Illustrations. Harry and Hazel equal H2, and they combined his work and local art with rare books and their specialty: original illustrations from famous novels and fairy tales.

Hazel carefully steps down the worn eighteenth-century carved stone stairs that lead into the back room where the sun is sending honey hues through the windows. This is Harry's art studio hidden from the rest of the gallery. Barn doors, which they refurbished and painted bright blue, separate the two spaces. She slides the doors open to step into the main gallery.

The caterers bustle about, a bartender sets out the glassware, and the guitarist strums a lazy tune. The front doors remain shut. Hazel pauses to take it all in before rushing to greet her friends. If she dreamed of a hand-curated gallery, she would have dreamed this. On floating wooden shelves, painstakingly hung by Harry, sit blond-wood-framed colored illustrations leaning against the wall. Each one is a Pauline Baynes drawing from the Peggy Andrews Whisperwood collection.

Scattered about in groupings are handmade jewelry, drawings, paintings, etchings, cushions, pottery, and any fare Harry's artist pals bring to sell in the wide bright space.

And in the middle of it all, on a round wooden table, rests a pile of books by Hazel Mersey Linden. *The River Child: A Memoir of Whisperwood.* With a cover of the starry-winding river rushing through an enchanted woodland, each book is wrapped in a red silk ribbon, just as the original package that once landed on the back table of Hogan's Rare Book Shoppe.

Hazel sets her hand on the pile and smiles; warmth fills her as her child kicks inside, as if she knows what this book is about. No, Hazel isn't absolutely sure her child is a girl, but she suspects. And although she hasn't yet told Harry, she would love for them to name their child Flora Lea Aberdeen.

Hazel walks to the locked front door and laughs to see Midge's face squashed against the iron mullioned windows, her palms on either side of her eyes. Hazel slides the iron bolt of the double door and opens it so that Midge falls into her arms. "Auntie!"

Hazel hugs Midge while taking Kelty in her arms, Midge squeezed between them. "Oh, look at you!" Kelty places a hand on Hazel's stomach. "It's only been a month since I've seen you. Are you sure it's not twins?"

"Take that back right now," Hazel says. "I'm glad you're early, you can help me finish setting up."

Kelty glances around the gallery and tears fill her eyes. "I am so proud of you. So damn proud of you."

"Well, I hope people show tonight! You know what Edwin used to say." She pauses for a moment and thinks of the *click clack* of his cane, of his papery skin and kind eyes. "God rest his soul. He used to say that there are those who are collectors and those who have no idea what any of the fuss is about. I'm hoping the first kind show tonight."

"He also used to say that he lived for the great discovery," Kelty says. "I remember that, too."

Hazel feels the wash of sorrow that her child will never know Edwin along with great gratitude that she herself knew him.

The back barn door slides open and Harry strides into the gallery. "Well, look who's first." He hurries to Midge, scoops her into his arms.

*He's going to be a damn fine father*, Hazel thinks. For a man who never did find out what happened to his own father, he is the finest man she's ever met. Even when he was a boy, he was the finest man she'd ever met.

Within the hour, the gallery bustles with patrons, friends, and family. By twos and threes they come through the door faster than Hazel has time to greet them. Her mum and Alastair dressed in their finest for an art show and book signing in a seaside town. Tenny has a date hanging on his arm, a young girl trying to look like Jean Shrimpton's famous photo with the velvet-bow headband and fringy bangs. Dot and her husband, Russel, and their son, six-year-old Connor, stand together in front of the Baynes illustrations. They've visited St. Ives at least every two months since Hazel and Harry moved here last year. Dot and Hazel are more than sisters now; they are the dearest of friends.

In London, Mum and Dot have fashioned a new relationship out of long walks and leisurely teas. And each time Mum looks at Dot, Hazel sees Mum's face shine with the sheer miracle of Flora's existence in the world, here with them, alive as a woman with her own child.

Peggy and Wren arrive to a smattering of applause for those who know who she is: the author of the Whisperwood series. They rush to Harry and Hazel with hugs and kisses all around. Peggy looks so stylish wearing a shift dress of bright yellow crepe with a shawl that falls over her back in waves. Peggy sets her hands on Hazel's shoulders and steps back to stare at her. "You are a wonder."

"As are you," Hazel says.

It has been over a year since Book Two of Whisperwood sailed into England with a huge splash, and the publishing house sent Peggy to London for an extended book tour. Since then, there have only been letters and brief phone calls between Hazel and Peggy, but the deep sense of connection flows between their stories.

"How's the next one coming?" Hazel asks, holding Peggy's hands.

"Slow. But steady. I've been a bit preoccupied . . . planning." She holds up her left hand and a diamond ring surrounded by emeralds flashes in the candlelight.

"Oh, congratulations!" Hazel hugs Peggy and kisses Wren on the cheek. "And your mother? How is she faring with you in Boston?"

Peggy sighs. "She's adjusting."

Hazel laughs. She's long since granted forgiveness to Linda. It isn't Linda's fault that a poor young nurse, who'd been unable to save the most wounded of the war, had "saved" a young girl who didn't need it. In her best moments, Hazel feels sorry for Imogene Wright, whose mind was bent and twisted by the gore and carnage of young boys she could not rescue. Yet in Hazel's worst moments, when the midnight fear awakens her from a dream where she is running along the river's muddy edge screaming for Flora, she feels anything but sorry for Imogene; she senses only fierce and piercing rage. The feeling passes, it always does, and yet the anger still lives in the recesses of Hazel's childhood heart, visiting in the darkest night.

Bridie and Mr. Nolan walk through the door and Hazel runs through the crowd to hold them tight.

"You are radiant," Bridie says.

"That's what Harry said!" Hazel kisses her mother-in-law and takes Mr. Nolan's hand. "I am so happy you're both here."

Mr. Nolan looks to Bridie. "You want to tell her?"

Bridie nods and a mischievous grin lifts the corners of her lips. "We're not only here; we're not leaving until well after you've had that baby. We're here to help and to be with you and Harry."

"Oh, Bridie!" Hazel cries out. "This is the best news of the night."

"No." Bridie points to the table of Hazel's books. "That is the best news of the night. Now go greet your fans."

Even if these are the only people who attend the grand opening and book signing, Hazel's heart will be full to overflowing. But there are so many more. Aiden Davies has come, holding his felt hat in his hand and gazing around with awe. He holds a scotch on the rocks in a glass tumbler and follows Dot around like he will never let her out of his sight.

Friends from St. Ives, including Ethan, other artists, shop owners who have shut down early, and tourists wandering by, fill the gallery with conversation as they gaze over the latest handmade fare.

Hazel's literary agent, Meg, bursts through the door with a smile as bright as sunrise, her long caftan bright blue and flowing behind her. "I hate being a know-it-all," she says as she approaches Hazel and takes her by the shoulders. "But I told you." She nods at the book.

"I like when you're right," Hazel says with a laugh.

Harry climbs onto a wooden platform he'd built just last week and dragged in for this purpose. He holds out his hand for Hazel and she joins him. With the end of a paintbrush, he clinks his crystal. "A toast," he calls out.

The room hushes in increments until it is quiet enough for Harry to continue. "Hazel and I want to welcome you to the grand opening of H2 and my beautiful wife's book signing." He turns to her. "All good things have come from your stories, and I love you so much."

"As I love you." She smiles at him. "And you are one of my favorite stories." She then catches Dot's gaze and winks, for she knows that Dot, and her return, is the best story of all.

Hazel lifts her glass, and whoops and hollers fill the room. Midway through his toast while he offers gratitude to everyone he can remember to thank, Tim and Poppy walk through the door.

Hazel lifts her glass to the duo of Hogan's and smiles. Sensing a pause, Dot raises her hand and calls out with laughter, "Dorothy Bellamy from *Vanity Fair* here asking—Hazel, why would you open this place in St. Ives?"

Hazel laughs and sets her hand on her stomach where it seems the child within her heard the joy of Dot's voice, of Flora's voice. "The Celts speak of thin places," Hazel says. "And if such a place exists outside of Whisperwood, it exists here. This land is liminal, transporting . . . mystical, even." She smiles. "And within every package that arrives here, there might be another adventure, another quest, another mystery. I know someone else might see the package as something simple: a rare book or signed illustration, but here's the secret—nothing is simple."

Hazel pauses and it seems as if the tide outside, her breath inside, and the crowd around her wait for whatever might come next. "For when you see that the world shimmers just like the outline of Whisperwood's doors, mystery and enchantment are everywhere just waiting to be noticed. In an unmapped realm in your own souls, I hope all of you find the land made just and exactly for you."

# Note from the Author

Dear Reader,

"Not very long ago and not very far away, there once was and still is an invisible place right here with us. And if you are born knowing, you will find your way through the woodlands to the shimmering doors that lead to the land made just and exactly for you."

This is the start of *The Secret Book of Flora Lea*, a reminder that we are a myth-making people; it is how we make meaning of the meaningless and sense of the senseless. It is why we tell stories.

Often, for me, those stories that matter are born from wondering, and it was no different for this novel. While researching another novel, I was struck by a tidbit of 1939 British history. In Operation Pied Piper, children from large British cities were sent away from their families to protect them from the German bombs that were sure to come. With luggage tags around the children's necks, gas masks dangling from their knapsacks, and a stamped addressed note for their parents when they found out where they'd ended up, these children were bundled onto trains and ships and sent off to unknown locations.

I shuddered with fear when I imagined sending any of my three children away in such a manner. How could these parents send their children away?

Didn't the British authorities know the fearsome legend of the Pied Piper? The original story dates all the way back to the Middle Ages, to

1300s Germany. Like most legends, it has shifted and morphed through time. But at its heart, "The Pied Piper" is set in a small German town called Hamelin. The children in the story are seduced by the flute of a brightly dressed piper who then leads them to drown in the River Wesser. Many versions of this story have appeared through time, from an 1803 poem by Johann Wolfgang von Goethe to Brothers Grimm stories to the 1842 poem by Robert Browning. Through numerous adaptations, musicals, operas, plays, and books, we reach present day, where even a young adult graphic novel by Jay Asher was published in 2017. It is a legend told in different ways over and over.

Why would the government name their safe-haven plan after a legend of drowned and disappeared children? I could only assume it was because they didn't truly know the story, that they chose the name without looking closely at the lore.

It has been reported that this scheme was a difficult and emotional decision for the British government. The goal was to relocate children out of areas where bombing attacks were most likely, and to transport them to low-risk places. Some children were sent to the countryside (as my fictional sisters, Hazel and Flora, were sent to Oxfordshire), and some children were sent overseas to South Africa, Australia, America, and Canada.

After the declaration in September 1939, over eight hundred thousand children were remarkably evacuated in just four days. In the end, over three and a half million children were relocated. There were extraordinary stories of children finding lovely homes in the country, and there were horrifying stories, too. Not all evacuees were safe. Seventy-seven children were killed when a ship carrying evacuees to Canada was torpedoed and sunk by a German submarine.

The scene in my novel where Hazel and Flora are being chosen by Oxfordshire families was an imagined reenactment of a very real scenario that was repeated over and over in the years between 1939 and 1944, with the call of "I choose this one" echoing across the country. Posters hung all around England encouraging mothers to send their children away, and other families were urged to fulfill their duty to the crown and billet the evacuees.

While I read about this government plan, I was also researching fairy tales and what they mean to us and why they affect us the way they do. Fairy-tale history is long, beautiful, and complicated, related to but different from mythology. I was fascinated by J. R. R. Tolkien's statement that fairy tales are so vitally imperative to children's inner lives, and that they offer what he calls "the consolation of a happy ending."

As I sat with the ideas of a wartime operation being named after a fatal legend, and the world of fairy tales that simultaneously nurtured so many children through time, I imagined two sisters named Hazel and Flora from Bloomsbury, London. I saw them being sent to shelter in the countryside of Oxford. I heard Hazel comforting her little sister with a fairy-tale land she called Whisperwood, a mystical place of their own imagination told in the riven hollow of an oak tree. Here the girls are safe . . . until they aren't, and six-year-old Flora disappears.

I've always been fascinated with the unseen world, with the natural world as both salve and escape, and with the ability of children to survive with story in a world gone mad. I've been consistently fascinated with the metaphor of a river, with its final destination and its source.

In *The Secret Book of Flora Lea*, I wanted to tell a tale in a mystical landscape that echoed with the enchantment of storytelling, a story of sisterly bonds, and first naïve love, of innocence lost and maintaining hope against all odds. I wanted the girls to live in a magical land of both their imagination and of nature, and I set them in Binsey (a hamlet with its own myths and legends), outside of Oxford.

But most of all I desired to tell a tale that might ring with these words by Mary Oliver: "Said the river: imagine everything you can imagine, then keep on going."

With love and imagination,
Patti

If you have any interest in reading more about Operation Pied Piper, here are some book and site recommendations.

*When the Children Came Home* by Julie Summers

*Torpedoed* by Deborah Heiligman

*Evacuees: Children's Lives on the WW2 Home Front* by Gillian Mawson

*Out of Harm's Way* by Jessica Mann

*Don't Forget to Write: The True Story of an Evacuee and Her Family* by Pam Hobbs

The British Evacuees Association

# Acknowledgments

A novel is written alone and yet never in isolation: a paradox to be sure. There are so many people who have made this novel possible, and I am both humbled and grateful.

My agent, Meg Ruley, you are both an extraordinary visionary and a stalwart ally. I am the luckiest to have you by my side for this incredible journey! Your ideas, humor, good-natured alliance, and your changes to this tale have been invaluable. To the geniuses at Jane Rotrosen Agency, starting with Jane Rotrosen Burky and Andrea Cirillo, to Jessica Errera, Rebecca Scherer, Annelise Roby, Chris Prestia, and the whole team at JR Agency, I bow to your expertise and enthusiasm. To Dana Isaacson, I've said it before, I'll say it again—you are a book-whisperer. Thank you for reading early pages and gently, kindly, and firmly pushing the story in new directions.

To the Simon & Schuster Atria Team, you are remarkable. I am honored to be part of your swirling mass of creativity, whip-smart fun, and sheer story-smarts. To my editor, Trish Todd, I am so happy we found each other in this mad world. Your keen eye and wise input took this story to a new place, and I am grateful. To my publisher, Libby McGuire, thank you for bringing me into this creative fold and supporting this book. To the extraordinary Flora Lea team of Lindsay Sagnette, Dana Trocker, Lisa Sciambra, Megan Rudloff, Morgan Hoit, Dayna Johnson, Karlyn Hixson, Paige Lytle, Jade Hui, Sean Delone, and to the artist

Laywan Kwan who designed my beloved cover—your imaginations and ideas create new worlds.

During the start of the pandemic Friends and Fiction began, and it has become a ballast in a sea of uncertainty these past years. As you see in the dedication, my cohosts are Mary Kay Andrews, Kristy Woodson Harvey, and Kristin Harmel (and Mary Alice Monroe, who helped found the group back in 2020!). One writing day in the mountains, I said to Mary Kay Andrews, "I want the fairy-tale world to be in the woodlands, and a secret." She said, "Whisperwood." This alone set the story off and running. In addition to the dearest friends you see on the screen, you don't often see librarian Ron Block, managing director Meg Walker and AV guru Shaun Hettinger who have been keeping the oars in the water and humor in the chaos.

Meg Walker of Tandem Literary—our Jersey girl—has been my steadfast marketing guru for years now, and her upbeat enthusiasm, wise words, organizational skills, wicked sense of humor, and creative ideas are a true force of nature. Judy Collins keeps my website tip-top and my newsletter coming. Her attention to detail is astounding—I am grateful!

The arrow of these acknowledgements is also aimed straight at my author pals who told me, "Of course you can do this," who believed and listened and played character-psychoanalyst with me. To those whose words of advice are exemplified in the lives they lead: ones of integrity, honesty, and vulnerability. You know who you are, and I am grateful and would not and could not do this without you. To Paula McLain, I don't know how I could muddle through the sloggy parts without you. To Kristin Hannah, who kept me off the ledge more than a few times as I made huge changes.

In addition, I would be remiss not to bow to the authors I admire so much who supported this novel with their blurbs, time, and energy before the novel was released: to Christina Baker Kline, Jamie Ford, Sarah Penner, Sadequa Johnson, Fiona Davis, Janet Skeslian Charles, and Chris Bohjalian.

To my dearest friends, to those who listen about an imaginary world and still nod their heads with interest. I love you all. Madly.

To all those behind the scenes who opened their heart and life to me when I needed interviews, tours or information. To Jan Pardy, the extraordinary child evacuee who let me into her private world, and her niece Jane Pennell. To Tim Byars the London antiquarian bookseller who never tired of my questions or my handling of his precious books. To my tour guide Tabby Lucas who took me through the magical world of the real Binsey and shared my fascination with Saint Frideswide, leading me to her shrine. To the tour guide in London—Ann Marie—for traipsing through gardens and libraries and book shops while regaling me with stories of lost lore. I am so grateful to all of you. This book would be a different book without you.

And to *you*, the ones for whom I write: the readers, librarians, booksellers, bloggers, podcasters, and the entire literary community. This book is for you.

To Pat Henry, Meagan, Evan, Bridgette and Beatrix Rock, Thomas Henry and Rusk Henry, to my extended family, all of you. To Bonnie and George Callahan, who have supported every word I've written whether those words deserve it or not, and my sisters, Barbi Burris and Jeannie Cunnion, the same. I love you to all the moons and back—thank you for putting up with me while I live half in and half out of two worlds. I am yours.

# About the Author

PATTI CALLAHAN HENRY is the *New York Times, USA Today,* and *Globe and Mail* bestselling author of sixteen novels. She is the recipient of the Christy Award for Book of the Year, the Harper Lee Award for Distinguished Writer of the Year, and the Alabama Library Association Book of the Year award. She is the cohost and cocreator of the popular weekly online *Friends and Fiction* live web series and podcast. Patti is also a contributor to the monthly life lesson essay column for *Parade* magazine. A full-time author and mother of three, she lives in Mountain Brook, Alabama, and Bluffton, South Carolina, with her family.